UTAH!

The twelfth exciting story
in the WAGONS WEST saga—
new heart-stopping episodes of high adventure
among intrepid frontiers—
men and women fired with an undaunted spirit
that made America's promises come true.

OTTO SINCLAIR—
Like an evil ghost, he returns from a
long-forgotten past . . . his plans for the present
include blackmail, terror, and death.

KALE SALTON—
A voluptuous courtesan, she knows men in an
especially intimate way, but in teaching one
certain man a lesson, she learns the
unsuspected needs of her own heart.

RALPH GRANGER—
One of the last true pioneers, his vast ranch in
Utah Territory is his reason to go on living,
and he'll kill before he lets another take it.

IAN CAMERON—
A rough-riding foreman, money can persuade
him to carry out any order, even if it puts
his head in a hangman's noose.

MILLER AND BRADY—
Two old sourdough wagon drivers,
their kind of rare courage opens up the West
. . . but they have the help of Jughead,
a one of a kind Missouri mule.

WAGONS WEST ★ TWELFTH IN A SERIES

UTAH!

DANA FULLER ROSS

Created by the producers of
White Indian, Children of the Lion,
Saga of the Southwest, and
The Kent Family Chronicles Series.

Chairman of the Board: Lyle Kenyon Engel

BANTAM BOOKS
TORONTO • NEW YORK • LONDON • SYDNEY • AUCKLAND

UTAH!

*A Bantam Book / published by arrangement with
Book Creations, Inc.*

*Bantam edition / January 1984
5 printings through January 1985*

*Produced by Book Creations, Inc.
Chairman of the Board: Lyle Kenyon Engel*

ISBN 0-553-23921-X

Published simultaneously in the United States and Canada

PRINTED IN THE UNITED STATES OF AMERICA

H   14 13 12 11 10 9 8 7 6

TO ALL AMERICANS . . .

As the rails that span this great country are joined, so may men and women in our fifty states work hard to get along with each other and achieve a union of happiness and fulfillment.

★ UT

IDAHO

PROMONTORY
GRANGER'S RANCH

CENTRAL PACIFIC R.R.

OGDEN

Great Salt Lake

NEVADA

Territory 1867 –

© BOOK CREATIONS INC. 1985

UTAH!

I

The late afternoon sun was hot in the vast desert of Nevada in the summer of 1867 as the crews building the Central Pacific Railroad worked overtime. First came the surveying crew, led by tall, red-haired Rob Martin, the young expert who had more experience than anyone else in the country in laying out railroad lines. Directly behind his team came the crews of common laborers, those who had done the grading and laid the track through the mountain passes and valleys of California, across the chasms and rivers of the Sierra Nevada, and now over mile after mile of arid Nevada desert. Their goal: the territory of Utah, where crews of the Central Pacific heading east and the Union Pacific heading west were destined to meet and join the silver rails spanning the North American continent.

Ordinarily the grading and track-laying crews didn't labor on the heels of the surveying team, but Rob Martin was admittedly behind schedule and struggling to get caught up. He had been absent from his job on two occasions when he had traveled to San Francisco to see his wife, Beth, who had been on trial for murder. Now, grateful that she had been exonerated in the killing of playboy Leon Graham, who had held her prisoner in his San Francisco house, Rob was trying to make up for the time he had lost.

1

Within a year, he felt certain, his surveying tasks would be completed and the work crews would finish the job of grading and laying the rails. Then, somewhere in Utah, an American dream would be realized as the Atlantic and Pacific coasts were linked by a ribbon of steel.

After laboring from sunup to sundown, Rob's surveying team returned to the work camp, where scores of canvas tents had been set up and where the Chinese cook was now serving food to the hungry men. After hastily downing his meal—a watery, highly spiced stew—Rob went off to the area of the surveyors' tents, where he was eventually joined by some of his men. Sipping a drink of cooled tea, Rob paid scant attention to the conversation of the surveyors. But eventually the words of one man—a newcomer to the team—intruded on his thoughts.

"The whole story was in a San Francisco Sunday newspaper that some friends sent to me," the surveyor said as he sat leaning against a log, filling his pipe. "Man, what a story it is! It seems like this fellow, Leon Graham, was pretending to be a respectable businessman, but actually he got hold of this good-looking girl and made her a prisoner in his house. Then he took all her clothes away and dressed her up in some fancy black lace and used her for his pleasure whenever he came home from his place of business. It isn't bad if you can get that kind of work!"

There was raucous laughter from the entire group gathered near the man.

Rob flinched. He had no idea whether his assistant knew it or not, but he was speaking of Rob's wife.

"I tell you true," the man continued, "it was as simple as all that. I reckon she didn't like his brand of lovemaking any too well, and so she put a bullet hole into him. It served him right for leaving a gun around where a girl could get it. If I had me some hot little dish hanging around, wearing nothing but a little black lace, I wouldn't take no chances and give her a gun. That isn't what I'd give her!"

Rob didn't stop to consider the consequences as he leaped to his feet and approached the man. There was a hard, strange look in his eyes as he strode to the surveyor, hauled him to his feet, and held him by the front of his shirt.

"It may be," Rob said, brandishing a fist in front of the man's nose, "you think you're being funny telling the story of Beth Martin. Well, in case you don't know it, Beth Martin is my wife, and I see no humor whatever in the ordeal that she was forced to undergo."

Realizing his mistake, the man tried to mumble an apology. The others who had been listening to him were equally abashed and tried to shrink back into the shadows.

"If you know what's good for you," Rob declared stridently, "you'll make no more jokes at Mrs. Martin's expense. She was forced into a living hell by that man, Graham, and I thank the Almighty that she emerged from the ordeal without any permanent harm." He shoved the surveyor from him with such force that the man staggered backward and fell to the ground.

Seeing Rob's expression, the man made no attempt to rise. He had never seen a man so overwrought, and he certainly didn't want to tangle with the big, red-haired six-footer.

Feeling empty and strangely unsatisfied, Rob looked around at the faces of the half-dozen spectators, then suddenly stalked away from the group. He had made an exhibition of himself, he knew, but that couldn't be helped. He hated the thought that his wife was a topic of lewd conversation and humor wherever men gathered these days.

He hurried on until he reached the simple tent

that was the only home he knew while on the survey-ing assignment. There he lay on his cot and tried in vain to go to sleep. In a way he couldn't blame his subordinates for the interest they showed in the re-cent murder trial. He guessed that he would feel much as they did if he weren't so intimately involved in the case.

Thinking of his relationship with Beth caused Rob renewed anxiety. Though they had been married now for two years, they seemed to be growing farther apart instead of closer. When her mother, Cathy Blake, had died in a rockslide, Beth's perspective on the world had been completely jarred. Then, when her father, Major General Lee Blake, had remarried the past year, Beth had withdrawn from Rob more, possibly because he was so close to the former Eulalia Holt, the woman the general had married. Rob had approved of the marriage, but Beth had felt not only that she herself had been betrayed but that the memory of her mother had been betrayed, also.

These events had caused Rob's marriage to the blond-haired Beth Blake to get off to a rocky start, so that even before the murder trial had begun, their lovemaking had come almost to a complete halt. Then there were the facts surrounding the trial itself. Even though Beth had been exonerated of all wrongdoing in the murder of Leon Graham, who had held her captive, Rob could not rid himself of the suspicion that Beth had been having an affair with Graham.

But Beth had not asked to be held as Graham's prisoner, Rob reminded himself, or to be subjected to the degrading sexual acts that the depraved man had demanded of her. After all, Beth had killed Graham, something she wouldn't have done if she had been en-joying his company.

Rob told himself that he must not let what had happened in Graham's bedchamber color his feelings for his wife. Doing so would not be fair to her. Yet he could not control what he felt, and each time he thought of Graham with his wife, a new surge of jealous anger welled up in him.

Now he wondered how well he knew his wife. The young woman who had been held by Graham, who had satisfied the man's sexual demands, and finally, unable to tolerate his crudities any longer, had put a bullet in him, was not the same woman he had known, loved, and married. It appeared that he was married to a total stranger.

Eulalia Blake, handsome and impeccably dressed, the wife of Major General Lee Blake, United States Army, glanced at her stepdaughter, Beth Martin, then looked out the window of the hotel suite she shared with her husband overlooking San Francisco Bay. She and Lee had just returned to San Francisco after visiting several army posts in California and Oregon under his command, and while he was off at the Presidio on military business, she had a delicate task to perform.

Eulalia's relationship with Beth had improved marvelously since the young woman's trial, and that was one blessing for which Eulalia was grateful. The misunderstandings that had marred their relationship had been cleared away, and Beth seemed at last to understand that Eulalia's marriage to Lee, Beth's father, had been all for the good. Beth now realized that while she herself had lost her mother in the tragic mountain slide, Eulalia had also suffered when she had watched her husband, Whip Holt, the renowned mountain man, trapper, and guide, lose his life in the same accident. If Eulalia and Lee, old friends who had made the first wagon train journey across the continent more than a quarter of a century earlier, could find happiness in their marriage, then Beth realized she should only feel happiness for them.

In brief, Beth's trial had made her far more human, far less self-centered and overconfident.

Eulalia smiled at the young, blue-eyed blonde who sat opposite her, sipping fragrant tea that a busboy had just served them in the room. "I must say, Beth, you look wonderful—healthy, happy—infinitely better than you did when your father and I last saw you."

Beth nodded, her smile radiant. "I feel like a different person," she said. "For one thing, I'm sleeping again, and for another, I'm sorry to say, my appetite has returned with a vengeance. I've got to be careful of what I eat, or when Rob comes back to me after he finishes his assignment with the railroad, I'll be as fat as a hog."

"Hardly that," Eulalia said. "You've got a superb figure." She took a sip of tea. "You know," Eulalia went on, "your father and I have been terribly worried about you, and we've thought of little else the entire time we've been on tour."

"I told you I would be just fine," Beth said.

The older woman nodded and took another sip of tea. Then she launched into the subject that was foremost in her mind. "We think," Eulalia said, "that you should come home with us to Fort Vancouver and wait for Rob's return there. The staff will pamper you, as you know, and so will we. Your father wanted me to present this idea to you in the most favorable way possible, and I told him that I intended to resort to no subterfuge. You're an adult now, and I said I would present the facts as they stand and hope that you'll agree."

Beth reached out a hand and put it on her stepmother's arm. "I'm grateful to you, Eulalia," she said. "Far more grateful than you'll ever know. But I think it would be wrong to go with you. I think my place is right here until Rob returns."

Eulalia realized she would have to get right to the heart of the matter. "Beth, dear," she said quietly but firmly, "the fact is, we would much rather have you at home with us than living here in San Francisco with Kale Salton."

"But I'm deeply indebted to Kale," Beth said, her blue eyes displaying her sincerity. "Her intervention in my trial and her testimony were the turning point. It was her admission that she had been treated by Leon Graham as he treated me that saved my life and won my freedom for me."

"What you say is true," Eulalia admitted, "every word of it. It had to be difficult for Kale, and she had nothing to gain personally by stepping forward and admitting that she's a professional courtesan. Her testimony undoubtedly was the factor that influenced the court in your favor." The older woman nervously patted her still thick, dark hair into place. "Please don't take offense at this, Beth," she said, "but your father and I feel rather strongly that you're doing yourself no good by staying on in San Francisco as Kale Salton's houseguest. No matter how great your debt to her, she *is* an acknowledged, highly successful prostitute."

"I would be a fine friend," Beth protested, "if I walked out on her now. I owe her my life and my sanity. It was she who helped me regain my self-respect, who helped me to face reality and stop wallowing in self-pity, and I think I've got to take the risk with my reputation."

"That's very loyal of you—and typical, too," Eulalia replied. "I can't argue with that stand. Your father will try, of course, but he's the first to admit that loyalty is an enduring asset."

"Let me tell you," Beth said—and it was clear that she was speaking with great difficulty— "what I could never mention to Papa. I have things to worry about that are far more important than my so-called reputation. Rob and I, ah, lost our sexual compatibility before my trial . . . before I ever heard of

Leon Graham. I don't know why it happened, but it did."

"Oh, dear," Eulalia murmured, her eyes fixed on her stepdaughter.

"The facts that came out in my trial have only intensified the absence of a relationship. I'm sure that Rob has been influenced by the revelation that I was forced into intimacies with Graham, intimacies such as I never had in my marriage."

"I see," Eulalia said. "I wondered about that, and I'm sure the thought has occurred to your father, too. It's a dreadfully delicate situation."

"It's all been just awful," Beth replied. "I'm sure Rob has felt sexually inadequate, which is far from the truth, and the revelations that came out in my trial can't have done anything but intensify those feelings in him. Anyway, whatever the reasons, he hasn't touched me in months. He went back to work right after the trial, and we haven't been to bed together in all this time. And now—now I wonder whether I'll ever be able to let Rob or any man touch me again. Not after what happened in that—that awful man's house."

Eulalia put her arm around Beth, whose eyes were filling with tears. "Things will work out, dear. You'll see. I must admit, though, that the problems you face are extraordinary and unique." She gave her stepdaughter a squeeze. "I so wish I could help you, but I don't know what advice I can possibly give you, other than to try and make yourself available to Rob when he comes back to you and hope that he is understanding and gentle enough to cure you of your fears."

Beth nodded. "That is my only hope," she said.

Their cups of tea had grown cold as they had talked. "I just wish, for your father's sake, as well as for your own," Eulalia continued, "that you would reconsider this visit you are paying to Kale and that you would come back to Washington with us. Then we'd know you'd be safe and in good hands."

"Even if I had valid reasons for wanting to return to Fort Vancouver, I wouldn't go now," Beth replied firmly. "I would insist on staying with Kale. Kale is a real friend, and she's proved it. And believe me when I say I'm going to need her friendship more than ever in the months to come, when Rob at last returns. I'm going to need all her support when I try to win Rob back!"

Arranging to return to the hotel later and meet her father and stepmother for dinner, Beth walked back to the house on Powell Street that she shared with Kale Salton. The San Francisco weather was at its best: The sun was bright and hot, but a steady, cool breeze was blowing in from the bay, and the temperature was comfortable.

Arriving at the attractive two-story brick house, she rang the bell, and her summons was answered by Irma, the uniformed maid.

"I'm so glad you're here, Miss Beth," she said. "There's a gentleman who's here callin' on Miss Kale, but she ain't home, and he insisted on waitin'."

Indicating that she would take care of the matter, Beth raised a hand to her pinned-up hair and then went directly to the parlor.

A tall, husky man with dark hair and eyebrows was seated in a large, stuffed armchair near the windows. When he saw the lovely blond-haired woman standing in the entranceway, he rose at once to his feet. "How do you do?" he said. "My name is Dudley. Watson W. Dudley. I'm a friend of Kale's."

Beth smiled at him politely and extended a hand. "How do you do?"

He held her hand slightly longer than was necessary, which made her uncomfortable.

"Was Kale expecting you? I believe she's out shopping this afternoon."

The man shook his head. "No, she don't even know that I'm in town. I just arrived in San Francisco at noon."

"I see." Up till now, Beth had not met any of Kale's clients, the other woman always having been present to greet them. Nevertheless, Beth was poised and polite and played the role of hostess. "She should be back before too long. Could I offer you a drink?"

"That's right nice of you, ma'am," he said. "A drop or two of whiskey with some beer to chase it down wouldn't be a bad idea."

She tugged a bellpull, summoning the maid, and ordered him his drink. Irma waited a moment, as if she expected Beth to order a drink for herself, but the young woman shook her head, and the maid left the room.

Irma soon returned carrying a silver tray with a decanter of whiskey, several crystal tumblers, and a tankard of beer. She deposited these on the sideboard and served the guest, then departed as Dudley downed his whiskey in a gulp and then sipped his beer. "That's more like it," he said. "A man does develop a thirst by this time of day."

"Where's your home, Mr. Dudley?" Beth inquired primly, sitting opposite him and smoothing her skirt.

"I got me a ranch about a hundred miles north of the city," he said. "I get down here once every three or four months." He looked at her appreciatively, taking in every detail of her appearance.

His close scrutiny made Beth uncomfortable, but she gave no sign of it as she continued to chat with him. She felt perfectly safe in her friend's home.

He absently twirled the empty glass, and Beth, taking the hint, went to the sideboard and refilled it. He grinned at her and launched into a long recital about his ranch and his way of life there.

It occurred to Beth that he made no mention of family or whether he lived alone. She had an idea that he was married and was deliberately refraining from disclosing that fact to her. Perhaps he thought that she, like Kale, was a courtesan.

Without warning, he reached out and caught hold of her hand. "Look here," he said. "I don't got to see Kale. If you ain't busy, how 'bout comin' out for a few drinks and some supper with me, and then we can come back here? I don't know what you charge, but I'm certainly willin' to pay you what I give to Kale, and if need be, I can even go a little higher."

Beth snatched her hand away. "You've got the wrong person, mister," she said. "I don't play those kinds of games."

Not giving her a chance to withdraw, the man rose from his chair and walked to Beth, putting his arm around her shoulders and pulling her to him. Beth froze. The man's action brought back a terrifying memory of Leon Graham. Then his hand reached down and grabbed her breast.

Now a wave of intense anger overwhelmed her. Summoning all her strength, Beth freed her arm and jabbed her elbow into his stomach, causing the man to release her and gasp for breath.

"I told you," she said fiercely, "you've got the wrong woman. Now get out of here before I call one of the servants to throw you out."

Still clutching his stomach with one hand, the man retrieved his hat from the armchair and hastily departed, all the time looking back at Beth with an expression of disbelief.

Waiting until she heard the front door open and close, Beth left the parlor, mounted the stairs, and locked the door of her bedroom behind her. She supposed she should have known that living in Kale's house, she might be approached by some of her clients, but having a stranger touch her, let alone manhandle her, was too much to bear. Never again would she allow a man to take advantage of her; never again would she allow anyone to hurt or abuse her.

Lee Blake, gray-haired and dignified, the sun shining on the twin stars of rank that he wore on each shoulder, alighted from the carriage and reached out a hand to help down his wife. Eulalia, trim and graceful in her dark traveling dress, stepped to the ground and took in with a glance the many buildings of Fort Vancouver. She was glad to be home after weeks of touring the army posts in Oregon and California. They had most recently sailed from San Francisco on a coastal steamer that took them up the Columbia River to Portland. Then they had traveled the rest of the way to the fort in an army carriage provided to Lee.

"Glad to be home?" Lee asked affectionately as he took his wife's arm and escorted her up the walk of their house. Two young enlisted men were unloading the Blakes' baggage from the carriage.

"Oh, yes," Eulalia said. "But I'm not going to be able to enjoy it for long."

"What do you mean?" Lee asked, coming to a stop and studying his wife's face.

"Well, dear," Eulalia replied somewhat demurely, "I want to pay a little visit to the ranch." She was referring to the Holt property she still owned in Oregon, where her daughter-in-law, Clarissa, the wife of her son, Toby Holt, was living at the moment with her grandson, Tim.

"I should have known you'd want to see your grandson the minute you got back."

"Of course," Eulalia replied. "Our visit to the ranch a while back while we were on tour was much too brief, and I want to spend some time with my grandson. According to the last letter Clarissa sent, the one that was waiting in San Francisco for me, Tim is recovering from a bout of teething, so I should have no problem exercising my grandmother's prerogative of spoiling him and holding him on my lap. I daresay that the youngsters will be less than delighted to see me, however, because they'll know they're expected back at school."

By the youngsters, she meant her daughter by her first marriage, sixteen-year-old Cindy Holt, and her inseparable companion, seventeen-year-old Hank Purcell, the orphan boy whom Clarissa and Toby had befriended in Montana and who had since become the young girl's closest friend and protector. Both attended a public school near Fort Vancouver, where they made their home with the Blakes, but they were spending their summer vacation at the ranch in Oregon.

"I intend to ride to the ranch today, just as soon as I'm sure you have everything you want and need in the house," Eulalia went on. "I'd be much obliged, dear, if tomorrow you send your gig across the river to fetch the children and their things."

"By all means." He grinned at her. "Kiss Clarissa and the baby for me, and tell the youngsters that I'm expecting them to be on time to report to school tomorrow." He leaned toward her, and his kiss was far warmer than seemed suitable in front of the house belonging to an officer of his high rank.

Eulalia quickly saw to it that the house was in good order, that the baggage was unpacked, and that Marie, the housekeeper, had her instructions about what to do. Then, while her husband hastened to his office to begin looking through all the correspondence that had piled up while he was away, Eulalia changed into a riding dress, went to the fort's stables to obtain a horse, and headed for the ranch.

Taking the ferry across the Columbia River, Eulalia arrived in the vicinity of the ranch in a short time. Directly ahead was the Holt property, where Eulalia Blake and her late first husband, Whip, had raised horses, where her son and daughter had been born, and where she had lived as a widow. Her son, Toby, she knew would not be home. He had recently returned from his mission in the Dakota Territory, where he and Andy Brentwood's troops had subdued the warlike Sioux, but according to a message he had sent to her and Lee at Fort Vancouver, he was now off for a few days to visit the lumbering property he and his partners owned in the Washington Territory.

Behind Eulalia lay the town of Portland, whose first residents had been her friends on the first wagon train to cross the United States. To her right loomed the snowcapped peaks of the mighty Cascade Mountains, which separated coastal Oregon from the lands that lay to the west.

Eulalia felt somewhat breathless as she rode onto her property and started up the long, winding path that led to the imposing brick and clapboard house where she had been mistress for so many years.

Clarissa Holt, who was tall and majestic, with upswept red hair and clear, green eyes, saw her mother-in-law approach through the kitchen windows and hurried out to greet her, Tim in her arms.

Eulalia halted and dismounted before Clarissa reached her side. She moved toward the younger woman, then took the baby from her and kissed him soundly.

"Grandma missed you, you little rascal," she told him. "I'm so glad to see you again, Clarissa. So much has happened since we've been gone."

"Yes, Beth won her trial, thank the Lord," Clarissa said. "What a relief that is to all of us. I was worried sick about her."

"So were we all." Eulalia hugged her grandson.

"The worst of it," Clarissa said, "was the feeling

that we couldn't do a thing about it. It seemed as if we were all suffering from a very bad dream."

"I know exactly what you mean. Where are Cindy and Hank?"

"They've been expecting you, so they've gone out for a last ride around the ranch. In fact, they have their belongings all packed, and they're ready to go as soon as you like."

"That's a surprise," Eulalia said, and laughed. "I told the general that I wouldn't need his gig until morning."

"It's just as well," Clarissa said, and sounded mysterious. "That will give us time to talk tonight."

Something in her tone caused her mother-in-law to stare at her. "Is something wrong, Clarissa?"

The other woman apparently did not hear her. "I'll send one of the ranch hands to look for Cindy and Hank."

"That won't be necessary," Eulalia said, smiling. "Let them enjoy their last day of freedom." She led the way into the kitchen. Stopping, she shifted her grandson to her other arm and took in the scene at a glance. "I honestly believe that this is my favorite room in all the world."

"Mine, too," Clarissa replied, evading her mother-in-law's searching gaze.

Before Eulalia had the opportunity to question her, they heard the drumfire of rapid hoofbeats, and soon two horses came into view, racing across the fields toward the house. In the saddles were a teenage boy and girl, both heavily tanned after spending virtually the entire summer outdoors. The girl's horse was in the lead by a neck, and when she reached the house, she flung herself to the ground, her sandy-colored hair streaming behind her, and shouted exuberantly, "I won! I beat you fair and square, Hank."

The boy was full of hearty scorn as he, too, dismounted, tied up the horses to a rail, and followed his

companion toward the kitchen. "Like fun, you beat
me. Don't you know yet that I let you win whenever
we race? Toby says I've got to learn how to behave
like a gentleman, and that includes letting ladies
win."

"Ha!" Cindy replied. "You wouldn't let me win if
we were the last two people on earth."

"I would, too!" he shouted. "I'll do whatever I
have to, to show you I can be a gentleman."

They came racing into the kitchen, and Cindy
hurled herself at her mother, almost knocking her and
Tim over.

"Easy does it, dear," Eulalia gasped, handing
Tim to his mother so he wouldn't be crushed. Then
Eulalia hugged her daughter. "There's no point in in-
quiring after your health. Obviously you've never
been heartier." She turned to the boy, who had removed his hat and stood shifting his weight from one
foot to the other. "How are you, Hank?"

"I'm mighty fine, thank you, ma'am," the boy replied, feeling abashed when Eulalia planted a kiss on
his cheek.

"Mama," Cindy interrupted, "are we going back
to Fort Vancouver tonight?"

Eulalia shook her head. "General Blake isn't sending his gig across the river for us until morning, so
we'll be spending the night right here."

"And that means you can both do your chores, as
usual," Clarissa interjected. "Hank, you may collect
wood for the cooking fire—after you've tended to the
horses you were riding today. And, Cindy, you were
saying last night that you wanted to cook a meal by
yourself, so here's your chance."

Cindy and Hank raised their voices in a joint
protest. "But, Clarissa," Cindy said, "it's our last night
at the ranch!"

Clarissa paid no attention, however, and silenced
them with a wave and a laugh. "Until now," she said,

"you've accepted your chores gracefully. Like adults. So don't spoil your records the last night you're here. Your mother and I are going into the parlor, and we'll be there if you need us for anything." She preceded her mother-in-law out of the room.

As Eulalia followed her, it occurred to her that Clarissa was in a great hurry to have private words with her.

"I'm sorry, Mama," Clarissa said as she laid the baby on a blanket on the floor. "Would you like a cup of coffee?"

Eulalia shook her head. "No, thank you, and if I did, I certainly know where to get it here. I've got to hand it to you, Clarissa. You've learned the secret of making those teenagers jump when you give them an order."

"That's not my doing, really. It's a little trick I picked up from Toby. When I speak to them, I sound authoritative, as though I mean every word, and I don't give them a chance to object. That's the secret of dealing with people of their age. Give them no chance to protest, and they'll do as they're told." Her smile faded as she plucked a small handkerchief from the pocket of her apron. She sat down, and a look of pain crossed her regular, classical features. She lowered her voice and said, "I hate to burden you with this, Mama, but I'm in trouble."

Eulalia's premonition had been right. "What kind of trouble?" she asked, taking a seat across from Clarissa.

"My marriage," Clarissa said, speaking so softly her voice was just above a whisper. "I—I'm not sure it can be saved."

Eulalia felt as though she had been kicked in the stomach. When Toby had been married to his first wife, she had known that their relationship was going to end catastrophically, as it had, but she had liked and admired Clarissa from the first time she had met

the woman and had applauded her son's good judgment when he had married her. She could not imagine what could have caused such a serious rift.

Clarissa plucked nervously at the handkerchief
clutched in her hand. "When Toby came home from
Dakota," she said, "he admitted to me that he had
been unfaithful to me there."

"Oh, no!"

"I, too, found it very hard to imagine Toby's
breaking his marriage vows to me," Clarissa said. "But
he did. The girl's name was Gentle Doe. She was a
member of the Sioux nation, and she apparently died
a heroine's death, losing her life to save Toby's. She
was buried at Fort Shaw in Montana with full honors.
Colonel Andy Brentwood attended the ceremony himself."

Clarissa's news, coming on top of Beth's revelation that she and Rob were having serious marital
problems, was the last straw, and Eulalia was convinced that she could tolerate no more. "Why, Clarissa? Did he tell you why?"

"He says he's told me everything there is to tell,"
she said, wiping her eyes with the handkerchief. "He
claims that he wasn't really attracted to her, that she
made herself available to him. She was there, and he
gave in to temptation without quite realizing what it
meant and what the consequences would be. Does
that seem possible to you?"

The hollow that Eulalia felt in her stomach persisted. "I honestly don't know what to say to you," she
replied.

"There have been so many problems right from
the beginning," Clarissa said, taking a deep breath,
"that I don't know which way to turn. To begin with,
Toby fell in love at one time with Beth Blake, but
when he learned that Rob, his best friend, had asked
her to marry him, he bowed out. That's a fact, even
though he would rather be shot than admit it. Also,

his previous marriage ended tragically when his wife lost her reason and killed herself. Right on the heels of that came the tragedy of his father's death, and you know even better than I do how much Toby worshiped his father. And finally, as you and I also know, he was badly upset when you remarried. He's accustomed to the idea now, and I know he approves wholeheartedly. But for a time he didn't know quite how he felt, and when he asked me to marry him, I'm not sure whether he did it out of love or out of the confusion he was feeling. All of these factors add together to make the problem of his infidelity worse. All I can say is that every time I picture him with that Indian girl in his arms, I choke inside, and I don't want him ever to touch me again."

"I find it very odd," Eulalia mused, "that history has a way of repeating itself. Listen, my dear. Many years ago, when we were on the first wagon train to cross the continent, there was a very attractive Indian girl who appeared out of nowhere and joined the train. Forgive me if I don't remember her name, but it all happened at least thirty years ago. She had been Whip's mistress, and when she appeared unexpectedly and threw herself at him, he didn't have too much choice in the matter, and before you know it, he was sleeping with her again. Apparently she knew he didn't love her, that he couldn't love her, because when we were at our camp in the Wyoming mountains, she disappeared and has never been seen again from that day to this. I'm sure she killed herself. It was shortly after that that Whip asked me to marry him. I did, and I never had a moment's cause to regret it."

"I see," Clarissa said.

"Do you really see?" her mother-in-law demanded. "I do hope so. Whip acted contrary to his strongest feelings, and apparently Toby has done the same thing. But it made no difference in the end."

"That's what he says," Clarissa declared. "He swears that he loves only me and that he loved me the entire time that he was having the pointless affair. I just don't see how it's possible, and I'm afraid my jealousy is so great that a true reconciliation is impossible."

"I'm afraid that Toby is very much like his father," Eulalia said. "When this Gentle Doe gave herself to him, he could not resist taking her, even though he knew better, even though he really loved only you."

"If it's true, I can't see it," Clarissa declared. "I just can't imagine it."

"For the sake of your future with him and for the future of that dear little baby, I wish you would spend a great deal of time thinking about all this," Eulalia told her.

"I've thought of little else," Clarissa muttered.

"I mean, think about it from Toby's point of view, if you can. Try to understand his position, the way he felt, and the way he feels. I hold no briefs for him; I make no excuses for him. But if I understand my son at all, I know that he loves only you, and I'm sure that he's wild about his baby son. Don't deprive him of those who are nearest and dearest to him, because I know you'll be depriving yourself, as well."

The army lieutenant who served as General Blake's aide-de-camp appeared at the Holt ranch house early in the morning, accompanied by the general's gig and driver. Cindy and Hank's belongings were piled into the gig, and a short time later, Eulalia Blake left with the two teenagers for the short journey to Fort Vancouver.

Clarissa Holt discovered that the relief she had felt after confiding in her mother-in-law was only temporary. Eulalia, who was a wise and experienced woman, could offer her no assistance, and she felt that no one could. For reasons that were beyond her ability to analyze, the future of her marriage continued to appear dim. She had no idea how she could ever completely accept Toby as her husband again, knowing that he had been unfaithful to her. She seriously doubted, too, that Toby really wanted her as his wife.

After taking care of her morning household chores, Clarissa went to review the account books, which had become her responsibility as the new mistress of the Holt ranch. But her mind wandered, and after she had tried unsuccessfully to add a column of figures for the third time, she closed the ledger and left the little room that she, as had Eulalia before her, used as an office.

For a moment she desperately wished Toby were back from his trip to the lumbering property in Washington so she could talk to him, so he could hold her in his strong arms and assure her everything was all right. But then the image of the Indian girl sneaked into her mind, and she could no longer picture her husband holding her.

She played with her baby for a time, and then after putting him to sleep in his crib, she wandered into the parlor and picked up a book. It did no good to go over her situation again and again and again in her mind, and perhaps she could find some relief in a novel by Harriet Beecher Stowe.

She was just settling into a chair when the deep voice of a man caused her to jump.

"You look well, Clarissa," he said. "Damned if you don't."

She stared at the burly, clean-shaven man, dressed in a suit that was too tight for him. "How did you get in here?" she demanded.

"The usual way, I reckon." He stood grinning down at her. "I opened the door and walked in."

She cursed the ranch hands for not intercepting

the stranger before he managed to enter the house.
"Who are you, and what do you want?"

He stuck his thumbs into his broad belt and
rocked back and forth on the heels of his boots. "You
don't know me, huh? That's a hot one!"

Clarissa stared at him, and gradually an expression of horror crossed her face. One hand crept to
her mouth, and she whispered through her fingers,
"Otto?" The question was tentative, as though she
couldn't believe her eyes. She had been a young
bride, living in Philadelphia, when the War Department had notified her that her first husband, a ser-
geant in the Union Army, had been killed in battle.
She had accepted the report. But here he was, close
enough to touch and very much alive.

His booming laugh filled the ranch house. "Otto
Sinclair in person, ma'am," he said, his tone boastful.
"I'm like a cat who has nine lives, and I have eight of
them still to live. Never thought you would see me
again, did you, wife?"

Clarissa had to press her knuckles against her
mouth to prevent herself from screaming loudly and
bringing the entire ranch staff hurrying into the room.
"I—I don't understand," she murmured.

Sinclair laughed again. "It's very simple," he said.
"The War Department made a mistake. I was wrong-
ly identified as one of the victims of a Confederate
bombardment when the bodies of a half-dozen soldiers were found. I never wanted to miss an opportunity or to let grass grow under my feet, you know.
So I acted good and fast. Once I was reported dead, I
left the army for good, and I also walked out on a
marriage that I knew was a failure."

She nodded, still wide eyed. "I see," she murmured.

"Anyway," he continued boastfully, "I been living
pretty doggone high on the hog, using one name or
another. I been having real fun, and I've been respon-

sible to nobody but myself. It's been a grand life, and I've enjoyed just about every minute of it."

Clarissa didn't know what to reply, and her mind whirled. All she knew was that the man to whom she had been unhappily married years earlier in Philadelphia had reappeared, as though he had risen from the dead, and her own sense of security was completely shattered.

Otto Sinclair had been right when he had called their marriage a failure. She had been so young then, and so pitifully innocent, that he had taken unfair advantage of her in every possible way. Whenever she had objected to his many excesses, including his over-indulgence of liquor, he had resorted to physical violence, and she had soon become afraid to protest for fear of receiving another cruel beating from him.

As she looked at him now, the unhappy past rose up and came to life, and again she had all she could do to stop herself from screaming in sheer frustration.

Sinclair grinned at her, his expression mocking. "Ain't you glad to see me, sweetie?" he demanded, holding out his arms to her.

As Clarissa shrank from him, he whooped with laughter. He caught hold of her upper arms, and still showing the considerable physical strength with which he was so liberally endowed, he pulled her to him.

She was a big woman, and strong, but she knew from experience that her strength was no match for his. She also knew, however, that by acting indifferent and not protesting, Sinclair would lose interest. Indeed, with the challenge gone, Sinclair acted accordingly, dropping her arms and making no further attempt to fondle her.

She was relieved beyond measure, but her face revealed nothing.

"I could've swore we'd have us a high old time, a

real bang-up reunion," he said mockingly. "Oh, well. You never know these days."

Her mind whirling, Clarissa faced him courageously. "What do you want of me, Otto?" she demanded. "Obviously you know I've married again because you traced me here, and you must know, too, that I've had a baby."

"Sure, sweetie," he said. "I know all kinds of things about you from reading the newspapers. Just because I was reported to be dead don't mean that I really disappeared. I knew when you went west to Washington with the cargo of brides, and I found out when you married this here Toby Holt that you had gotten into one of the leading families of this part of the country. Your father-in-law was a very special fellow out here. He was a mountain man, and they blame near made him a god. His son is quite a war hero and has all kinds of exploits to his credit after the war. And I hear tell he's part owner of a gold mine, too. So, you see, I'm wise to you and to everything you've been up to."

Clarissa's one desire was to be permanently rid of the man who had made her so unhappy. She had to know the answer to the question that hammered at her brain, even though she felt certain that she already knew it. "If you've been enjoying your freedom so much," she said, "why did you bother to search me out?"

His smile seemed plastered to his face. "Well, now," he said, "I got to thinking that I didn't want to be selfish. After all, you are my wife, so I wanted to share my good fortune with you."

She felt ill. "That's a lot of damned nonsense, Otto, and you know it," she said angrily. "In the years we've spent together, you never wanted to share anything with me, and I'm sure you haven't changed for the better. I demand to know why it is you've bothered to look me up now."

It's exactly like I say," he answered, unperturbed. "I figured that I wanted to share my good fortune with you, and by the same token, I felt sure you'd want to share your good fortune with me."

She clenched her fists so tightly that her knuckles whitened. "Just what does that mean?" she demanded.

He grinned easily at her. "Let me see," he said. "You're the daughter-in-law of the late Whip Holt, which makes you somebody awful special out in this part of the country. Not only that, but you're also the daughter-in-law of the woman who's now married to the commanding general of the Army of the West, so you have powerful connections there. And as for your husband, he's got himself a national reputation as a peacemaker with the Indians and a surveyor for the railroads. You live on this big ranch that would sell for a million dollars, including all the horseflesh on it, and as the mother of a boy who represents the next generation of Holts, your place is secure. You don't want to lose any of that, do you?"

Her heart sank. He had come here to blackmail her, she thought.

"You want me to get out of your life again and to leave you all comfy and cozy and secure, like you were before I showed up and you discovered I was alive, after all. Am I right? You want to pretend that the War Department notice telling you that I had been killed in action was accurate and that the army don't make mistakes. You want to be safe for the rest of your days as Mrs. Toby Holt, instead of Mrs. Otto Sinclair. Am I right?"

Clarissa was a clearheaded young woman, whom few things in the world could rattle. But uncharacteristically, she felt a mounting wave of panic assail her. Otto was openly threatening all that she held dear in the world. If he chose, he could reveal the fact that he was still alive and invalidate her marriage to Toby.

Similarly, little Tim would become a bastard in the eyes of the law. She was shaken to the roots and was prepared to grasp at any straw. She had been complaining because of Toby's confessed infidelity to her, and that problem was compounded by the one that confronted her now. Would Toby stay with her if he knew her first marriage had not been dissolved by Otto's death? Would Toby take this opportunity to free himself of his ties to her? The knot in Clarissa's stomach tightened.

"I want you to get out of my life, Otto, and stay out!" she said, her voice sounding harsh and grating in her own ears. "I have no intention of sharing with you the life I've made for myself. Not in any way, now or ever. I want you to leave me alone!"

Again he rocked on his heels. "I can't say as I blame you for feeling the way you do, although I have to admit I'm kinda hurt. I was expecting a real warm welcome back to the land of the living from you."

"I don't want to see you ever again, Otto—or whatever you call yourself these days. And I don't care what happens to you," Clarissa said flatly. "I just want you to get out of my life for good!"

He stared hard at her for a moment and then lifted his right hand above his head in a gesture that was all too painfully familiar to her. She knew, not only from his action but also from the expression in his eyes, that he intended to slap her hard across the face.

But Clarissa was no longer the helpless youngster she had been when she was married to Otto Sinclair. She had survived on her own for years; she had made her way in the world, and she had learned a great deal about human nature. So instead of flinching, she stood her ground and faced him coolly. "If you touch me," she said, "I shall call our ranch foreman, an Indian named Stalking Horse, and he'll do what the

Confederate cannon failed to do. He'll kill you in cold blood, without a moment's hesitation, and then he'll dispose of your body. Believe me, he'll do it, and nobody will be the wiser."

Sinclair slowly lowered his arm to his side again. "All right," he said. "So you don't scare easy these days. That's kinda good to know, ain't it?"

"I advise you not to forget it," she told him.

Nevertheless, he continued to be at an advantage, and he realized it. "Your other husband," he said, "is off on business up in Washington, where he's tending to some lumbering property that he owns there. I've made it my business to be well informed, you see. So suppose I just hang around, and when he comes back, I'll introduce myself to him, and we'll see where we go from there."

Again blind panic assailed her, and she could not think clearly. "You know that's the last thing in the world I want."

He pretended shocked surprise. "What do you want, then?"

"I've already told you. I want you to get out of my life and to stay out."

"Well, now," he said, "I suppose that could be arranged. I'm none too happy about it, but I'm willing to do just about anything to oblige you. Naturally, I'd expect a favor or two from you in return."

"What kind of a favor?" She heard her voice tremble, and she held her breath while awaiting his reply.

"I'll take cash," he said. "Pure, unadulterated cash. That's the only language that means a damned thing these days."

"How much?"

"How much have you got or can you scrape together?" he asked.

At least he was making a concrete demand, and she prayed that she would soon be rid of him. "I don't know," she replied. "Wait here." Turning quickly on her heel, she raced off to the bedchamber that she and Toby shared at the other end of the ranch house.

Sinclair waited for her in the parlor, as she had requested. He was amazed at how easily his plan was working out. For whatever her reasons, Clarissa seemed mighty eager to keep Toby Holt in the dark about her first husband's existence. *Good!* he thought. This venture could prove even more lucrative than he had hoped.

Once in her bedroom, Clarissa emptied her purse, and while she was at it, she rummaged in a drawer and added the funds that she kept apart for emergencies. There was no other money to speak of on the ranch, for Stalking Horse paid the hired hands their weekly wages with money orders drawn from the Portland bank. She remembered that she had put ten dollars aside in another purse to make purchases for the baby, and she added that money to the sum. In all, she had one hundred and fifteen dollars, and she hurried back to the parlor, clutching the bills.

Sinclair saw the green money in her hand and nodded pleasantly. "You and I are getting along better than we ever did before. How much are you giving me?"

"One hundred and fifteen dollars," she replied. "That's all the cash I have on hand, and I have no way of obtaining more before Toby comes home."

"I ain't gonna get rich on a hundred and fifteen smackers," he said, "but I'll take it because I know you want me to have it, and I'd be the last one on earth to disappoint you." He reached out and took the money from her, glancing at it quickly and stuffing it into his trouser pocket.

"Will you get out now?" Clarissa pleaded.

"Sure, I'll go," he said.

She felt a spasm of relief as he began to move toward the front door, but the next moment her mind was clouded by doubt. "I'm not playing games with you, Otto," she said. "I expect you to clear out and stay out."

"Oh," he replied airily, "your expectations are real clear to me, but your payment leaves a lot to be desired. I'm afraid, Clarissa, my dear, that if you expect me to get out of your hair entirely, I'm going to need a lot more than a measly one hundred and fifteen dollars. Your husband is a well-to-do man. He and his partner have a very healthy income from a gold mine that they own in Montana, and he's making a handsome profit every year on this ranch and the lumber mill. Not to mention the amount that he must have inherited from his father, which had to be plenty."

"Those are Toby's funds, not mine," she said. "What he does with them is strictly his business, and I have no say regarding his money."

He regarded her for a moment. "If I know you, Clarissa," he replied, one hand on the front door latch, "and I know you pretty well, I think, you're not going to stand by idly and watch those funds being spent on causes and on purchases that you don't approve of. You're going to demand the purse strings, aren't you? That way you can get me a tidy little fortune together, and then—but only then—will I get out of your life forever. You think about what I've said, and I'll see you again before very long." In a gesture of supreme insolence, he blew her a kiss and took his leave.

Even though the bewildered Clarissa knew she had not seen the last of Otto Sinclair, she was relieved that he had departed. But the relief turned to despair when she thought of Toby. She realized she would be wise to tell him about her situation the very moment that he returned home. But she knew that she lacked the courage to come out with the truth. She was afraid that Toby's love for her was too weak to withstand such a shocking disclosure and that he would see it as an easy way out of a bad marriage.

Her fright and confusion, compounded by the fact that she had given in to Otto's demand for blackmail, were so great that she was making herself doubly vulnerable. The past had come to life again, and in the future she would be forced to live a lie.

II

Ralph Granger's property was one of the most extensive spreads in all of the Utah Territory, and the young man and woman who were sitting astride their horses at one end of the ranch could look down from the heights over thousands of rolling acres to the valley below. The real estate agents in San Francisco had said that the old widower, now in his late sixties, was one of the biggest landowners in Utah and that his property was as choice as any in the West.

Dark-haired Millicent Randall, a talented young musician from Baltimore, and her cousin, Jim, a one-eyed veteran of the Civil War, had good reason to believe this estimate. They had been spending many weeks traveling through Nevada and Utah, looking at properties they might want to purchase. Originally they had come west in search of the man who was Millicent's fiancé and Jim's close friend, an army officer in the Corps of Engineers, who they discovered had been murdered en route to Montana Territory. After learning of the death, their intention had been to tour the region for a time, for they felt that such a trip would take their minds off their loss. But in time the cousins fell in love with the area, and they decided to buy land and start a ranching operation. Although city bred, they had already demonstrated their adeptness at working with livestock, dealing with Indians, and hunting for food. The great advantage of buying in Utah or Nevada, Jim Randall had learned, was that the coming of a coast-to-coast railroad through those territories would increase the value of the land enormously. Prices were certain to skyrocket as soon as the railroad was completed in the months ahead.

"The agent made it clear to me," Jim had said during breakfast at the hotel where they were staying in Ogden, "that no part of Granger's property is for sale. Nevertheless, he insisted that we see it as a perfect example of the type of land we're looking for. He said that once we've seen it, we're going to have a hard time being satisfied with less."

"Isn't it a waste of time, then, to pay a visit to his ranch?" Millicent had asked gently.

Adjusting the patch that he wore over his sightless eye, Jim shook his head. "Not at all," he said. "This is the sort of land we want and need, and once we've seen it, we'll be able to approximate it more closely somewhere else."

Now as the cousins surveyed the scene, they saw huge snow-covered peaks looming high in the background. In the foreground were the rolling hills of the ranch, covered with green grass that would be perfect pastureland for the horses the two cousins wanted to raise. A single glance at Millicent's sensitive face told Jim that she had already fallen madly in love with the place.

Sitting his mount next to the Randalls was none other than Ralph Granger himself, who had agreed to show the young couple around his property. Tall, with a thick chest and huge arms and hands, Granger was a big man in every sense; his head was leonine and was topped by a great mane of shaggy silver hair. He was said to have a ferocious temper to match his bulk. According to the real estate agent in San Francisco, he had lost his wife and two children many years earlier in an Indian raid and now lived alone on the ranch, his sole surviving relative being his nephew, Paul Granger, who was currently attending his final year of college somewhere in the East.

As the ranch owner and his two visitors rested their horses at the crest of the high hill, Granger rolled a cigarette, then lighted it with a kitchen match, which he ignited with his thumbnail. "This whole country grows on you after a while, you know," he said. "I feel as though I was born here and that this land is part of my bloodstream. I can't really explain it to you, but it's a wonderful feeling."

"I think I know what you mean, Mr. Granger," Jim Randall replied carefully, "and it's a feeling that I would like to enjoy myself. Is there any chance that my cousin and I could buy a parcel of land from you, perhaps a hundred or a hundred and twenty acres?"

"There's not a chance in hell," the old man replied firmly. "I'm sorry, and I don't mean to seem inhospitable, but this land is mine, and I'm going to keep it in one piece as long as I live. I had hoped to present it someday to my son as his heritage, but God had other plans for him, and now it's going to go to my nephew, Paul, once he finishes college and comes home."

"I don't mean to press the point," Jim said delicately, "but you can name your price per acre, and we'll gladly pay it. We, fortunately, inherited some money, and we're in a position to meet any financial demand."

The old man shook his head and gave them a thin-lipped smile. "I take your interest as a compliment," he said, "but I don't think you understand. I was one of the first settlers to come to these parts a good half-century and more ago, and I've watched the territory develop from a complete wilderness into what it is now. I think Utah has undergone enough change, and I want to keep it just as it is. That's why

I keep holding my property together. It just makes sense to me. A single landlord is in a position to resist encroachment far better than a half-dozen people who have subdivided a large plot. No, Mr. Randall, these lands bear the name of Granger, and that's what they're going to keep doing as far ahead as we're capable of seeing."

Millicent spoke with complete innocence as she replied, "If you're going to keep your entire property, Mr. Granger, I guess the government's claim of eminent domain doesn't apply to you. But I've heard that they're taking all kinds of properties and are paying a set price for them because they need the land for the building of the railroad across the country."

Granger sucked in his breath and held it for so long that his face became very red. Jim was afraid the big man would faint, but instead he suddenly began to curse loudly, unmindful that he was in the presence of a woman. "To hell with the government and to hell with its claims of eminent domain!" he shouted, shaking a fist. "Government lawyers have written me letters saying that they've made such claims against me, and they're planning on laying their damned railroad line right across the heart of my land, if you can imagine such a thing. They're going to bisect my ranch with a railroad! Well, I'll be damned if they're going to do any such thing. I'm going to fight them, in court and out of court, and in every damn way I know. But they're not going to get one square inch of my land. That I can promise you!" His whole body was shaking as he spoke. "No damn government lawyer knows how hard I worked to put together this whole spread, and nobody who works for the government, from President Johnson right on down the line, is going to take away any land from me."

Jim was alarmed and feared that the old man

was so angry he well might suffer a heart attack or a stroke.

"Right now I'm fighting legally to safeguard my property, but I'm also prepared to fight illegally." Granger patted the rifle that was laid across his saddle. "Either way, I can promise you this much: The government is not getting one bit of Ralph Granger's land!"

Millicent was abashed that she had caused such an outburst, but when she started to apologize, Granger's attitude changed instantly. His anger vanished, and his manner became courtly. His voice was subdued as he said with chagrin, "I'm sorry, Miss Randall, but I'm the one who should apologize. I had no right to take out my annoyance with the U.S. government on you. It's just that their attitude is so cavalier and unfair that I see purple whenever it's mentioned. Won't you and Mr. Randall come back to the ranch house for a steak dinner with me?"

"Thank you all the same," Millicent replied, "but I'm afraid we can't this noon. We have an old friend, Rob Martin, who just arrived in the area, and we're planning to meet him at our hotel for dinner."

"The world is full of coincidences," the old man said. "I have a meeting scheduled with young Martin just before dinnertime. If I had known ahead of time, I could have told my cook, and we could have arranged to have all of you out to the ranch. Well, we'll do it another day, then."

"Thank you, sir," Jim said, removing his hat, "and thank you for your hospitality this morning."

"Think nothing of it," Ralph told them. "You seem like decent people. I almost wish circumstances were somewhat different and that it would be possible for me to sell off a chunk of my ranch to you."

They went their separate ways after saying good-bye, Granger riding to the west toward the spot he had designated for his meeting with Rob Martin,

the Randalls turning their mounts in the direction of
Ogden.

Millicent, riding beside her cousin, was silent for
a time. "The real estate agent in San Francisco," she
said at last, "wasn't exaggerating when he said that
Mr. Granger has a violent temper. I've never seen
anyone react as he did when I mentioned the government claiming the right of eminent domain for building the railroad."

"He's rather set in his views," Jim admitted. "I
thought he was going to shoot me down before he
was through."

"That wouldn't have surprised me any, either,"
she said. "I wonder what his business with Rob might
be. Mr. Granger is such a violent man that I hope
Rob doesn't suffer any harm at his hand."

Jim studied her. Something in the tone of her
voice and the pained look on her face told him that
his cousin was feeling more than normal concern for
the well-being of Rob Martin. Millicent had met Rob
on several occasions—first in Montana and then a few
times in San Francisco during Beth Martin's trial—and
each time Millicent had responded to Rob with great
sympathy and interest. She knew, of course, that he
was a married man, but sometimes such considerations could not stop what one was feeling in one's
heart. Millicent might be particularly vulnerable because of the loss of her fiancé, or perhaps her heart
went out to Rob because of the loneliness he had felt
during his wife's trial, but whatever the case, Jim intended to keep a close watch on his cousin and advise
her if she seemed to be getting too involved with a
married man.

Ralph Granger headed up into the hills and at
last saw Rob Martin and some of his surveyors operating with a plumb line a short distance from the
edge of his own property. The railroad men had

made excellent time surveying through Nevada, and now, in early 1868, had managed to leave the work crews behind and had arrived in the hills of Utah.

Rob, peering through a surveyor's transit, was unaware of the older man's approach until he heard the sound of hoofbeats. Then he looked up at the figure riding toward him and waved cheerfully. "Time for our meeting already, Mr. Granger?" he called. "This morning has passed even faster than I thought it would. I lost all track of time."

Rob temporarily abandoned his efforts with his surveyor's instruments as he watched the old man dismount. He had to hand it to Granger; the rancher kept fit and had the agility of a man half his years. "What can I do for you, sir?" Rob asked.

Ralph hooked his thumbs in his broad belt as he moved closer to the younger man. "It's not so much what you can do for me as it is what I can do for you, son," he said. "I hear tell you're a Westerner, too."

"That's right, Mr. Granger. I was born and reared in Oregon."

"You sure have to have a real feel for all this." Ralph waved an arm expansively. "It's beautiful land—the kind you can only find in the West." Suddenly the old man seemed to change the subject. "I don't suppose you've heard if the rumor is true that the railroad line will bisect my ranch."

"I wouldn't say it will bisect it," the tall, redheaded surveyor said, "but it certainly looks as if it will cut across your property. Here, look for yourself." He pointed toward his instruments.

Ralph shook his head. "No, thanks," he said. "I would just work up a head of steam, and that wouldn't do anybody any good, least of all me. There's no point in my making a speech to you about how much my land means to me. Let me just say that it's my property, and I aim to keep it that way."

Rob realized that he was being thrust into a ticklish situation, and he wanted to avoid it. "I'm just a surveyor, Mr. Granger," he said. "I'm under orders from everybody from the President of the United States on down to lay out the straightest and most direct line for the railroad that I possibly can. I was told to ignore private property and that anytime the government had to claim land, they would pay well for it. They've done it previously, all across the country, and I'm sure they're going to be doing the same thing right here in Utah."

Ralph spoke softly but vehemently. "I don't give a hang what they pay," he said. "It won't be enough for me. If they take some of my land from me, it's like robbing me of all that I own."

Rob saw that the silver-haired man meant every word and felt sorry for him, but there was nothing that could be done to alter the situation and make matters easier for Ralph Granger. The building of the railroad was foreordained and took precedence over all else.

"I'm basically following and rechecking the route originally surveyed years ago by the Army Corps of Engineers," Rob said. "The only time that I make deviations that amount to much are when we've got to build a new bridge or cut a tunnel. Neither is necessary across this particular stretch of terrain, so I think it's safe to say that the line that originally fell across your property is definitely where the railroad is going to be built."

"Don't say that." Granger plunged a hand into his pants pocket and brought out a silver dollar, which he laid in the palm of his other hand. He held it out for the younger man's inspection. "I have a thousand of these little beauties that say they're looking for a new home and will be very happy to belong to the man who changes the route of the railroad so that it doesn't touch my ranch."

Rob flushed but did not lose his temper. "I'm

afraid," he said firmly, "the line won't be altered to a less efficient route for a hundred thousand silver dollars. I'm not amenable to bribery, Mr. Granger. Never have been. I'm not making any patriotic speeches, but I was given a job to perform by the President, and I'm doing it to the very best of my ability. I hope I've made myself clear."

Contempt showed plainly in the old man's eyes. "You have, sir. You've been eminently clear. I was hoping to settle this matter in a quiet, gentlemanly way, without any fuss being created and without anyone being hurt. But if that isn't to be, then we'll have to let the chips fall where they may. But I can assure you of one thing, and that is that not one track will be laid across my land. I give you my solemn word on that."

Rob watched Granger as the big man mounted his horse, pulled his broad-brimmed hat lower on his forehead, and cantered off in the direction of his ranch house. The younger man sighed and shook his head. His surveying job for the Central Pacific was nearing an end, but it looked as if problems for the railroad were just beginning.

Ralph Granger looked calm as he rode his gelding at a rapid canter toward his ranch house, but he was seething inwardly. Rob Martin was a damn fool, he thought. By refusing to change the railroad route, he was not only working himself out of a very considerable sum of money but was placing himself in acute danger. Ralph had no intention of allowing the tracks to cross his property, and the knowledge that grading and track-laying crews would soon be trespassing on his land filled him with despair.

In spite of his disturbed state, a feeling of intense pride welled up within him when he rode down from the hills and across the small stream that bordered his vast property. There was no way to fence in so much acreage, but he didn't need fences to know that he was on his very own land once again, and he felt secure riding across the rolling hills and the pasturelands. This soil was his.

He had devoted more than a half-century to acquiring this vast, lucrative property. He had built his holdings slowly but surely, claiming free land whenever it was possible and paying cash for the rest. This ranch was a testimonial to all that he had represented over a lifetime, and he was damned if he was going to allow a railroad line to cut through the heart of it. No matter what the United States government wanted, no matter what the railroad men wanted, no matter what the territory of Utah ruled, his land was going to be intact and free.

He half stood in his saddle, searching for his foreman as he made his way toward the spacious, rambling ranch house made of wood and stone. He felt relieved when he saw the man on horseback coming toward him from the direction of one of the large barns.

Ian Cameron was in his forties, bewhiskered and burly, his clothes always covered with dust from the trail. He had been in Ralph Granger's employ for a quarter of a century and had been shaped by him, having been a drifter and sometime cowhand before finding his first real job with the wealthy rancher. By now he knew the old man's thinking automatically and understood his moods merely by glancing at him.

Racing at a gallop until he reached Ralph's side, Cameron reined in sharply. "You had no luck with Rob Martin." He made a statement, rather than asking a question.

Ralph nodded glumly. "I was prepared to give him a thousand in cash," he said, "but he didn't even want to discuss my offer. He took a holier-than-thou attitude right from the start. He just point-blank refused to deal with me."

They rode together in silence to the ranch house, where they dismounted and tied their horses to a hitching post.

"Are we being forced to take the law into our own hands?" Cameron demanded as they entered the ranch house.

Ralph Granger nodded. "I've kept the law most of my life," the big man said heavily. "I haven't gone beyond its bounds more than any other rancher hereabouts, but all that is coming to an end." His expression was grim as he led the way to his study at the rear of the main floor, looking out over the pasturelands that extended as far as the eye could see to the rear. "Ian," he demanded as he settled into his overstuffed leather chair, "how many of the hands are boys you can rely on completely, lads who will do what they're told and keep their mouths completely shut?"

Cameron, who was deep in thought, said, "Well, let's see now. I know we can always count on George. Phil is with us all the way, and so is Bruce. I would say there are maybe a half-dozen of the boys we can depend on, no matter what."

"You make it clear to them," Ralph said, "that I intend to defend my ranch in any way I can, and those who stand with me are going to be rewarded accordingly. I'll pay them enough money so that they'll have a few nights on the town that they'll never forget, with all the women and all the liquor they want."

"I'll tell them," Cameron said.

"I want the railroad sabotaged," Ralph said succinctly. "When tracks are finally laid in the territory, I want them torn up or destroyed in any way you can. I want you to dip into the principal funds and take enough cash to pay the local Indian tribes handsomely for attacking railroad work crews. Use your imagination and consider that I've given you a free

hand. One way or another, we've got to stop the railroad from being built."

Cameron favored him with a taut smile. "I've got
you, Ralph," he said. "It will be done just like you
say."

"I don't care how much it costs or how much
blood is shed," Ralph said emphatically, "but one way
or another, we've got to keep the railroad off my
ranch!"

It wasn't long before the railroad work crews of
the Central Pacific, following the route laid out by
Rob Martin and his surveyors, entered the western
portion of the Utah Territory. No sooner were the
first signs of the Chinese work crews detected than
the old rancher and his hirelings began their reign of
terror, designed to stop the railroad from being built
now and for all time.

Ian Cameron had ridden hard, day and night, for
two days to reach the rendezvous high in the mountains. One of the hands on the Granger ranch, a
Shoshoni Indian who had come to work for the
rancher a few years earlier, had managed to arrange
for Cameron a meeting with representatives of the
Ute nation, a ferocious Indian tribe, many braves of
which had refused to honor peace treaties with the
United States.

Cameron's journey was attended by many risks.
The trail through the mountains was an arduous one,
requiring great stamina on the part of both horse and
rider and of the packhorse that followed. Then there
was the danger of being spotted by unfriendly Indians, who would ask no questions but instead would
take pleasure in acquiring a scalp and two good
horses. But the greatest risk of all, perhaps, was that a
rancher or settler in the area would somehow learn of
Cameron's mission and look askance on the purpose
of his ride.

Cameron knew beyond all doubt that if he should be observed and reported to the authorities, he would have a very difficult time. At best, a federal territorial judge would sentence him to a long prison term for having dared to consort in private with Indian braves who considered themselves at war with the United States.

At last he reached the appointed place, a plateau high in the mountains, where several large boulders offered concealment. Cameron was a physically rugged man, but after two full days of nonstop riding, he was grateful for the respite. He gathered firewood on the plateau located just below timberline, and as he warmed himself by the fire, he ate a tin of baked beans and some jerked venison, the only foods that he had eaten since leaving Ralph Granger's ranch.

After a wait of several hours, he was recovering his strength when the three warriors of the Ute nation made their appearance, riding agile ponies. Rising and extending one arm Indian-fashion in greeting, Cameron studied the trio surreptitiously.

They were young men, short and slightly built, as were most Ute. Their faces reflected their deep-rooted antagonism for the white man. They neither returned Cameron's greeting nor actively acknowledged his presence in any other way.

He was satisfied, however. These three representatives of a hostile Indian tribe, who were regarding him with such obvious hatred, were precisely what he needed. Pretending to be unaware of their attitude, he offered them a tin of baked beans, which they haughtily refused.

Ignoring the snub, Cameron silently waved them to a place beside the fire. After their long, extended climb, they were chilly and grudgingly accepted his hospitality. He rose, took a bottle of whiskey from his saddlebag, and removed the cork.

The three Indians watched him with brightened, expectant eyes. He silently handed them the bottle, and each, in turn, took a long drink of the whiskey. Then, wiping their mouths on their bare arms, they sat back on their haunches and at last appeared to be mollified.

"My brothers," he said to them, addressing them in their own tongue, which he had learned fairly well during his years as a vagabond, "I wanted this meeting with you because we have enemies in common. Enemies we should destroy and crush."

The warriors exchanged swift glances and then turned back to the ranch foreman, puzzled expressions in their eyes.

"You know him who employs me," Cameron said, "and you know his ways well. Ralph Granger has lived as your neighbor in peace for many years. But now other white men, who have great greed, have come to this peaceful land of mountains, and it is their wish to change everything that they find. They wish to seize the very land itself and build an iron horse that will cross the entire land from one great sea to the other. If they have their way, they will be sending many men, women, and children to occupy all the farmlands that are available in this territory. You will have no choice, and we, too, will have no choice. We will see our paradise on earth destroyed by those whose appetite for land is insatiable."

The eyes of the Ute warriors glittered. "Why do you tell us this tale about your own kind?" one of them asked.

"Because like you, Granger is determined to halt the greedy men before they have a chance to devour the rivers and lakes, the forests and the plains of this great territory."

Again he removed the cork and handed them the whiskey bottle. Again they drank.

Satisfied that he was making progress now, Cameron spoke with greater assurance. "Granger and others who feel as he does have declared war on the unrighteous who would bring their civilization and its evils to Utah. But his enemies are as numerous as the trees in the great forest, and they have much money to spend on their desires. Therefore, he needs help, and he seeks the aid of his natural allies, the Ute."

Again the trio exchanged quick looks. "What is it that Granger has in mind for us to do?" one of them asked.

"I will tell you," Cameron said, "but I have something for you first." Rising to his feet, he placed the whiskey bottle near them. Then he went to his saddlebags and returned with three more bottles of whiskey, placing one in front of each brave.

The warriors were elated. It was a rare treat for them to be offered a drink of hard liquor at any time, as the United States had firm rules against giving drink to Indians. Here was a generous man, who not only was allowing them to drink what they pleased from his own bottle but was making them gifts of bottles of their own. They could ask for little more.

"Now perhaps you will come with me, and I can show you a foolproof way to prevent the iron horse from being built and from crossing the territory. If you and your other warriors will do as I instruct you, all will be well, and the land will be saved."

The warriors nodded, and the apparent leader of the group rose solemnly. "We will accompany you, brother," he said, his hostility having vanished. "Instruct us in what needs to be done, and it will be done."

They began their descent from the mountain heights soon thereafter, and they reached the rolling plains and valleys of Utah shortly before dark. In no hurry to illustrate what needed to be done, Cameron proposed that they eat supper first. Obligingly, the braves found and shot a mountain deer, and after butchering it, they cooked ample meat for supper that night.

Later, darkness having descended on Utah, Cameron took them out and showed them a length of railroad line, glistening in the moonlight. "You'll notice that these rails are made of steel," he said. "They are driven into the wooden ties with spikes of iron, and they are supposed to last for a very long time. If only metal were used in their construction, we would have a difficult time destroying them. But I want you to watch." He dismounted, opened a container of kerosene, and poured liberal quantities over the wooden railroad ties.

Then cautioning the Indians to keep their distance and moving his own horses out of harm's way, he lit a sulfur match and threw it onto the nearest tie.

To the warriors' surprise, a flame, bright and intense, leaped toward the sky.

Ian Cameron grinned at the three warriors, who were blinking in astonishment at the fire. "I will supply you with this magic fluid," he told them, "and with it, I'll give you a supply of white men's sulfur matches. In return for the ties that you and your comrades destroy, you will be rewarded. For each one hundred ties that are no more, you will be given a bottle of whiskey as a reward from Ralph Granger as his way of showing his appreciation for all that you do."

The Indians nodded happily, and after Cameron had distributed the kerosene and matches and had arranged a relatively safe place to meet with them a few days hence, they galloped off on their ponies, eager to set as many fires as they could.

Within days the results of this meeting were evident as the warriors' destruction was discovered. The

railroad workers found the progress they had made
reversed and were forced to spend their days repair-
ing the track they had already laid.

But these disturbances were mild compared to
what took place next. Continuing to meet the Ute at
the rendezvous in the mountains, Cameron—well
pleased with the results of the Indians' work so far
—offered the braves additional incentives if they
created even greater havoc.

"Ralph Granger will give you each a gift of a gun
and ammunition if you attack the supply wagons that
travel along the trail, bringing goods and supplies to
the work crews of the railroad. Prevent those wagons
from getting through—however you must—and you
may keep the guns, as well as whatever you want
from the wagons."

And thus a terror spree began, the likes of which
had rarely been seen. The damages the Ute caused
were incalculable, and the man-hours of work that
they rendered useless were staggering.

Returning to Ralph Granger's ranch one night
after hearing the Indians' latest report on damages
done—two supply wagons raided, their drivers
killed—Cameron smiled in satisfaction. At very low
cost, he had assured his boss a major victory over the
forces building the coast-to-coast railroad.

The project supervisors of the Central Pacific immediately sent urgent telegrams to their headquarters
in Sacramento and San Francisco. Rob, who was finishing his surveying assignment for the railroad,
added his voice to these complaints, saying he would
do whatever was needed. It was obvious that bold
measures would have to be taken to put a stop to
these tragic disturbances.

Naturally, America's leading financiers were
deeply concerned about the violence taking place in

Utah, and an emergency meeting of the board of
directors of the Central Pacific Railroad was held in
San Francisco. The discussion in the oak-paneled
boardroom of a San Francisco bank seemed far removed from the scene of strife, but the underlying
tension was great.

The distinguished, impeccably attired board
members were no strangers to violence, and they
were hard-eyed as they listened to their chairman
reading an account of recent developments in Utah.

"Troubles in Utah are endless, and violent flare-
ups have become a way of life. Supply wagons are
being hijacked and looted, trains are being derailed,
and there have been head-on crashes between work
engines that have completely wrecked both engines."

Leland Stanford, whose gradual acquisition of
Central Pacific stock was placing him in the position
of being the railroad's driving force, raised his voice.
"To what extent are deliberate acts of sabotage by the
opponents of our railroad responsible for the series of
catastrophes?" he asked.

"I'm afraid, sir, that I can't answer that question,"
the chairman replied.

"These troubles," Stanford said firmly, "must be
stopped immediately. It's necessary that we find the
right man to do so!"

One of his associates seated at the far end of the
oval-shaped table nodded emphatically. "This is a situation," he said, "that requires the supervisory
presence of an extraordinarily strong man like the late
Whip Holt. If he were still alive, I would offer him a
fortune to take charge."

A murmur of approval ran around the table, and
then Stanford said, "Unfortunately, Whip Holt is no
longer among the living. But if my sources of information are accurate, his son, Toby, is creating a
formidable reputation in his own right. What's more,
he and his partner, Rob Martin, have been responsi-

ble for laying out large sections of the Northern
Pacific route in Montana and Dakota, and Martin has
been working for us on the Central Pacific in Utah.
His work there is nearly completed, and young Holt
has already finished his work on the Northern Pacific,
if you get my meaning."

The chairman smiled faintly. "The reports I've received from the directors of the Northern Pacific state
that Holt and Martin indeed did a superb job laying
out a practicable route for a northern transcontinental
line, just as Rob Martin has now done for the central
line. I was particularly interested when we received
Martin's recent telegram describing the troubles he
encountered in Utah, namely the fact that there's a
wealthy rancher in the area, a Ralph Granger, who
tried to bribe him to change the location of the
tracks. Martin said he believed Granger might be
causing some of the trouble, though it's difficult to pin
anything on the man."

Stanford raised his voice. "Mr. Chairman," he
said, "I move that we get in touch with Toby Holt
and Rob Martin and offer them any inducements
necessary to persuade them to take charge and put an
end to our troubles in Utah at once. Before doing so,
however, I recommend contacting in New York
Thomas Durant and other members of the board of
the Union Pacific, to enlist their cooperation in this
vital campaign. Surely the Union Pacific crews working on the eastern portion of the railroad are also facing difficulties."

The mood of the directors was such that the motion was seconded and passed by unanimous vote,
without further discussion.

Once the board of directors of the Union Pacific
approved the plan, and once railroad stockholders
gave their consent, an agent would be chosen to contact Toby Holt and Rob Martin and inform them that

they had been selected to reduce the terrorism in Utah. The two young men would be able to choose their own terms, just as long as the railroad was finished on schedule.

III

Tall, sandy-haired Toby Holt sat at the breakfast table in the ranch house kitchen and did his best to demonstrate that he was in a good mood. He had played with his son, who was now back in his crib, and he watched Clarissa as she cracked some eggs and put them into a pan to fry with several slices of ham. "Where did you learn that deft touch in cracking eggs?" he asked, a forced smile creasing his rugged, tanned face. "You make frying eggs look easy."

Ever since he had returned home from the lumbering camp a few months earlier, Clarissa had felt as though her world were coming to an end. Her reaction to the sudden appearance of Otto Sinclair had been overwhelming, and in spite of her best efforts, she was unable to reply in kind to Toby's attempts to patch up their differences. She knew that he was feeling bad, that he was convinced she was being distant and standoffish because of his affair with Gentle Doe. That was not entirely the case, however.

As she knew only too well, she had mishandled Otto badly. Allowing her panic to rule, she had given in to his bullying precisely as he had hoped she would. Now she felt guilty for holding back from Toby the knowledge that her first husband was still alive, but Toby's affair with Gentle Doe had shaken the foundation of Clarissa's security, and she believed Toby would leave her for someone else if given the opportunity.

Like his father, Toby was a straight-thinking man, uncomplicated and unworldly in dealing with people. If she told him now about Otto, she was sure that he would be stunned, shocked beyond measure, and would blame her for not having revealed the truth to him the very moment that he had come home from Washington. Her fear, she realized, had been her worst enemy, and with each passing day, her situation became even worse.

Her greatest worry now was that Otto would reappear. Every knock at the door, every unexpected footstep, caused her to jump. But so far he had not shown up. Perhaps he had finally got in trouble with the law as he deserved; perhaps he was staying clear because of Toby's presence. Whatever the case, she was beginning to convince herself that maybe, he never would come back.

Toby forced himself to make conversation. "The way you cook, we could always open a restaurant in Portland," he said. "How does that strike you?"

She knew that he was clumsily trying to make conversation, but she was in no mood for his sense of humor. She replied in an abrupt, unfriendly tone, "No, I don't want to open a restaurant."

He felt as though she had slapped him. He averted his face and tried desperately to think of something else to say. But only a heavy silence descended, and there was no sound in the room but the sizzling of the eggs as they fried in the pan.

The silence was leaden by the time Clarissa finished cooking the eggs and slid them onto a plate, along with the slices of ham. She silently placed the plate in front of her husband and then sat down opposite him.

Toby tried to smile his thanks, but his face felt

too wooden, and his features would not respond as he wished them to.

She searched for something to say, but her mind was blank, and she could think of nothing.

He took two bites of egg and ham and suddenly lost his appetite. He pushed the plate away.

Clarissa knew what was troubling him but could not bring herself to admit it aloud. She knew she had to say something, though, so she asked, "Is something wrong with the ham? Are the eggs stale?"

"No, they're just fine," he said. Realizing how flat his statement sounded, he felt compelled to add, "I ate a lot last night at supper, and I guess I'm not hungry today."

"Oh," she said, and wanted to congratulate him on his inventiveness.

At last he thought of an icebreaker. "Did you take the baby to Rob's father for his checkup?"

She nodded, then realized that she had to say something. "Yes, he's just fine, Dr. Martin said. He's gaining weight, and all his reactions are very normal."

"Good," Toby replied emphatically, and then ran out of words.

"Stalking Horse," she thought to say, "wanted to take Tim with him for a pony ride, but I insisted that he wait until you thought he was ready. I knew that you would want to be in charge of that."

"Yes, I do, and thanks very much." He appreciated her thoughtfulness, and it occurred to him that the baby might be the only link between them at the moment.

Toby's heart ached as he stole a glance at his wife across the table. It was too much to expect her to forgive him and to go on with their marriage with the slate clean between them. He had thoughtlessly given in to temptation when he had bedded Gentle Doe, and even though he had not been in love with her, he could not expect his wife to see or accept the truth. Another man could understand his position, but he felt sure that no woman could. He had made a serious error in judgment and in his loyalties, and now he had to pay the consequences.

They sat miserably, avoiding each other's eyes, as they drank their coffee. The marriage had deteriorated almost beyond the point of repair, and each of them wrestled with troubling thoughts, unable to communicate.

They were agreed on only one thing: Their young son was all that was holding their marriage together.

Rob Martin, rolling up his maps, felt as though a great weight had been lifted from his shoulders. Having surveyed as far as Ogden in central Utah, his work for the Central Pacific Railroad was completed at last, and he had been told to return to California and report to the Sacramento offices of the railroad. Other men could worry about the grading and the laying of tracks in Utah.

He arranged to take advantage of the hard labor in which he had engaged for so many months by reserving a space for himself on the work train that traveled back and forth between Utah and the Pacific coast. His quarters on the train were crude, but he had a lower berth to sleep in and decent meals to eat in the "chow car."

Rob's trip was uneventful. It was impossible for him to read, so he spent the better part of the journey gazing out the window at the scenery that had become so familiar to him as he had done his surveying work. He thought about the major impact this railroad would have on the people of America. Instead of struggling to cross the great mountain range that separated the western states from the eastern ones, it would be a painless, effortless journey, made in infinite comfort and in an astonishingly short time. No longer were California, Oregon, and Washington separated from the rest of America by an almost insurmountable mountain barrier. Travelers would be able to ride at their ease, eating normal meals and spending their nights in comfortable beds as they crossed the continent. Thanks to his efforts, and the efforts of others who had been equally selfless and hardworking, the continent had shrunk dramatically from the days when Lewis and Clark had made their first journey under the direction of President Thomas Jefferson.

Above all, Rob remembered the stories he had heard his father and mother—Dr. Robert Martin and Tonie Mell Martin—tell of their journey across the face of America in the first wagon train to traverse the continent. Those days were now gone for all time.

The railroad would alter the whole face of the continent. The differences could already be seen in many places. Laramie, Denver, Salt Lake City, and Sacramento were growing into large cities. Soon they would be joined by rail to other communities in the mountain states and territories, and these places, too, would grow. Above all, the cities on the Pacific Coast would benefit and flourish. The frontier that had originated in New England and had moved westward had now all but vanished, thanks to the railroad.

Rested and somewhat awestuck by his own accomplishments, Rob arrived in Sacramento and went straight to the headquarters of the Central Pacific. There he was greeted warmly and was given a four-day leave in order to join his wife in San Francisco. Thereafter, he was to return to Sacramento, where officials of the company would listen to his appraisal of the situation in Utah and particularly would discuss with him ways and means of ending the violence that was disrupting the last stage of the construction of the railroad there.

The fastest way to travel from Sacramento to San

Francisco was by steamboat, so Rob made the day-long trip that way. He reached San Francisco without incident and hired a carriage for the final journey that would deposit him at Kale Salton's house. He had misgivings about Beth's living at Kale's house, but he tried to dismiss them from his mind. Kale might be a high-priced courtesan, yet Beth owed her freedom and her very life to the testimony that Kale had given on her behalf in court.

What bothered him most, as he rode in the horse-drawn cab, was the thought that he would have to behave normally in Beth's presence. But how could he, when all he could think was that Beth might have been having an affair with Leon Graham before he had taken her as prisoner? How could he act as if nothing were wrong when he kept remembering that she had been forced to wear suggestive, black lace lingerie while she had been the man's captive, that she had been forced to submit to his advances, to give in to his natural and unnatural demands? His wife, who had been exclusively his, had belonged to another man. Never again would he be able to rest secure in the knowledge that he alone had bedded her.

This thought had been driving him almost to distraction ever since he had learned of the infidelity that had been forced on her. Granted, she had killed Leon Graham with his own pistol because she had been so ashamed, so driven to despair by the degradation to which she had been submitted. Intellectually he knew that she could not have enjoyed the experience. But intellect and emotion were strange mates. His heart refused to accept what his mind told him, and he felt a deep stirring of jealousy, which he was incapable of erasing.

When he reached Kale's house, he got out, paid his driver, picked up his bag, and walked slowly toward the front door.

As it happened, Beth had been looking out the

window, and seeing him arrive, she had hurried to the door. Opening it, she stood on the threshold, then spread her arms wide and hugged Rob hard when he reached the top step.

Embracing Beth, Rob closed his eyes, and as he kissed her, he wondered how often Graham, too, had kissed her and whether she had been forced to simulate pleasure as she had responded to his embraces. Then he chided himself for giving in to such thoughts.

All that Beth knew was that his kiss was cold, remote, and impersonal. Never before her trial had she known such a distant quality in Rob. But since that time, she had known nothing else.

The sense of disappointment that she felt was crushing. She had last seen him many months ago, at the celebration that her father and stepmother had given her when she had won her freedom in court. Rob had departed that same night to conclude his surveying job on the railroad. Since that time, she had hoped that he would overcome his feeling of hurt and would once again become the loving, caring man he had been when they had become betrothed. To find that he seemed to be still carrying a grudge against her for something that she had been unable to prevent was a disappointment too great to be borne.

She could not help but wonder whether he realized that had she failed to obey Graham's harsh commands, he would have beaten her severely and would have enjoyed the effect that his leather strap had on her. She had given in to his demands because she had had no alternative.

She wanted to force Rob to listen while she poured out the whole story of the degradation and shame that she had suffered. But common sense told her that she would be far wiser to let the past bury itself and to live in the present for the future. Consequently, she said nothing.

At last Rob released her, and she hated to admit it, but she felt only a sense of relief.

Rob followed Beth up the staircase and into her bedchamber, with Kale's hired hand carrying his luggage. A large, four-poster feather bed dominated the room. The thought came into Rob's mind that perhaps Beth had slept in it with other men since she had been Kale's guest. No, that was an unfair thought, he chided himself. Beth was the same sweet young woman she had been when they had first been married, and nothing she had experienced had changed her. He had to keep that ever-present in his mind. It was going to be difficult, very difficult, for both of them, working together to achieve the happiness they had once known, and he could not allow himself to be carried away by jealous images.

The hired man deposited Rob's suitcases on the floor of the room and took his leave. Beth, still ill at ease and uncertain of the position her husband was taking, was by no means anxious to spend time alone with him at this moment in the privacy of her bedchamber. "Are you just on leave," she asked, "or have you come back to stay?"

"You could say that my work in the mountains is finished," Rob replied. "I stopped in Sacramento this morning, and I've got to go back there in two days for a day or so to receive new orders. Then we can decide just what we're going to do next with our lives, where we'll live and what job I'll take on next."

"That will be nice," Beth said unenthusiastically, her mind racing. "We'll have dinner right here tonight," she said. "Kale had an engagement that will keep her out for most of the evening, so we'll have the house to ourselves."

"We'll go to a restaurant for dinner," Rob said. "I see no reason why you should go to all the trouble of preparing a meal for us tonight."

She laughed. "It's no trouble whatsoever. We

have a very competent staff here. Our meal will be prepared by Kale's cook and will be served by her housemaid, Irma. Kale lives in great style, you know."

He grinned weakly. "That sounds very elegant. I just hope you won't be spoiled when we get back to normal again and you have your own household to run."

"I'm Cathy Blake's daughter, and Eulalia Blake's stepdaughter," Beth replied firmly, "so you have nothing to fear. I give you my word that I'll know what to do in a kitchen as soon as it becomes necessary for me to do it."

That sounded more like the Beth he knew, and a faint hope stirred within him.

She had no idea what he was feeling and immediately spoiled the image she had presented. "In the meantime," she said, "I believe in taking advantage of every luxury that we can."

He could not help wondering if that love of luxury was what had got her into trouble with Leon Graham in the first place. "To be sure," he replied stiffly.

She couldn't possibly know the reasons for the sudden change in his attitude, and because of this she also began to draw back. "Shall we go downstairs?" she asked, and realized then that she sounded rather formal. "Kale has the finest liquors, and you can have just about any drink you want." She started toward the door.

Rob followed her but deliberately allowed a space of some feet to intervene between them. "My tastes are still very simple," he said. "I prefer a beer on ordinary occasions and a single drink of whiskey before supper on festive occasions."

"What sort of occasion is this tonight?" she asked, and deliberately refrained from looking back at him as they descended the staircase.

Following her, Rob chose not to answer.

They reached the drawing room, and Beth went off to the kitchen to tell the cook that her husband had returned to San Francisco and was joining her for supper. When she returned to the elegantly furnished room, she found Rob pouring himself a whiskey at the small bar in the corner. "What can I get for you?" he asked.

"Oh, I've asked Irma to bring me a glass of lemonade. I don't want anything alcoholic."

Rob was surprised. "Why is that?" he asked.

"I lost my taste for alcoholic drinks," she said.

Even as she spoke, he recalled the testimony she had given during her trial when she revealed that Graham had forced her to drink alcoholic beverages until she became intoxicated, and that she hadn't minded too much because it was easier to comply with his sexual demands when she was under the influence of hard liquor.

The very reminder of the ordeal that Beth had undergone served to put still another damper on their reunion. A spurt of jealousy flamed within Rob, and no matter how he tried to quench it with the knowledge that Beth had not chosen to be Graham's captive—and had killed the man to gain her freedom—he could not subdue his emotional torment.

Unaware of his reaction, Beth knew only that she had been reminded of what she had been forced to undergo, and she became even more withdrawn. Neither could shake the effects of what they felt, and their conversation was stilted until they were called to the table. Then Beth had the presence of mind to inquire about the surveying job.

Rob responded willingly and told her in detail not only about the surveying he had done but also of the troubles that were brewing in Utah.

"What's going to happen?" she asked. "Will the railroad ever be built?"

He shrugged. "Under present conditions, I very

much doubt it," he said. "I think that it's going to be necessary to make some changes in the territory's security forces and they'll need someone tough enough to enforce the law. Otherwise, the killings will go on, and the building of the lines will be permanently interrupted."

"That's horrible," she said. "Can't the railroad companies call in the army to restore and maintain order?"

Rob shook his head. "President Grant would be criticized," he said, "for using federal troops to support private enterprise. Most Americans badly want the railroad, but they're unwilling to see taxpayers' money used to help insure that it gets built. I'm afraid this is one task the railroads will have to perform themselves, in their own way, and I honestly don't know what that way will be. All I can tell you is that it's not going to be easy."

He had answered her question to her satisfaction, and all at once she realized she had nothing more to say. They finished their meal in virtual silence. Beth rang for the maid and announced, "You may clear the dishes, Irma. We're finished now."

Sitting opposite her at the table, Rob began to fidget.

"You must be tired after your long journey," Beth said politely.

The thought hadn't crossed his mind, but he realized he might find escape in sleep. "Yes, I reckon I am," he said.

Beth suggested that he precede her upstairs while she, acting in Kale's place, stayed to discuss the following day's menu with the cook. Glad of the respite, Rob took his leave. Once upstairs in Beth's bedchamber, he undressed quickly, donning his pajamas, and took the precaution of extinguishing the oil lamp before he climbed into the feather bed.

His heart ached for Beth, and he desperately

longed to hold her in his arms. But the ghost of Leon
Graham continued to intervene, so he turned his back
to her side of the bed and pretended to sleep.

He continued to maintain that pretense when he
heard her enter the bedchamber. After lighting a
small candle, she went into her dressing room, dis-
robed quickly, then vanished into the bathroom.

He was taut, every nerve end quivering, as he listened to the sounds that she was making. When she
reappeared in the bedchamber, he lay very still
with his eyes closed.

Beth climbed into the opposite side of the bed,
extinguished the candle, and sighing faintly but au-
dibly, held herself as far from her husband as the bed
allowed.

Hours passed before either of them fell asleep. A
feeling of misery and a spirit of despair seemed to fill
the bedchamber.

Rob fell asleep shortly before dawn, and in spite
of his troubled mental state, he was sufficiently exhausted that he slept until late in the morning. Beth
became increasingly restless, and at last she arose, put
on a wrapper over her nightgown, and went off to the
bedchamber of Kale Salton, where she joined her
hostess for a cup of coffee.

Kale, wearing an elegant black dressing gown,
greeted her with a broad smile. "Well," she said, "I
understand your husband came home last night. You
should be in a very happy mood today."

"Yes, he's here," Beth replied glumly. "He might
just as well have stayed in Utah, though."

Kale's smile vanished as she poured her friend a
cup of coffee. "Do you feel like talking about it?"

"Why not?" Beth said listlessly, and leaned back
in her chair. "He's not the Rob I knew. He gave me a
grandfather's kiss when he first arrived, and since that
moment, he hasn't as much as touched me."

"You're telling me that you didn't make love last night?"

"He didn't come near me," Beth said shortly.

"Oh, dear." Kale sipped her coffee. "What was responsible, do you think? Was it the trial and the ghost of Leon Graham hovering overhead?"

"I think so," Beth replied. "He didn't spell it out in so many words, but I gleaned that my experience shook him up rather badly."

"I see," Kale replied thoughtfully. "Can't he understand that you were forced to submit to Graham under duress?"

Beth shook her head. "I'm afraid not. Not Rob. He's a wonderful man and a splendid husband, but he's sexually unenlightened and is quite puritanical."

"That," Kale said, "can create difficulties. What do you intend to do about it?"

Beth took a large swallow of her coffee. "I'm afraid I have no idea. I've been too confused. All I know is that Rob will be here until tomorrow, when he's got to go back to Sacramento for a day or so. After that, we'll probably head up to Oregon or Washington, and we'll live there unhappily ever after."

"You can't possibly go anywhere with him until your personal relationship is straightened out."

Beth shook her head. "That's asking for the impossible."

Kale grinned at her. "Take my word for it, Beth. Nothing is impossible in a relationship between a man and a woman." She was lost in thought for a time. "Where is Rob right now?"

"He's sound asleep."

"Then let him sleep. I think this is an opportune moment to let a little air into your relationship. I suggest that you get dressed and go shopping. Buy yourself a new dress, a new hat, and a pair of shoes to cheer you up."

"I'd love to," Beth replied. "That sounds like wonderful advice. But what if Rob wakes up while I'm gone?"

Kale simulated casualness but actually replied with infinite care. "Don't worry about him," she said. "Half the fun of shopping lies in taking your time. If he should wake up, I'll entertain him until you return. And don't worry, Beth, dear. Between us, we'll figure out some solution to your problem."

As soon as Kale was alone, she made her preparations for the day, bathing quickly, then dressing. First she put on her most provocative undergarments, complete with a pair of black net stockings with frilly garters holding them up. Her dress was one of her favorites, featuring a very low neckline and a skirt that was slit high on her thigh so that when she sat down, a long, shapely leg was revealed. She applied her makeup with a heavy but professional hand, combed out her long auburn hair, and, as a last touch, dabbed her favorite French perfume behind her ears and on her neck, adding a final bit of scent between her half-exposed breasts.

Hearing the front door open and close, she knew Beth was departing. It was time to put her plan into operation.

She tugged at the bellpull that summoned her serving maid.

"Yes, ma'am," Irma said when she came into the dressing room.

"Is Mr. Martin awake as yet?"

"Yes, he is, ma'am. He's just going down to the dining room for breakfast."

"When he's through, ask him to join me in my sitting room, if you will," Kale said, "and be good enough to make up my bed. With the silk sheets."

The maid was stunned. She guessed what her mistress had in mind—her provocative attire and the request to make up her bed with silk sheets spoke for themselves. Knowing that Beth Martin was Kale's close friend, the woman continued to stand in her mistress's dressing room with a raised eyebrow.

Kale became annoyed. "Be good enough to obey orders," she said. "I know precisely what I'm doing."

As soon as she was alone again, Kale adjourned to her sitting room, where she stretched out artfully on a chaise and deliberately arranged her skirt in such a way that her thigh, covered with the net stocking, was revealed. She also undid one more button of her dress so that the cleavage between her breasts showed even more plainly. Confident of her powers, she felt she was irresistible.

Kale knew that any number of incidents could occur to spoil her bold, carefully made scheme, but she had to take the chance. Beth Martin had become her dearest friend, and it was for the sake of Beth's marriage that the courtesan had to try to seduce Rob, something that Beth would obviously disapprove of if she were aware of it.

Picking up a book, Kale opened it and pretended to be absorbed in it. She had no sooner settled in this position on the chaise when a light tap sounded at the door and Rob Martin came into the little sitting room.

He stopped short when he saw the provocatively attired young beauty.

Kale's smile was friendly and indicated nothing unusual was taking place. "Hello, Rob," she said. "It's nice to see you. Sorry I wasn't on hand last night to greet you." She extended her hand to him.

Since she was his hostess, he had no choice but to walk over to her and take it. Kale deliberately held his hand far longer than was necessary. "Beth has gone shopping. She felt she had nothing appropriate to wear to celebrate your return."

"I see," he replied, and the minor mystery of Beth's whereabouts that morning was solved.

"Join me for a little chat," she said, "but first help yourself to a drink." She pointed to the bar at the far side of the sitting room. "While you're at it, you might pour me a little whiskey and water. You'll find the water in a pitcher on the bar."

Although it was only noon and he had just finished breakfast, he obeyed and poured their drinks. Approaching the chaise, he handed one glass to Kale.

With her free hand, she patted the space at the foot of the chaise, inviting him to sit, and she simultaneously moved in such a way that more of her leg was exposed.

Feeling trapped and embarrassed, Rob sat on the chaise and tried to relieve his feelings by taking a large swallow of his stiff drink.

"Beth tells me you've finished your work for the Central Pacific." She spoke impersonally, in contrast to her sultry appearance.

Rob nodded. "Yes," he said. "As far as I know, I'm about finished."

"You've done a great deal of work surveying for the railroads."

"Well," he said, "I reckon I have." Glad for something to talk about, he went on. "I worked for the as yet unbuilt Northern Pacific in Washington, Montana, and Dakota. And in Nevada and Utah, I worked on the Central Pacific, which we hope will be joined with the Union Pacific in the not too distant future."

She managed to consume a token swallow of her drink. "You've covered the better part of the West, then," she said, her voice filled with admiration.

"I guess maybe I have." Her exposed breasts and leg, as well as her powerful perfume, were making him extremely uncomfortable.

Kale pretended to be totally unaware of his reactions as she carried on a prolonged conversation about railroad surveying.

Trying to relieve his embarrassment, Rob quickly

gulped the remainder of his drink. Kale, who had been keeping a sharp eye on his glass, immediately suggested that he refill it.

He hesitated but decided that the liquor helped him relax with this provocative woman. He rose, went to the bar, and refilled his glass, then returned to sit on the divan, all the while aware that Kale's intense scrutiny made him feel naked.

After delving to the roots of her knowledge of railroading, Kale proceeded to question him about life in the deep forests of the Washington Territory, where he and Toby owned a lumbering property in partnership with their friend Frank Woods. Even though her talk remained impersonal, Kale knew that Rob stayed keenly aware of her shapely body. The trick she was playing was as old as the art of seduction itself. While simulating interest in a subject that could by no means be termed intimate or personal, she was wooing him with every twist and every turn of her shoulders, of her arms and hands, of her hips and legs, and of her face.

In spite of himself, Rob was becoming more and more aroused. He had known no women during his long sojourn in the wilderness, and his jealousy of his wife's relations with the man she had eventually murdered had left him unfulfilled and frustrated. And now a lovely woman was silently offering him her body, and he knew it.

When he had finished his second drink, Kale did not suggest that he refill it immediately. She had decided that the time had come for a brief respite. Instead she again began to talk, and casually, seemingly by accident, she placed her hand first on his hand, then on his arm, and ultimately on his leg.

Rob stirred beneath her touch.

The moment had come, Kale realized, to intensify her efforts, and lowering her voice, she raised her head to his and moved closer to him. Her enormous green eyes looked into his, promising him untold delights if he wished to take advantage of her. Her lips, moist and parted, were demanding to be kissed. Her breasts insisted that they be fondled.

Rob Martin was an honorable man who had always been faithful to his wife, but he was only human. He resisted temptation as long as he could, and then suddenly his powers of reasoning deserted him, and he gave in to the insistent demand of his body. Scarcely realizing what he was doing, he grasped Kale by the shoulders and proceeded to kiss her. Her lips parted, and his kiss became passionate, intense.

Although sure that he was now won over, Kale nevertheless took no chances and proceeded to curl her arms possessively around his neck. Their embrace became prolonged, and at last Rob breathlessly moved several inches from her.

"I'm so sorry," he muttered. "I had no intention of—" He was so flustered that his voice trailed away.

Kale took further advantage of him by raising her face to his again, and before he could stop himself, one of his hands slid inside the front of her dress and closed over a bare breast.

That was Rob's finish, and he was unable to resist any longer. Casting all caution aside, he stretched out on the chaise beside her, and his caresses became more insistent and more intimate.

Kale, of course, made no objection, and in fact she gave the impression that she was enjoying herself thoroughly.

To her own astonishment, that was indeed the case. So many men had made love to her in the years that she had been a courtesan that she had lost count of their numbers, and without exception, they had left her cold and unmoved. But Rob Martin was proving to be an extraordinary exception.

His kisses inflamed her like those of no other man she had ever known. She found herself quivering beneath his touch, eager to be fondled and embraced even more, eager to complete the sex act so she could gain maximum fulfillment.

Acting instinctively now, without simulation, she moved with him from the chaise to the adjoining bed-chamber, where they undressed swiftly and stretched out on the silk sheets. Hardly aware of the luxurious feel of the sheets, Rob knew only that he wanted this woman, that he had to have her, and that she was his for the taking.

Kale, too, was lost, the victim of her own unre-quited passion. Her scheme had boomeranged on her, and she knew only that she had to have this man, that he was providing her with an experience that was unique in spite of the life that she had led.

Neither of them was acting consciously now, but the passion of one fueled the desire of the other. They writhed on the bed, their naked bodies linked to-gether, their hands caressing and exploring. A subtle parting of Kale's knees was a silent invitation that Rob eagerly and swiftly accepted, and he entered her.

Thereafter, both of them became increasingly frenzied as their desires fed each other, and their in-satiable longing at last found its natural outlet and re-lease. They reached a climax together, and Rob pumped wildly, using his full force, his full strength, while Kale clung to him, her long nails digging into his back.

Then it became very silent in the room, and the couple on the bed lay still, panting for breath, and slowly recovering their senses.

They kissed again and then drew apart.

"I—I'm so sorry," Rob muttered at last. "I don't know what came over me. I had no intention of dishonoring you or myself."

With a great wrench, Kale pulled her mind back to the reality of the situation in which she found her-self. Her plan had worked perfectly, far more effectively than she had imagined it would. Now was the time to take full advantage of the situation and forget that for the first time in her life, she had been sexually satisfied in her lovemaking.

She propped herself on one elbow and looked at him. When she spoke, her voice was calm and clear, and only someone who knew her extremely well could have detected the huskiness that underlay her words. "Do you love Beth?" she demanded.

Rob couldn't help squirming beneath her gaze, but he felt compelled to answer honestly. "Yes," he said. "I do."

"Even though you've been intimate with me?" she went on. "Even though we've had what I can only describe as enormously, wildly successful sex relations?"

He closed his eyes for a moment, but when he opened them again, he found Kale close to him, staring at him, her deep green eyes demanding a reply. "Yes," he said. "I've never had sex like this in my life, but that doesn't affect my feeling for Beth. She's my wife, and I love her, and only her. She's the only woman I'll ever love, as long as both of us live."

His words cut deep, and Kale suffered a sense of hurt greater than any she had ever before known. But at the same time, she had to congratulate herself. Her scheme had been completely effective.

"How could that possibly be?" Kale asked with pretended innocence.

"I don't honestly know," Rob replied. "I'm afraid that I can't answer your question. But I know that what we've just done has only strengthened the depth of my love for Beth. It's strange, I'm sure, and I can't explain it. But that's the effect that our relationship has had on me."

A faint smile appeared on Kale's face. She reached for the negligee that was on the chair beside them and donned it. The fact that she was now at least partly clothed, while he remained totally nude, gave her an advantage that she intended to exploit to the fullest.

Again she smiled faintly, and there was a challenge in her tone as she said to him, "What you feel at this moment toward your wife is anything but unusual. It's true love. This I know, and this I can guarantee you. Perhaps now you can understand that she cannot be blamed for her infidelity to you. It was forced on her. You had a free choice in your relationship with me. She had none with Leon Graham. She had gone out with him in the first place because he was a seemingly upright man and she had needed an escort to the theater and concerts. But then he drugged her and made her his prisoner, and she was trapped. If she had failed to do his biding, he would have beaten her severely and possibly maimed her for life. Remember, she was dealing with a madman. The result of what she went through was a strengthening of her love for you, an increase in her appreciation of the qualities you possess, a thankfulness for your love toward her."

He was listening now, his entire being concentrating on the wisdom that this beautiful young woman was imparting.

"From the moment that Beth was arrested for murder," Kale said firmly, "your behavior toward her has been abominable. You've acted like a damn fool toward her." She paused, and there was a hint of scorn in her voice. "Please be good enough to get dressed and to leave my bedchamber." She rose and disappeared into the bathroom.

Badly shaken, Rob Martin dressed swiftly. He understood completely now the mistake he had made in his treatment of Beth. Furthermore, he realized that Kale had deliberately seduced him in order to teach him a lesson that he could have learned in no other way. He was eternally in her debt but could not bring himself to explain this to her right then. He would have to wait until time healed the passionate flow that had erupted between them, and then—only then—could he thank her for her incredible kindness toward him and for the deliberate sacrifice of herself that she had made on his behalf and his wife's. He knew now what had to be done, and the way ahead was clear. But he would have to act surely and swiftly, and he could afford no more errors.

Before leaving, however, he felt compelled to go back on his own better judgment and to say something appropriate to Kale for the service she had performed for him. Walking to the bathroom door, he tapped lightly on it and then called softly, "Thank you, Kale. I appreciate what you've done." Turning, he walked out of the room and down the stairs to the drawing room, where he would await Beth's return.

Kale heard him through the closed bathroom door, and the very sound of his voice caused her to shiver uncontrollably. Removing the heavy makeup, she stared bleakly at her reflection in the mirror above the washbasin. She had tried to play God, and now she was called on to pay the consequences. Beth was her close friend and trusted her implicitly. Kale had entered into the game she had played so successfully with only one intention in mind, that of teaching Rob a valuable lesson that he appeared incapable of learning in any other way.

What she had not counted on, what she had not dreamed would happen, was that she herself would react to him as she had reacted to no other man she had ever known. Of the dozens with whom she had gone to bed, he was the first who had aroused her and then given her complete satisfaction.

But because he was Beth's husband, he was untouchable. She would return to her existence knowing one man after another and being forced to simulate sexual satisfaction with all of them, yet realizing that the one who could fulfill her own needs was beyond her grasp.

What made Rob so different from every other man with whom she had ever been intimate was beyond her understanding. Certainly he was no more virile than most, and if the truth be known, was not as virile as some others. He was courageous and upright, but he had no great intellect, and his personality, although pleasant, was not overwhelming. Nevertheless, as she thought of him, she remembered the way he kissed her and the way he touched her, and her body began to quiver all over again. There would always be a special, soft place in her heart for Rob.

Kale hurried into her dressing room, where she began to don more modest, suitable attire. As she tried to sort out her feelings about what had happened, Rob, too, was thinking about the same situation as he paced the drawing room, awaiting his wife's return.

Never could he admit to Beth that he had committed adultery with her closest friend. She had been hurt enough, and he had no desire to devastate her. What was all important to him was the lesson that Kale had taught him. Now he had to apply it to his own life, to his relationship with Beth, and act accordingly. They would leave Kale's home today, tonight at the latest. They would put San Francisco behind them and get on with their own lives. That was paramount: to put everything that had happened in the past behind them and to make a fresh, clean start. That would be their only salvation, and he told himself that no matter how much Beth might protest, he had to have his way in this matter. Their whole future depended on it.

After a wait that seemed interminable, he heard Beth come into the house. She was surprised to see her husband, who leaped to his feet as she came in.

"I had no idea that I would sleep so late," he told her. "I—I had a chat with Kale, and she told me you had gone shopping."

"Yes, that's right," she said, her arms full of packages. "Where's Kale now?"

"I don't know, but I assume she's in her private quarters."

Beth took a step, as though intending to leave the room.

"Wait a minute," Rob commanded, and took her packages out of her arms, and set them on a table. "I've got to talk to you about something."

She heard a new tone of command in his voice. Curious, she looked at him.

"I've decided," he said, "that we're going to move out of here this very day. This place conjures up too many memories, and we're going to go to a hotel where we'll rent a suite and make a fresh start."

"But what about Kale?" Beth protested.

Rob grinned at her. "What about *us?* Let's do something for ourselves for a change," he said. "We're going to have another honeymoon. We deserve it."

She looked at him, so taken aback by his changed attitude that she was unable to speak.

"I don't want Kale to think that we're in any way ungrateful to her for her kindness and her hospitality," he said, "so we'll invite her to dine with us tomorrow before we go to Sacramento."

"You want me to come with you to Sacramento while you have your talks with the railroad people there?" she asked incredulously.

"You bet!" he replied emphatically. "We've been separated long enough, and we're not going to be separated again, even for a single day. We'll head straight from Sacramento up to Portland, so we can see your father and stepmother and my parents, and we'll have a chance at least to say hello to Toby and

Clarissa and see their baby." He spoke firmly, leaving no room for argument.

Beth was in no mood to argue. She had been longing for just such a display of firmness from Rob, and the fact that he was exhibiting it now seemed little less than miraculous to her. "I'll be ready to go," she said, picking up the purchases, "as soon as I pack my belongings. I would like a few minutes to see Kale. I don't want her to think that I'm just racing out on her now that you've come back."

"Take your time," Rob told her as he sat on a small divan. "We have the rest of our lives."

Bewildered and puzzled by the sudden change in his attitude, Beth smiled at him vaguely and left the room. When she reached the second floor, she quickly dropped the packages on her bed, then went straight to Kale's bedchamber and tapped on the door.

Kale's voice came to her from the dressing room, telling her to come in.

Beth entered the room and found her friend modestly attired in a high-necked, ankle-length dress. Her face was devoid of makeup, and she was just pinning up her hair in a demure style at the crown of her head. "You're back, I see," she said cheerfully, feeling anything but cheerful. "What luck did you have?"

"Everything fell into place beautifully," Beth said. "I got a dress that was just right, and I found a pair of shoes and a hat to match."

"Isn't that nice," Kale said, and beamed at her.

"But I'm badly thrown by the change that's taken place in Rob. Did you feed him any strong medicine or raw meat while I was gone?"

Hoping that her emotions did not show, Kale shook her head. "We talked about railroading and life in the lumbering country in Washington," she said. "I can't recall whether he had a drink or not." She spoke glibly and hoped that her friend would not know that she was lying.

Beth was too involved with her own emotions to be aware of Kale's quandary. "Rob wants us to move to a hotel tonight," she said. "He says we're going to have a second honeymoon. Tomorrow he would like you to meet us for dinner, and then I'm going with him to Sacramento. We're going to leave from there for Portland, so it will be in the nature of a farewell dinner."

Kale told herself that for Beth's sake, she would have to meet the couple and go through the torment of pretending to enjoy herself. At least she would be saying good-bye to them, and it would be a great help not to see Rob again.

Beth's next words jarred her.

"I'm not certain that I want to go," she said. "I see no reason to leave your house, and I think it would be much more sensible if I waited right here for him until he finishes his business in Sacramento and comes back to San Francisco for me."

Kale knew her task was far from completed, that she had to play Cupid a little longer. "I gather," she said, "you're not sure you want to return to a full-scale marriage to Rob Martin."

"Maybe I do, and maybe I don't," Beth replied. "I just find this sudden shift in his attitude almost too much to accept. He was cold and remote and seemed to be pushing me away from him when he showed up last night, and now, today, he's falling all over himself being glad to see me and making plans for our future together."

Kale was satisfied that at least she had turned Rob in the right direction. Now she had to do the same with Beth, and she decided to act swiftly and ruthlessly.

"I was glad I had the opportunity today to become acquainted with Rob," she said, speaking with great sincerity. "You had told me what a wonderful man he is, and I couldn't quite believe you. But now that I know him, I find that you didn't exaggerate in the least. All I can say is that if you don't want him, Beth, just say the word, and I'll be glad to step in." She smiled gently to show that although she was serious, she had no desire to hurt her friend.

Beth was startled and reacted in precisely the way that Kale had anticipated. "Of course I want him!" she cried. "He's my husband, and I've never wanted any other man." That was not strictly true, but in Beth's present emotional state, she believed completely what she was saying. "Thanks for the warning, but don't waste your time because I'm going to hang onto him, if it's the last thing I ever do in this world!"

Kale's laugh, which she had to force, followed Beth down the corridor.

Her mind made up, Beth packed her clothes in record time, throwing them into her valises and packing Rob's belongings, as well.

When she was finished, she called the serving maid to help her, and together they carried the luggage down to the drawing room. There she found Rob and Kale engaged in a somewhat stilted conversation.

Kale's groom harnessed a team of horses to the carriage and put the luggage in it. The two women arranged to meet at noon the following day, and then Rob and his wife took their leave. At last they were alone, completely on their own, for the first time since she had been released from prison.

He said nothing, but held her hand tightly on the ride to the Palace Hotel. When they reached the hotel, an assistant manager showed them to their suite and left them contemplating the spectacular view of San Francisco Bay stretched out below them.

Beth stood at the window looking out at the

steamers and sailing ships making their way in and out of the great harbor. "When I was a little girl," she said, "I used to look at that view by the hour from our house in the Presidio. I used to daydream about the happy life I would lead someday, and somehow, the bay was always mixed up in my dreams."

Rob came up behind her, slid his arms around her narrow waist, and buried his face in her neck. "Even as a very little girl," he said, "you had a special quality, an ability to foretell the future accurately." He turned her around and kissed her with a fervor and tenderness greater than any she could ever remember him having shown.

"I'm going to have a bottle of champagne sent up," he said. "Do you want to order supper here, too, or would you rather we go downstairs for it?"

Beth was still breathless from his kiss. But she regained her equilibrium and, a smile playing on her lips, said at last, "If we dined downstairs, I could wear my new dress and hat. But I think I'd much rather have dinner served up here in our room. I want us to be together, just the two of us."

"That's fine with me," he said, and smiled as he walked to a bellpull to summon the waiter who would bring them their champagne and dinner. "The whole night belongs just to us."

Beth nodded, then slipped into the adjoining bedroom after giving Rob a quick kiss and telling him that she intended to change into a dressing gown. The whole night indeed stretched out ahead of them, and they were going to spend every possible moment of that time making love. She smiled in anticipation, and she felt wonderful. Rob was a new man, and she felt like a new woman. For the first time since her release from Leon Graham's house, she felt the genuine desire to share physical love.

Rob, watching her go, felt his own stirrings. He

was eternally grateful to Kale Salton and could never repay his debt to her. She had saved his marriage and shown him how to make it succeed. That was the greatest gift that she could have given him.

IV

No force yet existed in the territory of Utah to end the depredations taking place there. Counties were just in the process of organization, and consequently, there were no sheriffs or other law enforcement agencies to deal with those who broke the peace. In addition, the United States Army had no permanent troops stationed in the territory since they were needed in Wyoming, Montana, and Dakota, where Indian uprisings were occurring with greater frequency. Though Toby Holt and Colonel Andy Brentwood of Fort Shaw in Montana had signed a peace treaty with the Sioux, Cheyenne, and Blackfoot, everyone knew the treaty was temporary and would last only until the Indians could arm themselves and go to war against the white man, who they felt was invading their hunting grounds. Thus Andy Brentwood's troops had to remain in Montana.

So the violence along the line of construction of the railroad tracks grew steadily worse. The Indians, members of the Ute tribe, encouraged by Granger and well paid by him, continued their reign of wild terror, destroying track and attacking the work camps of the Central Pacific Railroad. And some of Ralph Granger's ranch hands added to the unfortunate situation, doing their own dirty work, usually at night when they could not be identified.

One effective technique of terror developed by Ian Cameron and his band of henchmen was to deal harshly with ranchers who consented to allow the railroad to build its lines across their property. Such ranchers were regarded as fair game, and soon after they signed papers granting the railroad a right of way, they were subjected to strange attacks.

In each case the plan was the same. A band of masked men—some who worked on Granger's ranch and some who were drifters hired by Ian Cameron—appeared out of nowhere, either at dusk or at dawn. The first that the rancher and his family learned of their presence was the fire that sprang up in his corral and his barns. When he raced out to see what was happening, heavy gunfire whistled overhead; it was some time before any of the family members figured out that no real attempt was being made to shoot them, that the purpose was merely to frighten them.

The rifle fire seemed in earnest, however, and as it continued in the direction of the ranch house, the rancher's cattle and horses were scattered over a wide area by riders who drove them without mercy. In almost every raid, the rancher, reasoning that he had been outnumbered by a band of robbers, gathered his family and fled into the wilderness.

That was all that Cameron and his band needed. The ranch house was invariably destroyed, its contents being subjected to axes and then scattered across the landscape before the house itself was set on fire with cans of kerosene.

The net result of these raids was that the ranchers lost not only their homes and all of their belongings but also their capital in the form of their livestock. Unable to cope with such disaster, the victims vacated their property, and once they had gone, Ralph Granger's henchmen returned and tore up any railroad tracks that had been built there.

It seemed virtually impossible for the good people of Utah to fight such raiders. The honorable citizens were simply too few in number.

The hardest hit of all, however, were the supply wagons that brought food, cooking utensils, tools, lumber, and other supplies to the site where the tracks were being built. It was becoming a common occurrence for wagons to be held up and robbed by the Indians.

These wagons, all of them pulled by mule teams, provided the lifeblood on which the building of the railroad depended. Consequently, the drivers, acting in self-defense, formed convoys and traveled in groups. They were far less likely to be attacked when there were several of them on the road together.

Among the independent drivers, those who owned their own wagons and mule teams, were two veteran frontiersmen by the names of Miller and Brady. They had a natural rivalry in that each man hoped to sell the railroad crews more of his wares than the other. But the violent attacks on the supply wagon trains forced them to join up as members of the same convoy. They were fearless on the road, and the other drivers in the convoy enjoyed the company of the two crusty old-timers and felt relatively safe with them. As the long-haired, gray-bearded Brady sometimes commented, "Never fear, lads. Any time Miller and I smell trouble a-brewin', we'll be off and runnin'. We don't aim to lose our mules, our wagons, or the goods that we're paid hard cash to transport."

Miller and Brady and the others in their convoy followed a regular routine, picking up at least once a week the goods for transfer in the booming frontier town of Ogden. They would load their wagons with supplies, spend the evening downing schooners of beer in a saloon—where they invariably whiled away the time by arguing about any subject that arose—and then the next morning, they would start out for the railroad terminus, which usually took two or three days to reach. After delivering their goods, they would return to Ogden, taking care to travel only in daylight and forming their wagons into a circle at night in order to discourage potential raiders.

One night when they were about a day out of Ogden, having delivered their goods at the railhead and now on their way back, they were finishing their supper of baked beans, bacon, and sourdough muffins when something of a commotion was raised at the far side of the fire. Miller, his lanky form resting against a wagon wheel, immediately reached for his old Pennsylvania long rifle and, standing, called, "What's the trouble yonder?"

The disembodied voice of a fellow driver floated back to him. "There's an Indian here tryin' to sell us somethin'," he called. "He's Shoshoni, an old fellow. I don't know if he's legitimate or if this is a trick."

"Let him through, so's we can keep an eye on him," Brady replied, and a moment later, the brave, wearing the war paint of the Shoshoni, approached him and grinned broadly.

"You good fellow," the Shoshoni said.

"Never mind all that," Miller replied brusquely. "What do you want?"

"I got mule for sale," the brave responded. "Good lead mule for wagon team. Best one you ever see."

It was likely that he had stolen the animal, and Miller started to wave the brave away. But Brady was curious. "Hold on a minute," he said. "Where can we see this here mule?"

The Indian pointed to a spot just outside the circle of wagons.

"I think I'll mosey over and have a look," Brady said, quickly picking up his long rifle and sauntering toward the place.

Miller was not to be outdone, and snatching up his own rifle, he followed his rival.

The Indian was at their heels, obviously pleased by the opportunity to make a sale. He jabbered incessantly about the wonderful qualities that this particular animal had and how fortunate the driver who bought him would be.

Somewhat to the surprise of Miller and Brady, the Shoshoni did not exaggerate. The mule was a sturdy, long-eared animal, about eleven hands high, with a pair of the most intelligent eyes that the two drivers had ever seen. Perhaps it was true that here was a lead mule for a wagon that was really a superior beast of burden.

"How much you want for him?" Miller demanded.

"Fifty dollar," the Indian replied.

The two veterans were stunned. Fifty dollars was a fortune, and almost no man who drove a wagon on the trail had that kind of money in his pocket. On the other hand, a dependable lead mule that started to move when requested and kept up a steady pace all day was worth its weight in gold.

The two drivers exchanged an uneasy glance. "I'll give you twenty-five," Brady said.

The Shoshoni shook his head. "Fifty dollar," he repeated stubbornly. "That's what I charge."

Again the two veterans exchanged a long look. There was no need for conversation between them. If the animal was all it was said to be, it would well be worth the fifty-dollar price.

"I reckon," Brady said, "that maybe we could put up twenty-five dollars each."

"If this here animal is all he's cracked up to be, we can take turns using him for a day," Miller said. "But how do we know that this Injun's right and that the critter's all that he says he is?"

The Shoshoni spread his hands. "You pay me half now," he said. "Tomorrow night I meet you at Last Chance Saloon in Ogden, and if you satisfied, you pay other twenty-five dollar. If you not happy with Jughead, you give him back to me, and I give you back your money."

The terms sounded satisfactory, and Miller grunted his agreement.

"What'd you say the mule's name is?" Brady demanded.

"Jughead," the Indian replied.

The two drivers were certain now that the animal had been stolen from its previous owner. No Shoshoni would name a mule Jughead. Miller scratched the animal between the eyes, and the mule looked at him soulfully. "Jughead," he said, "me and Brady here is gonna share you, so you see to it that you give both of us fair value. You look after us, and we'll take care of you."

"That's right," Brady added. "We ain't never gonna take a stick to you, and we'll treat you plenty good." He reached in his pocket and produced half of the twenty-five-dollar down payment.

Miller did the same, and the mule was theirs. They led the beast into the circle of wagons where the other animals were tied, and then Brady said, "I'll flip you to see who gets to use him tomorrow."

"Fair enough," Miller replied, and removed a silver half-dollar from his pocket. "Call it," he said, as he tossed the coin into the air.

"Tails," Brady replied, and crowed with delight when he found he had won. "Jughead," he said, "me and you is gonna get acquainted right fast!"

Jughead proved to be all that the Shoshoni had claimed—and a great deal more. He was a thoroughly reliable beast, took his place at the head of the column of mules automatically, and needed only a slight jiggling of reins to start the rest of the team forward, pulling the load. He trudged uncomplainingly and halted only when told to. The other mules meekly followed his lead, and Brady, whose team was being led by Jughead this day, had to slow his animals so that he did not outdistance the other drivers. By the time they reached Ogden, he and Miller were sold on the new lead mule.

After supper, which they ate at their campsite just outside town, the two drivers were ready to leave for the Last Chance Saloon in order to pay the Indian the second half of his fee when Brady had a bright idea. "Let's take Jughead with us," he said. "I don't want to let him out of our sight for a minute."

"Good idea," Miller replied, patting the mule on the head and taking the loose end of the rope that was looped around his neck. Jughead started off immediately and accompanied the pair.

The Shoshoni was waiting and showed no surprise when he saw the mule come inside the saloon with the two men. They paid him the remaining twenty-five dollars that was his due, and he promptly disappeared before any questions could be asked, confirming their suspicion that Jughead had been stolen. But the animal was far too precious for Brady and Miller to be too concerned about his past ownership.

They ordered their customary two beers and were oblivious to the stares of the bartender and the patrons who were amazed to see a mule in the saloon. Soon newcomers were entering the bar to see the mule for themselves, and the bartender quickly realized that the two old frontiersmen and their mule were actually good for business.

Miller felt that something was needed to convince the lead mule that he had become a highly valued member of a very special team. He reached into his shirt pocket and removed a stogie, a slender cigar made of a pungent tobacco and twisted into a rather strange shape. He extended the cigar to Jughead.

The mule sniffed the object, opened his mouth, took the stogie between his teeth, and proceeded to chew.

The animal seemed to enjoy the cigar enormously. Belching quietly, Jughead chewed rhythmically until the last of the cigar disappeared.

"You gotta hand it to the critter," Miller said. "He sure knows what he wants."

"He sure does," Brady echoed, and shaking his head, he ordered a refill of the mugs that he and the other driver had emptied.

The two veterans chatted amiably as they drank beer after beer, but inevitably, as their consumption mounted, both became increasingly cantankerous. Ultimately, they began to argue about where the rails of the Central Pacific and Union Pacific would eventually join. It was impossible for them to come to terms, and their voices rose as both of them became increasingly annoyed.

Soon they were shouting, not caring who heard them or how much they disturbed others at the bar. They stood facing each other, almost nose to nose, shaking their fists and cursing. Suddenly Jughead shoved his way between them, forcibly separating the two combatants.

Miller and Brady tried to push the animal aside, but Jughead demonstrated the main characteristic of a mule by refusing to budge. The animal could not be made to move even a fraction of an inch.

Brady and Miller tried talking over the mule's head, but once again Jughead thwarted them. The mule raised his head, lifted his ears, and then moved his head from one side to the other, making it impossible for the two old codgers to carry on a conversation, much less a quarrel.

The thwarted drivers had to stop drinking and knew the time had come when they would have to return to their campsite. As they started off down the street, the mule walked between them, and every time one of them tried to renew the dispute, the mule nudged him with considerable force.

Miller fell silent, and finally Brady's unhappy chuckle seemed to break the spell. "Damned if this here critter ain't smart," he said. "Damned if he ain't just about as smart as they come. He ain't gonna let us get near each other until we're cold sober again tomorrow mornin'."

Miller sounded somewhat forlorn. "I never knowed I'd have to do what a mule wanted in order to get along in life," he said, "but I guess that's the way it is. This critter is worth every cent that we paid for him, but he ain't my boss."

"Like hell he ain't," Brady replied, and laughed without humor.

Jughead continued to walk serenely down the main street of Ogden, keeping the two drivers separated.

Cindy Holt, having celebrated her seventeenth birthday several months before, was pleased, as she nowadays always was, to be seen with Hank Purcell. They finished their classes at the Fort Vancouver high school at the same time every day and customarily walked home together on the path that led from the school through the woods to the military post on the northern bank of the Columbia River. Cindy did not try to hide the fact that she had a serious crush on the blond-haired, freckle-faced Hank. He was an extraordinary boy, as she so often reminded her friends at school. He was the best rifle shot she had ever seen, not including her brother, Toby, or her late father, the legendary Whip Holt. Hank was completely self-reliant, and he had a maturity that often astonished her.

When they reached the post, they went straight to their house. There, Eulalia Blake gave them slices of apple pie and glasses of milk, which they ate ravenously. Then, following their regular custom, they went to their respective rooms to do their homework. So far, this appeared to be an ordinary day.

The first indication that something out of the ordinary was taking place occurred when Eulalia tapped at Hank's door. The boy looked up from his exercises in mathematics, a subject in which he showed a considerable proficiency, and then rose to his feet. "Yes, ma'am?" he asked tentatively.

"General Blake has come home from the office and would like to see you in his study, Hank."

The boy swallowed hard. "Did I do something wrong?"

Her smile broadened. "I wouldn't worry about it if I were you. Just don't keep the general waiting."

"No, ma'am, I won't." He sprinted down the stairs to the center hallway and walked to the open door of the study, where the two-star general sat at his desk.

As always, Hank felt somewhat ill at ease when he saw Lee Blake in full uniform. "You wanted to speak to me, sir?" he said politely, his manner reserved.

Lee waved him to a chair. "I think," he said, reaching into an inner pocket, "you'll be interested in a letter I received today from an old classmate of mine, General Pete Devereaux." He handed the letter to the boy.

Hank's heart hammered more rapidly when he saw the postmark on the envelope: *West Point, New York*. He knew there could be no mistake when he read the heading at the top of the communication that was inside the envelope: *Office of the Commandant, United States Military Academy.*

The message was self-explanatory:

Dear Lee,

I know you'll be interested in the outcome of your ward's application. Hank Purcell has been accepted as a member of the class of 1872 and will report as a cadet in the autumn of 1868.

Congratulations.

Yours,
Pete

The boy stared at the letter, unable to believe his good fortune. He privately breathed a long, deep breath of thanks to God. His prayers had been answered. Where not so long ago he had been an orphan in Montana, drifting aimlessly, he knew now that his future was assured.

Lee Blake guessed what was going through the teenager's mind. "This isn't an end in itself, Hank," he said. "It's the beginning of something. It's the foundation for the career you're going to have."

The boy looked at him and swallowed hard. "I know, sir, and I'm more grateful to you than I can ever tell you. You have no idea how much this means to me."

"I think I can guess," the gray-haired man said, and smiled. "But there's no need to thank me, you know. You were accepted on merit, on the basis of the scores you achieved in the various tests that you had to take."

Hank shook his head. "I think the fact that the commanding general of the Army of the West acted as my sponsor didn't do me any harm."

"I suppose it didn't," Lee admitted, "but all the same, your own record is what mattered. The fact that you're my ward has no bearing on your standing, and it won't have once you're there. You're entering a system where you're going to be judged strictly on your own merits."

"I'm glad of that, sir," Hank answered fiercely, "and I aim to make you proud of me by the time I graduate and win my commission. Just you watch me, General."

"I'll do that, boy, with the greatest of pleasure," Lee said.

"Does Mrs. Blake know about this?" Hank asked.

The tall, dignified man nodded. "I told her when I got home, but I asked her not to mention anything to you. I wanted the pleasure of surprising you myself."

"All I can say is that it's some surprise." Hank stood erect, drawing himself to attention as he had seen so many soldiers at the fort do in General Blake's presence, and then raised his right hand to his forehead in a smart salute. Lee Blake was touched as he returned the salute.

Hank then dashed out of the general's study and rushed down the hallway at a breakneck pace. Eulalia was in the kitchen conferring with the cook when Hank burst into the room, then kissed and embraced her exuberantly. "You knew," he said accusingly, "but you didn't say a word to me!"

"I couldn't spoil my husband's pleasure," Eulalia replied, beaming. "He was so proud of you, Hank, and so eager to tell you the good news himself."

"I think," the boy told her, wide-eyed, "that this is the most important day of my life."

Eulalia guided him from the kitchen into the parlor. "Yes," she said. "It's terribly important right now, but there are many more important days to come. The day you enter the academy will be one, and the day you graduate and are granted your commission

will be another. I just hope that you're making the
right move, Hank, and that you really want a career
as an army officer."

"Oh, I do, ma'am," he replied.

"The army can be a cruel and hard profession,"
she told him. "The army demands that it come first at
all times, ahead of your family, and that you serve
with unswerving loyalty, even when you don't agree
with the position your superiors have taken on an issue. I've known several people who have become
high-ranking officers, and none of them is more prominent than General Blake, who has served his country
with a loyalty second to none. If he were forced to
make a choice at this moment between his daughter
and me on one hand and his career on the other, I'm
sure that the army would win. Fortunately, we don't
face that choice, and neither do you, but you'll be
wise to keep it in mind."

"I will, ma'am," the boy promised.

Cindy came into the room, her natural seventeen-year-old boisterousness vastly reduced. In fact,
she looked quite shy as she said to Hank, "Mama told
me you've been accepted as a cadet at the academy.
Congratulations." She extended a hand to him.

The boy clicked his heels together and shook
hands formally with her. "Thank you very much,
Cindy," he said primly.

This mutual show of manners was so unusual
that Eulalia had to avert her face so the two teenagers would not see her laugh.

General Blake came into the parlor to join his
wife for their customary predinner drink, and although they usually spent this hour by themselves,
they asked Cindy and Hank to join them. Cindy was
soon behaving naturally and talking incessantly, but
Hank, much to the surprise of the older couple, drew
back into a shell and became very quiet. He seemed
lost in thought.

Eulalia knew that by rights the boy should be in high spirits, and she glanced at her husband, then asked, "What's wrong, Hank?"

Hank was startled. "Wrong, ma'am? Nothing!"

"We wondered," Lee commented quietly, "because you're so quiet."

"Oh, that." The boy was silent again for a few moments and then took a deep breath. "I was thinking, that's all. You know, my mother died giving birth to me, so I never knew her and had to depend on my father for a description of her. I never even seen, I mean, I never saw as much as a picture of her. Then I lost my pa when that gunslinger in Montana shot him, and ever since that day I was alone in the world until first Clarissa took me in, and then you folks did. So I've been kind of wondering."

"Wondering what, Hank?" Eulalia prodded, her eyes revealing her bewilderment.

Hank clenched his fists, and it was obvious that he was having a difficult time as he forced himself to continue. "Anyway, you've been so blame good to me that I feel I owe you something in return, and now that I know I'm going to go to the academy, where I'm going to start earning my own way, I would . . . well, I would kind of like it if you folks saw fit to adopt me. You're the only family I have, and I'd like to make our relationship permanent."

Eulalia and Lee exchanged a single, swift glance. They had frequently discussed the possibility of adopting Hank but had thought that perhaps the boy would feel he was too old to be adopted. Clearly, that was not true.

Lee took charge. "We've often discussed the possibility of adopting you, Hank, and I can tell you there's nothing in the world that either of us would like more."

The boy beamed. "Gee," he said. "That's just great, then."

Out of the corner of her eye, Eulalia caught a glimpse of Cindy and saw that her daughter looked horrified. But this was not the moment to think of Cindy. "We'll be very happy and proud to welcome you into the family, Hank," she said, "and I know that Toby and Clarissa will agree heartily with that. They've said as much to me when we've talked about you."

The boy's sense of excitement grew. To be accepted as a full-fledged member of such a distinguished family was beyond his wildest dreams, and his voice shook as he asked, "Will I have your last name instead of my own?"

"Certainly, if you wish it," Lee told him.

Hank looked down at his hands, then said softly, "I'll always remember my real father, but I'd be awfully proud to be a Blake."

Eulalia kissed Hank and embraced him, and Lee shook the boy's hand, then did away with formality and gave in to his feelings, hugging him. When the excitement began to subside, Eulalia noted that Cindy was no longer in the room but had quietly vanished. Again she put the girl out of her mind for the moment.

"I'm probably crazy to take on the extra burden at the academy of being your son, General," Hank said, "but I can't help it."

"For one thing, you had better stop calling me General and start referring to me as Father," Lee told him with a smile, "and for another, I don't think you are at all stupid to give yourself that extra burden at the academy. The incentive just could be a help to you."

"I know it will be—Dad." Hank turned fiery red, and Lee beamed at him in pleasure.

"Supper will be ready any minute," Eulalia said. "I had better round up Cindy. Don't go to the table without us." She left the room and hurried up the stairs to her daughter's bedchamber, where she tapped on the door.

"Come in," Cindy called, her voice sounding sorrowful.

Her mother stepped inside the room and saw Cindy lying on her bed, her face buried in her pillow. Eulalia closed the door behind her and leaned against it. "What on earth is the matter, dear?" she asked.

Cindy looked up at her, and the girl's expression was little short of tragic. Her face was flushed; she had obviously been crying. "It's bad enough," Cindy declared, "that Hank is going to be spending four years at the military academy and that we'll be separated by a whole continent. The fact that he's going to be my brother is just too much, though. I don't think I can stand it." The tears started to roll down her cheeks again. "How can I ever admit to my friends that the man I love is my brother? How can I possibly ever look forward to marrying my brother?"

Eulalia was vastly relieved to learn the source of Cindy's unhappiness. She had feared that Cindy disapproved of the adoption plan for another reason, possibly jealousy. Now she understood that her daughter's tears resulted from her fondness of Hank, not out of competition with him. To Cindy, his adoption was an insurmountable obstacle to future romance.

"You can take my word for it, dear," she said gently. "Although Hank will become your brother, he'll be an adopted brother, not a blood relation, so there will be no barrier to a romance between you."

"Are you sure of that, Mama? Really sure?"

"Of course. I'm quite positive. If at the end of four more years, you and Hank should decide you want to be married, nothing will stand in your way. But in the meantime, I think you're a bit premature

in your thinking. I would urge you to let the four
years pass as they will and take one step at a time."

Cindy seemed to accept her mother's advice, and
they went downstairs together to the celebration of
Hank's acceptance at West Point and his new status
in the Blake family.

Kale Salton had to force herself to keep her noon
dinner engagement with Beth and Rob Martin. She
dressed demurely in a dark blue jacket and skirt and
put only a trace of makeup on her lips and eyes. Then
she had her driver bring the carriage around and take
her to the hotel.

The Martins were in their suite when she arrived
at their door, and her heart turned over when she saw
them. Beth, wearing a stylish new green dress that
complimented her blond hair and emphasized her
trim, lovely figure, was radiant, more so than she had
been at any time since Kale had known her. Beth embraced her friend warmly and whispered, "Thank you
for your help."

The tall, stolid Rob was so reserved that it was
hard to believe that twenty-four hours earlier he had
been making passionate love with Kale. But he
warmed when he saw her, grinned, and shook her
hand at length. "You're the perfect person to meet us
for dinner today," he told her. "If it hadn't been for
you, Beth and I wouldn't be here together at this very
moment."

Beth had no idea what her husband meant, but
Kale understood completely, and her heart sank.
Looking at the red-haired, handsomely attired Rob,
his face glowing, Kale found it inexplicable that after
her years of experience with so many men, she should
have lost her heart to one who was not available to
her. There was nothing that she could do to alter the
situation now. She would never forgive herself if she
came between a happy couple.

They went to the hotel's elegant, gaslit dining room to eat, and there Rob ordered a bottle of champagne and then proposed a toast to Kale.

"Here's to Kale," he said, lifting his glass. "With our thanks for saving our marriage."

As Beth drank, she assumed that he was referring only to the help and advice that Kale had given her. Not in her wildest imagination did she dream that Kale had seduced her husband in order to illustrate to him how little sexual intercourse meant without love.

They chatted amiably throughout the meal, and Kale put up a marvelous front, never for a moment admitting that she had been generous at the cost of her own happiness and fulfillment.

The couple's plans for the future were made. They intended to leave that same afternoon for Sacramento, and after Rob finished his conferences with the representatives of the Central Pacific Railroad, he and Beth would go first to Portland, where they would visit his parents, as well as Toby and Clarissa Holt, who lived on their ranch outside the city. Then, after a stay of indeterminate length, they would go up to Washington and vacation in the lodge Toby and Rob had built in the heart of the lumbering district. It was there that Beth's mother, Cathy Blake, had died with Whip Holt in the tragic rockslide, and Beth had expressly asked to go to the lodge so that she could pay her respects at her mother's grave.

While they were at the lodge, Beth and Rob would decide on future plans—where they would build their house and whether Rob would continue to work for the railroad or perhaps become a businessman in Oregon or Washington. He could always count on a position in the firm of Chet Harris, an old family friend who had met Rob's parents and the Holts and Blakes as a boy crossing the continent with them in the first wagon train. Chet had become a financier and now managed the Holt-Martin gold mine in Montana. But, Rob thought, whatever career he chose, it was clear that his future with his beautiful wife was secure.

"We've talked quite enough about us," Beth said suddenly. "What are your plans, Kale?"

"I have none, really," Kale replied slowly. "I'll still be doing business at the same old stand, so to speak." Her candor cast a temporary pall over the dinner. Rob and Beth were not surprised that she would be continuing to live as a courtesan, but there was something in her voice and expression that indicated she was far from happy with her lot. It was all the more disturbing because the stunning, auburn-haired Kale was usually such a hearty, self-confident individual.

"Perhaps you can come up and visit us as soon as we get settled in our new home," Beth said, her blue eyes sparkling. "How does that strike you, Kale?"

"We'll have to wait and see," Kale answered, uncertain that she would have the courage to face Rob again in the future.

Rob had the uncanny feeling that he was responsible in some way for Kale's reticence. "Please do come and see us," he said. "There's nothing that I would like better, and come to think of it, there're some mighty fine men up in Washington who are still bachelors, only because of an absence of appropriate women to marry."

Kale was flattered that he should think of her as someone who would be "appropriate" as a wife. Apparently he did not hold her dissolute life against her, and perhaps it was this very innocence and lack of complexity that had caused her to fall in love with Rob.

They parted company in the hotel lobby after the meal. The women embraced warmly, and kissed, and then Rob gave Kale a friendly, light kiss.

As she climbed into her carriage, Kale's fists

clenched, and she fought back tears. She was voluntarily giving up the one man on earth who meant anything to her and was condemning herself to a dreary life of loveless relationships, with an endless string of faceless men.

V

The visit that Rob and Beth Martin made to Portland was wonderful. They were greeted enthusiastically by their fellow second-generation Oregonians, the sons and daughters of those who had crossed America on the first wagon train, and they enjoyed themselves thoroughly. Among this group, they were closest to Toby and Clarissa Holt, who had not seen the couple for a very long time. There was a joyous reunion at the Holt ranch, with Rob and Beth delighted to see the new baby and with the friends filling one another in on all that had taken place. Rob and Beth were so happy with each other that they failed to see the great tension between Toby and Clarissa.

Rob and Beth found particularly pleasing their ongoing relationships with Rob's parents. The white-haired Dr. Martin, who still worked as hard as a man half his age, took time off from his patients to enjoy a number of outings with his son and daughter-in-law, fishing and picnicking in the beautiful countryside of Oregon. At Beth's request, her mother-in-law, Tonie, spent a great deal of time with the young couple, too, shopping in Portland with them or attending plays and concerts at the newly opened opera house, which was Portland's pride.

In Sacramento Rob had received a request from the Central Pacific Railroad for specific information about the terrain adjacent to the tracks along the route he had laid out for the line. He was also told that in due time, he would be approached by an agent of the railroad to discuss the possibility of further employment, but until then he should concentrate on writing his report and then take his holiday in the Washington mountains.

Rob went to work at once on the report for the Central Pacific. It was a major effort and took him much longer than he had believed would be necessary. After six weeks of living at his parents' home while he completed his assignment, the report was finished by early summer. He and Beth intended to go on after that, stopping one last time at the nearby ranch of the Holts before going up to Fort Vancouver and then to the lodge in Washington.

On the last day of their visit, Beth sat at a table in the Martin kitchen shelling peas, while her mother-in-law was busy peeling potatoes. An air of great harmony was prevalent, and Tonie, looking matronly in middle age, smiled a trifle wistfully as she said, "You don't know how much Dr. Martin and I have appreciated this visit of yours, Beth. Rob hasn't spent this long with us since he went off to the war in sixty-one."

"Rob has been very busy working on his special report," Beth said, "but I've loved every minute of it."

"I'm so glad," her mother-in-law said.

"It's fortunate that we're so close because I have something important I want to talk to you about."

Tonie continued to peel a potato. "And what might that be, dear?"

Beth put down the bowl of green peas and, smoothing her skirt, looked into her mother-in-law's face and smiled coyly. "There are times in life," she said delicately, "when things of great importance take place."

"Oh?" Tonie's mind seemed to be elsewhere.

Beth continued to bait her mother-in-law. "I suggest," she said, "that you check with Dr. Martin. He'll find it far easier than I do to tell you the results."

"What results, dear?"

Beth had to keep from giggling at the game she was playing with her mother-in-law. "I saw him yesterday, and he gave me a thorough physical exam."

"I didn't know that," Tonie said, "but then he never discusses medical matters with me." Beth had begun to pique her mother-in-law's interest. "What caused you to go to my husband for an examination in the first place?"

Beth was now laughing openly. "Oh, it was one thing—and another. Actually, I haven't had an examination in a long time, and I was overdue, so I thought as long as I was here, I might as well take advantage of the time—" Her voice trailed away inconclusively.

Tonie looked at her, and the older woman's eyes sparkled. "Beth Martin," she declared. "You're going to have a baby!"

Beth nodded, smiling shyly. "You guessed it, Mother."

"And you're all right? You're in good health?"

"Yes, ma'am. The doctor says I'm as strong as a horse."

Tonie embraced and kissed her and held her at arm's length. "I think," she said, "this is just wonderful."

"Me, too." Beth giggled and suddenly felt very girlish again.

"Does Rob know?"

"No, not yet. I wanted him to finish his report before I told him."

"When are you going to tell him?"

"Tonight, I guess, before we go on to see Toby and Clarissa. I would rather he learn about it here under your roof than under the roof of friends."

Tonie couldn't help taking charge. "Unless you have some particular reason for waiting until tonight, why don't you tell him right now?" she asked. "Then we can have a real celebration at supper tonight."

"You're right," Beth said, and she rose, suddenly looking uncertain.

Tonie inspected her carefully. "Beth, dear," she said slowly, "I know you and Rob had a number of serious problems and you went through a very rough time. I've been very grateful in the weeks that you've been here with us that you seem to have solved your difficulties."

"We have," Beth said fervently. "We've never been so close."

"Good," her mother-in-law responded. "I was afraid that your reticence to mention your news to him might have been caused by some residue of your trouble."

Beth shook her head. "I believe with all my heart," the younger woman said, "that our problems are behind us now. The reason I was hesitating to tell Rob was a silly one, I'm afraid. I'm sure he's going to be as ecstatic as I am, but I was putting off the moment of telling him because I wanted everything to be just right. I want so very badly to have him feel as happy as I do. Do I make sense?"

Tonie nodded. "Of course, dear. And he *will* be very happy when you *do* tell him. So don't keep this to yourself any longer. I saw him come in from his father's office while we've been in here, so he must be upstairs in your bedroom right now."

"All right," Beth said, and her voice became tremulous. "I'll break the news to him this very minute."

She left the kitchen and took her time as she mounted the stairs to their bedchamber on the second floor.

Rob was sitting at a little desk by the window, making notations in a small notebook that he carried. He looked up and grinned. "You and my mother were so deep in conversation down in the kitchen just now that I didn't want to disturb you," he said.

"You wouldn't have disturbed us," Beth replied lightly. "We were talking about something very personal that your father already knows, and I thought your mother deserved to know, too."

He made another notation or two in his notebook; his mind was obviously not on what his wife was saying.

"Would you put away your pen and papers?" she asked.

Rob decided to humor her. "Sure," he replied, placing the pen on the table beside him and pocketing the notebook. "I'm now devoting my full attention to you."

"We're about to perform a rather ambitious experiment in the months to come," Beth said mischievously. "We're going to find out how much you've learned from Dr. Martin."

Rob stared at her blankly. "What have I to learn from him?"

"The fine art of fatherhood," she replied softly but distinctly.

He stared hard at her for a moment, and then his face was lighted by a beatific smile. Suddenly he whooped at the top of his voice. His shout carried to the attic above and to the cellar below.

Throwing his arms around his wife, he began to dance around the room with her, hugging her wildly as he did. All at once he realized what he was doing and stopped instantly, leading her to a chair and insisting that she sit in it. "I'm so sorry," he muttered. "I've got to be more careful. I'm so sorry."

Beth couldn't help laughing aloud. "I'm not all

that fragile," she said. "I'm not made of glass, you know."

"All the same," he insisted solicitously, "we've got to be careful. We can't afford to take any risks with your health."

"Your father said that I'm in perfect health, and he advised me not to indulge myself."

"When did you see him?" Rob could not erase the broad grin from his face.

"Yesterday," Beth said. "I suspected as much several weeks earlier, but I wanted to make certain, and he confirmed my guess."

"This is the best news in the world," Rob said, "but obviously we'll have to change our plans. You either have to stay here with my folks or go to your father and stepmother at Fort Vancouver. You don't want to be out of touch with my father at any time in the weeks ahead."

Beth shook her head vehemently. "No, Rob. You're very wrong, and I won't be either staying here or going permanently to Fort Vancouver. I discussed the whole matter at length with your father, and he agrees with me that our troubles were caused by the fact that we were separated. I'm never going to be separated from you again, no matter what."

"But the lodge is no place for a woman who is about to have a baby," he protested.

She shook her head. "That's pure nonsense," she said. "When I had that talk with your father, he told me that there were any number of women who were pregnant when they crossed the continent in wagon trains. If they could put up with those hardships, I'm sure I can tolerate something only a fraction as rigorous. If you disagree with me, have it out with your father. But I'll tell you one thing right now. No matter what may happen, I refuse to be separated from you again. We're together now and always, for the rest of our lives!"

*   *   *

Beth and Rob Martin beamed at each other and then at Clarissa and Toby Holt as they all sat in the dining room of the Holt ranch house. The Martins had arrived only an hour earlier and, unable to keep their secret to themselves, they had revealed Beth's condition to their host and hostess.

Toby poured four glasses of a fine port he had been saving for a special occasion and then lifted his glass in a toast. "To Beth, to Rob, and to your son or daughter," he said. "You've had a rough time, and you deserve all the happiness that is going to be yours."

"May your baby be as perfect as our Tim," Clarissa said, then added silently to herself: *And may you have the marital happiness that we've missed. May you succeed where we have failed.*

The joy of the Martins was so great that Toby, too, felt the contrast. He and Clarissa had lost their way and were floundering. Rob and Beth had faced obstacles as great as those that he and Clarissa faced, but they had overcome their difficulties and achieved a rapport and an understanding.

Feeling inadequate and unhappy, Toby glanced to the place where his wife sat opposite him at the table. Their eyes met, and both of them froze. Even after all this time, he was sure that she held his affair with Gentle Doe against him. She, of course, was overwhelmed with guilt because of her failure to tell Toby about the reappearance of Otto Sinclair.

The long-standing friendship of the two couples worked a chemistry of its own, and it was not too difficult to present a festive air, even though neither Toby nor Clarissa felt like celebrating.

They were sharing their dessert when one of the hired hands came in and announced that a stranger on horseback had just arrived at the ranch and wanted a word with Toby. Toby excused himself, and before long the others could hear him talking to a man in the front hall. A few moments later, he ushered the visitor, a portly, balding man wearing a business suit, into the dining room. Clarissa, who had been alarmed when the stranger was announced, was relieved to see it wasn't Otto Sinclair.

"My wife, Mr. Andrews," Toby said, "and this is Mr. and Mrs. Robert Martin. Mr. Andrews is a special representative of the railroad."

"I'm in luck finding both you men together," Andrews said. "I've been sent out here as a representative of Leland Stanford and Thomas Durant, major stockholders of the Central Pacific and Union Pacific railroads, on a mission that involves both of you. You, Mr. Martin, perhaps had an inkling that the railroads would be in touch with you sooner or later, but with one thing and another—reaching an agreement of Union Pacific and Central Pacific boards of directors, getting stockholders' approval—it took longer than we thought to come up with a plan of action for the problems in Utah."

Clarissa invited Mr. Andrews to sit at the table and offered him a piece of pie and a cup of coffee, which he accepted gratefully. "I guess," Andrews said, "that the violence that's prevalent in Utah where the railroad line is currently being built is no secret and no surprise to either of you gentlemen."

"No, it isn't," Rob replied. "I just came back from Utah a couple of months ago, and conditions were very rough then and were getting much worse. There are those who are opposed to the establishment of a railroad, and they're doing everything they can to thwart the building of the lines. Add to that the fact that Indians of the area are being bribed to raise havoc, too, and you have an explosive situation that makes the construction of the railroad that much more difficult to finish. Frankly, I don't know when the line will be completed."

"You've saved me the need for a great deal of ex-

planation, Mr. Martin," the representative of the railroads said. "You've summed up the unfortunate
situation in Utah very handily. The American people,
however, are demanding that the railroad be completed. President Johnson and the Congress have issued land grants to the railroad companies, and
freight is already piling up, both in the major industrial cities of the East and out here in San Francisco
and Portland and Sacramento, as manufacturers await
the opportunity to exchange goods freely and easily."

"We can understand the frustrations that officials
feel," Toby said. "The time is ripe for the establishment of a railroad line that spans the continent, and
every week of delay is expensive, as well as frustrat-
ing."

"Gentlemen," Andrews said, "at the instigation of
Mr. Stanford and Mr. Durant, the boards of directors
for the Central and Union Pacific railroads have authorized me to approach you two and to make you a
flat offer of one thousand dollars per month, each,
plus all of your expenses, if you will take charge of
our affairs in Utah and restore law and order."

The offer was so surprising that Toby and Rob
inadvertently exchanged a shocked glance.

Andrews misunderstood the look. "If the financial
terms are not satisfactory," he said, "I'm authorized to
increase our offer to fifteen hundred dollars per
month for each of you."

Toby couldn't help smiling to himself. The railroad man had no idea that he and Rob owned a gold
mine in Montana that made them independently
wealthy. By hesitating for a moment, they each had
increased the amount offered to them by a sum of five
hundred dollars per month.

"How long do you reckon it will take to establish
peace in Utah?" Toby asked.

Andrews shrugged. "I would say, Mr. Holt, that
it is strictly up to you and Mr. Martin," he said. "If

you could work wonders and achieve a lasting peace there in one month, it would be miraculous, and I'm sure the boards of directors would give you a very handsome bonus. But don't misunderstand me. They're not expecting miracles of any kind. We're thinking in terms of six months to a year."

"That's far more realistic," Rob commented.

Beth, who had been listening carefully, suddenly raised her voice. "May I inquire about the living quarters in Utah?"

Andrews wondered why she should ask, then decided she was concerned for her husband's well-being. "The gentlemen will occupy a pleasant house in Ogden, Mrs. Martin," he said, "and whenever they go into the wilderness, they will have as many comforts as we can provide them, as well as reasonable protection from violence."

Rob knew exactly what his wife was thinking, but before he had a chance to protest, Beth spoke out. "It sounds to me as though I would get along just fine in Utah. You came home on a Central Pacific work train, Rob, and I could use such a train—even if full passenger service hasn't been established as yet—when the time comes for me to see the doctor and have my baby."

"I suppose you're right," he said reluctantly.

Andrews was surprised. "You would accompany your husband to Utah in spite of all the troubles there, Mrs. Martin?" he asked.

Beth nodded emphatically. "Being the daughter of an army general, I've been in many troubled areas in my life. So I'm well accustomed to upheavals and dangers."

She turned to her husband and spoke quietly. "You make up your mind as to whether you want to take this assignment, Rob," she said. "I would be the last to interfere and try to make up your mind for you. All I can say is that if you do take it, I'm going with you. And that's final."

Her husband sighed and nodded, but he did not look displeased. He, too, wanted to avoid another separation, despite the risks to her in the lawless territory.

Andrews could foresee complications with such an arrangement but accepted them. The acquisition of Rob Martin as a troubleshooter was worth the difficulties involved in having his wife with him in Utah. "What about you, Mrs. Holt?" the representative of the Union Pacific asked. "Do you also plan to move to the territory with your husband?"

Not looking at Toby, Clarissa shook her head. "Toby certainly knows that he's free to make up his own mind as to whether to accept your offer. As for me, much as I'm tempted to go with him to Utah, I'm afraid I can't even consider the possibility. Our son is too young to be forced to withstand the rigors of life in a primitive territory, and I intend to stay right here at the ranch in Oregon with him. Perhaps I'm being selfish, but I feel that the needs of our baby come before our own desires."

That ended the subject, and Toby was relieved about her decision not to accompany him. Not only would she and their son avoid the risks of living in a lawless area, but the separation might even do them some good.

Andrews could scarcely believe his good fortune. Aside from the disparate viewpoints of the two young wives, their husbands seemed to accept the offer of the Union and Central Pacific without further discussion. The representative of the railroads wanted to make sure of the ground on which he stood. "Do I assume correctly that you'll agree to sign on with us, Mr. Holt?" he asked.

"Sure, why not?" Toby asked recklessly. At the moment it was easier to go to Utah and wage war against the unscrupulous elements trying to disrupt the establishment of railroad lines than it was to fight in vain to reestablish a solid basis for his relationship with Clarissa.

Clarissa heard his tone and wanted to cry out that, in truth, she would love to go with him, that she wanted to be with him. But she could not say a word and sat glumly, her expression frozen. She, not he, was now responsible for the failure of their marriage.

"Do you also accept employment by the railroads, Mr. Martin?" Andrews asked.

"I do, sir, provided it's understood that my wife will be going with me and that we'll be given quarters suitable for her wherever I need to travel in the territory," Rob replied.

The representative nodded and then smiled with satisfaction. His condition would be easy to fulfill, if that was what he and his wife wanted. They would be taking all the risks, Andrews knew, while he would be able to report to his employers that he had contracted the two men they wanted.

The plans to vacation in the lodge in Washington were put off for the time being. Rob and Beth immediately left the Holt ranch and hurried to Fort Vancouver so that they could spend several days with Beth's father and stepmother. Eulalia and Lee pampered the mother-to-be, and they held their peace when she announced she was going to Utah. They, too, knew the importance of the young couple's avoiding another separation. From Fort Vancouver, Rob and Beth would return to Portland and join Toby, boarding a coastal steamer to San Francisco, then going on to Sacramento, where a special passenger car would be put on a Central Pacific work train to Utah for their convenience.

Toby delayed his family farewells until the night he left the ranch to join his partner and Beth. With

his belongings packed in two trunks and his rifle and
pistols cleaned and ready for use, he went into the
nursery and looked down for a time at his sleeping
son. "Timmy," he said softly, "behave yourself, and I
pray to the Almighty to look after you. If anything
should happen to me, do what your mama tells you,
grow up to be strong and smart, and don't make the
damn fool mistakes that your father made."

Clarissa heard him through the open door that
separated the nursery from their own bedroom, and
she wanted to weep. What if indeed this were the last
time she would see her husband? She thought once
again that it was her own weakness, her own cow-
ardice, her own inability to face reality and openly
condemn Otto Sinclair for reappearing and successfully blackmailing her that was making it impossible
to heal the rupture with Toby.

Toby came into the room and forced a smile. "I
guess this is good-bye again," he said.

"I suppose it is," she said with forced lightness.

"If you need any help for yourself or the baby,"
Toby said heavily, "my mother is no farther away
than Fort Vancouver, and she and the general will be
glad to pitch in anytime, no matter what the problem."

"I know." Clarissa's voice was virtually inaudible.

"You can get in touch with me by telegraph in
Ogden, and if there's a serious emergency, I can always get home in a hurry."

"Thank you, Toby," she said politely.

He looked at her and was about to add something but refrained. Her cool response discouraged
closeness of any kind.

In truth, Clarissa wanted to throw her arms
around his neck and beg his forgiveness for her lack
of honesty to him in her dealings with Otto Sinclair.
It was unfortunate, however, that she had waited too
long for that, and her nerve failed her when she

thought of making a full confession to him. Sooner or later she hoped she would find the courage to speak the truth to him. Then and only then would she know if he would leave her or if he would stay, if they could save their marriage and work their problems out.

The Central Pacific Railroad provided a special board of directors car, attached to the end of a work train heading to Utah from Sacramento, and Toby Holt and the Martins traveled in style. They had a private drawing room, a dining room, and two large bedchambers in the car, and Beth, less accustomed to travel by train than were her husband and his partner, marveled at the ease with which they crossed the Sierra Nevada.

Sitting with Rob and Toby in the dining room of their railroad car after being served a delicious meal by a porter provided by the Central Pacific, Beth looked out the window and was awed by the view. They passed through deep timberlands, over high trestle bridges nearly half a mile long, and into long tunnels blasted through the mountains. For the first time, Beth understood the tremendous problems that had confronted Rob in surveying for the railroad, and she suddenly felt great pride in the job he had done.

Ultimately they crossed the vast state of Nevada and made their way through desolate stretches to where the tracks came to a halt in Utah, about twenty-five miles west of the growing town of Ogden.

Ogden was a community that provided the elements of a settled town and, at the same time, had those of a new, raw frontier community. Established where the Ogden and Weber rivers meet, it began as a trading post back in the 1820s, and in 1847 it was transformed into a substantial community by the arrival of a large number of Mormons. The Mormons who had settled there were hardworking, sincere ranchers and farmers and served as a stabilizing influence. Law-abiding folk, they minded their own business, and they augured well for the future of Ogden.

The floating population of the town created trouble, though. Made up of railroad workers, unemployed ranch hands, down-and-out prospectors, and ne'er-do-wells who looked for any way to make a dollar honest or otherwise, they crowded the town and frequented the saloons and brothels.

The Central Pacific owned much of the property in Ogden, and there was a house waiting for the new arrivals. Rob, who was familiar with the town from the time he had spent in Utah before, hired a wagon to take them there. They rode from the railroad along the well-traveled dirt road leading into town, and after a full day's ride, the buildings of Ogden came into view. It was a typical frontier town, with a dusty main street and a variety of recently constructed, wooden buildings, including saloons, hotels, a general store, a bank, a territorial office—but mostly saloons.

Because of the railroad and the increasing number of settlers, the town was bustling. As they rode, Toby and Rob carrying their rifles with Beth seated between them, it was obvious that the young woman was creating something of a furor. Virtually every man who saw the attractive, blue-eyed blonde on the wagon seat gaped at her, and only the presence of her companions saved her from the embarrassment of their comments.

"Beth," Rob said, flicking the reins to increase the pace of the horses, "the first law of living in Ogden is very simple. You stay indoors most of the time, and you venture out only when I'm with you or when Toby is with you. In that way you'll stay clear of trouble."

"I reckon it's the only way," Toby added solemnly, then observed, "You'll notice, Rob, that the town appears to be full of idlers. That's why there's so much stew and fuss and ferment hereabouts. Whenever you find idlers, you find real trouble. I'm going to go out on an inspection trip in the field in the next day or two and see what I can dig up."

"Do you want me to come with you?" Rob asked.

Toby shook his head. "No, you stay here with Beth. I think you're going to have more than enough to do keeping the peace in Ogden. I want to get to know what groups are either kicking up trouble or have the potential for doing so. We'll work out our schedules over supper."

At last they arrived in the residential section of town, where there were several well-built clapboard houses with neat yards and wooden fences surrounding them. These were the houses owned by the professionals and businessmen of the town, and among them was the tidy-looking white house owned by the railroad.

Soon they were settled in the house, which was pleasantly furnished and well supplied with linens and kitchen utensils. The railroad also provided the tenants with a combination housekeeper and cook, who would be a great help to Beth as her pregnancy advanced.

The morning after their arrival, Beth expressed her intention of going into town to the general store for some food staples. Naturally Rob insisted on accompanying her. They started out at once, on foot, and when they reached the store, Beth busied herself examining the produce. For a mountain state, Utah was provided with a great variety of vegetables and usually hard to find food items, due to the presence of the railroad and the market created by the industrious and affluent residents of the community.

Suddenly the cultured, ladylike voice of a young woman cut through the air. "You see, Jim? I told you it's Rob Martin! I would know him anywhere."

Beth watched from a distance of about ten yards as her husband removed his hat and was warmly greeted by the dark-haired young woman, who, although not a beauty by any means, nevertheless had a self-confidence and poise that made her definitely attractive. Her escort, whom Beth remembered was the woman's cousin, was a tall, slender, dark-haired young man who wore a patch over one eye. The attire of both was expensive; it was obvious that they were people of means.

Rob appeared very pleased to see them. After chatting for a moment or two, he looked up and beckoned to his wife to join them. Feeling very much the outsider, Beth approached slowly.

Rob presented her to Millicent Randall and her cousin, Jim Randall. They greeted Beth warmly, having last seen her in San Francisco after her trial. Beth responded politely but somewhat shyly to all their questions concerning her welfare.

"For all the good it's doing us, Rob," Jim Randall said, "we're keeping after Ralph Granger to sell us a piece of his property. But he appears adamant." Then in a confidential tone of voice, he added, "If you ask me, I'm reasonably sure that Granger's responsible for most of the violence and upheavals in this territory. He's so powerful, however, that no one has the strength or the courage to stop him."

Rob, remembering Granger's attempt to bribe him the previous year, concurred with Jim Randall's observation. "If he is at fault," Rob said, "Granger will pay for his transgressions. I guarantee it."

"You've returned to Utah to restore order here?" Millicent ventured to guess, and the concern in her voice was evident.

"Something like that," Rob admitted.

"Well, do be careful, Rob, dear," Millicent replied. "Mr. Granger could be a very dangerous and wicked man, and anyone who clashes with him could be in great peril."

"Maybe he's the one who could be in peril," Rob replied.

The Randalls were staying at the one decent hotel in town, the Ogden House, and invited the couple to dine with them there the following evening. After conferring with his wife about the invitation, Rob accepted for both of them. Then the Randalls paid for the goods they had selected and left the store. Beth once again went about choosing her own items.

As the Martins stood at the counter, waiting for the clerk to tally what they had selected, Beth smiled thinly. "Miss Randall and her cousin seem to be enjoying their sojourn in the West very much," she said, her voice tart. "If you ask me, as a purely biased observer, I would swear she has a distinct crush on you."

Rob started to object but then suddenly laughed. "I guess there's no point in denying the obvious," he said. "It's been plain to me for some time now that Millicent Randall indeed sparks to me. But I've paid no attention to her attraction to me, and I advise you to do the same. She's a lady, every inch of her, and she would never raise a finger to make a direct play for me."

"You're quite sure?" Beth asked hopefully.

"I'm very sure," Rob replied firmly. "Besides, the fact is she isn't my type. She gets no encouragement whatsoever from me."

"Aha!" Beth was in a good mood and raised an admonishing finger. "The fact that you don't encourage the woman to make advances is most reassuring. See that you keep that in mind at all times."

"Yes, ma'am," he responded with mock seriousness. "I hear you, and I obey accordingly."

"I am certainly glad I came to Utah with you," she said as Rob paid the bill and she began to put her

purchases into the basket that she carried over one
arm. "This is a very primitive country, so primitive
that a wife has to fight for her rights, which is precisely what I intend to do."

Rob joined her in laughter, but it was apparent
to him that behind her jesting manner she was serious. Her concern and protectiveness pleased and flattered him, and when they left the store, he put his
arm around her waist and held her close to him.

As they walked down the street to their house,
Beth looked up at her husband and, with a twinkle in
her blue eyes, asked, "And just who is your type of
woman, Mr. Martin?"

The tall, red-haired Rob stopped walking and
faced his wife. "Now that, Mrs. Martin, is a silly question. There's just one woman for me—you. And if you
don't believe it, just wait till we get back to the
house. As soon as we're alone, I'm going to make
good and sure you know just how much I love you."

Beth laughed gaily and, feeling marvelous, began
to walk down the street again.

The following evening the Martins joined the
Randalls for supper in the Ogden House dining room.
During the meal, Beth was again able to tell from the
way the dark-haired woman looked at her husband
and the way her cheeks glowed that Millicent Randall
had a strong personal interest in Rob. When she conversed with the other woman, Beth subtly indicated
her own devotion to her husband and further let drop
the fact that she was now carrying his baby.

Millicent was far from insensitive to the situation
and was genuinely pleased that Rob had found happiness after suffering through such a rocky time.
Aware that she had perhaps let her feelings for the
stolid, upright young man get out of hand, she repeatedly told herself, "Millicent, don't act like a silly

young thing. He's a happily married man, and there's no place in his life for you."

While the women were talking—neither of the men aware of the topic of their conversation—Jim quietly had a lengthy discussion with Rob about the state of affairs in Utah. The net result of this talk was a meeting the following morning with Toby Holt in the kitchen of the house.

There, for the first time, Rob revealed to his partner his own aborted meeting with Granger and told of the rancher's attempt to bribe him. Jim Randall listened carefully to what Rob had to say and then expressed the opinion that Granger was probably the most dangerous man in Utah and the biggest troublemaker. "He's been living by himself for so long that I wouldn't be surprised if he's become demented," Jim said. "Certainly he has a fixation about the railroad. He won't sell a square inch of his property for fear that the railroad will get hold of the land, and he threatens to exterminate anyone connected with the railroad who stands in the way of his independence. He isn't rational on the subject any longer."

"As Rob knows," Toby said, "I'm going out in the next day or so to make a personal survey of the entire situation. I reckon I ought to look in on Mr. Ralph Granger and size him up for myself."

"Size him up all you please," Jim Randall replied. "I realize I've got an awful lot of nerve telling a Holt how to conduct his business, but I urge you to be careful. Having this fellow Granger as your opposition is little short of lethal."

The following morning, Toby mounted the stallion he had purchased in town and left on his inspection trip through the territory of Utah.

Not far from Ogden, he found the Chinese crews on the Central Pacific hard at work in the shadow of the snow-covered hills, and he marveled at their industry. Strung out over a long distance were numerous crews, some of them grading the land and some of them laying rails. The graders, armed with pick-axes and shovels, removed boulders, leveled the ground, and otherwise prepared the way for the crews that came behind them, laying first the ties and then the tracks, which were made firm by driving stakes through them. At several points along this stretch of activity stood an odd assemblage of shacks and tents. These were the work camps, where the crews and their foremen lived.

Some of these Chinese workers had been brought to the United States under false pretenses by unscru-pulous agents who had recruited them in China and had promised them high wages and other advantages that existed only in imagination. These Chinese didn't realize they were trapped until they actually went out into the field, and then they made the best of their situation, working from sunup until sunset without pause.

Later in his inspection tour, Toby found that a similar situation was true at the Union Pacific work sites in the eastern half of the territory, where the Irish crews labored. Like the Chinese, they were being cruelly used, but they were given cheap whiskey, which prevented rebellions and made them more compliant.

The two railroads approached each other from the East and West, but no point had as yet been agreed upon for the joining of the lines. Conse-quently, the foremen of both railroads and their grad-ing crews worked on, and eventually the two lines actually passed each other, going in opposite direc-tions, as the men leveled the ground for the tracks. For the time being, they bypassed Ralph Granger's property, since the rancher had posted armed men around his land in order to keep railroad crews from trespassing.

In these places where the lines ran parallel, trouble often started among some of the rival crews working side by side. Either the Chinese or the Irish rioted daily, and these race riots invariably ended in the death and disfigurement of one or more workers. So far, there seemed to be no way to stop the killings and the mayhem.

It was inevitable that serious, constant friction should develop between the Chinese and the Irish. Neither spoke the others' language or understood the others' customs. All they knew was that here there were strangers who were performing the same work that they themselves were doing, and their rivalry asserted itself with a vengeance. The supervisors did their best to keep them apart, but when they were working within shouting distance of each other, this proved virtually impossible.

At night Toby camped not far from the railroad worksites. It had been some time since Toby had been on his own, out in the open country, and he thrived on this kind of existence. This was the life for which he—and his father before him—had been bred.

One evening after finishing his supper of jerked beef and roasted corn, Toby was sitting by his campfire, drinking a mug of coffee, when he heard the noises of an outbreak in the distance. Mounting his stallion, he rode rapidly toward the noise and found small groups of Irish and Chinese beginning to fight.

Knowing that great tragedy could occur, he quickly dismounted, drew his rifle from its sheath, and entered the melee. The workers were engaging in a vicious free-for-all, swinging pickaxes and shovels, as well as fighting with their fists and with knives they carried in their belts. Supervisors for the two railroads milled about helplessly, unable to intervene.

Attempting to separate the Chinese and the Irish, Toby used the stock of his rifle, pounding it on the shoulders and backs of the fighting men. Several times he was knocked about by the brawling workmen, but he continued to work his tall, lanky body into their midst, using his rifle as a club.

"Break it up! Break it up now!" Toby shouted repeatedly, and his tone of command soon had the workers lowering their weapons and moving away from each other. By now, the railroad supervisors were also assisting Toby as best they could.

Eventually the rioting was halted, and the Chinese and the Irish workers appeared to be tamed. Gradually they retreated and returned to their respective camps, giving evidence that they intended to mind their own business, at least for the night.

Breathless and bruised in several places, Toby was joined by an exhausted railroad supervisor. "I'm afraid this was a bad one," the man said as he watched his comrades looking after the unconscious or wounded. "Two Chinese and one Irish worker have been killed."

Casualties in senseless brawls were becoming common. Toby sadly shook his head as he returned to where he had left his horse. It seemed as if the problems in Utah were even worse than he expected.

This was confirmed when the following day, shortly before noon, he encountered a convoy of mule-drawn wagons en route to the building site. He halted, as did the convoy, and he had an opportunity to question the wagon drivers, Miller and Brady among them. They informed Toby that the wagons were constantly threatened by parties of mounted Ute warriors, who roamed through the wilderness seeking victims.

"Sure as the snow falls all year long up there beyond timberline," Brady said, "the Ute are lookin' for trouble. They ain't a nasty tribe by disposition, and some of us have the idea that they're bein' paid to raise cain with the supply wagons."

Toby feigned innocence. "Who would want to create such troubles?"

"The way we hear it," Miller replied, "there's a big ranch owner hereabouts who'll give half his fortune to prevent the railroad from touchin' on his property. His name is Ralph Granger, and he eats nails for breakfast. I want no part of him, and neither does Jughead, our lead mule here."

As Toby chatted with the drivers and, at their request, met Jughead, their incredible mule, he became aware of three figures in the distance observing the halted caravan. All three were Ute warriors mounted on ponies, and they were studying the convoy, as though trying to determine whether it would be worth their while to launch an attack on it.

Here was an opportunity that was too good for Toby to miss.

Immediately calling the attention of the drivers to the savages, he said, "Don't panic, lads, and keep your heads. I'll appreciate it if you'll stay right here where you are and not resume your journey for at least another hour. That will give me a chance to sneak up on those three through the forest from the rear and, I hope, detain them. I want to question them about who's putting them up to their belligerent acts against the wagon drivers."

Brady's eyes widened. He had heard tales of the exploits of Whip Holt and his son for years, but this was his first actual exposure to one of them. "Look here," he said. "You're takin' one whale of a risk. There's only one of you and there's three of them."

Toby nodded complacently. "But I'll have two advantages," he said. "First, the element of surprise will be in my favor, and secondly, my firearms are superior to any weapons they may be carrying. I think the odds are about right for me to take the risk and learn what I can." He walked to the edge of the woods, and when he was shielded by the trees from the sight of the braves, who were looking down at the convoy from the heights, he mounted his horse. Then he rode rapidly toward the place where the three Ute were sitting their mounts. He took care to approach them silently from the rear.

He reached their general location after riding for about a quarter of an hour. As he neared the spot on the trail where he judged the three Ute to be, he was pleased to see through a break in the foliage that the braves were still keeping the convoy under observation.

Slowing his horse's pace to a walk, Toby cocked his rifle and held it ready for instant use. Then he drew closer to the warriors. They were conversing in low tones and had no idea that Toby was approaching from the rear.

"Stay where you are," he called to them in their own tongue. "I mean you no harm and bring you greetings of peace."

The braves, who were indeed the ones working for Granger and Cameron, were instantly alert, but when they discovered that only one white man had approached them, they relaxed. It was odd to find someone who knew their tongue, and the senior member of the group, acting as the spokesman, demanded, "Who are you who speaks to us like a brother?"

Toby allowed his reputation and that of his father to speak for themselves. "I am Holt," he said, and they seemed satisfied. They were only too familiar with the name. As a trapper and trader years earlier, Whip Holt had become a legend among the Indians as a giver of gifts and a protector of the red man's rights. Like his father, the son had also achieved a considerable reputation among the Indians of the Plains and in the Pacific Northwest, cooperating with them and helping them achieve peace with the white man. Thus Toby was no ordinary foe, and although they knew they were in no immediate danger from him, they were nevertheless alert.

"Why do you study the supply wagons of my

countrymen?" Toby asked them. "Surely the Ute, who have kept the peace all these years, have no intention of stealing from the white men and doing them harm?"

The brave nodded somewhat sheepishly and made no reply.

"Is it not possible," Toby demanded, "that one who has no love for his brothers in his heart offers gold and silver to the Ute in return for their stealing from the supply wagons?"

It was too much to expect a complete admission from the warriors, but the senior brave said, "It is possible."

Certain that he was on the right track, Toby persisted in his questioning. "Is it not possible that he who is known as Ralph Granger is responsible for the activities of the Ute?"

Again the senior warrior replied, "It is possible."

That was as close to a confession as Toby could reasonably expect the Indians to give, and he was satisfied. Now he knew for sure where the attacks originated. Raising his left arm in a rigid salute, he turned his horse and started down toward the halted convoy below.

The Ute would not attack the wagons that day because of his presence, Toby knew, and by the time they decided to act, the convoy would have safely arrived at its destination. So after reassuring Miller and Brady and the other drivers of their safety, he immediately headed for Granger's ranch.

He was obliged to spend another night in the wilderness and arrived at the Granger property late the following morning. No one seemed to be present as he let himself in through the gate and headed up the dusty trail that led to the ranch house.

Suddenly two ranch hands appeared on foot. Both brandished cocked pistols.

Toby carefully laid his loaded rifle across his saddle. "How do," he said.

The pair made no reply and continued to stare at him in a sinister way.

"I'm here to see Mr. Granger," Toby said. "Does he happen to be in?"

"Who wants to see him?" one of the pair demanded.

"My name is Holt. Toby Holt."

The identity of the stranger caused a sudden change in the attitude of the two ranch hands. They were familiar with the name of Toby Holt and knew of his many exploits. Furthermore, they had no desire to tangle with someone who had the reputation of being the fastest and best shot in all the West.

"Why didn't you say so in the first place?" one of the men demanded, and he began to lead Toby toward the ranch house, his companion hurrying ahead of him to notify Ralph Granger that distinguished company had arrived.

As Toby drew closer to the house, the door opened, and the silver-haired Granger came out onto the stoop. He ran a hand through his thick mane of hair and grinned amiably. "Welcome, Mr. Holt," he called. "It's nice of you to call."

Toby was encouraged by his attitude and dismounted, hitching his horse to a rail. He shook the old man's hand.

"You'll stay for dinner with me, I reckon," Granger said.

"I don't want you to make a fuss over me," Toby replied.

The old man shook his head. "No fuss," he said. "We seldom have visitors here, and when someone stops by, it's always a cause for celebration."

"I've heard on all sides," Toby said as he removed his hat and accompanied his host into the house, "that you're opposed—lock, stock, and barrel—

to the establishment of the railroad line that is being erected across Utah."

Granger replied with great caution. "I'm not so old-fashioned that I blind myself to the need for progress. I realize that the population of the United States is increasing rapidly and that there's a great need for the goods of the East in the West, and vice versa. The days of wagon trains are numbered. I'm sure there will be half a dozen rail lines that span the continent before the financiers and the builders are finished."

Toby was encouraged. In spite of what he had heard, this man did not appear to be a fanatic.

"What I resent," Granger went on, and sheer hatred began to throb in his voice, "is the government's position in decreeing that a railroad is going to be built across my land, whether I like it or not. I've spent over half a century building this ranch. It's one of the largest and most successful in the entire territory, and I'm damned if I'm going to have it desecrated by the appearance of rail lines across it. That's asking too much of a man." Controlling himself with an effort, the big man headed toward the dining room and guided his guest to a chair there. Ah-Sing, the ranch's Chinese cook, served them ham, baked beans, and sourdough biscuits, and Toby enjoyed the simple fare and the noncontroversial small talk that he shared with the rancher as they ate.

Relaxing in the old man's presence, Toby said casually, "I wonder if I might see your foreman and talk to him for a little while, Mr. Granger. I've been given to understand that he's offered bribes to the Indians in this area so they'll attack convoys of supply wagons."

"I've known Cameron for a long time, a very long time," Ralph Granger said after a moment's pause, "and I've never known him to say or do anything that's against the law. I think your information has got to be erroneous."

Something in the old's man tone convinced Toby that he was being glib and was not telling the truth. But it was impossible to prove.

"I've never met Mr. Cameron," Toby said firmly, "and I would appreciate the opportunity to have a little chat with him."

"I can understand the way you feel, Mr. Holt, and I certainly sympathize with your position. But I'm afraid I can't oblige you at the moment. Ian Cameron's away for a while, visiting a sick relative. However, when I next see him, I'll sure pass along your message."

Toby felt his stomach muscles tighten but nevertheless nodded as though accepting what the old man had to say to him, which was the only polite course of action he could take. But in truth, Toby felt badly disappointed. He was willing to bet his soul on the fact that Ralph Granger was lying to him. He could hear the hollowness behind the man's voice.

They discussed the problems of ranch owning, with which Toby was thoroughly familiar, and inevitably the subject came around to the railroad again. They had finished their dessert—a lemon sherbet Ah-Sing had made—and Granger was now drinking brandy and smoking a cigar, Toby having declined the rancher's offer of an after-dinner drink and smoke.

"I would be a happy man," Granger said, blowing out a great cloud of cigar smoke, "if it weren't for the threat that the railroad holds over my head. Can you imagine them insisting on cutting across my property with their damn tracks? They're not going to do it! They're not going to get away with it!" He struck the table hard with his fist.

"They're offering generous compensation, of course," Toby said tentatively.

"No compensation is generous if it interferes with

my ranch! When I go, this property will belong to my nephew, and I'm keeping it intact for him, just as I'm keeping it intact for my own sake. If anyone starts building a railroad on my property, I'll have my men shoot first and ask questions later!"

"I see," Toby said, and realized that the old man was indeed as fanatical on the subject as he had originally heard. "It strikes me," Toby said, "that the odds against you are pretty strong, Mr. Granger. They've already built the railroad up to the border of your property, and they're continuing to build on the other side of it. It's just a matter of time before the government insists on a right of way through your land so that the rails can connect."

He paused and braced himself before continuing, "President Johnson is on record. He badly wants a coast-to-coast railroad. The two houses of Congress are favoring the establishment of a railroad and offering generous compensation, both to the railroad companies and to any individuals who are displaced or otherwise put out by the establishment of a line. Some of the leading financiers of the country are members of the boards of the Union Pacific and Central Pacific, and they add up to some formidable opposition."

The old man's eyes were bright, and his jaw jutted forward pugnaciously. "I've spent my adult life fighting alone," he said, "and frankly I don't care what the odds are against me. I've made up my mind that, come hell or high water, there isn't going to be any railroad line built across my property, and you can depend on it!"

The rancher got up, poured himself another glass of brandy, then said, "You have a great heritage, Mr. Holt. I remember meeting your father many years ago and admiring him tremendously. From what I've read of your exploits, I've developed an admiration for you, too. So let me tell you plain. Don't mix into things that are beyond your capacity. Don't take the side of the railroads in this fight of mine, because if you do, you're going to be hurt. Anybody who stands in my path is going to be hurt bad!"

By the time Toby took his leave of Ralph Granger a short while later, he knew the old man was a dangerous, treacherous foe. Toby realized that he would need to exercise great care in handling the crafty old man, who clearly was avoiding getting himself incriminated by having his foreman do all the dirty work. There was no evidence whatsoever against Granger himself, and there was no way to arrest him. Still, Toby would need to keep an eye on the man at all times in order to ascertain what he was doing. Somehow he had to gain control of the situation in which he found himself. Granger could not be allowed to continue to exercise jurisdiction over the people and the property of Utah.

No sooner was Toby clear of the ranch than Granger summoned one of the ranch hands who was on duty at the time. The rancher said, "Go ride up to the mountains and make sure that nobody—absolutely nobody—is following you. Find Ian Cameron where he's hiding out and tell him I want to see him as soon as he can get down here. But stress to him that he is to travel only after dark and to make sure that nobody is following his movements."

Several days passed without incident, and it was late one evening when an insistent tap sounded at the door of the old man's ranch house. Carrying a candle in one hand, with the flap removed from the holster of his Colt repeater pistol, Ralph Granger went to the door and looked vastly relieved when he saw his foreman standing in the dark outside. "Come in, Ian, come in," he said impatiently, and closed the door behind his subordinate. "Anybody see you coming down here from the mountains?"

"No, to the best of my knowledge. I've been on the move only after dark, and I haven't seen one person in the wilderness or on the trail."

Granger led him to the parlor, where he placed a bottle of whiskey and a glass on the table beside the younger man.

Cameron poured himself a stiff drink. "I knew you wouldn't have brought me back here except in an emergency, so I lost no time getting here."

"The opposition is growing stronger," the old man said, "and we've got to take firm steps in order to counter them. I had a visit from Toby Holt, Whip Holt's son, the other day. He's been enlisted by the railroads, I suspect, and he's a formidable opponent. Which means we're walking on eggs. Holt is an expert at smelling out conspiracies and plots, and with him breathing down our necks, it won't be long before he discovers the very considerable role we've been playing in the incitement of the Indians. Right now, he can pin nothing on me, but with you it's another story."

Cameron's smile was without humor. "It's very possible," he said, "that Mr. Holt could suffer an unfortunate accident that would put him out of commission for quite a spell, maybe even permanently."

Granger shook his head and looked exasperated. "Did you ever see a buzzsaw?" he demanded. "It's a circular saw, and it spins around and around. It has enormous teeth in it, and it cuts blame near anything. You try attacking Toby Holt, and you're taking on a buzzsaw. I want no part of any such activity, and if you've got any brains in your head, you'll run the other way before you try to attack him."

Cameron's forced laugh was not convincing.

"If you're smart," Granger said, "you'll avoid Toby Holt at all times. Remain in hiding, if you have to. You're not being cowardly, you're being sensible. So lay low. If you have any thoughts as to how to end the threat the railroads represent, without incriminating either of us, let me know immediately, without delay."

Cameron saw he was serious and sobered accordingly.

"We've got to take steps," the old man concluded, "that even Toby Holt cannot counter."

The following morning, Ralph Granger and Ian Cameron, each of them lost in his own thoughts, ate breakfast in silence. The foreman of the ranch had spent the night in the main house, reluctant even to make an appearance at the bunkhouse, lest one of the hired hands accidentally slip and tell someone in town of Cameron's whereabouts.

Ah-Sing padded in and out of the kitchen with fried eggs, bacon, and steaming sourdough muffins, which he placed in front of the pair. The Chinese man made no attempt to converse. He was well accustomed to the old man's moods by now and adjusted his own behavior accordingly.

Suddenly Granger broke the silence. "Ah-Sing," he said, "every now and then you visit your friends who work on the railroad. What do you know about the workers?"

The cook paused and shrugged. "Know plenty," he replied noncommittally.

Granger peered intently at his cook. "What do those coolies fear—more than anything else in the world? Answer me that!"

Ah-Sing did not hesitate. "Easy question to answer. Boss man hear of tongs?"

The old man was irritated by the question. "Of course," he said. "The tongs are the criminal gangs that operate in the Chinese districts in every city in America where they exist. They're said to exert absolute control over the residents."

"Is true," the cook said, nodding emphatically,

"and men most afraid of hatchet men for tongs. Hatchet men have very great power and hatchet men very strong. Go cut—and coolie lose arm, lose leg. No go to police because then hatchet men kill."

The hint of a smile appeared at the corners of Ralph Granger's mouth. Taking a thick roll of paper money from an inside pocket of his buckskin coat, the old man removed a ten-dollar bill, which he handed to the cook. "This is a bonus for you, Ah-Sing," he said. "Add it to this month's salary and enjoy yourself. You have no idea how much trouble you've saved me."

The cook promptly took the money and disappeared into the kitchen with it, moving rapidly before Granger had a chance to change his mind.

"Simple plans are best," Granger said sharply to Cameron. "They're the easiest to follow, and there's less opportunity for making mistakes. You know San Francisco, am I right, Ian?"

His foreman nodded. "Sure," he said. "I lived there for over a year, and I got to know my way around."

"I want you to go to San Francisco immediately," Granger said, and his smile broadened. "Do it in the least amount of time possible, which means take advantage of the railroad to get you there. Bribe whoever's in charge of one of the work trains. Go to Chinatown and speak to the leaders of the two biggest and most powerful tongs in town. Then pay whatever is necessary—I don't care how much it is or how badly they hold you up—for the services of the biggest, toughest enforcer that they have on their payroll. When you come back here, be sure you have the hatchet man with you."

Cameron began to grin. "I think I understand," he said.

"Sure. It's basically so simple it's a stroke of genius!" Granger rubbed his hands together. "You heard Ah-Sing say that the coolies who work on the railroad are more afraid of the tongs' hatchet men than they are of anything else on the face of the earth. So much the better. We'll turn a hatchet man loose in their midst, and that will be the end of their work effort. They'll throw down their picks and shovels, and I don't think we'll need to resort to any other tactics to keep the railroad from being built. The best part of it is, there'll be no way the trouble can be pinned on either of us."

Night came, and quiet gradually enveloped the Holt ranch outside Portland, Oregon. The bunkhouse where the hands lived had gone through its final noisy flurry for the evening, and now the men who looked after the horses were settling down to read, to tell stories, and to sit in front of their hearth for an hour or two before they retired.

Stalking Horse, the foreman, returned to his own quarters from the house, carrying the ledgers with the financial records of the preceding month. Miss Clarissa had gone over them and pronounced them accurate, so his work was done until morning, when he would begin again. As he knew from a lifetime of activity, work at the ranch never stopped.

In the main house, Clarissa Holt tucked the sleeping Tim more securely into his bed, then went into the kitchen to fix herself a belated supper. She had been working hard all day, so hard, in fact, that she had not noted the passage of time, and she had eaten nothing except a small sandwich at noon. Not really very hungry, she fried some ham and eggs and carried her dish to the kitchen table, where she sat and ate halfheartedly.

It had been nearly a year since she had last seen Otto Sinclair, and though there was no way she could forget that her first husband had virtually returned from the dead in order to haunt her, she had nevertheless successfully convinced herself that he would not reappear. Perhaps it was a false hope, but this was the only way she could get along on a day-to-day basis at the ranch.

That afternoon, she had received a brief, hastily written letter from Toby in Utah. She was determined to answer it that night, writing in length and, she hoped, displaying a warmth that her inhibitions prevented her from showing him in person. She wanted him to know that she loved him, that she prayed every day for his safety and well-being. She couldn't help recalling her mother-in-law's words when Eulalia had learned of Toby's present appointment. "He's just like his father," she had said. "He automatically attracts trouble, and whenever he's involved in something, you know that there's going to be violence and mayhem and gunfire."

As she ate, Clarissa began to compose the letter to Toby in her mind, and she was so intent on her task that she failed to hear the window in the pantry next to the kitchen slide open. She first realized that an intruder was in the house when she looked up and saw Otto Sinclair emerging from the pantry into the kitchen.

Rather than show any alarm or surprise, she was indignant, as if she had, despite her hopes, been expecting him to show up but was severely disappointed that he had. "Don't you know yet how to use doors and how to knock on them when you go calling?" she demanded. "I can't tolerate your sneaking in and out of this house."

He laughed easily and was pleased with himself for his accomplishment.

Clarissa's meal was forgotten. "What do you want, Otto?" she demanded.

He slid into a chair opposite her and looked at her plate. "I think the least you could do," he said, "is offer me a cup of coffee or, better yet, something stronger like a drink of whiskey. I think I deserve such treatment."

"If I give you what you deserve," she said, "you'll get no coffee from me, and no liquor, either." Her voice became strident. "Now what do you want?"

"Come on, Clarissa. What do you think I want? Do you think I'd be satisifed with the measly sum you gave me last time I was here? You and your new husband—your illegal husband—are extremely well-to-do people who, I think, would be mighty glad to share some of that wealth in order to keep things the way they are. I've been lying low this past year, but when I read in the papers that Toby Holt had gone to Utah in behalf of the railroads, I decided to pay you another little visit and remind you of your obligation to me."

Her heart pounded so violently against her rib cage that she felt faint. "You had best understand one thing now and for all time, Otto Sinclair," she said. "Because my husband has access to substantial sums of money does not make me rich. I get along on a very limited allowance for household expenses, and that's all I get. I have no access to Toby's gold or to the profits from his lumber business. Those are strictly his own concerns, and there's no way that I could get my hands on any money from either source."

His smile faded. "You better find ways of gaining control of those sources," he said, "if you know what's good for you. Otherwise, I'll have to reveal that you're still married to me and that your relationship with this fellow Holt is illegal."

"I know of no way that a single penny could be made available to me," she said insistently. "You'll have to be satisfied with what I've given you, and there's an end to it."

He was not in the least surprised by her attitude. "All I can do is warn you, Clarissa," he said. "Beyond that, everything will depend on what you do and what you say and what you arrange. I'll give you a little more time to work out the plan as best you can, but I urge you, for the sake of your future happiness, to be generous with me. Very generous." Still smiling, he strolled to the door and let himself out of the house.

In spite of the threat that he had made, Clarissa was infinitely relieved to be rid of him so quickly and easily. She had no idea whether he intended to make good his threat or not, but she had been telling him the truth when she said she had no access to Toby's income. If Otto insisted, then she would have to take the consequences and see her entire life collapse around her in ruins.

Meantime, Sinclair was in no way surprised or disappointed by the results of the brief encounter. He had expected nothing more. By applying pressure on Clarissa, he might be able to push her into obtaining substantial amounts of money, but he couldn't push too hard. He had to keep in mind the fact that she could grow panicky at any time and could totally destroy the good thing he had built for himself.

As Sinclair started back toward Portland, where he had taken up residence in an inconspicuous hotel in a rundown section of town, an idea occurred to him, and recognizing its worth, he began to develop it slowly. It was an ingenious plan that promised him a far greater return than any he had planned previously. If he was careful and observed all the rules of society, he could acquire great wealth and not be dependent on Clarissa and her mercurial temperament for a single penny.

The scheme was predicated on the assumption that Toby's principal heirs were Clarissa and her child. Once that point was established, the rest would be quite simple. Sinclair would follow Holt to Utah and would dispose of him there. He recognized that his own anonymity would serve as a protective shield. No one except the terrified Clarissa knew he was even alive, and thus no one would suspect him of being the killer.

In the normal course of events, Clarissa would inherit a very large sum of money as Toby's legal heir. Having killed Holt, Sinclair would bide his time and then would suddenly appear on the scene. He would reveal the true facts of his situation, including the gross error in identification made by the War Department when they had declared him killed in action in the Civil War. Once he had officially proved that Otto Sinclair was very much alive, the rest would follow quite naturally. Clarissa would still be married to him, and her inheritance legally would belong to him and to him alone. Therefore, he could proceed to relieve her of the fortune quite naturally and without any fuss.

Similarly, any money that her young son inherited would be Otto's by virtue of the fact that Clarissa would be the legal guardian for her son's estate, and it would be only natural for Sinclair, as her husband, to step in and take charge of it for her. After Holt had been done away with, Sinclair would be able to proceed step by step within the law and without any danger. In fact, killing Toby Holt was the riskiest part of his plan.

Toby was a dangerous man, a highly skilled adversary. But Sinclair believed he had a great advantage in that he would be performing the deed in the wilderness, where there would be no law and order and where violence was a way of life. What was more, he had killed a number of enemies in the war and was known to be a fairly skilled shot himself.

Meanwhile, still sitting at the table in the kitchen of the ranch house with her head in her hands, Clarissa thought of her tangled relationship with Otto Sinclair. She was confused and frightened. Usually clearheaded and knowing exactly how to proceed in any given situation, she felt lost and did not know what to do next. She could not bring herself to write the truth to Toby because their relationship was already so strained. As before, she feared that upon realizing she was not his legal wife, he would be so relieved that he would refuse to set eyes on her again.

Perhaps the best course of action for her would be to accept her unhappy fate, leave Toby, and go back East. Perhaps such a move would spare her and Toby considerable pain in the long run.

The only trouble with such a solution was that it did not deal with the problem of Timothy. He was a Holt, and no matter what happened to her marriage, he was the son of Toby. She knew that Toby would never willingly give up the boy, and she could picture Toby's mother and stepfather—people of enormous influence and power—putting up a spirited fight for the child, as well.

Therefore, if she decided to accept the inevitable and relinquish her title as Mrs. Toby Holt, she knew she would be forced to give up her son. The prospect was so awful that she could not face it, and she therefore put it out of her mind. All she knew was that she would rather die than give up her child.

VI

Ah-Sing had prepared one of Ralph Granger's favorite dishes for his noon meal. It consisted of chicken livers sauteed in a rice wine Ah-Sing himself had fermented in the ranch house kitchen, mixed with scallions and served on a bed of rice.

The old man ate large quantities of the dish. He knew he would feel stuffed later and perhaps suffer indigestion, but that was a small price to pay for the enjoyment he got from eating Ah-Sing's cuisine. Ralph was a man with hearty appetites, and he denied himself nothing.

He raised his head from his plate when he heard a horse cantering up to the house, and a few moments later Ian Cameron came into the dining room and joined him. The foreman was wearing the same black city suit and cravat with a white shirt that he had worn when he had left for San Francisco. Greeting his superior, Cameron sat down opposite him and happily accepted the food that Ah-Sing heaped in front of him.

"Well?" Granger demanded sharply. "How was your luck?"

Cameron smiled. "It couldn't have been better," he said. "First, fortune was with me both to and from San Francisco in that no one questioned me, and no one knew what I was up to. But the best is yet to tell.

For a total expenditure of two thousand dollars—a thousand to the tong and another thousand to the man himself—we've acquired the services of one of the most proficient and frightening hatchet men in the business."

Granger relaxed for the first time in several days. "When does he start work?"

"He traveled with me from San Francisco," Cameron said, "and I saw that he was situated in one of the Chinese work camps outside Ogden. To the best of my knowledge, the hatchet man's already started to go to work. We ought to see results very shortly. Believe me, if he told me not to work on the railroad, it's the last place in the world that I would try to earn a living. He's the most ruthless, frightening monster I've ever seen in my life!"

Ian Cameron did not exaggerate. The tong hatchet man, Wang, was a giant from northern China who weighed over three hundred pounds. Most of his bulk was muscle, and he was very tall, so he loomed like an avenging giant above his fellow men. When he arrived at the Chinese work camp, he was wearing a black, Western-style suit that did little to conceal his bulk, and on his feet, out of custom, he wore felt-soled slippers that enabled him to walk silently. He had dark, brooding eyes, and his face was screwed into a perpetual scowl.

No one missed seeing the razor-sharp hatchet that Wang carried menacingly in one hand. It was said that he could throw it with great accuracy or could wield it in hand-to-hand combat, a blow to any-one who dared to stand up to him was inevitably leth-al. In all, he was a thoroughly frightening specimen.

The Chinese work force in Utah had grown considerably. Most of them coolies, they continued to be inveigled into accepting positions in the New World by agents who had made false promises. Also included now in the ranks of the workers were a num-

ber of young men of substance who had been
abducted right from the streets of Shanghai, Canton,
and other major cities, and then shipped across the
Pacific to take part in the building of the railroads.

As always, these men were treated little better
than slaves. Paid tiny wages and charged more for
their meals and their lodging than they earned, they
were perpetually in debt to their employers and had
no hope of getting even. The overwhelming majority
of them understood no English and hence were in no
position to complain of the treatment that they received. They could appeal to no one. They were su-
pervised by brutal foremen who severely beat any
man who complained or otherwise tried to rebel.

The activity at the railroad camp was summa-
rized in a single word: work. The coolies labored
seven days a week, never taking a rest, never enjoying
a respite for as long as twenty-four hours. They had
been imported for one reason only—to build the railroad line—and they were being used for that purpose
exclusively, regardless of the effects on their health
and on their mental state.

After a breakfast of rice, mixed with chopped
vegetables and bits of meat, the coolies went to work.
They were divided into four units or teams. The first,
following the path laid out earlier by Rob Martin's
surveyors, graded the land and made it level. The second group laid out ties, the third placed the steel rails
on them, and the fourth drove long spikes into the
ground, making secure the ties and rails. Every man
knew what was expected of him, and consequently
the supervisors gave virtually no orders. The coolies
behaved like parts of a well-oiled machine.

Gradually those working at the rear of the line
became aware of the presence of an outsider in their
midst, a huge, hard-eyed, overweight giant. The
hatchet in his hand identified his profession, and no
other introduction was necessary. As he strode east-

ward along the tracks that had not yet been fixed in place, he spoke a few words. "No work," he said. "No work."

It was unnecessary for him to repeat the phrase more than a few times as he strolled past a group of workers. The words spread like wildfire among the men. As he passed the other work teams, the gigantic hatchet man repeated again and again, "No work." All work halted.

The Central Pacific Railroad supervisors were responsible for keeping the crews active, regardless of what might transpire. But they were in no mood to argue with the surly giant. They valued their own necks far too much for that, and they did not interfere when the coolies dropped their sledgehammers, picks, and shovels and wandered back to their camps.

For the first time since the Central Pacific had initiated activity on the construction of its tracks, labor ceased entirely.

Knowing of Rob Martin and Toby Holt's presence in Utah, the railroad supervisors sent a messenger to the pair in Ogden requesting immediate assistance. The rider arrived at suppertime that same evening, and Toby, who had just returned to the town after many days on the trail, did not hesitate.

"Let's start off right now," Toby said to Rob, "and we'll eat our supper in the saddle. This may be just the opportunity we've been waiting for. It's possible that, if we play our cards right, we can finger Granger as the man who's behind all this."

Beth hastily prepared sandwiches, which, as Toby had suggested, the two men ate as they rode their horses. They arrived at the work site late that same night and slept in the open, rolled up in their blankets. The following morning they arose at dawn in order to ride out to the railroad line. It seemed strange to find the work area deserted. There were picks and shovels scattered about on the ground, as well as sledgehammers here and there, all of them dropped by coolies who had wasted no time in leaving the scene to return to the work camps not far away. Examining the abandoned tools, Toby dismounted, and after a few moments, Rob joined him. "This is eerie," Toby said. "Ordinarily the whole area would be bustling by now, but there isn't a soul at work."

Rob caught hold of his arm and muttered, "It wouldn't surprise me any if the direct cause of it all is heading toward us this very minute." He nodded down the line toward a huge, burly figure in black who was walking steadily toward them. "I don't blame the coolies for being scared," Rob murmured. "This creature is big enough to frighten anybody, and look at the hatchet he's carrying. It looks so sharp that it wouldn't surprise me if you could use it to shave. I'd sure hate to have it thrown at me."

Toby calmly took the hatchet man's measure. He not only was enormous but also seemed to be totally lacking in fear. Although Toby and Rob were armed with rifles and pistols, he continued to advance toward them.

As he came closer, his eyes met Toby's, and the young Westerner knew that he had met his match. Wang's dark eyes gleamed malevolently, and his lips parted in the suggestion of a sneer. He was issuing a challenge to the pair, daring them to force him to withdraw.

As Wang continued to advance, Toby deliberately blocked his path but did not raise his firearms. He preferred to settle the issue without violence. "Hold on a minute, my friend," he called. "I'm told that you chased all the workers back to their camp yesterday. How come?"

The hatchet man's lips parted in a bloodless smile, but he made no reply as he continued to move forward.

Toby was unsure whether or not he spoke English but chose to act as if he did. "You didn't dream up this work stoppage all by yourself," he said. "Somebody has undoubtedly paid you a goodly sum to act for him. Who was it?"

The huge man continued his advance, and the contempt in his eyes was so great that when Toby saw it, he felt that he had suffered a physical blow. Never had any human being looked at him in such a way.

Rob, who lacked Toby's patience, bridled and was about to issue a challenge. But Toby, sensing his partner's intent, clamped a hand on his shoulder, steadying him, and prevented him from talking out of turn.

The one thing that Toby refused to do was to move out of the path the Chinese had chosen. The man was heading straight toward him, and even though Toby thought it likely that Wang would crash into him and step over him, he braced himself but refused to budge.

At the last possible instant Wang shifted his weight and avoided smashing into Toby, instead brushing against him as he passed.

For whatever satisfaction he could take from the incident, Toby knew that he had outbluffed the hardbitten hatchet man.

"You win that round," Rob said. "For whatever it's worth, the big hulk knows that he can't scare you. But what good you've actually done is beyond me."

"You're right. I've accomplished precisely nothing," Toby replied. "Not one Chinese coolie is going back on the job, and that's all that counts."

Together they watched the big man as he continued to saunter along the line. He was alone, and no one else was in sight.

"I'm afraid we're stymied—for now," Toby said. "Assuming Granger is somehow behind all this, we're dealing with a mastermind who understands the mentality of the Chinese. We're up against a stone wall. Sooner or later, we've got to figure out some way of breaking the impasse, and for the sake of the future of the railroad, I would say we've got to do it sooner rather than later."

Precise routines were being followed, as they were every morning, at the San Francisco office of the financiers Chet Harris and his partner, Wong Ke. Both of the partners received information vital to their interests that morning. Some of the information was supplied by telegraph and consisted of figures on the quantity of gold and of silver removed from their various mining interests in the past twenty-four hours, together with current prices quoted on the gold and silver markets of London and New York. Then from their hotel division came written reports describing the percentage of rooms occupied the previous night and the profit made. Finally, their newspapers and magazines supplied them with circulation and advertising figures that were up to the minute. Had either of the partners cared to, he could have estimated their current net worth to a figure not far removed from the accurate total.

Chet looked up in surprise when his usually imperturbable partner came into his richly appointed, mahogany-paneled office. He was obviously upset. "What's wrong, Ke?" he demanded.

Wong Ke, impeccably attired in a black suit coat and striped trousers, sat down and adjusted the razor-sharp edge to his trousers. "I've had some very disappointing news," he said, and flourished a letter.

Chet reached for the document and frowned. The envelope was printed in English, and the postmark was that of Ogden, Utah Territory. When he opened the epistle, however, all he found was handsome Chinese calligraphy. "I'm afraid I need a bit of help in translating this," he said with a smile.

His partner took the communication from Chet. "This," Ke said, "is a letter from my nephew, from my brother's son, Wong Wu, in which he begs for my immediate help. He was abducted one morning after leaving his parents' home in Shanghai and was placed on board a ship bound for San Francisco. After suffering many hardships at sea, he arrived and was sold to a contractor, who whisked him off to Utah, where he's been forced to work on the building of the railroads. The conditions are primitive and brutal, and he's been threatened with death or with severe punishment, at the very least, if he complains and calls anyone for assistance. There is a foreman there, a man named McManus, who would do him great harm if he found out. But my nephew has taken that risk because he isn't sure how much longer he can tolerate the treatment he's been receiving."

"How awful!" Chet exclaimed. "Please, Ke, tell me how I can be of assistance."

"I've already engaged a private railroad car on the Central Pacific to take me to Utah," Ke said, "and I'll be grateful if you'll explain the circumstances to my wife. Also, I'd appreciate it if you'll send a telegram of explanation to Holt and Martin and ask them to be prepared for any eventuality after I get there. From the way my nephew speaks in his letter, he took a very considerable risk to write me, and my attempt to free him from service appears to be unprecedented. Nevertheless, I shall do it even if it's necessary to buy out the railroad."

Chet grinned at him. "I wouldn't advise that," he said. "You and I aren't accustomed to paying off blackmailers. With Whip Holt's son assisting us, I have an idea it won't be necessary for us to pay one red cent!"

* * *

Toby and Rob restlessly paced up and down outside the ramshackle wooden structure that served as the temporary Utah terminal for Central Pacific work trains. Toby looked frequently at his watch, and ultimately his friend became annoyed. Both men were on edge because of the continued trouble on the rail lines and their inability to get to the bottom of it.

"You're not going to speed its arrival by staring at your watch, Toby," the tall, redheaded Rob said.

"I know," Toby replied, "but the blasted train is over an hour late right now."

"It isn't observing any regular schedule as yet. Just remember that much," Rob said. "So whenever it gets here is all for the good."

Even as he spoke, they heard a rumble in the distance, followed by the high-pitched blasting of an engine's whistle. Both of the young men brightened.

"I'm blamed if I know why I'm so anxious for Wong Ke to get here," Toby muttered half to himself. "We have absolutely nothing to report to him, and our prospects look mighty glum."

A few minutes later the train pulled in. The partners heartily greeted Wong Ke, and Rob insisted on carrying his luggage to the buckboard they had brought to transport him to the Chinese work camp.

"I know how anxious you are to confront this foreman McManus with the facts you've accumulated and to obtain the release of your nephew," Toby said. "But it won't be all that easy. I've tried on three separate occasions to make an appointment with McManus for you, and the boys on his staff say that he's busy and can't see anyone."

Wong Ke's jaw grew taut. "He'll see me, you can be very sure of that. Let's go directly to his headquarters right now, if you will. Everything else can wait."

They drove to a compound of many tents, most of them quite large, which was located on the site of the building of the tracks. Raw materials were piled nearby, but no one was at work, the Chinese workers milling about the compound, sitting by campfires, and drinking tea or smoking pipes. The hatchet man was not to be seen, but there was no question that his continued presence had called a halt to all work on the railroad.

Alighting from the buckboard, Ke made his way to a tent set apart from the others. He walked steadily, without fear, flanked on his left by Rob and on his right by Toby.

A man in an open-necked woolen shirt emerged from the tent and looked at them inquiringly.

"I've come here from San Francisco for the purpose of seeing Mr. McManus," Ke said, and he presented the man with a calling card from a gold case that he carried in an inner pocket.

The man had already been instructed by McManus to get rid of the influential visitor from San Francisco, but seeing the Chinese man, impeccably attired and carrying himself with great dignity, caused the assistant to hesitate. Everyone in the West knew the identity of Wong Ke, and no man had the temerity to refuse a direct request from him. He was too wealthy, too powerful, and far too influential for that.

Accepting the card and beckoning, the man led the way inside the tent. Ke followed, still flanked by his two young associates. Both of them, he noted, had their hands resting on the butts of their pistols.

Reclining on his bunk was a balding man with red hair, a freckled face, and burned skin that almost matched his hair. His blue eyes were hard, and as he leaned up against the wall of the tent, he looked without expression at the small, dapper Chinese who approached the desk.

Toby noted instantly that the gigantic hatchet man named Wang was sitting on a barrel in a dark corner of the tent, casually leaning on the weapon that gave him his name. His eyes, as before, were filled with hatred and bore into Toby, who guessed that McManus, like all the other railroad foremen, was totally intimidated by the hatchet man and gave him free rein in the work camp.

The dapper Ke inquired politely as he approached the bunk, "Are you Mr. McManus?"

"That's me," was the surly man's response.

"Wong Ke." The little Chinese bowed gracefully and paid no attention to the giant in the corner of the tent. "I daresay you've heard of me."

"Maybe I have and maybe I haven't," McManus replied in a surly voice.

Ke ignored his manners and his tone. Instead he explained in detail that he had had a letter from his nephew, who had been abducted in Shanghai, brought to America, and forced to labor on the railroad in Utah. He was being charged so much for his weekly room and board that he remained far behind in his payments to those for whom he worked, and could never catch up.

"All in all," Wong Ke said in conclusion, his voice deceptively mild, "I would say that this is a most sorry situation."

"Assuming that it's true," McManus interjected swiftly.

"My nephew does not lie," Ke said. "Perhaps we could get an affidavit from him and from some of his companions, who are undoubtedly suffering in the same unfortunate situation."

The supervisor lost his temper. "What goes on here?" he demanded loudly, rising from his bunk and sitting upright. "Are you trying to hang me?"

Ke smiled gently. "Not at all, sir. But I can't help wondering if the board of directors of the railroad is aware of the means employed to obtain and keep the services of your so-called coolie crews. I should think that an exposé would do no harm. However, I can understand your natural inclination to avoid publicity, and I have no desire to embarrass you. For the present, my one aim is to obtain the release of my nephew."

McManus slapped his leg angrily with a heavy fist. "You got some nerve, Mr. Wong, coming out here and slinging dirty innuendos and accusations at me. I urge you to get the hell out and to leave me alone before I have you thrown out." He glared at Wong Ke, then at his two companions.

That was all the hatchet man, Wang, needed. He glowered unpleasantly, his eyes glittering as they narrowed. He took a firm grasp on his hatchet and silently rose from his seat on the barrel.

Toby took no chances. Before anyone realized what was happening, his pistol was in his hand, pointed at the huge hatchet man, and the weapon was cocked. "Mr. Wong," he said, "be kind enough to inform the big fellow that if he fails to let go of the handle of his hatchet instantly, he's going to be in trouble. No matter how big he is, he can't bounce a bullet off his hide."

Wong Ke spoke briefly in Cantonese.

Wang directed another look of pure hate at Toby and then released the handle of his hatchet. It fell to the dirt floor of the interior of the tent beside him, and he made no attempt to pick it up.

"As for you, Mr. McManus," Toby went on, "I beg to remind you that Mr. Wong is one of California's most distinguished citizens and happens to be one of the most well-to-do individuals in the entire West. He deserves politeness, and when he fails to get it, he gets somewhat annoyed. So I would urge you to apologize to him and get on with the business at hand."

McManus found himself staring down the barrel of Toby's Colt and muttered an apology.

"Now," Toby concluded reasonably, "perhaps you'll be good enough to send for Mr. Wong's nephew. You might want to go with the messenger, Rob, just to make sure that nothing funny happens and that the young man isn't abused in any way."

It was plain that McManus wasn't being trusted, and he flushed a deep scarlet. He summoned his assistant, who had waited outside the tent, and sent the man off, accompanied by the hatchet man. Rob quietly accompanied them and, for good measure, had his pistol drawn.

Ke and Toby stood waiting inside the tent. McManus lacked the courtesy to ask them to sit, but Toby ignored this insult. He had something of much greater importance on his mind.

"McManus, Mr. Wong has told you he has no intention of exposing you to the railroad board of directors. That's far from the case with me, however. I work for the railroad, and it's my duty to tell my employers how you and some of the other supervisors are virtually holding the Chinese workers in bondage."

"Now you hold on!" the foreman shot back. "I've already agreed to turn over the Chinaman's nephew. What more do you want?"

"For the moment, nothing," Toby said. "As long as the hatchet man has all the foremen and the Chinese workers cowed, there's nothing anyone can do. But sooner or later I'll think of a way to get rid of the hatchet man, and then the coolies will go back to work. When they do, I want you to give your men the rest they need to remain healthy. No more than ten hours of work per day, with all day Sunday off. I've seen the swill that passes for food around here, and I want that changed, too. Do you get the picture, Mr. McManus?"

The unshaven man scowled. "All right, Holt," he

said with resignation. "And assuming I cooperate, what then?"

Toby smiled at the burly foreman. "Then I won't write to my employers and tell them you and certain other foremen have been mistreating the workers. It will be business as usual, with the railroad getting built but with working conditions vastly improved."

At last a young slender Chinese, with a long queue braided down his back, came into the tent. He was obviously frightened. Seeing Wong Ke, however, he made an immediate recovery, crying out in the Mandarin dialect used by the educated classes and bowing respectfully to his uncle. Both uncle and nephew exchanged extensive, flowery, polite speeches before they embraced.

Ke flicked a glance at the alert Toby, who knew what was expected of him and responded immediately. "Mr. Wong," he said to McManus, "thanks you for your cooperation." Toby was rubbing salt into McManus's wounds, and the man snarled at him. Indifferent to the opinion that the supervisor had of him, Toby bowed politely and dismissed both McManus and the hatchet man from his mind. The reunion of Wong Ke and his nephew was a joyous occasion, and he wanted to enjoy it to the utmost.

Toby and Rob escorted the Chinese financier and his nephew to the buckboard, and Toby drove the wagon back to Central Pacific's rail terminal. He and Rob waited there with Ke while his private car was made ready for the journey back to San Francisco. Meanwhile, Ke's nephew had been frightened so badly that he continued to look over his shoulder, though Toby assured him that there was no longer anything to fear.

Ke had ideas of his own on the subject. "Toby, I urge you to exercise great caution. I know my fellow countrymen, and the giant hatchet man has lost face. He can recover it only at your expense, which means that he is likely to attack you or come after you when you least expect it. Be on your guard, please."

Toby listened carefully and nodded. He knew enough to follow Ke's advice, and he had virtually no experience with Chinese strong-arm men himself. Thanks to Wong Ke, he would not run a needless risk by being overly complacent.

Seeing Wong Ke and his nephew off at last, Toby and Rob rode back to Ogden. Toby was silent the whole time, and he scanned the hills and valleys with great care as they rode.

The following morning, when Toby emerged from the house in Ogden, he found a stake driven into the ground. The top had been shaved to a point.

He was uncertain regarding the significance of the shaft, and Beth and Rob, whom he called outside to take a look, were equally in the dark. They all returned to the kitchen to finish their breakfast and were soon joined by Jim Randall, who had ridden over from his hotel.

"Have some coffee," Beth offered Jim, and he took a cup and sat with them at the table.

"Where's Millicent?" Toby asked.

"She's tired today and is spending the morning in her hotel room," Jim replied, but he knew that was not exactly the case. Millicent was keeping more and more to herself lately, practicing her flute or reading, and Jim believed she was avoiding Rob Martin, for whom she had developed such a strong affection.

The conversation turned to the stake that Toby had found driven into the ground, and after Jim took a look at it, he was able to offer some explanation of its appearance. "When Millicent and I were in San Francisco last year, we met a number of interesting people and learned some fascinating things. One person we met, an old Chinese merchant living in Chinatown, had a collection of artifacts, among which were similar shafts of shaved wood. I wouldn't swear to this, Toby," he concluded, "but it seems to me that this is a residue of an ancient warrior's tradition, something that has existed in Cathay for many years."

Toby nodded. "Then what does it mean?"

They were all silent for a time, puzzling out the riddle. Then Rob suggested, "Maybe the hatchet man is challenging you to combat, Toby. Maybe he's daring you to meet him, as an equal, in a fight to the death. Let's wait and see if the challenge is repeated. If it is, then I'm sure that I'm right."

The very next morning another shaved post appeared in the ground outside the house. The three occupants were beginning to believe that Rob's theory about the hatchet man was true.

At noon dinner that day, the challenge was very much a principal topic of conversation.

"The hatchet man," Beth said, "is going to great lengths to try to prod you, Toby. He must be very annoyed with you."

"I reckon he is," Toby replied quietly.

"That's just too bad," Beth said indignantly. "Even in a wilderness district like this, we observe civilized codes. Duels are barbaric."

"Nevertheless," Toby said, "any duel I fight with the hatchet man will be for the good of all."

The others stared at him, and Beth was the first to find her voice. "Surely you don't intend to fight him, Toby," she said. "You told me he weighs at least three hundred pounds. You'll be taking your life in your hands if you engage in combat with him!"

"She's right," Rob said. "I've never seen a bigger or meaner-looking individual in all my life."

Toby concentrated on his roast lamb, which the cook had prepared to perfection. "I think," he said casually, "that we're in for a very interesting time. I'm looking forward to meeting the hatchet man in combat."

Having known Toby all her life, Beth was aware

that he could be stubborn beyond compare. She groaned aloud.

Rob realized that he alone had the potential power to change his friend's mind. "Why, you can't do it, Toby," he said flatly. "You have a wife and a young son waiting for you out in Oregon, and you can't risk your life needlessly. The hatchet man is the biggest, toughest human being I've ever seen, and I don't care how proficient a fighting man you are. You can't possibly be a match for him."

"We'll see about that," Toby said quietly. He looked at his old friends. "You should know by now, Rob, and so should you, Beth, that a Holt never allows a challenge to pass unanswered. I'm compelled to reply in kind and to take my chances, whatever they may be, in personal battle."

"Then you're mad," Beth muttered. "You're taking an awful chance, and you're risking your life without reason."

"Not without reason," Toby said as he shook his head. "I've been worrying for days now about a problem that has seemed insoluble to me. The Chinese workers are frightened half to death of the hatchet man, and they'll do anything in their power to avoid him. He's already ordered them not to work, and there's no power on earth strong enough to drive them back to their picks and shovels. Of course, if he should be beaten in personal combat, if he should actually be destroyed and proved to be impotent, his loss of face will be so great that he would have no further influence on the coolies. He could scream at them until hell freezes over, and they would pay no attention to him. Can't you see the point I'm trying to make? If I can beat the big man in personal combat—and I'm quite certain that I can—our problem is solved. The coolies will be back at work the following morning."

"What would Clarissa say if she knew the choice that you're making?" Rob asked.

Clarissa was so indifferent to his fate, Toby thought, that it wouldn't matter in the least to her what he did. But he refrained from expressing his feelings. Instead, he said, "It's been a long-standing tradition in my family for a man to make up his own mind when his honor is at stake. I'm quite sure my wife would agree to anything that I decide, and I've decided that, hell or high water, I'm going to have a showdown with the Chinese hatchet man."

A third shaved post in as many days proved to be the last straw, and Toby strapped on his six-shooters and went into town in search of the hatchet man. He made his purpose clear as he traveled from bar to bar. To everyone he saw, he said the same thing: that he was looking for the giant named Wang who had offended him.

His search quickly narrowed when he discovered that the Chinese hatchet man frequented a large, noisy tavern called Smitty's, which was located on Main Street. According to one report, Wang showed up there almost daily and, shunning all company, downed several beers before he went back to the work camps. Surely he would appear at Smitty's within the next day or two.

The tension built for thirty-six hours. Three times each day—at noon, late in the afternoon, and at night after supper—Toby dropped in to Smitty's saloon in search of his opponent.

Eventually it became evident that the giant was aware that his challenge had been accepted and was biding his time. A dozen or more men came to Toby with the news that McManus, the foreman for the railroad, was wagering the enormous sum of one thousand dollars in cash on the hatchet man's winning the duel.

Many habitués of Smitty's, although ignorant of the Cantonese dialect and Chinese customs, nevertheless reported that the hatchet man was supremely confident that he would emerge victorious from the combat. Attempts were made to needle Toby, to goad him into saying things that he might subsequently regret, but no matter what was reported to him, he smiled slightly, nodded, and kept his opinions to himself.

Rob and Beth privately agreed that Toby was at his most dangerous now, that the slightest spark would set him off.

"He's like the strings on a fiddle," Beth said. "They're turned tighter and tighter until they're right at the breaking point, and then anything can snap them. I remember seeing his father reacting in the same way whenever danger threatened, and he was the most ruthless man alive at times like that. My father used to say that any sensible man would give Whip Holt a very wide berth when he was in that kind of mood."

In spite of the growing tension, the evening the duel finally took place started like any other. Ranch hands, men associated with the railroad, and wagon drivers ate their supper early, then drifted to the long bar at Smitty's and ordered their favorite drinks. Prominent in the crowd were Miller and Brady, who were accompanied, as always, by Jughead.

Then the swinging doors at the far end of the long room opened, and the hatchet man came in. He paused, looked malevolently at the crowd, and then made his way slowly toward the bar. Those present gave him all the space he wanted.

Aware of his power, of his control over the emotions of the other patrons, Wang was arrogance personified. He swaggered as he walked, and his face registered supreme contempt for ordinary members of the human race.

Brady, watching as the giant drew nearer, removed his hat and wiped a film of perspiration from his forehead. "I don't like this one bit," he said. "I think we oughta get us out of here while the gettin' is still good." He hastily drank the last of his beer.

"You're right," Miller muttered. "We're peaceable folk, and this is no time for a big fight. Anythin' happens hereabouts, we can learn all the details of it later."

"Come along, Jughead," Brady said to the mule.

Ordinarily the most cooperative and amenable of animals, Jughead nevertheless could be extremely stubborn. Continuing to stand his ground, the animal paid no attention to the man who spoke to him.

Wang was drawing nearer. "Damnation, Jughead! Don't be that way," Miller told the mule. "You want to get yourself killed for your pains? You do, and you just keep on misbehavin' the way you're doing right this minute!"

The animal continued to stand where he was.

Brady reached for the loose end of the rope that encircled the mule's neck and tugged at it. The animal planted his feet apart and refused to budge.

"Damnation!" the frustrated Brady muttered beneath his breath. "We're gonna be dead as doornails because this damn mule ain't got the sense to mind his own business and to get out of here while the gettin' is good."

Miller cleared his throat. "Maybe we oughta let the dumb critter stay here and stew in his own juice while we get us the hell out," he suggested.

Brady disagreed. "No, that ain't fair. Jughead is the best lead mule in the whole territory, and we'd no sooner be rid of him than we'd miss him somethin' awful. I say we hang on to him and take our chances on his seein' the light and behavin' sensible." He leaned closer to Jughead, demanding loudly, "You hear me, animal? If you value your hide, hurry up and let's get out of here."

Jughead paid no attention whatever to the commotion he was causing.

Conscious of their nearness to the gargantuan hatchet man, Brady tried a new tact. He took one of his stogies from his pocket, then placed it a short distance down the floor of the saloon, closer to the door.

Jughead would have none of this. Using his nose, the animal nudged the cigar closer to him and then complacently began to chew on it.

The Chinese giant brushed against the mule, but Jughead was oblivious to everything and was determined to finish chewing the cigar in peace.

Brady became panicky. Edging away from the giant, he looked longingly at the sawdust on the floor beneath a table. The tabletop was stout, made of heavy oak, and seemed impervious to minor damage. At least it could serve to protect a careful man.

Then the swinging doors at the far end of the bar opened, and Toby Holt came into the room, his thumbs hooked in his belt. Conversation died away, and a deadly hush settled over the drinkers.

No one in the place was more influenced than was Jughead. The mule took one look at the grim-faced Toby and another at Wang. That was enough to satisfy the animal, who promptly lost all taste for the cigar and, pieces of tobacco hanging from his mouth, quietly trotted out into the night.

Miller and Brady followed instantly, both of them relieved to be leaving before the fireworks began.

"You! Tong man!" Toby called. "I've been told you understand enough English to get my meaning, so listen to me and act accordingly." His voice took on a hard, metallic note. "Get out of Utah! Now! And don't come back—ever! If you know what's good for you and you value your health, stay away!"

He was so bold that some men in the saloon caught their breath.

The giant turned slowly, lazily. He proceeded to draw a long, curved sword from his belt. In his other hand he grasped the hilt of his murderous hatchet.

Men shrank from his path, giving him clear access to Toby. No one knew whether he intended to advance or whether he planned to throw one of his weapons, but the onlookers were taking no chances.

Neither was Toby Holt. Drawing a pistol with lightning speed, he fired the weapon, and the sound of the shot echoed loudly through the bar. Those who were unfamiliar with Toby's marksmanship were astonished when they saw that the bullet struck the sword and knocked it from Wang's hand. It lay useless on the floor, some feet from him.

But the hatchet man was far from finished. With a fierce growl, he drew back his other hand and let fly his murderous hatchet, aiming it at his opponent's head.

Toby had no time to lose. He sighted the hatchet as it flew through the air, and then he squeezed the trigger. The bullet hit the blade with a loud ringing noise almost simultaneously with the explosion of the gun, and the hatchet spun to the floor. In a remarkable display of marksmanship, Toby had actually shot down the weapon in midair.

The spectators, badly shaken, stared at Toby in openmouthed astonishment. Wang may have been an expert at throwing his hatchet, but he could not compare with Toby Holt in self-protection. The hatchet had fallen not far from where Toby was standing. With his gun still aimed at his adversary, Toby nudged the hatchet with his toe, brought it closer still, and then with a swift sideways kick, sent it across the floor and out the door of the saloon into the dirt street beyond. Then he retrieved the sword in the same way, and a kick got rid of it, as well.

He felt infinitely better because he had regained control. "Hear me!" he called to his Chinese opponent. "I've only used two bullets. I have four left in one gun and six in the other. That makes a total of ten. I'm only going to need one of them, however, and that's the bullet that I'm going to put between your eyes if you don't do as you're told, and do it fast."

Even those who did not know Toby heard his measured, cold ruthlessness and knew that he was not a man with whom one could tamper.

Keeping one gun trained on the hatchet man, Toby took a fob from his pocket and nodded as he glanced at his watch. "It's as I thought," he said. "The night stage to San Francisco leaves in less than an hour's time from the depot on Main Street. See to it that you're on that coach, and stay on it until it reaches San Francisco. If I ever catch sight of you in these parts again, I'm going to shoot you on sight, and I assure you I will shoot to kill."

The big man had not only suffered total defeat, but—even worse—he had lost face so badly that there seemed to be no way he could recover. While Toby stood guard, his pistol drawn, Wang left the saloon slowly, his head lowered, and when he reached the street beyond, he picked up his weapons. Instead of being objects that inspired terror, they now caused pity for him among those who had seen the sorry spectacle to which he had been subjected.

Looking totally dejected, Wang ruefully examined his battered sword. Then he looked at his hatchet, the sharp edge of which had been badly nicked by Toby's bullet. His heavy shoulders sagging, Wang beat a slow retreat. Several score of men followed him, laughing and hooting as he made his way down the street to the stagecoach depot. Later, a number of volunteers informed Toby that the hatchet man had fled Ogden, undoubtedly intending to put Utah behind him for all time.

"I reckon the coolies will report for work tomorrow morning," Toby said, and felt vastly relieved. Thanks to his intervention and that of Wong Ke, he also felt reasonably certain that the lot of the poor Chinese laborers would be vastly improved, too. McManus and the other railroad foremen had undoubtedly learned a lesson from the fate of the hatchet man and, not wanting to share in his punishment, certainly would treat those under them with far greater consideration and kindness.

The sudden collapse of the menace posed by Wang caused a number of strange and unpredictable consequences, not the least of which became evident when a note was delivered to Jim Randall the following day. He immediately took it to the house of Rob and Toby, who were just returning from a visit to the rail lines, where they had been reassured that work had indeed been resumed. Jim showed them the epistle.

Mr. Randall,
Will you and your cousin do me the honor of dining with me any day at noon? It will be to your advantage to avail yourself of this opportunity.

Very truly yours,
Ralph Granger

"What in the devil do you think he wants?" a frowning Jim asked.

Rob shrugged. "Damned if I know, but it does sound promising. The old man is one of the great characters of Utah, you know, and like all the early settlers, he has his own code and his own ethics and moralities. Don't write him off because he doesn't think or act as we do. He's more like the early settlers were in Whip Holt's day."

"Then you think we should accept his invitation?" Jim asked.

"I think so," Rob said. "There's no way of telling what you may have to gain, and as near as I can see, you have nothing to lose. Sure, see him and find out what he has in mind. You may be very pleasantly surprised. Maybe we all will. Maybe the defeat of the hatchet man has made him see reason at last. What do you think, Toby?"

Toby, who had been sitting silently at the kitchen table, listening to the conversation, merely shrugged. "I'm not certain. As Rob says, go and see him, Jim. Maybe you will be pleasantly surprised. Whatever the case, I look forward as much as you to learn what's up."

The following morning the Randall cousins set out for the old man's ranch in their small, open carriage. Millicent was excited and hopeful that perhaps Granger was going to offer them some of his property and the cousins could begin to get settled at last. She was growing weary of their transient life. Jim, too, was optimistic that Granger had had a change of heart, though he was taking no chances and packed a small revolver in a holster under his suit coat.

Ralph Granger greeted the cousins with great cordiality and served them glasses of a rare, old sack that he had had in his possession for many years. Ah-Sing was delighted at the opportunity to cook a meal for a lady, and he outdid himself. His seven-vegetable soup was thick and luscious, and his fried pork with Chinese noodles was superb.

Millicent insisted on going out to the kitchen after the meal and congratulating the beaming Chinese chef on his accomplishments.

Not until they retired to the parlor after dinner did the old man reveal the purpose he had had in mind when he invited the couple to dine with him. "I reckon you know," he said, "that I've left all my earthly goods to my nephew, the only living relative I have."

"I believe you mentioned that before," Jim Randall replied.

"Well, sir," Ralph said, "I've got me to thinking lately, and you can't ever be too sure of where you stand. It's possible when the boy comes home this year, he won't want it. If that's the case, I'm going to sell it. So if you're still interested in my property, I'll be glad to give you a first option on it in return for a token payment."

Jim was very much surprised. "That's decent of you, Mr. Granger," he said. "Very decent."

The old man grinned. "You hear a lot of talk about what an old curmudgeon I am, but those who get to know me don't find I'm all that bad," he replied. "You folks have been square and decent with me, and I want to at least offer you a fighting chance to acquire this property. I'm not saying that you're going to acquire it. Far from it. But if anybody other than my nephew gets it, you stand first in line. Here, you might want to read this document over." He took a brief, one-page paper from his pocket and passed it to Jim Randall. "This is a very simple agreement that I had my lawyer in Ogden draw up," he said. "Nothing fancy or tricky to it."

Jim read the paper and had to agree. It was indeed a simple document, saying that in the event the ranch belonging to Ralph Granger should be sold, the first people to have the right to bid on it would be James Randall and his cousin, Millicent Randall. In return for this right of first option, they had paid Ralph Granger the sum of twenty-five dollars.

"This looks just fine to me," Jim said, "but I must say you're doing yourself out of a lot of money. Twenty-five dollars isn't a fair token payment."

"It's fair enough for legal purposes, and that's all that matters to me," the old man said. He produced a pen and handed it to Jim with a flourish.

The younger man signed, then removed the bills from his pocket and handed them to Granger. "I still feel that I'm cheating you," he said.

"Not a chance," Granger replied. "Dismiss it from your mind."

The agreement was simple indeed, but Ralph Granger's motive in having Jim Randall sign it was extremely complicated. Granger had learned of Toby's defeat of the hatchet man, but now the old man had another arrow in his bow that he could fire. If the government tried to crack down on him and force a sale of part of his property to the railroad, he could claim a prior written agreement with young Randall, and the "simple document" could tie up proceedings in court for several years at the very least.

The party ended on a festive note. The Randalls had no idea of Ralph Granger's ulterior motives and thanked him repeatedly for his generosity. He accepted their thanks and promised to look out for their best interests, so they were in high spirits as they started back toward Ogden.

When Toby Holt heard the story of what happened and read the agreement, his eyes narrowed, and he shook his head. "I admit this sounds just fine," he said, "but you'd better search pretty hard for an explanation that will make sense of this. Ralph Granger hasn't done anybody a favor in a half-century, and I don't see him starting now!"

Ralph Granger lifted the top from the soup tureen and inhaled blissfully as the steaming contents filled the dining room with their fragrance. Ah-Sing had no doubt come up with another of his masterpieces, and the old man was ecstatic.

He took a taste of the soup and bellowed for the

cook. Ah-Sing immediately appeared from the kitchen. "You no like soup?" he wanted to know.

"Of course I like it, Ah-Sing. What is the name of it?"

"It called hot and sour soup," Ah-Sing replied.

At the risk of allowing his anger to interfere with his euphoric state, Ralph replied, "I know it's a hot and sour soup. But it must be called something. It must have a name."

Ah-Sing shrugged. "In Canton, my home, all people call hot and sour. You ask for hot and sour, this what you get."

Ralph gave up. "All right," he said. "Fair enough."

The cook bowed and, satisfied with himself, disappeared back into his kitchen.

Ralph ladled a generous portion of soup into his bowl and began to eat. He had no idea what ingredients went into the making of the soup or what spices the cook used. All he knew was that the combination was exquisite and the dish was so spicy that it brought tears to his eyes as he ate it.

He would be sure to tell Ah-Sing to prepare the dish again the night his nephew arrived home. What a grand occasion that would be! Looking forward to it with great eagerness, Ralph knew that the day would be one of high points of his life.

He removed the brief letter from New Haven from his inner coat pocket, and although he was already thoroughly familiar with every word, he read it again.

Paul Granger, his late brother's son—Ralph's only living relative—was about to complete his course of study at Yale University, receiving highest honors. He would be returning to his uncle's home in Utah, and ironically, he would be traveling almost the entire distance by railroad. Though the Union Pacific was not yet joined with the Central Pacific, it was still possible to arrive in Utah from the Eastern Seaboard in a scant five days, as opposed to many weeks by horse-back.

The rightful heir to the ranch would soon be here, coming into his own, and Ralph was prepared to redouble his efforts to prevent the railroads from gaining possession of as much as one square inch of his land.

He would not be fighting for himself alone. The property would be Paul Granger's, and his son's after him, for as long as they lived.

Folding the letter and putting it back into his pocket, Ralph ladled himself another generous portion of soup and blinked the tears from his eyes as he happily ate it. His life was complete and fulfilled, and he was content.

VII

With the departure of the hatchet man, the problems that had beset the building of the railroad seemed to ease up, and there were now just a few places in Utah where construction needed to take place in order to connect the rails at last. One area, of course, was Ralph Granger's property, and railroad supervisors—unwilling to have a run-in with the hired men Granger had posted on the outskirts of his land—decided to tackle that problem last. But at least the Indian raids had stopped, and there were few outbreaks between Chinese and Irish workers, due in large part to the presence of Toby Holt and Rob Martin.

Toby still rode out and visited the work sites to make sure everything continued to run smoothly. The workmen, and even many of the supervisors, were glad to see him and gave him a hero's welcome when he showed up on his horse, sitting tall in the saddle, looking every bit the legendary figure who, like his father before him, had done so much for the West. Toby enjoyed his long forays into the Utah Territory, not so much a wilderness now, with miles of tracks having been laid and little communities—former work camps—springing up everywhere along the rails. It would be only a matter of a very short time, Toby and Rob thought, until Ralph Granger gave in and the tracks crossed his property, too. Then the rails would at last be joined, at a location in Utah still to be determined.

If Toby was lonely for his wife and baby, he admitted it to no one, not even to himself. For now, he pushed them from his mind. After he saw his present assignment through to the end—to the time the rails were joined and trains were running smoothly—he would face the issue of whether he had a marriage any longer. It was possible his second marriage, like his first, had failed; it was possible he and Clarissa would have to go their separate ways. But he would not know that until he returned to the ranch in Oregon and there confronted Clarissa once and for all.

Meanwhile, for the Martins, the time spent in Utah turned out to be idyllic, all the more so now that problems on the railroad were under control. Beth and Rob were able to spend a lot of time together, and they enjoyed every minute of it, going on day trips in their carriage, taking long walks, and frequently making love, sometimes in the seclusion of their house, other times on a blanket out in the open countryside during one of their excursions.

As the time drew nearer for the birth of Beth's baby, Rob became increasingly concerned. At breakfast one day, he revived an old argument. "As much as I hate to be apart from you, honey, I think that you would be sensible if you went home to Portland and had the baby there," he said. "Let my father take care of you now."

Beth shook her head cheerfully. "I see no reason to coddle myself," she said. "Dr. Smith here in Ogden is a very good physician, and he's had ample experience delivering babies. He says that I'm in fine health and should anticipate a normal birth, so there's no need for me to go to Portland or anywhere else."

"But—"

She gave him no chance to object. She rose, went

to where he was sitting, and put her arms around his neck. "I told you I was never going to be separated from you again as long as we live, Rob, and that's the way it's going to be. We've been so happy together in Utah, and I'm going to stay right here with you and have the baby."

He had known she would not be amenable to a sensible discussion of the subject, and he sighed. "What worries me," he said, taking her hand, "is that my mother won't be here with you, and neither will your stepmother. You have no real friend in the area, and I can't help but worry about you."

She gave him a kiss, then went to the stove for the coffee pot. She poured him another cup and smiled. "You're a darling, Rob, and I've given the matter a great deal of thought. I, too, would like to have a close friend with me here, and I have an idea. I had a long letter the other day from Kale Salton, and she stews and fusses over me as badly as you do. I would love to ask her to join me here and to stay with us until the baby comes."

"Wonderful!" he exclaimed. Rob had put out of his mind his earlier intimacy with Kale Salton, and now, hearing the woman's name, he thought of her only as Beth's dearest friend. "I'll arrange for her to come by rail whenever she wishes, and I can't tell you how relieved I am that you're going to have someone who is close to you, who will be nearby when you need help."

The arrangements were made quickly, and early in the morning two weeks later. Kale arrived by train in Utah. Rob came to the rail terminus in a light wagon pulled by a single horse to meet her.

Her long, auburn hair fell in loose waves below her shoulders, and her cosmetics, applied with an artful hand, brought out the green of her eyes and the full, moist quality of her lips. Her traveling gown showed off her superb figure to excellent advantage.

There were twenty to thirty men in and around the station, and the attention of every last one of them was riveted on Kale.

Kale kissed Rob lightly, full on the lips. She had steeled herself for this meeting with him, telling herself for the entire train ride not to pay any attention to his rugged good looks or his natural, easygoing charms. But she was annoyed because her heart beat rapidly and she was suffused with pleasure at the sight of him.

He took her luggage, placed it in the cart, and helped her up to the seat. "Thanks for coming, Kale," he said. "You have no idea how much your presence relieves my mind."

"Is Beth all right?"

"Yes, she's fine," he said. "But it's a relief to me to know she'll have her best friend with her when she has her baby." He patted her hand, then flicked the reins, and the wagon started off.

It occurred to Kale that he was treating her like a sister or a good friend, not like an attractive woman with whom he had made love. Well, that was just how it should be.

"Did you have any trouble on the ride out?" Rob asked as their wagon followed the well-traveled road back to Ogden. "I know more and more respectable people are traveling out here on the trains they've already got in service, but they're mostly businessmen, not stunning-looking women like you."

Despite herself, she flushed at his reference to her as a stunning woman. "I did happen to observe that I created a considerable flurry of interest," she said modestly.

"Kale," he went on a bit hesitantly, "I know, ah, that you're a woman of the world, but I don't think you've ever experienced a frontier town like Ogden. Women there are subjected to crude advances all the time, and by that I mean physical advances that aren't always possible to avoid. So I, ah, would urge you to tone down your use of cosmetics and to dress modestly and with care. If you've never seen the raging bulls of a frontier town in action, I assure you it can be a very frightening spectacle."

She was touched by his concern for her. "I wasn't thinking in such terms when I left San Francisco for this place," she said. "I'll exercise greater caution after this, you can be sure. I have no desire to create any problems for you, much less for myself."

He was pleased that she had accepted his advice in such a cooperative spirit, and he breathed a sigh of relief.

"The last thing on earth I would want to do would be to embarrass you," she said.

He grinned at her. "I don't embarrass easily, especially when I'm acting as a policeman here. It's your welfare that's my immediate concern."

She placed her hand on his and squeezed. "Thank you, Rob," she said, and seemed at a loss for words.

Rob was unaware of her tension. But Kale was aware of her hand on his, of the feelings she had for this man, and she was thoroughly annoyed with herself. She had promised to behave when she reached Utah and to put her relationship with Rob into its proper perspective.

From now on, she thought, withdrawing her hand, she would have to watch her step in dealing with Rob Martin. Under no circumstances could she allow him to see that she had lost her heart to him, and above all, she had to conceal the truth from Beth. Perhaps she had been unwise to heed Beth's request and come here in the first place.

But all other considerations were forgotten as Kale and Beth were reunited at the house in Ogden. They embraced happily, and then they began to chat as though there had been no pause in their relationship. They were in the parlor, laughing merrily, when Rob entered, strapping his pistols to his waist.

"I promised Toby I'd join him at a work camp just outside of town," Rob said, reaching for his hat. "Looks like a little new trouble is brewing between the Chinese and Irish. Nothing to worry about. Toby and I will be home for supper."

"I'm glad you'll be here," Beth said, going to him and giving him a kiss. "I've asked Millicent and Jim Randall over. And, dear, look after yourself."

"I will," Rob said, returning her kiss. Then he departed.

"How do you think Rob looks, Kale?" Beth asked when the women were alone.

"He's the picture of hardy good health," Kale replied. unable to get out of her mind the image of Rob and Beth kissing. "I would say that the mountains of Utah agree with him."

"What agrees with him is the responsibility of the life that he and Toby lead here," Beth replied. "They are exactly alike. Expose them to danger, give them a number of insurmountable difficulties, and they thrive on it. The way they respond to challenges is remarkable, and they're going to establish a rule of order on the railroads if it's the last thing that's ever done on this earth. Rob seems so gentle, but he has a backbone of steel."

"You're very fortunate to have each other," Kale said, hoping she didn't show the envy that she felt.

"I know," Beth replied. "All our troubles are behind us now, thank goodness."

"I'm glad for you," Kale told her. "You and Rob deserve each other."

"All I know is that we're happier than we've ever been. Our marriage was right, very right, and I'm glad that we had the good sense to stick it out and to overcome the bad times."

They spent another hour chatting, and Kale deliberately avoided the subject of Rob. It was bad enough to be aware of his relationship with Beth. There was no need for her to suffer unnecessarily by talking about him, as well.

In midafternoon the woman hired to cook and do the heavier housework arrived and went to the kitchen to prepare the evening meal. Beth and Kale joined her in the kitchen and prepared some of their own dishes for that night's repast. Beth had a recipe for coleslaw that she wanted to make, and with ingredients she found in the house, Kale was able to make a mince pie, which was her specialty.

Watching Kale roll out the pastry dough for the crust and prepare the pie filling, Beth was surprised. "You know," she said, "we've been friends for over a year now, and I even lived in your house, but I never knew you could cook."

Kale laughed gaily. "Oh, I'm full of surprises. The truth is, a lady of the evening has plenty of time during the day to learn about domestic matters like cooking and housekeeping. I honestly enjoy those things."

Beth marveled at her friend. Kale truly was a person of many talents.

As they worked in the kitchen, the subject turned to Toby Holt, whom Kale had never met and whom she was looking forward to seeing that evening. They also talked about the Randall cousins, whom Kale had last seen in San Francisco at the celebratory party given for Beth the night she won her freedom in court. Kale distinctly remembered observing the interest shown in Rob by Millicent, and she intended to keep her eye on the woman that evening at dinner.

Learning of the Randalls' search for a ranching property to buy in Utah, Kale said dryly, "I should think that anyone who voluntarily settles in this part of the world should see a physician. The scenery is magnificent, but the countryside is so lonely that I think I would scream if I had to settle here."

"I felt the same way when we first came here," Beth said, "but the scenery has a way of growing on one. I mean, the Randalls are from Baltimore, but they love it out here very much. Of course I lived all over America when I was growing up because my father was stationed at army posts in odd places. I grew accustomed to the mountains when he was first stationed at Fort Vancouver, so I'm not as much a stranger to the heights here as you might suppose."

The evening was going to be festive, in celebration of Kale's visit. The two young women dressed in pretty outfits and helped each other do their hair, Kale showing Beth the latest style being worn in San Francisco. Then, laughing like two schoolgirls, they rushed downstairs when the housekeeper announced that the Randalls had arrived.

Jim Randall, of course, had met Kale in San Francisco, but he wasn't prepared for the beautiful, laughing woman who greeted him. He was instantly smitten and couldn't keep his eyes off her all evening.

Millicent, it was immediately clear, was in a very quiet mood. She looked very plain because she wore no cosmetics. Her dress was long-sleeved, high-necked, and full. On examination, however, Kale noted her clean-cut features, pretty eyes, and attractive nose and mouth. Similarly, her figure was slender but very feminine, and it appeared that, if she chose to bother, she could be extremely attractive.

Kale knew that music was the principal, abiding interest in life for Millicent. She had been a prize student at the conservatory in Baltimore, where she had often given flute recitals, and apparently she had won a considerable reputation for herself as a soloist and as a composer. Kale could not help envying the other woman. She herself had never been so deeply interested in anything beyond her own well-being.

They were just getting comfortable in the parlor, talking about music, when Toby Holt and Rob Martin rode up. Leaving Kale to act as hostess, Beth ran out to the back of the house to greet the men. They were both grimy, with a layer of dust on their boots and on their skin. In addition, Toby had a discolored welt high on one cheekbone where he had suffered a cut.

Beth became alarmed, but Rob calmed her with a hug and a kiss. "We're fine, honey. Just let us get cleaned up." He and Toby removed the gunbelts from which their pistols were hanging and then wearily climbed up the stairs to clean up before supper.

Toby was the first to reappear. He had washed the grime from his hands and face and had changed his clothes. Also, he had applied some medication to the bruise on his cheekbone, which made his injury seem far less significant. Beth, who had rejoined her guests in the parlor, introduced him to Kale, and they greeted each other warmly. Toby also exchanged cordial greetings with Jim and Millicent Randall and then, at Beth's suggestion, poured himself a drink of whiskey. "Sorry we were late," he said, "but a sudden confrontation between the Chinese and the Irish blew up and had to be handled. It took us a spell to get things quieted down."

The others might be too polite to ask, but Kale's curiosity got the better of her. "What happened to your face, Toby?" she asked.

"Well," he replied, "a first-class riot was developing, and men on both sides got to heaving bricks. Either their aim was bad, or else I got my face in the way." He shrugged. "It'll look a heap worse tomorrow, but I'm lucky I didn't suffer any real damage." He downed his whiskey in a single gulp.

"How bad was the riot?" Jim asked,

"I reckon it was just about the same as the earlier fights that took place on the railroad lines," Toby replied. "A couple of Irishmen and a couple of Chinese start insulting each other, with none of them understanding a word of what's being said about them. The next thing you know, a huge crowd has gathered, and they start throwing things. Give them enough time, and they'll charge each other with axes and shovels and, for that matter, firearms, as well."

"How did you stop them?" Kale asked, and her voice reflected her deep concern.

When Toby hesitated, Rob, who was coming down the stairs from the second floor, answered in his stead. "It was quite simple," he said. "Toby spurred forward and rode between the Irishmen and the Chinese like a bat out of hell, and he flourished his six-shooters and fired a couple of shots over the heads of the mobs."

"Don't make me sound like a confounded hero," Toby said. "I didn't do anything single-handed, you know. You were right behind me, flourishing your own six-shooters as you rode hell-for-leather, and I would say between us we managed pretty well to put the combatants to flight."

"Well, now that you mention it," Rob admitted, "I did mix in a mite. I didn't want you to be alone with all those Irishmen and Chinese. There must have been a couple hundred of them, and one man by himself isn't nearly as impressive a sight as two men can be. Especially when both of them are firing their weapons."

"True enough," Toby said, and chuckled. "The only good thing I can say is that at least we haven't had any new trouble from Granger. These riots are a result only of the natural animosity between rival work gangs, and I think we can keep a lid on them."

As they continued to discuss the violent events of the day, the listening Kale was aware that Jim Randall was studying her, and she smiled at him warmly, telling herself to be careful not to encourage the man overly much. Jim was a gentleman and had dashing good looks, but Kale had no room in her heart for another man.

There was one fact above all others, however, that preoccupied her: Millicent Randall was very much attracted to Rob Martin. Her attitude showed all too plainly in the way she looked at him, and Kale suspected that the reason Millicent was so quiet was because of her deep feelings for Rob. It was astonishing that no one but Kale was aware of the dark-haired woman's state, and even Beth, who had earlier put Millicent out of her mind as a source of competition, seemed completely oblivious to it.

Kale felt ill. To know that another woman was secretly pining for Rob was too much for her, and she wanted to scream, to claw Millicent's face with her nails, to create a terrible scene.

Too upset to think straight or to take part in the conversation, Kale sat silently. Then they moved to the dining room for dinner, where another surprise awaited her.

"Millicent," Toby asked, after they were seated at the table, "are you still determined to go ahead with your performance tomorrow night?"

"Of course," Millicent replied quietly. "Why shouldn't I?"

"I can think of several good reasons," Rob told her. "The most obvious is the problem that we had this very evening. It's clear that there's no love lost between the Chinese and the Irish, and they may be spoiling for a fight tomorrow."

"I'm convinced," Millicent said, "that they'll both behave themselves."

Beth turned to Kale and smiled. "Millicent," she explained, "has decided to give a flute concert tomorrow night at the local opera house. In addition to the townspeople, laborers from the two opposing camps will be there. I thought the idea of Millicent's performing was mad myself, but I'm not so sure of that anymore. Millicent has pretty well convinced me that she knows what she's doing."

"I don't want to sound like I'm an expert on the subject of music, which I'm not," Millicent said, "but I've studied the flute long enough that I'm convinced of my ability to give a reasonably entertaining performance. What's more, music is a great softener, a great persuader, and I'm hoping that, by the mere fact that the two warring factions are going to come to my concert and are going to listen, maybe they'll be better friends by the time they leave."

"Maybe," Rob said sourly.

"In any event," Toby said, "we've got a number of respectable townspeople—farmers and businessmen and professional people—who have promised to show up and police the event. So, one way or another, we should be in fairly good shape tomorrow night."

Millicent nodded brightly. "I think you're going to be surprised, Toby. You, too, Rob."

"I hope so," Rob said curtly.

Millicent turned to her hostess. "What about you, Beth? Are you going to be there?"

Beth's lower jaw jutted forward. "You bet your life I'm going to be there," she said with determination. "Rob tried to talk me out of it, but there's no way I'm going to miss the one social event in Utah that has taken place in the months we've been here."

Rob sighed and shook his head as he said to Kale, "I tried to persuade Beth that it might be dangerous for her to go to the concert. If the Chinese and Irish start acting up and get ugly, there's no telling what will happen to her. But she's taken Millicent's word that there won't be any serious problems, and I'm powerless to prevent her from going."

"I think that Beth is brave to be going," Toby said, "and I think that you're showing great courage by performing tomorrow night, Millicent. You have a very considerable stake in the outcome."

"I wouldn't miss the excitement for anything in the world," Kale replied vigorously, telling herself that she wished Millicent no permanent harm, but she wouldn't mind if one of the workmen happened to hit her with a rock and made it impossible for her to perform in the near future again. More than that, Kale hoped Millicent would be too incapacitated to engage in her maddeningly unconscious flirtation with Rob.

Ranch owners and their wives, their sons and their daughters, came long distances to Ogden for the concert and filed eagerly into the opera house on Main Street. The leading merchants of the town were present in force, as were the owner of the hotel and other leading citizens.

Beth Martin and her party occupied a box at one side of the stage, and Kale, deliberately inconspicuous in her appearance, sat beside her friend. Jim Randall had offered to escort the women, and Kale again warned herself not to let the young man get too involved with her. She could feel him staring at her as he sat behind the two women in their box.

On the floor of the auditorium, a short distance away, Rob Martin stood at the foot of an aisle, his back to the stage, and watched the audience coming in to take their seats. He had elected to take up a post closest to the place where his wife was sitting. In that way, if any trouble erupted, he would be near at hand in order to get her out of the theater before real difficulties broke loose.

Toby Holt was everywhere in the opera house, patrolling the aisles, making certain that the businessmen, ranchers, and other townspeople who came in were ready for any emergency.

This they were. About ten minutes before the performance was scheduled to begin, the Chinese

workmen filed into the left side of the auditorium and
took seats behind the tenth row. Orderly and clean,
they had obviously scrubbed hard after their day's
work and wore clean work clothes. They were in a
festive mood and laughed and joked in seemingly
rapid-fire Chinese as they took their seats.

No sooner were they in place than the opposite
side of the theater filled with the Irish laborers who
were working on the Union Pacific line. They, too,
had scrubbed their hands and faces and wore clean
and neat work clothes. The two groups had been
warned to behave themselves and to create no mis-
chief on this occasion, and they did their best to comply. But the strain threatened to be too great for
them. As they became aware of each other, a low,
steady murmur arose on both sides of the center aisle.

Toby strolled slowly, with simulated casualness,
down the center aisle until he reached the front row.
Then he turned and surveyed the audience.

Everyone present knew him. The merchants and
ranchers were dependent on him for their safety, and
after numerous brushes in which they had emerged
second best, the Chinese and Irish laborers had
learned better than to tamper with him. His hands
rested in his belt only inches from his repeater pistols,
and the workmen knew that he would not hesitate to
draw his weapons if he felt the need.

They looked around now and were in no way
surprised when they saw other members of the town's
citizenry standing every few feet all the way up the
center aisle to the rear of the theater. In the event
that trouble developed, these men, without exception
crack shots, could be depended on to quell a disturbance in short order.

This was the first time that Kale Salton had ever
seen Toby Holt in action, and she did not wonder at
the reputation he had achieved. He was superbly
self-confident, coolly in command of himself and of

the situation, and his attitude made it clear that he would not hesitate to meet force with force if it should be necessary.

She could not help but note the difference between Rob's attitude and that of his partner. Where Toby was calm and deliberate, Rob was on his toes and alert, his attitude reminding Kale of a coiled spring about to be released. If the Chinese and Irish were at all apprehensive, Rob Martin was even more so, and he made it plain by his attitude that he was protecting his wife, no matter what the cost. His hands actually gripped the butts of his pistols; he was ready to draw the weapons at a moment's notice.

Discretion proved to be the better part of valor, however, and the two groups, although conscious of the proximity of their foes, nevertheless remained sufficiently quiet for the rest of the audience to begin to anticipate the appearance of the soloist of the evening.

Beth had eyes only for her husband. She did not feel threatened or ill at ease in any way, but his presence nevertheless comforted her and seemed to assure her that she would come to no harm while he stood guard over her. She smiled at him from her seat in the box, and he grinned at her in return.

Then his look strayed to Kale. She smiled in greeting to him, and on sudden impulse, she lowered one eyelid in a solemn wink. Rob saw nothing amiss and nothing forward about the gesture and returned it, winking back at her.

Millicent's accompanist, a talented music teacher, came out and seated herself at the piano. She was applauded lightly by the ladies and gentlemen who knew her, and a storm of applause from the Chinese and the Irish also greeted her.

Millicent appeared from the wings and walked shyly onto the stage. Her manner was completely self-effacing, and as she raised her flute to her lips and took a stance with her feet apart, she reminded Kale of the way a woman stood when she was putting on a pair of earrings. Looking at the other woman critically, Kale decided that she either did not know how to dress herself appropriately, or she deliberately underplayed her appearance. As on the other night, her dress was dark and full, with a high neck and long sleeves. It covered her trim figure so thoroughly that she might as well have been wearing a heavy overcoat.

There was no way of determining what the Chinese and Irish workmen in the audience were anticipating, but it was clear that they were disappointed in the plainly dressed, unglamorous-looking woman on the stage. They stirred restlessly in their seats and muttered to each other. Kale saw Toby signal to his colleagues to be alert for trouble, and she expected an eruption at any time.

At that moment Millicent began to play her flute.

From the very first note, she demonstrated a mastery of both the instrument and the music. Kale had no idea what Millicent was playing, but the music intrigued her, and clearly the coarse laborers felt as she did. They gradually grew quiet and sat still, giving the flutist their rapt attention.

Millicent created a spell as she played the melodic flute piece by Bach, and little by little, as she wove the fabric of her net, she drew her listeners to her. Kale was aware of what was happening, not only to her but to the entire audience, and this confirmed her opinion of the other woman. When it came to music, Millicent knew exactly what she was doing, and she had such a rapport with her flute that she was in total command of her audience.

Kale had heard it said that music could have a hypnotic effect on large numbers of people, and she was witnessing the phenomenon for the first time in her life. The Irish and the Chinese forgot their proximity to their sworn enemies in the audience and were completely caught up in the spell of the music that Millicent coaxed from the flute. Her fingers flew up and down the length of the instrument, and the music she played was little short of phenomenal.

The tensions that had gripped the audience dissipated and vanished. When Millicent finished, she bowed slightly, and the audience sat in a stunned silence before applauding so loudly and vociferously that the very walls of the building shook.

By the time that Millicent started to play her second piece, a lively sonata by Vivaldi, she completely owned her audience and could do no wrong. The spell she had woven was complete, and she plunged into the number with the total self-confidence of a virtuoso.

Knowing what to expect now, the audience was behind her solidly, and willingly they gave themselves to her. The feuds of the Irish and the Chinese were forgotten, and Toby's citizen police force not only found it unnecessary to remain alert but also became caught up in the spirit of the music.

When the performance finally ended, the audience was reluctant to see Millicent depart and applauded her so steadily and vehemently that she was forced to give three brief encores. And afterward, as they made their way out of the theater into the star-filled night, the Irish and Chinese laborers actually rubbed shoulders.

As Kale accompanied Beth Martin and Jim Randall backstage, she realized that Millicent might be ignorant of her strengths as a woman, but she knew her even greater strengths as a musician. Kale was in awe of her.

Millicent, meanwhile, was sitting in the small, cramped quarters she was using as a dressing room. She was exhausted. Her performance had been not so much for the benefit of her music as it had been an attempt to clear her mind of all the misguided feelings she had unwittingly developed for a married man. By throwing herself into her performance with everything she had, thinking only of the music, she had put Rob Martin out of her mind. Now if she could continue to keep her affairs in proper perspective, she felt she could get on with her life—study her music, find a property where she could make a home with her cousin Jim—and let Rob and Beth get on with their own lives.

Early the following morning, the entire household was awakened by heavy pounding on Kale's door. "I've got to go fetch Dr. Smith," Rob called in to her, a note of frenzied panic in his voice. "I'm sure that Beth is having her baby."

By the time Rob returned with the physician, Kale had the situation well under control. Clad in a long robe of lightweight wool, which she wore over her nightgown, she had not taken the time to dress. Making Beth as comfortable as she could, Kale put a container of water on the stove to boil—this would be for washing the dressings—and she also put on a pot of strong coffee and placed on the table a plate of bread and rolls and butter. She was cheerful as she confronted Rob.

"I suggest," she said, "that you and Toby have yourselves some breakfast, and I'm sure all of us can use some coffee."

"Breakfast?" Rob looked at her in a daze.

Kale laughed reassuringly. "You'll be surprised how hungry you are," she said. "It's important that you eat, you know. I've put on the coffee, and you see the breadstuffs. I've got to look in on Beth." She hurried off to Beth's bedroom to assist the physician.

Rob dutifully sliced some bread. He was acting automatically, paying virtually no attention to what he was doing, and when his partner came into the kitchen a few moments later, Toby quietly pushed him aside and took charge. "Why don't you just sit down, Rob, and take it easy. I'm going to make you a good breakfast."

As Rob went to the table, his partner began to slice bacon and break several eggs into a bowl. "I saw Dr. Smith in the corridor upstairs just now," Toby said, "and he wanted me to remind you of what he told you."

Rob nodded solemnly, his expression unchanging.

Toby added more wood to the fire, then placed a frying pan with bacon on a burner. "Well," he demanded, "just exactly what is it the doctor said to you?"

"He told me," Rob replied, "that he's never yet lost a father."

Toby laughed, but Rob remained straight-faced.

"I don't see the humor of it," Rob said, and suddenly rose from the table, looking panicky. "I've got to see how Beth's doing." He hastened upstairs, and in the meantime Toby, still smiling, concentrated on preparing breakfast. By the time Rob returned to the kitchen, the bacon and eggs were ready, and the pot of coffee was bubbling on the stove.

"Kale wouldn't let me stay," Rob said helplessly. "The doctor seemed to be very busy. He's working in his shirt-sleeves now."

"Sit down and eat," Toby commanded him, and put a plate in front of Rob. Then he joined him at the table.

Toby, eating his normal breakfast, was in no way surprised to find that Rob was ravenous and ate most of the bacon and eggs and also devoured three slices of bread.

Toby was pouring the coffee when Kale came into the kitchen, her sleeves rolled up above her elbows.

"Well?" Rob demanded, leaping to his feet.

Kale put her hands on his shoulders and pressed him down into a sitting position again. "Drink your coffee," she said. "I'll let you know when there's any news to report."

"But it's taking so long," he protested.

She shook her head. "Beth hasn't been in labor all that long."

Toby grinned at her. "Would you like a cup of coffee?"

"There's nothing I would like more, but unfortunately I don't have time for it now." She picked up an armload of towels and disappeared up the stairs again.

Toby soon discovered it was impossible to converse with his friend. Rob paid no attention to anything that was said to him. Unable to take the suspense any longer, Rob leaped to his feet and began to pace up and down the length of the kitchen.

Toby tolerated the incessant movement as long as he could. "Why don't you go out and cut some more firewood?" he suggested.

Rob responded to the request with great gusto, and a pile of firewood began to build up in the yard outside. He appeared with several loads of wood, and then, after building the fire in the stove again, he resumed his pacing.

Toby was about to suggest that they ride out to see the progress the work crews were making on the railroad lines, but he knew better than to make that suggestion. Nothing would persuade Rob to leave the house until after Beth had safely delivered their child.

The morning dragged interminably, and Toby couldn't help but think that he had missed a great deal of the travail that Clarissa had suffered when their son had been born, for he had been in Dakota at the time. Thinking of her, he felt a sharp pang. Missing his wife and son, Toby once again wondered if he and Clarissa would ever resume a normal relationship.

A lusty infant's howl drifted down the stairs, and the electrified Rob stopped short. "My God," he whispered. "The baby is here!" He would have raced up the stairs had Toby not detained him.

"Wait until they're ready for you, Rob," he said. "I'm sure that Kale will come for you the minute Beth can see you."

They had only a few minutes more to wait, but the passage of time seemed endless.

At last Dr. Smith appeared, looking weary but triumphant, and he went straight to the kitchen sink to scrub his hands. "Congratulations, Mr. Martin," he said. "You're the father of a healthy, normal baby girl."

Rob found it difficult to gain his voice. "My wife," he said. "Is she—I mean—"

"Mrs. Martin is just fine," the doctor assured him. "She suffered no complications and had a normal delivery in every way." He shook Rob's hand and patted him on the shoulder. "Come up in about five minutes more. We'll be ready for you by then." He disappeared up the stairs.

Rob's smile seemed to cover his whole face as he accepted Toby's heartfelt congratulations. "I suppose," Toby said, "that you could tolerate a toast to your daughter about now. It's past noon, so maybe a drink won't taste too bad."

"I'm going to let it wait," Rob replied, "until I've seen Beth. I don't want to go up to her with liquor on my breath." He removed his watch from his fob pocket. "I guess it's about time for me to go upstairs by now," he said, and bolted up the steps, two at a time.

A weary but happy Kale emerged from Beth's room as Rob reached the landing. Kale came to him, put her arms on his shoulders, and kissed him lightly on the cheek. "I know you and Beth are going to have all the happiness and all the good things in the world that you both deserve," she said, then, not waiting for a reply, hastened down the stairs for the cup of coffee that she finally had time to drink.

When Rob entered his wife's room, he saw Beth reclining in bed, wearing a clean nightgown with fresh bedclothes around her. Her blond hair gleamed dully as it rested against the pillows, and as her husband approached her tentatively, he saw the tiny creature who was his daughter. Her face resembled a monkey's, but he felt certain that this was the most beautiful infant he had ever seen in his life. As for Beth, she was lovely beyond compare.

Beth looked up at him, her blue eyes shining, and it was unnecessary for her to speak. Rob bent down and tenderly kissed her. Then he stared at the infant. It was obvious that he was afraid she would break in two if he touched her, because he retreated several paces as he stared down at her.

"I think," Beth said, "that she has you buffaloed already. Daddy's girl is going to wrap you right around her little finger."

He cautiously stepped forward, reached out toward the child, and put his finger in her hand.

Suddenly, acting in slow motion, the infant squeezed her hand, and a tiny, perfectly formed fist closed around Rob's index finger. At that instant, he lost his heart to his daughter.

Beth was watching him. "I will always be in awe of the relationships between fathers and daughters," she said. "It begins now, and it will last for life."

He bent down and kissed his wife again. "Forgive me for being somewhat redundant," he said, "but just for the sake of the record, I love you."

"For the sake of the same record, I love you, and so does she."

"I'm already very fond of her," he said. "And are we still in agreement as to the name we would use if we had a daughter?"

"Of course," Beth replied without a moment's hesitation. "We're giving her my mother's name."

"Very well, then," he said. "Cathy Blake Martin, welcome to the world."

The Chinese and Irish laborers apparently had come to a permanent understanding the night of Millicent Randall's concert. For whatever the reasons, their mutual acts of violence ceased and were not resumed.

But the violence on the railroad erupted in other ways as at last the inevitable happened, and work crews began laying the rails across Ralph Granger's property. Construction foremen had delayed as long as they could, ordering that track be laid everywhere else in Utah but Granger's property, but now it was necessary to cross the rancher's vast spread if the rails were ever to be joined. A representative of the railroad was sent out to Granger's property to serve him a writ that the U.S. government had taken a right of way for the railroad, and the railroad man, escorted to the ranch by Toby Holt and Rob Martin, didn't wait for a reply.

Granger stormed into town and spoke with his lawyer about his first option agreement with the Randalls, but it soon became clear that the agreement would not affect the ability of the U.S. government to have a right of way through the property, no matter who owned it. Leaving town on his horse, Granger fumed all the way back to his ranch, deciding what to do next.

Ian Cameron was useless to him now. The foreman was still hiding out in the mountains, afraid to make a move and probably worried that Toby Holt—who had made the Ute braves back down and had thwarted the Chinese hatchet man—would get him next. Well, Granger thought to himself angrily, he didn't need Cameron anymore.

Arriving at the ranch, Granger impatiently left his horse with one of the hands, told the man to get George from the bunkhouse right away, then marched into his study. He poured himself a stiff drink of whiskey and waited for his hired man to come to him.

Like Ian Cameron, George had been a drifter before coming to work for Ralph Granger, and the rancher knew he could get the hired hand to do his bidding. When the big, burly man hurried into the room, Granger's eyes bored into him.

"How'd you like to earn some extra money?" the ranch owner asked.

The hired man hid his surprise. "I'd like it just fine."

"I thought you would." Granger grinned. "Well, what I want you to do is not going to be easy. But if you agree to do it, I'll pay you one thousand dollars in advance."

This was an enormous sum, more money than the hired hand had ever seen in his life, and it was only an advance.

The ranch owner continued. "I want you to leave the ranch in the middle of the night. You must sneak out of here and be extremely careful that no one sees you. Then you must ride to the village of the Ute in the mountains. . . ."

"But boss," George burst out, despite himself, "them Ute'll kill me sure."

"No, they won't, not when you tell them you're working for me. I got the Indians to do what I wanted before, and I'll get them to do what I want again, especially when you tell them what they'll get if they continue to work for me." Granger's eyes gleamed diabolically. "For every Ute brave who goes out and attacks the railroad, I'll give him two new rifles. If the Indians send twenty-five men out to create havoc, I'll give them fifty guns; if they send fifty men, I'll give them one hundred. But your instructions to them are to create holy hell in Utah. They can do whatever they want; they can attack wherever they like, whenever they like, just so long as the railroad is stopped. Now, can you do this, George? Can you ride out of here undetected and get the Ute to do my bidding? If you do, I'll make you a very wealthy man." Granger had already taken from his safe a bag of gold coins, and he now spilled them out on his desk. "These are yours, George, and there'll be more—much more—if you do what I want."

George was unable to take his eyes off the glittering coins on the desk. As if in a trance, he said, "Boss, I'll do it. You can count on me."

And so the violence on the railroad line erupted anew, and construction again was held up, since most crews had to work to repair the damages. Agreeing once again to do Ralph Granger's bidding, the Indians were given fine new rifles, and armed bands of Ute warriors—with each band consisting of from a half-dozen to forty or fifty heavily armed braves mounted on swift Indian ponies—conducted lightning raids up and down the line, from one end of Utah to the other. When possible, they concentrated on the supplies, which they destroyed or stole. When necessary, they attacked the columns of working men, who had been issued no arms for self-defense. They fired on the work trains themselves, and they attacked stagecoaches and small wagon trains, not caring whether they were railroad property or belonged to civilians.

Toby Holt and Rob Martin were busier than they had been at any time since they had been called on to head the defensive forces of the railroad. Arming themselves with pistols and rifles and enlisting the aid of some of the townspeople as well as some of the railroad workers, they formed groups and spread out across the territory.

Even though the Indians were heavily armed and had greater numbers than the whites, the Ute braves soon realized they were no match for these grimly determined men who were working for the railroad. Their accuracy with rifles and pistols was far greater than that of the Indians, and in any confrontation the Ute inevitably lost some of their braves, while the white men suffered no casualties. So the Indians worked in stealth, attacking the railroad lines, work crews, and wagon trains where they could, but for the most part avoiding Toby Holt and his men.

Still, it was impossible for Toby and Rob to be everywhere at once, and the Indians took their toll before retreating into the mountains after each raid. Only because of their determination to see that people and railroad equipment came to no harm were Toby, Rob, and the others able to keep the destruction to a minimum.

Then one evening, as the exhausted Toby and Rob were returning to the house in Ogden after a daylong foray in the countryside, a knot of men who were gathered on Main Street hailed them. The two men pulled up their stallions and halted. The group consisted of several of the more prominent of Ogden's citizens, and from their serious manner, Toby and Rob knew they were discussing a matter of some consequence.

One of them called, "Have you heard the latest?"

Toby braced himself. "Now what?"

"One of the recent attacks was on a passenger stagecoach crossing the Rockies," the man said.

"The way we heard tell," another said, "Ralph Granger's nephew, Paul Granger, was killed. The lad just finished college back East and was coming home to his uncle's ranch."

"I always said that no good would come of Granger acting up the way he's been doing, and the

Lord has seen fit to punish him good and proper," a third man declared grimly.

"Granger has been responsible for more trouble and more hell raising along the line than you can shake a stick at," the first speaker said. "But it serves him right, what's happened to him now. He ordered an attack on an innocent stagecoach, and blamed if his own nephew, his only living relative, didn't die. That ought to be a warning to anybody who raises his hand for the forces of evil. I tell you plain, it's a bad, bad business."

Toby thanked the men for their information.

"I think it's we who should be thanking you, Mr. Holt," one of the men said. "If it weren't for you and Mr. Martin here, the problems would be a lot worse. The people of Utah, as well as the railroad, are in your debt."

Toby shrugged off the praise and smiled thinly. Then he and Rob rode the rest of the way home in silence.

Their housekeeper was preparing supper in the kitchen, and Beth and Kale were chatting in the parlor while the baby slept in Kale's lap. Beth got up from her chair and rushed over to the men when they appeared in the hallway, looking grimy and tired but unharmed. "Everything's fine," Rob assured her. "We'll tell you the whole story after we clean up." He and Toby went upstairs to wash and change their shirts. When they came down again and joined the women in the parlor, Toby told them about a run-in they had had with a few Ute braves, minimizing as much as possible the dangers they faced. Then Rob told the women the news they had gleaned about Ralph Granger's nephew.

"This is terrible," Beth said softly.

"It *is* terrible," Toby replied, "but people are right in saying Ralph Granger got what he deserves. I've been sure all along that he's primarily responsible

for all of the troubles that have been breaking loose
along the line, and although I can't prove it in court,
I would have any local jury with me one hundred
percent of the way."

Sobered by the tragedy, they spoke in hushed
tones through supper. Finishing their meal, they adjourned to the parlor for coffee. Toby and Rob helped
themselves to glasses of whiskey. There was a knock
on the door, and Rob answered the summons. He
looked disbelieving when he returned to the room.
"Ralph Granger's foreman, Ian Cameron, is here," he
said. "He's anxious to see Toby."

"I'll see him in the dining room," Toby said, his
voice grim. Taking no risks, he buckled on his gunbelt
before going to the door and admitting Granger's
foreman into the house. Toby demonstrated his contempt by not offering Cameron a seat when they
came into the dining room.

"Mr. Granger told me a while back that you've
been wanting to see me, Mr. Holt," he said.

"It strikes me," Toby replied coldly, "that you're
awful tardy doing something about it."

The man nodded slowly, removed his ten-gallon
hat from his head, and twisted it slowly in his hands.
"I can't say as I blame you for being annoyed with
me, Mr. Holt," he said. "I've known right from the
start why you wanted to see me, and to be truthful
with you, I've been ducking you. I figured that if I
didn't see you, I wouldn't have to answer any embar-
rassing questions. I've been busy getting in the way
of the railroads being finished," the man said, "and
I'm the first to admit it. I arranged for those early Ute
raids on the supply wagons, and I've even led some
parties tearing up rails and destroying ties. I'm admitting all this to you in private, Mr. Holt, although, if
you take me into court, I won't repeat a thing that
I've said here, and I won't admit any wrongdoing.
Old Mr. Granger has wanted me to delay the build-

ing of the railroad and the opening of the rails, and I've done everything in my power to comply with his wishes. But I had no part in the recent raids, and that's the truth. At least a half-dozen innocent people have been killed in these raids, and I say that's going too blame far."

"So who *is* responsible for the recent tragedies?" Toby demanded coldly.

Cameron twisted his hat still harder. "I think we both know the answer to that, Mr. Holt, sir."

As nearly as Toby could judge, Cameron was speaking the truth in saying he had had no part in the recent raids. Feeling unexpectedly sorry for the man, Toby invited him to sit down.

Cameron gratefully perched on the edge of a chair. "Thanks, Mr. Holt," he said, his voice choking. "I knew you were a decent man. That's why I took the chance and came here to see you. I wanted you to know it was Granger and not me causing all the recent trouble." He paused and let out a deep sigh. It was clear he was near the breaking point.

"What an awful thing it was that young Mr. Paul was on that stagecoach," Cameron at last continued. "I tell you, old man Granger loved that kid like he was his own son, even more, because he was the only Granger left of the younger generation."

"How is Mr. Granger taking the news of his nephew's death?" Toby asked quietly.

Cameron shook his head and spread his hands helplessly. "You ever seen a horse that grazes on locoweed? The poor critter gets to running round and round and round in big circles and can't stop, no matter what he does. Before you know it, he froths at the mouth, and then he falls down like he was dead drunk, and half the time he can't even get up again until he sleeps off the crazy jag he's on. I tell you true, I thought old man Granger was like a horse that had just been nibbling on some locoweed when I saw

him late today. He didn't make any sense at all. His
face was deadly white, so pale that you wouldn't even
know that he had any blood in his veins, and he was
talking crazy. Said he was going to get even with the
whole world for killing his nephew. He made no
sense, and when he talked about burning down a
whole town like Ogden, that's when I figured I'd better come here to see you. Frankly, Mr. Holt, I'm
frightened half to death of what the man may do."

    "You're saying," Toby declared slowly, "that
Ralph Granger is dangerous."

    "Yes, sir, he sure is. But there's no news in that. I
would say the old man has been dangerous for a long
time," Cameron said slowly, moistening his dry lips
with the tip of his tongue. "But now he's gone off the
deep end because of his nephew's death, and there's
no telling what he might do. He knows that I've done
enough jobs not only to go to prison myself but to
send him to prison for one hell of a lot of years, as
well. He knows that, and I could see in his eyes he
was measuring what to do about me. I got scared, Mr.
Holt, and that's why I came to you. I made mistakes—serious mistakes—and I'm willing to pay for
them. If you think I deserve to go to jail, go ahead
and send me up. But don't let Granger kill me, please,
Mr. Holt."

    Frontier justice was not like ordinary justice. Vio-
lence ruled in this turbulent land, and men conquered
and held their places only as long as they proved
themselves the strongest. Therefore, their acts could
not be judged as they were in ordinary society. Toby
had been imbued with a recognition of the principles
of frontier justice from the time he had been a small
boy. He had seen such justice administered by his father, whose judgments had been sure and swift, and
he had grown up knowing that the wilderness was a
land unique unto itself.

    "I don't see anything to be gained," he said now

to Cameron, "by forcing you to spend years of your life rotting away in a prison cell. You've learned your lesson, and that's what prison is all about, isn't it? Now I'll help you out if you agree to help me. I'm not going to ask you to appear in court, but I do want you to write out a statement saying Ralph Granger is guilty of all you say he is. Then I'll let you go free."

Cameron straightened slowly. "You mean that, Mr. Holt?"

"I do," Toby told him.

"Then just give me a piece of paper and a pen, Mr. Holt, and I'll write whatever you tell me to."

Toby went to the sideboard and produced the writing materials, and Cameron, sitting at the table, wrote out in a scrawl all the information he knew about his employer.

Toby took the paper, read it over, and nodded. "Now I advise you to get out of the area. I'll ask my partner, Mr. Martin, to provide you with a personal escort and see that you're on the first stage out of here."

"I'm gonna put this last crazy year in Utah out of my head for all times," Cameron said as he rose and energetically shook the other man's hand.

Toby nodded.

"You're gonna do something about the information that I brought here to you tonight, Mr. Holt?" Cameron asked.

"I hope to utilize it the best that I can, yes."

The man again shook Toby's hand. "You're all right, Mr. Holt," he said. "You're a square shooter. Every bit as much of a square shooter as they told me you were. I couldn't believe it, but I guess it's true, all right. For your own sake, be careful. Be awful careful what you say and what you do with old Ralph Granger."

"I'll be careful," Toby assured him, "and thank you for your concern."

❊   ❊   ❊

While Rob escorted Ian Cameron to the stage depot, Toby, his pistols strapped around his waist, walked to the stables to saddle his stallion.

The information that Cameron had given him was enough to send Ralph Granger to prison for many years to come. Toby could now permanently end the threat to the railroads and see that at last the tracks were joined.

But the fact was that the young Westerner had a secret liking for Ralph Granger, in spite of the terrible things he had done. Perhaps because old man Granger was a contemporary of Toby's father, the young man was inclined to romanticize him. He represented a generation that no longer existed in Utah or in any other territory in the West. He was a fiercely independent old man, who was accustomed to having his own way and who would blast out of his path anyone who tried to stop him. He was one of the pioneers who had built the West, who had fought the mountains and the climate and the isolation and the Indians, who had ultimately lost his wife and his two children to the wilderness, and yet who had struggled on alone.

It was for these reasons that Toby thought he was in no danger in confronting Ralph Granger. He was sure the man would see reason, that he would promise to let the railroads be in peace if Toby agreed not to use Ian Cameron's information against him.

Setting out for the Granger ranch, Toby rode swiftly, his stallion traveling at a steady gallop. Passing the Union Pacific construction crew, Toby saw the Irish laborers hard at work. They were paying strict attention to business, and there was no loitering on the job, no wasting of time and energy hating the Chinese and plotting against them. Something of a miracle had occurred when Millicent Randall had given her concert, and animosities between the two labor forces had vanished as if by magic. Toby realized that he was hoping another miracle would occur when he spoke to Ralph Granger.

Eventually Toby came to the border of the Granger property and followed the trail until he came to the gate that marked the formal entrance to the ranch. There he dismounted and unlatched the gate. Then, as he was riding in, two hands, mounted and heavily armed, approached him.

Toby did not recognize these men from his previous visits to the ranch. Making no attempt to reach for his pistols, Toby waved a cautious greeting to them and called, "I've come from Ogden to see Mr. Granger."

One of the pair looked at him with narrowed, suspicious eyes. "Who are you, and what's your business?" he demanded gruffly.

"You tell Mr. Granger that Toby Holt is here to have words with him. He knows me, and he also knows that my business is strictly between him and me." Toby spoke cordially but firmly.

The man promptly rode off in the direction of the ranch house, leaving his companion to stand guard over the visitor.

Toby made no attempt to penetrate any deeper into the ranch, and he did not try to converse with the remaining hand. He sat in a companionable silence and waited.

The ranch hand was not accustomed to the silent treatment, and he glowered, tugging at his hat brim to force it lower over his eyes as he sat his mount, alert to any unexpected sign of trouble from the stranger.

Finally the hand who had gone up to the house returned. "Come ahead," he said, a note of strong disbelief in his voice. "Mr. Granger says he'll see you."

Toby remained poker-faced as he rode up to the

house with the two men accompanying him, one on either side. The pair escorted Toby into the house and walked down the corridor with him to the old man's private office. There, they reluctantly left him.

Toby tapped at the door, and a deep voice told him to come in. Opening the door, he saw Ralph Granger sitting behind his desk, a pistol resting on the desk top in front of him. There were deep smudges beneath his eyes, and it was obvious at a glance that he had been suffering heavily in recent days.

The old man rose slowly to his feet and extended his hand.

Toby shook hands with him with great cordiality. "Thank you for seeing me, Mr. Granger," he said. "I wouldn't have intruded on you in your time of sorrow if it hadn't been essential that I see you."

"Sure," Granger replied. "The world still goes on when something happens to a fellow. I've learned that much in my life, anyway." He pointed to a chair opposite his desk. "Take a seat."

When both men were seated, Toby said, "Please accept my condolences on the loss of your nephew. I know it must be a hard blow for you to bear."

Granger ran a hand through his thick silver hair. "I know there are folks who are saying what happened to Paul serves me right, that those who live by the sword die by the sword, and other observations like that. But it wasn't fair to the boy, you know. He had no part in what I was doing out here, and he knew nothing of the state of affairs in Utah. His whole life stretched out ahead of him, and to have it snuffed out like a candle that was just beginning to burn brightly was unfair, awful unfair. All I can do is grieve for him. He's the one who really suffered the loss."

"Mr. Granger," Toby said vigorously, "I have

come to see you for only one reason. The death of your nephew convinced me there's been enough killing, enough tragedy, enough disturbance over the building of the railroad across the United States. The time has come for it to stop."

The old man looked at him, his eyes cold. "You don't need to tell me," he said. "Let me guess. Ian Cameron went running to you."

Toby saw no reason to lie. "Yes," he said. "It's true that Cameron came to see me. He told me everything that you've done to put a crimp in the machinery of the railroads. He was very explicit, and he gave me enough information, which he put down on paper, to win a criminal lawsuit against you."

"I stopped the railroad, and I guess I can stop the government from trying to arrest me," the old man said, and tapped his pistol with a finger. "You've never seen anything bloody until you've seen me putting up a fight with my back to a wall."

"I have no desire to report you to the Justice Department, Mr. Granger. I have too great an admiration of you for that."

"Admiration?" the old man asked sharply. "What for?"

"For all you've accomplished here, taming the wilderness and creating a large property out of nothing, making it a financial success. I know something of the vision that was necessary to build such an enterprise, and I'm also aware of the hard work that was involved in the creation of this ranch and of the sacrifices that had to be made by you and your family to build it."

"By God," Ralph Granger said softly. "You sure as hell are Whip Holt's son."

"I know this is hard for you to accept," Toby said, "but the United States today isn't the country that it was when you came out here from the East and first settled in Utah fifty years ago. The country now extends from the Atlantic to the Pacific, and there are states along either ocean. I read in a San Francisco newspaper just recently that they expect the census in 1870 to reveal that the population of the country is now forty million people. Think of it! Forty million! Half a century ago, there were only nine and a half million in the country, and people thought then that the United States was getting too big and too spread out for her own good."

Ralph Granger buried his face in his hands for a few moments. Then he got a grip on himself and raised his head again. "I know," he said. "The United States I knew when I was young doesn't exist anymore."

"It's still the same country, make no mistake about it," Toby said. "People believe as passionately in individual liberties as they always have, and as they always will. And that's what America is all about. Freedom for the individual to lead his own life as he wants to live it. But there's a new quality now that's been added to the way of life as we see it. A nation of forty million people has needs far different and far greater than those of a nation that has fewer than ten million. The will of the people must be served; the needs of the people must be served; the rights of the people must be observed. The great industrial cities of the East and Middle West provide the nation with goods once made for Americans in Europe. Those industrial plants need raw materials, which come from the South, from the West, and from the Far West. The entire nation is tied together. That's the meaning of the United States. That's why this country is strong, because each section depends on the others, and their strength lies in their union. The railroads of America bind the whole nation together. They tie the North and South, East and West, to each other and enable them not just to coexist but to prosper."

The old man stared out the window at the rolling hills that led to the mountain range on the horizon, his face expressionless as he listened.

Toby tried still harder. "Anyone who prevents the railroads from functioning is cutting off the vital aid that different parts of the country render each other. There are thousands of immigrants to the United States, thousands more of disappointed people in the great cities of the East, who are eager to accept the free land that the government is offering them in these mountain territories and want nothing more than the opportunity to start life anew. It isn't practical for them to depend on wagon trains to transport them across the country. That day has passed. The railroad provides the only answer to the problem. Furthermore, it's necessary to move the raw materials and the finished goods, and also to transport the food that's grown in one part of America to the other part."

Ralph Granger sighed but remained silent. Whether he was absorbing Toby's words was impossible to determine, and his gaze remained steadily on the snow-covered mountain tops in the distance.

"Anyone who opposes the progress that is making this nation strong and great is fighting a losing battle," Toby said. "The odds against him are overwhelming, and he cannot and will not prevail because the demands of America for progress are overwhelming. And progress means that the transcontinental railroad must be completed and put to work for the good of all citizens. There is no alternative."

Ralph Granger nodded slowly, but it was impossible for the younger man to tell whether Granger was merely acknowledging what he had heard or if he was agreeing with Toby's estimates.

"You have a long and honorable record," Toby

told him. "You've played your part in making America a great land. For the sake of your nephew's memory, for the sake of the memories of your own children who didn't live to succeed you, end your opposition to the railroad. For the good of all the people of the United States, cooperate with the government, with the two railroad companies, and let the transcontinental line be completed! You can take my word as a Holt that if you cooperate, I will destroy this paper of your foreman's, and you will be able to live in peace for the years to come."

Toby was aware of the old man's deepening, growing depression and attributed it to his feelings over the tragic loss of his nephew.

Like his father before him, Toby was far more accustomed to action than to words, and his long speech had exhausted him. He knew he had done his best, that he could try no harder. His instinct told him not to press the old man for an answer but to let his words sit and take root as they would. He had done everything in his power to convince Ralph Granger to end his opposition to the building of the railroad lines, and he had to be satisfied. He would not consider an alternative until he became convinced that the old man remained unalterably opposed to cooperation with the government and with the railroad companies.

Pulling himself to his feet, Toby extended his hand. "Thank you for hearing me out, Mr. Granger," he said. "I hope my words made sense to you. At least they were the honest expression of an honest opinion."

The old man forced a smile. "I know, and I appreciate your efforts, Mr. Holt." He took a deep breath and added thoughtfully, "I'll do my best not to disappoint you."

"Thank you, sir," Toby replied.

"Can you see yourself out?" the old man asked him. "I would ask you to stay for dinner, but I'm afraid I'm not in a very festive mood these days."

"That's perfectly all right, Mr. Granger. I certainly do understand." Toby turned and left the office. The two ranch hands were awaiting him at the far end of the corridor, and he walked slowly toward them.

All at once the sharp, staccato crack of a pistol sounded from the room he had just left behind him. Toby froze. Then he turned and raced with the two ranch hands back into Ralph Granger's office. Toby had already guessed what he would find. Ralph Granger's lifeless body lay slumped across his desk, his right hand still holding the smoking revolver that he had fired into his head.

Toby knew the old man had been burdened with an enormous sense of guilt. He had become convinced that the accusing finger of God had been pointed at him and had come to the conclusion that there was no place in Utah left for him, no place on earth where he would be at home, as he had been at home on the ranch that he had built with his own hands. Therefore, he had done the only honorable thing open to him and had taken his life by putting a bullet into his head.

It was sad—tragic—but now the way was at last clear for the railroad line to be extended across the vast ranch and for the union of East and West to take place.

Assuring himself that the hired hands would take care of Granger's body, Toby slowly mounted his stallion and started back on the ride to Ogden. There he would find a minister to come out to the ranch and preside over Ralph Granger's funeral. Toby would himself be present.

The conclusion of Ralph Granger's story had not

been what Toby had anticipated, but nevertheless the dispute that had flared for so long and so violently was over. There was nothing more that needed to be said or done.

VIII

With the death of Ralph Granger, the Indian raids came to a sudden and complete stop. The Ute had already been severely thwarted by Toby Holt and his men, and now, without Granger to provide them with more guns and ammunition, there was no way they could conduct their raids. They retreated back into the mountains to their villages, and at least for the time being, they kept the peace and left the settlers of Utah unmolested.

Meanwhile, the hired hand named George, who had indeed made a great deal of money by working for Granger, had not been heard from since his boss's suicide, and the other hired hands at the ranch believed that George had taken his small fortune and left the area for good. But they felt no envy for their former fellow worker; they knew that wherever he was, he would spend the money as fast as he had made it, and before long he would become a drifter again.

Once the private funeral for Ralph Granger had been held and the community at large had begun to recover from the shock of his ugly passing, Jim Randall went into Ogden and paid a visit to the U.S. Circuit Court judge in his chambers.

Judge J. B. Brennan, an austere man of middle years with gray-flecked dark hair, smiled a trifle frostily. "I daresay I know why you're here, Mr. Randall," he announced, "and I think I can save you some time. You intend to put in a bid on the Granger ranch."

"Exactly, Your Honor," Jim answered crisply.

"I can't show any favoritism, Mr. Randall," Judge Brennan told him. "I'll accord you the same treatment that everyone else is getting. I intend to set a date for a public auction, and at the same time, you and anyone else who's interested in the property will be invited to submit your bids. The highest bidder will be awarded the Granger ranch."

Jim Randall smiled faintly and reached into his inner coat pocket. "Apparently you're not aware of a document that might change your mind on the procedures to be followed, Your Honor," he said, and produced his agreement with Ralph Granger.

The surprised judge looked at it and raised an eyebrow. "Everything seems to be in order here," he said. "This is a regular first option form, and I can tell at a glance that Granger's signature on it is authentic. All I'll need to do is to corroborate the signatures of the two witnesses."

"They're still out at the ranch," Jim said, "waiting until the dust settles and a buyer appears who will continue their employment."

"Assuming that I'm able to validate the authenticity of this document," the judge said, "I'll be in touch with you, and you'll have the exclusive right to purchase the property, at whatever price the territory establishes."

"Thank you, sir," Jim said.

"I would like to make one thing clear to you at the outset, Mr. Randall," he said. "The Granger ranch is extensive and is comprised of many, many acres of land, in addition to the ranch house and an unusually large number of outbuildings. It won't be cheap. I'm required to charge you the going rate for buildings and land in Utah."

"My cousin Millicent—whom you heard playing the flute at a recent concert—will be going into partnership with me, and between us, we have ample funds. I've taken the precaution of preparing a list of the banks with whom we deal in Baltimore, our former home. You can feel free to telegraph them and obtain any information you wish regarding my financial status and Millicent's."

The older man nodded complacently. "I anticipate no problems, Mr. Randall," he said. "Barring some very unexpected development, I think you and Miss Randall can more or less count on being the new owners of the Granger ranch."

Precisely as Judge Brennan anticipated, the Randall cousins passed the financial examination with flying colors. The judge validated the signatures on the option agreement and named a stiff but fair price for the property.

Jim Randall needed twenty-four hours to have the money wired to him and to Millicent by the banks in Baltimore, and the following day they went to the judge's office and signed the necessary papers. They were now the undisputed proprietors of what was still known as the Granger property.

It was late in the day when the transaction was completed, and that evening they invited Toby and Rob, together with Beth and Kale Salton, to have supper with them at the hotel. In honor of the occasion, Jim ordered a bottle of champagne.

The waiter served the champagne, and Jim raised his glass to Toby and to Rob. "Gentlemen," he said, "the railroad's troubles are over at the ranch. Millicent and I are going out there first thing tomorrow, and there should be clear sailing for the railroad from now on."

The following morning, the two Randalls rode out to the ranch, full of eager anticipation. For her part, Millicent was happier than she had been in a very long time. She was determined to put all her recent disappointments behind her and concentrate now on making a new home for her and her cousin.

Their first act when they got to the ranch was to assure Ah-Sing that they wanted him to remain in their employ. They also proceeded to give him a larger salary.

"You're far too valuable to us to lose," Millicent told the grinning Chinese man. "We want to be sure that we keep you and that you're happy in your work."

When she emerged from the kitchen, she found about two dozen ranch hands—the total number of employees—gathered in the yard just outside the corral behind the house. Jim was waiting for her to show up before he addressed them.

"Men," he said, "you don't need me to remind you that in months passed, you've engaged in a number of illegal acts encouraged indirectly by Ralph Granger, your employer, and by Ian Cameron, your foreman."

The men shifted uneasily from foot to foot.

"You were simply following orders, and as I understand it, you were offered funds sufficient enough that the temptation was too great for you to overcome. Consequently, as your new employers, my cousin and I prefer to forget the past. You're here to raise cattle, not to terrorize the neighborhood or to destroy the property of the railroads. I want to make that position very clear."

No longer afraid they were about to be discharged, the men grew infinitely more cheerful.

"Any man who offers resistance, direct or indirect, to the crews building the railroads will be dismissed instantly, without a hearing and without explanation. When you see railroad men working their way across our land, pay no attention to them. Take yourselves elsewhere, and don't come back until they've gone. This is the first rule, and I'll stand for no exceptions to it. Do I make myself understood?"

The ranch hands nodded their agreement.

"The position of foreman is open. Ian Cameron is not coming back," Jim said. "Rather than hire a new foreman and impose him over you, my cousin and I prefer to promote from within. So we'll be watching all of you, and in approximately one month's time, we'll be promoting one of you to be the new foreman on the Randall ranch. I guess that's about all that I have to say. All of you know what's expected of you, so there's the end of the meeting. I advise you to get back to work now."

The hands promptly scattered. The knowledge that one of them would be promoted to foreman acted as an enormous incentive, and it was plain that every man in Jim and Millicent's employ would be doing his best to impress his new employers during the weeks ahead.

Early in May 1869, the work joining the railroads was virtually completed. On the tenth of the month the ceremonial "marriage of the rails" took place at Promontory Point, northwest of Ogden. Here the tracks of the Union Pacific Railroad coming from the east were joined with those of the Central Pacific Railroad coming from the west.

The celebrities in attendance were numerous. On hand was Leland Stanford, the president of the Central Pacific, as well as the chief engineers of the two lines, Grenville M. Doge of the Union Pacific and Theodore D. Judah of the Central Pacific.

Three large brass bands were also present, and arrangements had been made for Millicent Randall to conduct the massed musicians in rendering a medley of patriotic airs. The occasion was heavily covered by the American and European press, with representatives of at least thirty newspapers in attendance.

Also there were the state and territorial governors
of California and Nevada, Utah and Wyoming, Nebraska and Iowa, through whose territories the two
railroads had been built. A silver sledge was provided
for the occasion, with gold spikes to be driven into
the ground for the connecting rails. The governors
were to take turns driving in the spikes. The U.S.
Army was represented by an honor company of the
Eleventh Cavalry Regiment, though Colonel Andrew
Brentwood, commander at Fort Shaw in Montana,
could not personally attend the ceremonies.

Sitting in the stands was the proud, beaming
Beth Martin, who was accompanied by the two men
who had done more than anyone else to create this
occasion: Rob Martin and Toby Holt.

The event was recorded in full in telegraph sta-
tions throughout the entire United States, where large
crowds had gathered. There were more people present
at Promontory Point than had ever gathered in any
one spot in Utah before. And in Washington City,
the newly elected President, Ulysses S. Grant, described the occasion as one that would change the
destiny of America.

The Union Pacific, which had originated westward from the Missouri River at Council Bluffs, Iowa,
was 1,086 miles long, while the central Pacific, which
came from California, was 689 miles long. The
crossing of the continent, which had once required
months of hard, laborious travel, was dramatically
reduced, as speaker after speaker emphasized. One
could now go from the Atlantic to the Pacific or vice
versa in the miraculous time of one week. As Leland
Stanford said in his speech, the vast expanses of
America had been magically lessened, and the opening of the entire West was assured.

Toby Holt pointed out in his brief address that,
at least for the present, armed guards would be required on all trains in order to protect them, their

crews, and their passengers in the event there were attacks by Indians or unscrupulous robbers.

Toby also emphasized that the difficulties of building the railroad line had been appalling. The road was literally handmade. Long tunnels and deep rock cuttings had been made in the Sierra Nevada and Rocky Mountains; long, high trestles had been constructed across ravines and deep gorges. The Chinese and the Irish workers, he said, were the unsung heroes of the day.

A large tent had been raised in the open fields adjacent to the place where the ceremonies had been held, and a huge cook tent had been erected beside it. Tables had been set, and an impressive banquet was held, with many of the ingredients brought to the site for the occasion by rail. There were Chesapeake Bay oysters, which had been transported on ice, as had crab roe from South Carolina used in the "she-crab" soup. Superb cuts of beef from the stockyards of Chicago and Kansas City were being served, and the half-dozen varieties of vegetables from California were completely fresh. Nowhere had there been a more compelling display of the power of the railroads to serve all the people with food from every part of the country. The banquet was enormously successful.

Leaving her baby in the care of the housekeeper, Beth was attending her first real social event since the birth of little Cathy. The young woman enjoyed herself thoroughly. She looked stunning in a tailored blue jacket and skirt, with a white scarf at her neck, and Kale looked equally attractive in a green velvet jacket, trimmed with lynx fur. Kale was escorted by Jim Randall, who was dashing with his eye patch and well-fitting brown suit, looking every inch the wealthy rancher. He was highly attentive to Kale, anticipating her every wish, making light and easy conversation, and she returned his attentions, since it was her principle to devote herself exclusively to any man with whom she had a social engagement. Still, she realized she would have to talk to Jim sooner or later, discouraging him from any notions of courtship. In actuality, it was Rob, the lionized hero of the day, whom she wished were escorting her.

The other hero of the day, of course, was Toby Holt. Looking at him sitting across the table with Beth and Rob, smiling good-naturedly at everything that was being said, Kale felt sorry for him. Having no knowledge of the Holts' marital troubles, it was Kale's opinion that Clarissa was being shortsighted and unaccountably stupid in not accompanying him to Utah. Her husband was exceptionally handsome, and he had a magnetic, charismatic personality; she knew that he could attract any woman he wanted. Like Rob, he was independently wealthy, and it was inevitable that the longer the time he spent alone, the more interest he would arouse in the opposite sex.

If Kale were acquainted with Clarissa, she would have warned Toby's wife to come to her senses and join her husband without delay. If she failed to do so, she deserved to lose him. After all, Beth had given birth to her baby in the remote backcountry of Utah and had never once complained. She was staying on here with her husband as long as he remained and would travel anywhere that he did. That was the attitude of a real wife who deserved to keep her man.

Toby and Rob had no chance to eat their meals without interruption. Members of the press clamored for their attention, each of them trying to outwit his colleagues and obtain a private interview with the pair. Scores of prominent officeholders and financiers from New York and San Francisco insisted on shaking hands with Toby and Rob, and they were joined by prominent politicians from Washington City. It seemed as though no one in the distinguished throng was satisfied until he had shaken the hands of Holt and Martin and had thanked them for the role they

had played in the successful development of the
building of the railroad line. Toby and Rob had been
working on railroads almost steadily for four years,
ever since the end of the Civil War. The time they
had taken, the effort they had expended, had been
well worth their sacrifice, as was evidenced by the
momentous occasion.

Among those who halted at their table was Millicent Randall, who, with her cousin, came in for a
minor share of glory because of the cooperative attitude she and Jim had held toward the railroad after
they had taken over the Granger ranch.

Millicent looked beautiful as she glowingly
described her new property and all the improvements
she wanted to make. She was clearly a very happy,
fulfilled woman, and Kale admired her anew for her
strength of character and resilience. Why couldn't
she, Kale, stop pining for a man she could not have
and get on with her own life?

At last the festivities were over. Jim Randall took
Millicent back to the ranch, while Toby and Rob escorted Beth and Kale to the area where their carriage
was waiting.

"This was a wonderful day," Beth said. "I
wouldn't have missed it for anything in the world,
and I'm so glad that you got the recognition that was
due you, Rob. But I don't mind telling you, I'm not
going to need any persuasion to sleep tonight."

Rob immediately showed concern. "You're tired,
honey," he said. "I shouldn't have let you come to the
ceremonies today. You needed rest."

Beth replied by yawning at length.

"She's exhausted," Kale said, "but there's no harm
done. She's sufficiently far from childbirth now that
she's had an opportunity to recuperate and gain her
strength back, so I'm sure this outing has done her no
harm."

"I hope you're right," Rob said as a boy

harnessed their team of horses to a light open carriage and the men handed the ladies in. Toby had ridden out on his stallion, so he mounted while Rob climbed up onto the seat beside Kale and Beth and took the reins.

The evening sky was overcast and gloomy, with a raw wind blowing down from the mountains. The smell of rain was in the air. Toby, riding his mount at a slow trot alongside the carriage, peered intently through the twilight as he said, "If we don't dawdle on the trail, we should reach Ogden in plenty of time before the rain starts."

"For goodness sake," said Beth, who was sitting on the outside of the seat, near Toby, "don't worry about it for my sake. I'm not the first woman who's ever had a baby, and I won't be the last. I assure you that if it rains, I'm not going to melt!"

All of them laughed, and Rob gave a flick of the reins.

Suddenly a rifle cracked in the distance somewhere to the south. Kale, who was sitting in the middle between Rob and Beth, gasped and then stifled a scream as she felt Beth slump against her and tumble forward off the seat. The horrified Rob pulled on the reins. He reached his wife's side in one moment and gathered her in his arms. She appeared to be sleeping, and there was a spreading patch of crimson on her breast.

Rob was so shaken that he could scarcely speak. "The bullet landed close to her heart," he murmured. "There's no way we can save her."

Kale bit her lower lip and looked at her friend, her eyes wide. She had known the mountain country was a land of violence, but the last thing she had expected was to see a young woman, a wife and recent mother, who had no known enemies, struck down by the bullet of an assassin.

Kale was vaguely aware of Toby Holt spurring

his horse as he galloped off in the direction from which the shot had come. He was bent low in the saddle, and she had never seen anybody ride so rapidly.

As Rob tried to make Beth comfortable, she opened her eyes and saw her friend bending over her. "Kale," she said faintly, her voice nevertheless clear.

"Yes, Beth? I'm right here."

"You saved my life in court," Beth said softly, "and now I must ask an even greater favor of you."

"Of course, darling," Kale told her. "I'll do anything."

"Do you remember telling me—just a day or two ago—that you didn't know what you were going to do with your life, that you felt at loose ends?"

Kale nodded. "Of course."

"My baby is still too young for Rob to care for by himself. He's a wonderful father, but she needs the constant attention of a woman." Beth was fighting for breath now. "I've watched you with her. You really love her. Will you look after her for me? Will you take care of her and supervise her as she grows to womanhood?"

Kale protested. "You're going to be all right, Beth, dear. There's no need to . . ."

"No," Beth said sharply, rallying momentarily. "You can't fool me. There's no need for it, and don't waste your time. I have only a few moments left in which to get things settled. Will you do it for me?"

"Of course," Kale said as soothingly as she could, ignoring her own sense of pain. "I'll do as you ask, darling. I'll look after little Cathy for you."

"Promise?" Beth's voice was strained, and Kale could see the anxiety in her friend's eyes.

"I give you my sacred word of honor, Beth, darling," Kale told her, not realizing the extent to which she was binding herself. "I'll raise your daughter as my own. I'll do for her exactly as I would for my own flesh and blood."

Beth's sigh was long and tremulous. "Thank you, Kale, and may God bless you and keep you. I always knew I could depend on you." Now she shifted her gaze to the man who continued to hold her in his arms. "Rob?"

"Don't strain yourself or use your energies trying to talk, honey," Rob said in a hoarse voice. "I'm going to get you a doctor, and you'll be much better when he gets the bullet out of your body."

Beth smiled slightly and shook her head. "No, darling," she said contradicting him. "It's no use, so please don't try. My time has come, and nothing is going to save me. I know it, and I don't want to waste the few moments I have left on earth talking non-sense."

Rob tried to reply, but he was so choked up that the words would not come, and he held her more firmly.

"Listen to me," Beth whispered, "and remember what I tell you. The nightmare we went through in San Francisco was partly my fault. I was so sure I could look after myself living alone there, but I was too young, too inexperienced. My one regret other than the degradation and shame that I felt was that I was forced to dishonor you."

"Never!" Rob assured her fiercely. "You didn't dishonor me for a single moment. You conducted yourself honorably at all times!"

"Then you forgive me?" she murmured, and it was clear from her expression that she was in great pain.

"I forgave you long ago," he told her, his voice choking, his eyes filling with tears.

She sighed gently and nestled closer to him. "Hold me tightly, darling," she said. "I—I feel I'm slipping away."

He clasped her even more firmly.

"That's better," she told him. "You heard what I asked Kale?"

His eyes met Kale's over his wife's face, and he saw the tears that welled up in Kale's eyes. "Yes," he said gently. "I heard every word."

"Will you provide her support as long as she takes care of little Cathy? Will you give her and the baby a home with you?"

"Of course," he replied. "You may take my word for it, Beth, honey. Our daughter will come first in my thoughts and deeds at all times. Never will I shirk my obligations to Cathy, and never will I be remiss in my love for her or in my duty to her."

"Tell Papa and Eulalia that I love them," Beth whispered, "and tell them I'm not afraid to die because I know I'm going to see Mama, whom I've missed badly in these years since she was killed."

In spite of his efforts to exert self-control, Rob's tears were rolling down his face. "I'll tell them," he promised.

"Most important of all, I love you," Beth told him.

"I love you," he replied intensely, as though the words would wipe away her injury and restore her to health.

"I've been spoiled and selfish at times," Beth said, "but I swear to you, I've only really loved one man in all my life. You, Rob."

He bent down to kiss her, in part to silence her because she was expending too much energy. She returned his kiss feebly but with all the fervor at her command.

Gradually Beth's body grew limp, and Rob realized that life had left her.

"Good-bye, darling," Rob murmured, and straightened his shoulders. He was too shocked now to weep.

Still holding Beth in his arms, he closed his eyes and prayed silently, *Lord, look after her.*

Kale could think only that the closest friend she had ever known had died. For the first time in her life, she suddenly felt very scared, very much alone.

Toby Holt rode hard, with all the skill he could muster, as he galloped toward the knob of higher ground that lay to the south. He felt that Beth Martin no longer was with the living, having realized after one quick glance at her that she could not survive the wound she had suffered.

Why she had been the deliberate victim of a killer's bullet Toby didn't know. He couldn't help wondering whether the bullet had been intended for him or for Rob; they had undoubtedly made enemies in Utah. Well, he would find out if the bullet had been intended for him or for his partner when he discovered the killer and cornered him.

There was no doubt in Toby's mind that his present mission would succeed, that he would find the killer and would deal with him. All of his life, all of his experience, all of his training had been in preparation for this kind of a moment.

Ultimately, after galloping for several hundred yards, he reached the small, higher hill from which he had been certain the shot had been fired. Vaulting from the saddle to the ground, he examined the earth in the dim light of the night.

He had been right! One man, and only one, had been here, riding to the summit on horseback, dismounting, and kneeling in the high grass as he had taken aim and fired the bullet that had killed Beth. As nearly as Toby could judge, there was nothing out of the ordinary about the hoofprints he saw, nothing distinctive about the bent grass and the print of one knee and one foot.

Wasting no more time, Toby mounted his stallion

again and started in pursuit of the rider who had withdrawn from the knoll. He utilized all he had learned from his father, all he had been taught by Stalking Horse, the Cherokee warrior who had been his father's foreman and now worked for Toby himself on the Holt ranch. He leaned, too, on the practical experience that he had enjoyed. Perhaps no other man in the West could have ridden so swiftly and with such self-assurance while following a trail on a dark evening.

His pace was vastly reduced, but he felt sure he was making certain progress as he headed due south across the open rangeland. It was odd, he thought, that the killer should have come this way, because there were no towns, no houses, no signs of human habitation for many miles to the south of the place where the murder had taken place.

Gradually the conviction stirred in Toby that the fugitive was deliberately trying to mislead any possible pursuers by going in a seemingly wrong direction. Only by heading to the east, toward Ogden, would the killer be able to hide out in a tavern or hotel. No other course of action made any sense.

Rain fell infrequently in the highlands of Utah, and Toby was dismayed when some large drops spattered his face and hands. He squinted up at the sky and knew he was going to be forced to endure a shower, at the very least.

He continued to ride forward grimly, following the tracks. Gradually the rain worsened until at last it was coming down so steadily that he pulled out of his saddlebag an oilcloth poncho and donned it, thus preventing the jacket, shirt, and necktie that he had worn to the festivities from getting soaked. He pulled his wide-brimmed hat lower on his forehead and, unmindful of the weather, halted to consider the situation.

Obviously the rain was obliterating all hoof-

prints, and he could no longer follow the trail left by
the gunman. His one consolation was that he felt reasonably certain the man had not continued to ride
toward the south or to the west. His best hope was to
turn toward the east and go into Ogden, which was
only a few miles away. He hoped that by following
this route, he would remain on the trail of the killer.

Rain fell for a quarter of an hour at the most,
then stopped by the time that Ogden loomed ahead.
Following his instincts, Toby took the one road that
was available and arrived at the outskirts of town. He
came to a tavern with which he was unfamiliar, and
on sudden instinct he decided to stop there. Perhaps
the killer had come this same way and was losing
himself in the crowd at the tavern.

The horses tied to hitching posts indicated that
there was a fairly large crowd gathered in the place,
probably men who wanted to come out of the rain.
Toby, looping his reins over a post, went inside, pushing his hat back on his head with his thumb.

As he entered the saloon and removed his wet
poncho, all conversation in the establishment halted
abruptly. There were perhaps fifty customers in the
place, all of them ranch hands or workmen. It was apparent instantly that they did not welcome the
presence of this well-dressed stranger.

Feeling the waves of hostility roll over him, Toby
walked slowly to the bar and ordered himself a shot
of whiskey with a schooner of beer as a chaser. The
combination of whiskey and beer was very strong, but
he forced himself to gulp down the whiskey and then
took a couple of swallows of beer.

As he had anticipated, the tension eased slightly
once he found a place at the bar and started drinking.
A number of the patrons seemed to take it for granted
that if he was drinking, he was one of them, and they
paid no further attention to him.

Still others, however, remained suspicious and

continued to watch him, their eyes narrowed, and their broad-brimmed hats pulled low over their foreheads. In all probability, Toby thought, these men operated outside the pale of the law. Some were cattle rustlers, perhaps, while others engaged in a variety of illegal activities that made them alert and resentful in the presence of strangers who might be representatives of the law.

The more Toby pondered, the more convinced he became that Beth's murderer had come here. Such a place would offer him a perfect sanctuary. In fact, it was highly possible that any one of a dozen or more of the patrons could have been responsible for Beth Martin's seemingly inexplicable death.

Yet there was an explanation for her death, and Toby did not have to seek too far in order to find it. It seemed likely that Beth, who had no enemies in Utah, had been struck by accident. She had been sitting on the end of the carriage seat, with Toby's mount on one side of her, and the killer probably had missed his target and had hit her instead.

Whether he or Rob had been the intended victim, Toby realized that further speculation was useless. Picking up his nearly full mug of beer, Toby wandered to a table, a plain slab of pine that had a bench behind it as a seat. Perhaps he could study the patrons more closely and learn to distinguish something about the guilty party.

Sitting at his table, glad for the warmth provided by the pot-bellied stove nearby, he was unable to determine anything that incriminated any one man. Many of those present were either still damp or mud-spattered from riding out in the rain; they all carried guns; and they all looked equally capable of using their weapons.

One patron, who had entered the saloon only moments before Toby had arrived, kept the newcomer under careful but disguised scrutiny. Otto Sinclair, standing at the bar, was both confused and badly disappointed.

Believing that he had killed Toby Holt, he had been rejoicing ever since he had fled from the scene of the murder. He had followed a well-laid plan and had ridden in a large circle before doubling back and taking refuge in this particular saloon. Now he found not only that Toby was very much alive but also that Holt had come to the same place that he had.

His mind spinning, Sinclair calmed himself with a drink and then tried to think logically and reasonably. At last he came to some conclusions. His shot had obviously not found its mark. Perhaps he had cut down someone who had been a member of Holt's party rather than Holt himself, but whatever the case, he had not stayed long enough to find out, for he had been anxious to get away. Now to compound the disaster, Holt, who was noted for having the tenacity of a bulldog, had managed to follow him on his headlong flight through the open mountainous country of Utah.

As Sinclair watched his quarry, he saw Holt study one patron and then another. It soon became apparent to him that no one man was being favored and that it was likely that Holt was unfamiliar with the identity of the person he was seeking.

Sinclair took heart. Suddenly a strong desire welled up within him, and he knew that he had an unprecedented opportunity. He had the chance to become acquainted with Holt before putting a bullet into him!

Not pausing to weigh the risks or the consequences of his impulsive act, Sinclair picked up his glass and coolly sauntered over to Toby's table.

"Mind if I set, mister?" he asked innocently.

"Help yourself, sir," Toby told him. The man looked no different from any of the others.

Sinclair's sense of inner security increased. He

saw no indication on Holt's part that he himself was recognized. "You live hereabouts?" Sinclair asked casually.

"I do temporarily," Toby replied. "My home is in Oregon, and I also have a lumbering property up in Washington."

"I'm kinda new to the West," Sinclair admitted. "The newspapers back East were full of stories about the new jobs that would be opening up in this part of the country once the railroad was built and operating. But so far I don't see much sign of them."

Toby smiled faintly. "Don't be in too much of a hurry," he said. "It will take time for jobs to develop, but you can be quite sure there'll be ample work in a matter of months now that the trains are going through. For one thing, there are going to be a great many positions open for armed guards who will go back and forth over a space of several hundred miles, to keep hostile Indians and possible train robbers at a distance. If you're at all handy with a rifle or a pistol, you should have no trouble getting such a position."

"I'm not what you would call a sharpshooter," Sinclair said, and told himself that was the truth. In face, Holt owed his life to Sinclair's lack of expertise. "But I guess I can handle firearms as good as most can," he went on. "I thank you for the tip, mister." Still sitting, he held out his hand.

Toby shook hands with him.

A perverse thrill shot through Otto Sinclair. He was actually shaking the hand of the man he intended to kill. In fact, there was nothing to stop him from fulfilling his promise to himself to do away with Holt that very night. As soon as Holt left the saloon, Sinclair would follow him and would put him out of the way with a single, well-placed shot.

The man appeared harmless to Toby. "My name is Holt," he said, in an attempt to be friendly.

A strange desire to expose himself to danger by

making his identity known caused the other man to say, "Sinclair, Otto Sinclair." He looked intently at Holt as he spoke and saw no light of recognition in the other's eyes or facial expression. If Clarissa had ever mentioned her first husband's name, Holt obviously did not connect it with the man with whom he was holding a seeming innocuous conversation at this very moment.

Pleased with himself, Sinclair asked, "Can I get you another drink?"

Toby shook his head. "I thank you, no," he said. "This beer will be just fine for me."

"I'll be back," Sinclair told him, and rising, went to the bar and replenished his drink.

As he continued to chat about inconsequentials with Sinclair, Toby recognized that the goal he had set for himself was beyond achievement. He could not simply determine Beth's killer by looking at the man. He would need concrete proof that would stand up in any court of law.

Deeply disappointed over his failure, Toby drained his beer mug, then rose to his feet. He again shook hands with Otto Sinclair, wished him the best of good fortune, and departed from the saloon. Untying his horse and mounting it, he headed home, too tired and drained to continue his pursuit.

Meanwhile, Sinclair was aware that he had a great opportunity. He waited for a few moments, and then placing his empty glass on the bar, he followed Holt into the night. No one was conscious of his leaving the saloon, which was all to the good, and he went to his horse, mounted it, and made sure that his rifle was loaded. This time he would not miss.

Following at a sufficient distance so that he did not arouse the suspicions of his quarry, Sinclair saw Holt far ahead of him on the road. He well knew that he had to exercise great care. If he missed again, he himself well might be a dead man because he knew that his aim could not compare with that of Holt's.

Stalking his prey became exceptionally difficult. The rain had stopped, but the night was still heavily overcast, and fog shrouded the figures. Holt seemed to know exactly where he was going, which was more than could be said for his pursuer, and he turned sharply left, rode a short distance, and then veered to the right.

Sinclair felt growing dismay when he noted that they passed an occasional house, and suddenly he realized that they had arrived on a town street, both sides of which were lined with private homes. He had waited too long and would have to wait for another occasion to do away with Toby Holt.

Dejectedly, he turned away, his mission unfulfilled.

Tired and bitterly disappointed, Toby arrived at the house, where he learned that his worst fears had come to pass and that Beth was indeed dead. Kale took one quick look at his face and knew that he had failed in his attempt to find the killer.

Kale now brought him up to date on other developments. Rob had sent a telegram to Toby's mother and her husband, Major General and Mrs. Leland Blake, and the funeral was going to be postponed until they arrived in Ogden, which she was sure would be within a few days. Beth's body had been taken to a local mortuary, and Dr. Smith had given the grieving Rob some medication to render him unconscious for the night. Finally, Kale told Toby about Beth's dying request.

Toby accompanied Kale into the kitchen, where she offered to make him a cup of coffee. He accepted gratefully, and as he sat at the kitchen table waiting for the water to boil, he saw Kale's worried expression. Still wearing the outfit she had had on during the festivities earlier in the day, she looked haggard and pale. She had not applied fresh makeup, and her usually meticulous hair was in disarray.

"May I ask you something?" she said to him at last.

"Anything at all," he replied.

"You know your mother well, of course, and I assume that you have a fairly good knowledge of General Blake's personality, too."

"I think I know them about as well as one generation can understand another," he said tentatively. "What's wrong?"

"I already told you about Beth's dying request that I take care of Cathy permanently, and you also know of Rob's promise to cooperate in the whole matter of my taking care of the baby. I take that charge seriously, Toby. Beth showed a greater trust in me than anyone has ever placed in me in all my life, and I can't let her down."

"Of course not," he replied.

"You know how I've earned my living for a number of years," she said. "There's no need for me to spell that out for you."

"None," he agreed.

"I'm going to give up my profession completely," she told him. "It isn't fitting for a substitute mother for little Cathy to work as a prostitute. I'm going to devote my entire time to the baby."

"Good for you," Toby said as she poured the coffee.

"But that raises a big question in my mind. Will General Blake and your mother object to my accepting this mission? Will my past stand in the way? I would fight anyone for the right to keep my promise to Beth, but I can't fight the baby's grandparents, especially when the grandfather is the commander in chief of the Army of the West. The cards would be stacked against me, and I'm afraid I would be certain to lose. I'm worried, Toby, and I don't mind telling you I'm frightened, too."

"I suggest," Toby said gently, "that you let Rob handle his in-laws on this matter and let him talk to them, saying what he will. If need be, I'll add a word on your behalf, too."

"Thank you," she replied fervently. "You're a grand fellow, and I wish you all the happiness in life that you deserve."

"I'm not so sure that I deserve it," he replied, suddenly plunged into gloom, "and I'm even less certain that I'm going to have it."

On Monday morning Rob received a telegram from Fort Vancouver to the effect that General and Mrs. Blake would arrive for Beth's funeral on Wednesday morning. Somewhat to Rob's surprise, his own parents also were coming on the same train. He was too shaken to do anything, however, and Toby engaged the minister for services to be held at noon on Wednesday.

The friends they had made in the area came by the house and offered their sympathies. Jim and Millicent Randall in particular visited them a few times and brought over food and milk for the baby, as well as other needed supplies from their ranch. Rob and Kale were extremely grateful, and Jim wanted to tell Kale that he would do anything for her, that he would marry and make her co-mistress of the ranch house.

Kale sensed what was on Jim's mind and realized she would have to talk to him at last. Whereas before she had simply intended to tell him not to get too serious about her, there was now the matter of the promise she had made to Beth Martin before she died. When they arrived in their carriage one afternoon, Kale greeted Jim and Millicent warmly, then asked if he would mind taking a stroll with her.

They had walked a little way down the street when Kale finally said, "Jim, you've been so nice to me—and to Rob—that I just have to thank you."

"No need for thanks," Jim said, and suddenly stopped walking. "Kale," he began, "this is probably as good a time as any to tell you what's been on my mind. . . ."

She gave him no chance to continue. "I think I know what's on your mind, Jim. I wouldn't be much of a woman if I didn't realize you were very attracted to me and hoped to get even more serious."

"That's exactly it, Kale, and I want to—"

"No, Jim, let me finish. Yes, I know how you feel about me, but I'm not able to return those feelings. You see, when Beth Martin died, I made her a very special promise to look after her infant daughter. I intend to do just that, to the best of my abilities. But because of this obligation, I am not able to think of having a relationship with you. I'm truly sorry. You're a fine man. Maybe under other circumstances . . ."

"You don't have to say any more, Kale. I understand. I won't say I'm not disappointed; I am, very much so. But I think you're wonderful to do what you're doing for young Cathy and for Rob."

For a fleeting moment Kale wondered if Jim had guessed what she felt for Rob, but a glance into his eyes told her that he did not suspect; his eyes registered only disappointment at his own loss.

"Jim," Kale said, "I wish you and Millicent the best of luck on that ranch of yours. May you both someday find people as wonderful as you to share your lives there."

He gave her hand a squeeze; then they turned and walked back to the house in silence.

Toby, of course, did all he could for his best friend and partner. Then, unmindful of his own gloom over the fact he had not found Beth's killer, he went out to complete his final work for the railroad: acquiring the services of men who would man the rail depots and patrol the track, safeguarding the passage of trains as they traveled through Indian country and through wilderness in which bandits were bound to start harassing them.

With Toby gone, Kale was thrown into direct and continuous contact with Rob. When they ate together or passed each other in the hallway or sat in the parlor to chat, occasionally their eyes met, and they were both reminded of their brief affair. They were also acutely aware that they were being forced, by Kale's promise to a dying woman, into years of proximity to each other. But there was no choice. Kale intended to keep her word, and Rob would do nothing to harm her relationship with his baby daughter. She was committed to substitute motherhood and a tenuous relationship with the man she loved, and he had no idea of the way she felt.

At supper in the dining room, they sat silently through the meal. Rob continued to sit at the table staring into space until Kale asked him, "Would you like another cup of coffee?"

He roused himself. "I suppose I would."

"A drop of brandy can't do you any harm, either," she told him.

He considered her statement and finally nodded. "You're right," he said, and rising, went to the sideboard, where he poured two small snifters of brandy, one of which he gave to her. Returning to his seat, he raised his glass to her but said nothing.

Both sipped in silence.

Then Kale said, "May I talk to you about something?"

He was surprised by her hesitancy. "Sure," he said. "Anything you like, Kale."

She sipped her brandy to restore her suddenly faltering courage, coughed, and took a swallow of water. "I've been doing a great deal of serious thinking," she said, "and I realize, as you undoubtedly do, that I was under the greatest of pressure when I promised Beth that I would always look after your baby. I don't want you to feel it's necessary to hold me to that agreement."

Rob shook his head. "Ah, but it is," he said. "She also got me to promise that I would abide by the agreement and see to it that it was kept. And that's what I intend to do. Don't you want to look after Cathy, Kale? I certainly wouldn't blame you for not wanting to become a nursemaid, so I'll release you from your pledge, if you prefer."

Twirling her brandy glass nervously, she replied slowly. "Regardless of whether I stay on to look after the baby," she said, "I've given up my profession. I've put aside enough money to live comfortably—"

"Hold on," he interrupted. "You're not spending your own funds as long as you're looking after Cathy. I have more than enough money, and I intend to support you. So let's be very clear on that point."

"Thank you," she said, and swallowed hard, astonished that it was proving so unexpectedly difficult to express what was on her mind.

He could see that she was struggling, and he smiled his encouragement.

"If you and I were alone in this matter," she said, "I would have no hesitancy in keeping my promise to Beth and allowing you to keep your promise to her. But we aren't alone. Cathy has four grandparents, and all of them are coming here to the funeral."

He looked at her in some bewilderment. "The primary responsibility is still mine," he said. "My parents are wonderful people, and so are General and Mrs. Blake. But none of them has any voice in the way I choose to spend my life.

"All the same," Kale insisted, "from all that I've

heard, Mrs. Martin and Mrs. Blake are wise ladies. They also must be very shrewd and very tough to have survived the long trek across the entire United States on the first wagon train to Oregon. So I'm sure they are not going to tolerate any arrangement that you may have made with a former prostitute, no matter what duress you were under when you made your promise. What am I going to do if they decide that I'm unfit as a substitute mother for little Cathy? Suppose they object to you having a former courtesan living in your house, living under your roof, permanently, being supported by you. They can make life extremely unpleasant for you, for me, and they can influence the baby against me when she grows a little older."

"I've never known my mother or Eulalia to be narrow-minded," Rob replied thoughtfully. "They're both women, who—to the best of my knowledge—judge people for what they are, not for what they once were. I think you're just borrowing trouble."

"Maybe I am," Kale replied, her voice a bit shaky, "but I can't help feeling as I do. If they object to my presence with you, our arrangement will have to end, Rob. I'm not going to come between you and your family, between you and Beth's family. I can't do that."

" 'I am the resurrection and the life, saith the Lord; he that believeth in me, though he were dead, yet shall he live; and whosoever liveth and believeth in me shall never die.

" 'I know that my Redeemer liveth and that He shall stand at the latter day upon the earth; and though his body be destroyed, yet shall I see God; whom I shall see for myself and mine eyes shall behold, and not as a stranger.' "

Kale, dressed in black with a heavy black veil covering her face, stood with the principal mourners at the graveside and listened to the clergyman intone the sad, familiar words. Rob stood on the opposite side of the grave, his head bowed. On Kale's left were General and Mrs. Blake; on her right were Dr. and Mrs. Martin. They stood apart from her, their heads lowered, the women dabbing their eyes with handkerchiefs.

Lee, who had lost both his first wife and his only child in a short period of time, clutched Eulalia's hand tightly, fighting hard for self-control.

Kale felt completely alone, completely bereft. Tears came to her eyes, and she had great difficulty concentrating on the service. At last she heard the clergyman conclude:

" 'You only are immortal, the creater and maker of mankind; and we are mortal, formed of the earth, and to earth shall we return; for so did you ordain when you created me, saying, "You are dust, and to dust you shall return." All of us go down to the dust; yet even at the grave, we make our song, Alleluia, Alleluia, Alleluia.' "

At last the service came to an end. Rob threw a handful of dirt into the grave on top of the coffin, and the gravediggers then went to work to fill in the hole above it.

Kale wiped her eyes with a handkerchief and turned away, starting to make her way toward the waiting carriages. She felt strangely, unaccountably weak, and she stumbled slightly.

Ashamed of herself and of the spectacle she was making, she was afraid she might fall, so she slowed her pace. A strong arm encircled her shoulders, and looking up, she saw Rob beside her. Grateful for his presence, she leaned against him, and they walked together to the lead carriage.

It was wrong, Kale thought, for her to take precedence over Beth's parents and over Rob's parents, who were certainly far closer to Beth and far more bereft. Perhaps Rob was thinking that his mother and mother-in-law had husbands to look after them and Kale did not; whatever the case, Kale knew that to protest would be to make a scene. Thus she remained silent and allowed Rob to help her into the carriage. He followed her, and picking up the reins, he flicked them. The two horses started off toward the house in Ogden.

Kale threw back her veil and wiped her eyes again. She tried to think of something adequate to say, but the words would not come, and she stared bleakly into space.

Then, stealing a glance at Rob, she saw the utter misery in his eyes, the deep sorrow etched in the lines of his face. She wanted to cradle his head in her arms; she felt an almost overwhelming desire to comfort him, to offer him what solace she could.

She could imagine how the Blakes and the Martins, riding in the carriage directly behind them, would react, however, so she sat rigidly and did nothing.

"I'm not much of a drinking man," Rob said at last, "but I'll be glad to get a shot of whiskey in me when we get back to the house."

"Me, too," Kale murmured, and his hand was so close to hers that she could not help covering it with her own. He glanced at her in surprise, then caught her hand and held it in silence for the rest of the drive. By the time they reached the house, her fingers were numb.

The Randalls and other friends had pitched in to prepare a full meal for the mourners, and Millicent and Jim brought food that Ah-Sing had cooked for the occasion. It was a fine day, so they would dine outside on tables Toby had set up in the backyard earlier in the morning.

Rob had already prepared a drink for Kale and handed it to her. But then the housekeeper, who had looked after the baby while the others were at the funeral, came outside with Cathy in her arms and said to Kale, "I can't do nothing with the little one, Miss Kale. She won't drink her milk, and if I put her in her bassinet, she starts wailing like a banshee."

"I'll look after her, Ruth," Kale said, and taking the baby in her arms, she sat at one of the tables and gave the bottle to Cathy, who began to drink hungrily.

While Kale fed the baby, Eulalia and Tonie served the food and began to pass the plates. At Eulalia's suggestion a blanket was spread on the ground for little Cathy, and Kale put her down so she could rest. Kale started to help the other women, but Tonie waved her away. "You're doing your share," she said. "Why don't you sit down and let us bring you a plate?"

The young woman meekly found an empty chair between Rob and Toby and sat down in it.

No sooner was she seated than Eulalia's blood-curdling scream brought her to her feet. The general's wife was pointing, and to Kale's horror she saw a full-grown rattlesnake slithering onto the baby's blanket. The infant was fascinated and reached out to touch it, and as she did so, the snake coiled up and raised its head to strike, its tail sounding ominous in the electric silence that followed.

Completely ignoring her own safety, Kale was the first to react. She dashed forward and scooped the baby off the ground a split second before the snake reared back its head to strike.

At virtually the same instant, a pistol shot broke the silence, and the snake's head was severed from its body. The body convulsed grotesquely for several seconds, and Toby Holt, his still-smoking pistol in his hand, stepped forward and kicked the offending rattler's head and body out of sight.

Breathless, Kale was hugging and kissing little

Cathy. Tonie collapsed into a chair, and Eulalia went up to Kale, automatically putting her arm around the younger woman's shoulders.

"I'm in your debt, Toby," the shaken Rob declared. "That was close—too close for comfort. As for you, Kale, I'm eternally grateful to you. You saved the baby's life at the risk of your own."

Kale was unmindful of anything but the infant that she continued to hug in her arms.

"I've seen many people respond to emergencies and to dangerous situations in my life," General Blake said, "but I've never seen anyone react more rapidly or with greater certainty than you did, Kale, or with a greater disregard for her own safety. I'm privileged to have seen a rather extraordinary exhibition of courage."

As the excitement died away, the plates were distributed, and everyone began to eat.

Kale refused to relinquish little Cathy, so Rob put Kale's plate on the table and sat her chair directly in front of it. She was being stubborn, perhaps, but he understood that she had no intention of releasing the baby again as long as they remained outdoors.

At another table Eulalia and Tonie sat beside each other, their heads close together as they conversed in low tones that no one else could hear.

Conscious of the conversation of the two older women, and especially of the glances that they cast frequently in her direction, Kale was certain they were talking about her.

This was the moment she had dreaded, and she felt certain they were tearing her to shreds. She was sure that her dress, although black, was far too snug and revealed too much of her figure. She felt she should have worn no cosmetics at all that day, but she had been so pale that morning that she hadn't been able to resist using rouge on her cheeks and kohl on her eyes.

The discussion was seemingly endless, and Kale was supremely uncomfortable. She felt color rising to her face and wanted to crawl beneath the table. Her future was being decided—adversely. And there was nothing she could do about it. Not that she could blame Rob's mother and mother-in-law for feeling as they did. These two eminently respectable women could not be expected to look with favor on the prospect of a prostitute sharing Rob Martin's home and bringing up his child, their grandchild.

If pressed, she could always claim that she had reformed and had turned a new leaf in her life, that she intended to live respectably. But she wouldn't blame Eulalia and Tonie for disbelieving her and demanding that she demonstrate her reform over a long period of time before she had anything further to do with their grandchild.

The meagerness of her prospects and the dullness of the life that stretched out ahead for her so depressed Kale that they killed her already stunted appetite. She merely sat there, her untouched plate in front of her, the sleeping infant in her arms.

She hoped the two grandmothers would at least have the grace to say nothing to her face about her unsuitability but would talk to Rob in private and let him tell her. When that occurred, she supposed she would simply go back to San Francisco and pick up her life there again as best she could.

Arranging the baby more comfortably in her arms, Kale rose and started toward the house, intending to put little Cathy into her bassinet and to remain indoors herself while her fate was being decided here in the yard. She saw no need to attend her own trial and execution.

To her astonishment and acute discomfort, Eulalia Blake and Tonie Martin were waiting for her in the corridor when she emerged from her bedroom, where the baby also slept, and closed the door behind her. The eyes of the older women seemed to bore into her, and she shuddered.

"May we speak in private with you for a moment or two?" Eulalia wanted to know.

"Sure," Kale replied, a note of bitter recklessness in her voice. "Why not?" She led the way back into her bedchamber and indicated a single chair. "I'm afraid I can't offer you very luxurious surroundings," she said, "but no place in Utah appears to be sumptuously furnished."

Eulalia took the chair, and Tonie seated herself on the foot of the bed. For want of another place to sit, so did Kale.

"You knew we were talking about you at dinner a few minutes ago," Eulalia said. "We could sense your discomfort, and we apologize."

"Indeed we do," Tonie added. "We had no desire to embarrass you."

"This whole experience has been a nightmare," Eulalia went on. "The news of Beth's death was a shock, and I would have collapsed long ago if it wasn't for the fact Lee needs me now as he's never done." She paused for a moment, summoning her strength, then continued. "When we arrived on the train from California this morning, we walked into a very peculiar situation. We were worried about our granddaughter, and we wondered what arrangements Rob was making for her care. When we got here, we were flabbergasted to find that you were in charge of the baby and that you and Rob both were responding to Beth's dying wishes."

"That's right," Kale replied defiantly.

"As I'm sure you can understand," Eulalia said, "our immediate reaction was one of dismay. We wondered how Rob could have been crass enough and unthinking enough to agree to allow his child to be reared by a woman who achieved great notoriety as an acknowledged prostitute during Beth's trial in San

Francisco. We realize that it was your testimony that
saved Beth's life and that she was eternally grateful
to you. But both of us thought that she was going too
far."

"Too far," Tonie Martin echoed. "Beth always
had strong romantic tendencies, and we felt certain
that those feelings colored her reactions in her last
moments on earth and led her to select the worst of
all possible female guardians for her daughter, for our
granddaughter."

Although Kale realized the two women had
voted her down, she thought she had given them no
cause to treat her like a pariah. "I may be a prostitute," she said testily, "but I can assure you that I
haven't harmed or infected the baby in any way. Nor
do I intend to."

Eulalia held up a placating hand. "My dear," she
said, "you have us figured wrong. I can't blame you,
but do me a favor and hear us out before you say
anything. In the first place, if you're tarred with the
brush of a courtesan, you'll be interested to know that
I am, too, and in a far worse way than you've ever
been."

Kale blinked at her in astonishment. "You, Mrs.
Blake?" She couldn't believe what she had just heard.

Eulalia's smile was sad as she recalled the past.
"I'm sure you remember, Tonie, when I was kidnapped by Indians as we were crossing Nebraska in
the wagon train. They took me to their village and
forced me to work in their fields by day and to entertain their braves at night. I had no choice in the matter. It was either agree or be killed, and any number
of the warriors in the tribe took me to bed before
Whip Holt managed to rescue me. I must say, it was
rather magnificent of Whip never to mention the incident in all the years that we were married, and it
made no difference in our married life."

Kale continued to stare at her, her eyes wide.

"I'm no less an honorable woman because of that experience," Eulalia said. "In fact, I may be a better person now because of it. I was a spoiled, brattish Southern belle, and I learned a great lesson in humility."

"As I told you many times, Eulalia," Tonie said, "you changed dramatically for the better. You were impossible before the Indians kidnapped you, and you didn't become human until you returned to the wagon train."

"Kale, General Blake and I haven't forgotten, nor will we ever forget, the way you stepped forward and saved Beth at her trial at the cost of your own reputation," Eulalia said with quiet authority. "That was a marvelous act and took great character and great courage."

Kale was thoroughly bewildered. "You're no longer looking down your noses because of the way I earned my living?" she demanded.

Tonie shook her head emphatically.

"I've already explained to you in so many words," Eulalia said, "that we've been in no position to look down our noses at you."

"You made a fine impression on us during the funeral," Tonie said. "Your grief was genuine, and your concern for Rob, as well as for the baby, was very clear to see."

Kale froze in horror. Her greatest secret was the depth of her feelings for Rob, and she didn't want him to gather the impression that she was using her newfound relationship with the baby to win his affection.

But the other women, if they did know what was in Kale's mind, were acting as if they didn't, and Kale smiled in relief.

"Then we come to the frightening incident with the rattlesnake today," Tonie went on. "I don't mind telling you that when I saw that creature advancing toward the baby, I turned to jelly inside, and I was incapable of thinking or moving."

"I could do nothing myself," Eulalia said. "But you had your wits about you, Kale, and you proved yourself utterly fearless. My husband paid you a great compliment, and you deserved no less. You were wonderful, Kale, and the baby owes you her life."

"That incident, more than anything else," Tonie said, "convinced me that Beth knew precisely what she was doing when she asked you to look after her baby, Kale. I'm thankful to the Almighty that she did, and I'm thankful to you that you agreed."

"I'm thankful, too, and I'm also curious," Eulalia said. "What possibly could have motivated you, Kale? Surely you didn't have to promise Beth you'd look after her child. And surely there hasn't been the time for you to become that closely attached to the baby."

Kale shook her head. "I don't know what made me promise Beth, but I'm glad I did. I've been increasingly dissatisfied with my own life, and here was my chance to improve my lot, as well as to do something useful for the baby."

Eulalia and Tonie exchanged a glance that told Kale that these two shrewd women did indeed know just what was going on in the younger woman's heart. Then Tonie said, "My dear, I know that my son will appreciate your help in the years to come."

"And, Kale," Eulalia said, tears shining in her eyes, "if there ever comes a time when *you* need help, know that you can come to us. We mean that." She put her arms around the surprised woman and hugged her, thereby demonstrating her complete approval.

IX

Toby Holt was remarkably like his father, keeping his problems to himself and making no mention of them to anyone until long after they were resolved.

Eulalia Blake recognized this quality in her son and therefore said nothing to him about his wife until the day she and her husband left for Fort Vancouver by train. Toby accompanied them in the hired carriage that took them to the railroad station and sat on the jump seat facing them. His mother and stepfather filled him in on the news since he had been away, telling him that Cindy had not come to the funeral because she was busy with her studies at Oregon State College and also relating how well Hank was doing at the military academy. At last his mother glanced at him, then asked innocuously, "How long did you say you expect to stay on in Utah to finish your work here?"

"I can't predict exactly, Mama," Toby replied. "It's a matter of hiring and training the security crews for the trains. There are two trains a day heading east, and the same heading west. So that means we have eight crews in training right now, so that each train will always have one, with another in reserve. If they learn rapidly and all goes well, Rob and I well may be finished in about two weeks. If they're slow learners and it takes them longer, we may have to re-

place a few men, so it could be as long a month before I can come home. But I would say certainly it
will be no longer than a month."

"I'm glad to hear it," she replied, "and I have no
doubt that Clarissa will be delighted. She was really
distressed she couldn't come to the funeral, but there
was little Tim to think about, and you know that she
and Stalking Horse just about run that ranch by
themselves in your absence."

"Sure, Mama," he replied, his overly casual attitude revealing that there was still serious trouble between him and his wife.

General Blake responded to a surreptitious nudge
from his wife. "We'll have Clarissa and little Tim over
to Fort Vancouver for supper the first night or two
that we're home," he said, "and I'm positive that she'll
inundate us with questions about you and the way
you look and your general health."

Toby smiled politely and shrugged but made no
comment.

His mother looked at him intently. "It doesn't
take a magician," she said, "to know that there's something amiss in your relationship with Clarissa. I'm not
prying, Toby, and I certainly don't care to know your
private business, but I hope that you can get things
straightened out in the very near future."

"So do I," he replied, and didn't bother to explain
that the only answers Clarissa sent to his letters were
very brief notes informing him of their young son's
health and welfare. At no time did she mention herself or anything concerning her day-to-day activities,
much less her thoughts and her feelings.

Lee Blake was not one to beat around the bush.
Eulalia had told him about her meeting with Clarissa
and the marital problems the young Holts were facing. "Is there anything that we can do to ease matters
for you, Toby, or to smooth the way for your return?"

"No, sir, I'm afraid there isn't," Toby replied. "To

be honest about it, sir, I created an unholy mess for myself, and now it's a matter of whether Clarissa is willing to forgive and forget or whether she prefers to make war against me."

"I see," his stepfather replied, and nodded thoughtfully.

"I visit the ranch once a week," Eulalia said, "and we have Clarissa and Tim over to Fort Vancouver for dinner at least one other evening a week. So I would say that I see her fairly regularly, and if I'm any judge, she bears you no ill will, and she carries no grudge against you, Toby."

He raised an eyebrow and looked at his mother quizzically but made no comment.

"You may believe me or not, as you see fit," his mother told him crisply, "but I know women. I know that Clarissa misses you badly, and I hear the longing in her voice whenever she speaks of you, which she does every time we see her."

"Indeed she does," General Blake added. "I would say that you're the principal topic of conversation at the supper table. In fact, you have a teenage sister whose nose is probably still out of joint because when she came home at Christmas vacation, she wanted to spend her whole time talking about Hank, on whom she has a rather violent crush. We heard nothing but Hank, Hank, Hank from her, morning, noon, and night, but with Clarissa visiting, talking about you, Cindy couldn't get a word in edgewise."

Eulalia laughed and patted her husband's arm. "You did very well to control your temper, I must say, dear," she said.

"I'll admit," he replied, "it's a great relief to hear Clarissa talking about you, Toby, but I get a bit bored with her, too, because it seems that when she isn't talking about you, she's got to tell us the latest incidents in the life of your son, who's sound asleep two chambers from our dining room. No, Clarissa doesn't sound like a woman who thinks ill of her husband."

Toby tactfully changed the subject and spoke to the general about security matters for the railroad, until at last they arrived at the station. There they were joined by Dr. and Mrs. Martin, whom Rob had driven out in a separate carriage. Kale was there, too, the baby in her arms.

When the westbound train appeared around a bend and approached the station, there was a flurry of handshakes and kisses. Tonie Martin, after embracing her son, turned to Kale and took her granddaughter from her for one final hug and kiss. Impulsively, she gave Kale a kiss, too, then returned the baby to the other woman's arms. As Dr. Martin helped her up the steps of the railroad car, Tonie turned and looked at Kale. Then slowly, deliberately, she winked at her.

Much heartened by her support, Kale grinned and returned the wink.

"I'm having the carriage take me to Promontory," Toby said, "and I anticipate I'll be there for the rest of the day, hiring security men for the railroad. So don't count on me for dinner this noon, Kale."

He went off on his own, and Kale accompanied Rob back to the carriage in which they had driven his parents to the station. Rob helped the young woman mount the buckboard, and she, sensing he had something on his mind, sat in demure silence beside him as he started on the homeward journey.

"Well, Kale," he said at last, "I'm anxious to learn what took place between you and my mother. I saw her wink at you just before she got onto the train. If that's any indication, then you two have become fairly friendly."

"Yes, isn't it wonderful?" Kale responded. "Both she and Mrs. Blake were so kind and encouraging. I can tell you, I was not looking forward to seeing them. When I saw them talking and looking at me after the funeral, I was sure they strongly disapproved of Beth's plan for little Cathy here. But then later the three of us discussed the arrangement, and I found out I was entirely wrong about their opinions. They even offered their help if ever I need it."

"That's a relief," Rob admitted. "They must have realized how much I need you. I'm grateful, Kale."

At that moment little Cathy, whom Kale was cradling in her lap, awoke from her nap and began to fuss.

Kale immediately picked her up, loosened the blankets in which she was wrapped, and quieted her.

When they arrived at the house in Ogden, Kale and the baby went inside, while Rob put the carriage and the horses in the stable. When he came into the house, he found Kale, as usual, being marvelously efficient. The baby was lying on her side in her bassinet in the kitchen, drinking milk from a bottle, while Kale busied herself at the stove, it being the housekeeper's day off.

"I hope," Rob said, "that you're not going to a lot of trouble with just two of us here for noon dinner."

"Not at all," she replied cheerfully. "I'm just making a simple bacon and onion omelet." She well knew that such omelets were his favorites, and he was greatly pleased by her thoughtfulness.

While Kale worked, Rob wandered toward the bassinet and admired his infant daughter. He was about to reach down and pick her up when Kale said, "Rob, don't disturb Cathy while she's drinking her milk. Let her finish."

"Yes, ma'am," he replied dutifully and retreated halfway across the kitchen.

"If you have nothing better to occupy you," she said, "you might slice some bread. And if you absolutely insist, you can put the coffee on, too."

"Sure, I'm glad to help," he replied, and quietly marveled that this woman, whom he had regarded as

the epitome of glamour and sensuality, should have
been transformed into a trimly efficient, crisp young
housekeeper.

Feeling him looking at her, Kale turned and returned his gaze. "I'm glad we're going to be alone at
dinner today," she said. "I have something I want to
discuss with you."

"You make it sound rather ominous," Rob said.

She shook her head, then flicked away a strand of
hair that had fallen in front of her face. "It will have
to wait until later," she said. "I can't hold a serious
discussion and cook an omelet at the same time. I'll
burn the eggs." She busied herself at the stove and
did not speak again until she cut the omelet in half
and put it on two plates.

Rob poured them cups of coffee. "We make an
interesting team," he said. "We could always hire out
as a butler and a cook if my mine suddenly runs out
of gold and if the demand for wood from my forests
drops off."

"It's none too likely," Kale told him and smiled,
"so I refuse to worry about it."

They sat opposite each other at the small kitchen
table and began to eat quietly. The setting was the
most intimate they had enjoyed since Kale had come
to Utah, and she felt that the time was right for her
to get something off her mind and to clear the air between them.

Forcing herself to meet his gaze, she said, "I
think now is a good time to bring up what's on my
mind."

"Sure," he replied amiably. "Go ahead. This omelet is great, by the way."

"Thank you." Kale forced herself to continue. "I
am sure you recall the occasion in San Francisco
when I—when I seduced you," she said.

Rob reddened but continued to look into her
eyes. "I would hardly forget that occasion," he said.

"As you know, I acted with great deliberation," Kale said. "Your relations with Beth were strained, and I was anxious to see you get together again. I seduced you purposely in order to demonstrate to you that you could have relations with someone else and still love Beth with your whole heart. You realized it, and I achieved my goal."

Her attitude was cool, almost clinical, which relieved Rob's acute embarrassment to some extent. Although his face was red, he forced himself to continue meeting her at eye level. "I know," he said, "and I'm eternally grateful to you."

"My methods were drastic," Kale said promptly, "but they worked."

He nodded, then lowered his eyes to his plate and took another bite of his omelet.

Kale felt weak from the great effort it took for her to speak of that afternoon of lovemaking with Rob. She was hard pressed to keep one important fact to herself: that she had unexpectedly fallen in love with him. She had not recovered her sense of independence from that moment forward, and it was her love for him, more than any other factor, that was determining her retirement as a courtesan. She could not love one man and accept money and favors from others in return for going to bed with them.

Yet under no circumstances could she reveal the way she felt to Rob. The recent death of Beth, to whom he had been totally devoted, had left him vulnerable, and Kale had too high a regard for him to take advantage of his feelings at the present time.

Too shy to face her, Rob continued to look down at his plate. "You did a wonderful thing," he said. "You sacrificed your own integrity to help a friend."

"I was eager to help my friend, it's true," she said, "but as a courtesan, I had no 'personal integrity,' as you call it, whatsoever. I would like to make that point very clear."

"I see," he said, and fidgeted nervously.

"Now," Kale continued, "you and I have been thrown together by circumstances over which we have had no control. We seem fated to live under the same roof for an indeterminate period of time, and there's nothing we can do about it without breaking a promise that we both made to Beth during her last moments on earth. My reason for bringing up the past to you is very simple. In case you're worried that I'll throw myself at you again, you may relieve your mind. I have no intention of making advances to you, now or ever. The fact that I'm living in your house, taking care of your daughter, in no way obligates you to me sexually." There. She had outlined her present position with the greatest of care and had avoided telling him that she had fallen desperately in love with him and was willing to do anything in order to win his affections in return.

At last Rob looked up from his plate. There was a gentle smile on his face. "Thank you, Kale," he said softly. "That could not have been easy for you to say. But I appreciate your bringing things out into the open, and I think everything's going to work out just fine."

Now, it was Kale's turn to look away. If only things *could* work out, she thought. If only he would learn to love me ...

His plebe year at the United States Military Academy was behind him, and Cadet Henry Blake, who had been known as Hank Purcell prior to his adoption by Lee and Eulalia Blake, sat ramrod erect at the desk in his room as he studied for the last of his examinations. As soon as he passed it and the next class of cadets was admitted to the academy, he would become a yearling, and his year of hazing would be ended.

Hank had good cause to be proud of himself and

his accomplishments during the past year. He ranked third in his class academically, and as anticipated, he had no equal as a sharpshooter. He was a member of the West Point rifle team, and he was the outstanding star of the team, outshooting cadets who had spent as long as a full four years at the academy.

He knew he had another year to serve before he would be granted a furlough that would enable him to return home for a holiday. That year would pass swiftly enough, and in the meantime, he would continue his correspondence with his stepsister, Cindy Holt, who was finishing her first year at Oregon State College.

Forcing himself to concentrate on his studies, Hank devoted his full attention to the military campaigns of Napoleon Bonaparte. He lost all count of the passage of time and occasionally made a brief notation on a sheet of foolscap in order to summarize the key aspects of the battles that Napoleon had fought.

The door opened, and his roommate came in, unbuttoning his tunic as he shut the door behind him. "I picked up a letter for you at mail call just now," he said. "Here you are."

"Thanks." Hank reached eagerly for the letter, hoping that it was from Cindy. He had heard nothing from her for several weeks, which he found a cause of concern, and he felt a stab of disappointment when he recognized the official seal of the Army of the West in the upper left-hand corner of the envelope. Apparently the letter was from his adopted father.

The communication from General Blake was short and pungent. He wanted Hank to know that his adopted sister, Beth Martin, had been shot to death by an unknown assailant in Utah. The general and his wife had just returned to Fort Vancouver from the funeral, and Rob Martin was doing about as well as could be expected.

Hank stared at the letter in dismay. In his year at the academy, he had grown accustomed to a neat, ordered world, and suddenly the orderliness of his existence was shattered. He found it difficult to believe that Beth was no more. She, along with Clarissa, had done so much for him when they first had met in Montana, and he grieved for her because of the utter waste of the life of a young woman who had so much for which to live.

Blinking away the tears that blurred his vision, Hank again sat erect, in the position he had been taught to assume at the beginning of his plebe year.

"What's wrong?" his roommate asked.

Instead of replying in words, Hank handed him the letter.

His roommate read it and then murmured, "I'm sorry, Hank."

"Thanks, Bud."

"Are you going to ask for an emergency leave when we go into summer camp?"

Hank shook his head but said nothing.

"We'll be playing soldier and breaking in the new plebe class at summer camp," his roommate said. "Remember, we'll have no classes for about six weeks, so this would be a perfect time for you to request leave."

Again Hank shook his head. "The academy curriculum insists that we attend camp for a month and a half, and the military training we get there is every bit as valuable as our classroom instruction. No," he said, "my father would be very disappointed in me if I came running home right now. My job is right here. I've got to establish the best record I can in every possible way as a cadet, and I can't do it if I run home. Besides, what good would it do? It won't bring back my sister, and commiserating with other members of the family would be a waste of time."

His roommate looked at him in silent admiration,

knowing his attitude was typical of the way he felt about everything that transpired at the academy. There was no doubt in the minds of every classmate who knew him well that Cadet Henry Blake would be graduated in another three years at the head of his class and would be given whatever branch of service he selected. His academy stature was secure.

"Toby," Rob Martin said to him as they were riding back to the house in Ogden after purchasing supplies, "I've just received word from Chet Harris that they've started construction on the Northern Pacific Railroad. It follows the route that we surveyed in Montana, after crossing the land that you covered in Dakota," he said, "and after crossing Idaho, it goes into Washington and heads across the mountains, straight for Puget Sound. That's going to be the next boom area in the United States, unless I miss my bet."

"I believe you're right, Rob," Toby replied thoughtfully.

"When we leave Utah," Rob said, "I intend to spend time in San Francisco. I've been giving some thought to settling there, as it would be a fine place for little Cathy to grow up, what with its educational and cultural benefits. Kale can close her house and put it on the market, and I'll buy a house of my own. I also want to sit down and have a little conference with Chet. I've decided that I want to invest a fairly substantial sum in Northern Pacific bonds, and I want Chet's opinion before I go ahead."

"I'm sure he'll approve," Toby replied.

"Why don't you come with me? You may decide to make an investment yourself," Rob said.

"I'm tempted," Toby replied slowly, "but I prefer to go straight to my ranch. I haven't seen Clarissa and my son for almost a year now, and I'm anxious to get together with them again." He refrained from adding, even to as close a friend as Rob, that he had serious, unfinished business with Clarissa that he needed to attend to and that his whole future hung in the balance.

That same day, a reporter for the *Utah Weekly Record* arrived to interview the partners and learned from them that Rob was heading for San Francisco, while Toby intended to go home to Oregon, now that their work in Utah was virtually completed and the security guards were posted for every train that crossed the West.

These facts appeared in the interview that was printed in that same week's *Record.* Other papers throughout the West also printed the story, which created great potential complications for Toby, although he did not know it.

Otto Sinclair read the article with great interest and immediately decided that he, too, would return to Oregon. Since his accidental murder of Beth Martin, he had had no opportunity to finish his business with Toby Holt, who seemed to be constantly surrounded by other people, whether it was family who came out for the funeral or the security guards he was hiring for the railroad.

The terrain of Toby's ranch was familiar to Sinclair, as was the surrounding territory, and he felt his chances there would be even better than they were in Utah to put a bullet into Holt and then to come into the open in due time as Clarissa's real husband.

Sinclair was not the only person who read the interview with great interest. Among those who found it fascinating was a Chinese giant who had recently visited Utah and who had returned to San Francisco in order to settle in Chinatown there.

Wang, the powerful hatchet man for the tongs, had not found it easy to resume his former place in the social hierarchy of San Francisco's Chinatown since his return to the city. News of the loss of face he had suffered when Toby Holt had met his challenge had followed him to the city. Although his bulk, combined with his physical prowess, was so great that no one dared to criticize him to his face, he heard the snickers behind his back.

Holt had done to him what no other enemy had ever been able to do, and Wang had sworn that he would obtain vengeance someday. The hatchet man studied the newspaper article carefully, then went out of his way to obtain a map of the Pacific Coast area and to examine the region in the neighborhood of Portland. Once his standing with the tong was fully recovered and his control once again firm beyond a doubt, he would have to pay a visit to Portland.

No one in the state would connect him with the sudden, unexpected death of Toby Holt. Holt would learn better than to make fun of a hatchet man, Wang reflected. In fact, he would pay for his error with his life.

Toby Holt neither wrote a letter to his wife nor sent her a telegram to announce his homecoming. Instead, he traveled to San Francisco on the railroad, then traveled north, by stagecoach. Stopping in Fort Vancouver long enough to say hello to his mother, General Blake, and his sister, who was home for summer vacation, he took a horse and made the brief ride to the ranch he had inherited from his father.

His heart hammered against his rib cage as he rode, and he told himself repeatedly that his whole future depended on the warmth of the greeting that Clarissa gave him. If she was glad to see him, then he knew there was hope that she would ultimately forgive him for his transgression with the late Gentle Doe. If she remained coldly indifferent, then he would be obliged to steel himself and discuss a possible separation with her. The idea of a separation pained him, yet he realized that unless his marriage was restored to a peaceful and amicable arrangement, it would be better by

far for Clarissa and for him, not to mention for their
son, if they lived apart. Children were sensitive to domestic strains, and he didn't want little Tim to suffer
unnecessarily.

After dismounting to open the ranch gate, Toby
mounted his horse again and rode on, pleased by the
knowledge that he had reached his own property at
last. Stalking Horse, the Cherokee foreman, rode up
to him with a few of the hired hands, and they exchanged warm greetings. Toby was pleased to see
that the ranch looked well kept and prosperous, that
the horses in the paddocks and pastures were looking
as fine as ever.

He halted near the front door and tied his horse
to a hitching post. Then he walked into the house. He
heard the clatter of pans in the kitchen and told himself that Clarissa was probably preparing supper.

Halting in the hallway between the kitchen and
dining room, Toby peered into the kitchen. What he
saw caused him to grin broadly.

His son, who had been at the crawling stage
when he had left, was running around in the kitchen.
Toby's grin brightened, and he called softly, "Hi,
Tim. It's Papa."

The child approached him cautiously. He did not
recognize this man, having not seen him for almost a
year, but he did remember his mother often telling
him about his papa. The smile on Toby's face and his
outstretched arms completely won little Tim over,
however, and screaming, "Papa! Papa!" the boy
hurled himself into his father's arms.

Toby hugged the child fiercely, not realizing until this moment how very much he had missed his
son. For unknown reasons, he and little Tim began to
laugh uproariously together, as though they were
sharing a great joke.

Clarissa, who was busying herself at the stove
around the corner in the kitchen, heard her son

scream and recognized Toby's hearty laugh. Hastily pushing an errant strand of hair back into the bun at the nape of her neck, she quickly wiped her hands on her apron and came forward, a fixed smile on her face.

Toby's smile slowly faded as he held Tim in one arm. "Hello," he said. "I don't know if it was a good idea or not, but I decided to surprise you, rather than let you know I was coming."

The fixed smile remained steady on Clarissa's chiseled features. "So I see," she observed coolly, and obediently lifted her face for his greeting.

He stepped toward her, and their lips met briefly. Their kiss was not the greeting that a husband who had been long separated from a loving wife might have expected. Clarissa's kiss was brief, almost impersonal, and Toby couldn't help thinking that it was the sort of kiss he might have expected from his younger sister, Cindy.

He felt as though a bucket of chilly mountain water had been poured over him. "If you'll excuse me for a few minutes," he said, "I'm going to go out and find one of the ranch hands who will take my borrowed horse back to Fort Vancouver and will pick up the trunks that have my clothes in them."

"You stay right here and get acquainted with Tim," she said. "I'll attend to getting one of the men to return the horse and pick up the trunks." Giving him no chance to protest, she went out the kitchen door quickly and headed in the direction of the nearby bunkhouse.

Putting his wife's cold greeting out of his mind as best he could, Toby held his son at arm's length. "Tim," he said, "you've grown so much in the time I've been away that I scarcely know you."

"Tim big boy," the child told him proudly.

Again Toby hugged the child fiercely and told

himself he hoped that never again would they be separated for any length of time.

Clarissa came in at that moment, looking unaccountably pale, and went straight to the larder. "The very least we can do to celebrate your return," she said, "is to broil some steaks and have some salad." She busied herself with the preparation of the homecoming meal.

Toby seated himself at the kitchen table, put his son on one jiggling knee, and watched her. His presence seemed to make her nervous.

Actually, Clarissa was so startled, so stunned, that she scarcely knew what she was doing. Wrestling alone with her problem in recent weeks, she had decided to make the grand sacrifice for her husband and son at her own expense.

She had made up her mind to tell Toby her whole, unhappy story. She would conceal nothing from him, and after revealing the facts of Otto Sinclair's return from the dead, she would take permanent leave of Toby and their son and go East. She would leave behind the two people she loved the most, even though the prospect of a permanent separation from either of them broke her heart. But she believed she had no choice. She needed time, however, to screw up her courage for such a drastic move, and Toby's unexpected return had compounded her difficulty.

Toby marveled at her manual dexterity as he watched her cut up tomatoes and cucumbers, which she threw into the salad bowl along with a number of leaves of crisp, homegrown lettuce. Almost simultaneously, her fingers flying, she stirred the potatoes browning in a skillet and flipped over the broiling steaks.

Clarissa was relieved to discover that concentration on the preparation of the meal made it unnecessary for her to converse.

The silence became increasingly heavy, and finally Toby broke it. "What does Tim eat these days?" he asked.

Clarissa did not look up from the stove. "He eats the same foods that we eat," she said, smiling slightly.

"Good!" he replied. "What a big bruiser he is!" Then he was silent again until Clarissa began to put out the food. "Do you want me to serve Tim's supper?" Toby asked.

"If you like," she replied. "Just be sure that you cut his meat into very small pieces for him."

"You hear that, boy?" Toby asked his son jocularly. "Your mother thinks I don't know how to cut up meat for you. We'll have to see about that." Holding his son on his lap, Toby cut a small piece from the steak and proceeded to slice it into bits suitable for a small child. Then he scooped some potatoes onto the plate and added a small quantity of salad. "I don't suppose he gets any oil and vinegar," he said.

"It will be better," she replied, "if you don't use any dressing. He prefers it plain. He still uses the special chair you made for him."

Toby looked around the kitchen and spotted his son's high chair. He picked up his son in one arm, stood, then brought the chair to the table. He placed Tim in it and handed him a fork and a spoon. "Here you go, boy," he said. "You get first crack at supper. We'll be eating in a couple of minutes, so don't let us catch up to you."

He seated himself at Tim's left.

Clarissa served them their own plates. She filled a pitcher with cold water, then placed it and three glasses on the table before deliberately taking a chair to the right of her son.

Toby thought it was not accidental that she had chosen to seat herself as far from him as she could.

He had to admit, however, that she could still do

wonders with food. "I haven't eaten a meal this good in all the time I've been gone from home," he said.

The compliment sincerely pleased her, and she murmured her thanks. Such an attitude, she knew, was going to make it all the more difficult for her to tell him her news and the decision that she had reached.

The presence of little Tim at the table, however, inhibited serious discussion of the future, and instead Clarissa said, "Your mother and General Blake asked me to go to Utah with them for Beth's funeral, but I felt I was needed here more."

He nodded and waited for her to continue.

"I wrote a long letter to Rob, instead," she said weakly.

"I know," Toby replied. "He told me."

"I was surprised when your mother told me that Kale Salton is staying on with Rob to take care of Cathy. Is it possible that a romance is budding there?"

The very idea shocked Toby. "I should think not!" he said emphatically. "Rob was very much in love with his wife."

Clarissa turned beet red at the mention of the word "love." What had happened to the love she and Toby had once shared? Could it be he still loved her, that if he heard of her plan to go East, he would not be able to tolerate her news and would put up a fight to preserve his marriage? All she knew, she thought, her mind whirling wildly, was that she needed more time to sort out the situation in her mind, time to determine right from wrong, time to weigh her decision and then act accordingly.

The presence of their son at the supper table made the meal bearable. Tim demanded his full share of attention, which his parents proceeded to lavish on him. Eventually, however, the meal was done, and it was time for Tim to be put to bed.

Clarissa tucked him into bed, while Toby lingered behind to tell his son a brief story. She returned to the kitchen to prepare coffee for them.

Her footsteps on the hardwood floor told him when she was finished with the chore, and then he kissed the boy good night and extinguished the oil lamp in his room. Going downstairs, Toby found that Clarissa had taken their coffee cups into the parlor, and when he went in to join her, he discovered a small glass of brandywine sitting at his place, as well.

Her formality surprised him, but he said nothing, and draining his brandy in a single gulp, he proceeded to sip his coffee.

"Will you have another brandy?" Clarissa asked politely.

Shaking his head, Toby felt like a stranger in his own home. "No, thanks," he said.

He was eager to learn the state of their marriage, actually to hear whether Clarissa had forgiven his infidelity with Gentle Doe. But he believed he already knew the answer from his chilly homecoming.

"Rob is intending to invest at least some of his profits from our gold mine in the new Northern Pacific Railroad," he told her, for want of something else to say. "He's planning to discuss the whole thing with Chet Harris. He wanted me to join him, but I preferred to stand aside."

Clarissa showed a trace of her former spirit as she smiled and said, "Don't tell me that you've grown tired of railroads."

"Quite the contrary," Toby replied seriously. "I have complete faith in the future of the railroads that are connecting the East and West. In fact, I would say this part of the Pacific—Oregon and Washington—is going to be the next boom area in the country. The population growth in this state has been phenomenal, but it's nothing compared to what it will be when a direct rail line to the East comes through Dakota and Montana and then cuts across Idaho before it reaches Washington. One track will head toward Puget Sound, and another will come down to Portland. It guarantees the future of this state. This ranch, for example, should treble in value within a few years."

"Your mother may regret turning the ranch over to you," she said.

"I think not," he replied. "Her future is assured as long as she lives. For that matter, so is mine. I'm half expecting to receive an offer to go to Idaho in the near future."

"Idaho!" Clarissa echoed.

"I've heard nothing definite, and I have no idea whether or not I'll actually be offered a position. But if I am, I don't see how I can refuse."

"Must you accept such an offer?" Clarissa asked.

He nodded slowly. "Idaho is the last untamed region in the West," he said. "The terrain is probably more diverse and more difficult than in any other part of the country. If the railroad is ever going to get built there, someone will be needed to maintain law and order, to see that the Indians are kept in line and that the riffraff who inevitably show up in a frontier region are kept out of trouble. So I see it as my duty to go to the Idaho wilderness if I'm asked. For whatever this is worth to you, it would be my last trip, however. I don't know how long the job would take—presumably a matter of months—and then I would be free to come back home and to stay here."

Clarissa nodded, too overcome to speak. She could not bear the thought of leaving Toby and her young son to make their temporary home in the raw, unsettled Idaho Territory. If she was forced to desert them, she wanted to take comfort in the fact that they were at home on the Oregon ranch, where they had every convenience and where they were close to civilization. True, Toby, like his father, had grown up familiar with the wilderness, but it was too much to expect that little Tim be subjected to the same rough atmosphere.

"I thought," Toby said, his enthusiasm waning appreciably, "that I would mention the possibility of a transfer to Idaho to you before an offer actually materializes, because it occurred to me that perhaps you would like to come with me. Tim is old enough now to tolerate the so-called rigors of a wilderness atmosphere."

Clarissa neatly evaded his suggestion. "What makes you think you're going to get such an offer? Certainly you aren't basing your thinking on a pure hunch."

"Indeed I'm not," he said. "The day before I left Utah a stranger came to see me and interviewed me on my reactions to Idaho. He refused to identify himself and could have been anybody from a U.S. government representative to someone in the pay of the directors of the Northern Pacific Railroad. In any event, I answered him honestly, and by the time the interview ended, he indicated that I would be hearing again from his principals—whoever they may be."

"I see," she said, and nodded.

There was a long, uncomfortable silence, which Toby interpreted to mean that Clarissa would not come with him to Idaho. "My father," he said, "devoted many years of his life to the service of his country, and I feel obliged to follow in his footsteps. The least I can do for the development of this whole part of the country, to which my father contributed so much, is to make certain that conditions are safe for people to come in and settle and for the railroad to be built."

"I understand," Clarissa said, "and I'm sure that you'll do everything that's needful for the future of Oregon and Washington and the whole of the United States. . . ." Her voice trailed off. She didn't know

what to say. Her own future with Toby seemed
hopeless, and she prayed for the strength and courage
to tell him where she stood and why he would be
forced to go on in life without her.

Little Cathy slept soundly in a portable crib erected in the bedchamber of Kale Salton's San Francisco
house while Kale sorted through piles of her dresses
and hats, lingerie and stocking and shoes, carefully
packing her belongings into several leather trunks.
She was concentrating so hard on her task that the
doorbell rang several times before she heard it and
went downstairs to answer the summons.

Rob Martin waited patiently on the stoop, and
when she opened the door for him, he grinned and
shook his head. Her hair was disheveled, she wore
only the lightest of cosmetics, and a dirt smudge
stretched across the bridge of her nose.

"It's you," she said briskly. "Come on in. I'm in
the middle of packing, and wouldn't you know that
my housekeeper chose this of all weeks to take a vacation." She turned and hastened up the staircase.

Rob took his time following her, marveling at the
progress she had made in two days. Boxes were filled
with books and bric-a-brac, and various items of furniture were already tagged for moving. Kale had
been sincere when she had said that she intended to
dispose of her belongings and sell her house, and only
the greatest of persuasion had changed her mind to
the extent that she had agreed to keep most of her
furniture and to move it into Rob's home, which he
had just purchased in the fashionable Nob Hill district of San Francisco. The least he could do for her
would be to surround her with her own furniture.

He shook his head when he followed her into her
bedchamber. Piles of her clothes were everywhere except on the crib where his daughter was sleeping, and
when he saw the number of clothing trunks that Kale

was packing, he hoped that the house he had bought had enough space to accommodate her extensive wardrobe.

"The attorney who handled legal matters for me for a number of years dropped by a few hours ago," she said, "and I charged him with responsibility for the sale of this house. He said the location is a good one—not Nob Hill, of course—but he's sure he'll have no trouble getting a good price for it."

"That's splendid," Rob said. "If you would like, I'll arrange with Chet Harris to buy some Northern Pacific bonds for you. They have a fine yield because they pay a high, steady rate of interest, and you may as well put your funds to work for you."

"Mr. Harris won't mind?" she asked, raising an eyebrow.

"Certainly not. He's investing rather heavily for me in Northern Pacific bonds, and as a matter of fact, he's buying quite a few of them himself. So it should be easy enough for him to invest for you, too. In fact, I took the liberty of bringing up the subject with him."

"What did he actually say?" Kale insisted.

Rob chuckled and then looked embarrassed. "If you must know," he said, "he made several remarks indicating that I was wasting no time in the formation of a liaison with one of the leading courtesans of San Francisco. He refused to believe that our relationship is strictly impersonal and that you're simply looking after my baby for me and acting as my housekeeper."

The sleeping baby stirred slightly, so Kale lowered her voice as she perched on the lid of a closed trunk. "I was afraid something like this would happen," she said. "Your good name is being ruined and is being dragged through the mud with mine."

"To hell with it," Rob replied. "You and I know the truth of the matter, and that's good enough for me. I have no intention of explaining to the world that we are simply keeping a promise that we made to my late wife."

"Well," Kale replied dubiously, "if you're sure you don't mind—"

"I don't!" he replied curtly. "We may be the talk of San Francisco for a few weeks, but they'll forget us when the next gossip sensation arouses their interest."

Kale wished fervently that she would be forgotten not only by San Francisco but by anyone who had known her over the years. She could succeed in putting her past behind her and in starting out on a fresh life, with a clean slate, only if her past was not used against her.

X

On Toby's second day at home, he crossed the Columbia River and went to Fort Vancouver to have noon dinner with his mother and stepfather. Clarissa refrained from accompanying him, feeling it would be only right to give him the opportunity to speak in private with his mother and stepfather. So she found a convenient excuse to remain at the ranch, and he went alone.

In the dining room of the commandant's house, Lee Blake spoke briefly about the situation in Idaho. The Shoshoni Indians disliked not only the railroad but all of the incursions of the white man into their wilderness retreat, and bands of hostile braves were beginning to wreak havoc with the settlers there.

Eulalia waited patiently until the subject was exhausted. Then she glanced at her son and asked him quietly, "How do you find Clarissa and Tim?"

Toby elected to answer only the second part of the question. "Tim is growing so fast that I scarcely knew him," he said. "He's walking, and he's actually stringing words together into sentences now."

"Was Clarissa glad to see you?" she asked, pressing her point.

Toby hesitated. "Do you know of any reason that she should be other than pleased to see me, Mama?" he replied.

Lee looked down from his place at the head of the table. "I suggest that both of you stop fencing and that you get to the point you're trying to make, Eulalia," he said. "Toby isn't a child anymore."

His wife shook her head. "I suppose you're right, dear," Eulalia said, and turned back to her son. "Toby, I won't beat around the bush any longer. Clarissa confided in me some time ago and told me about your affair in Dakota with an Indian girl."

"I can only plead guilty," Toby said. "I tried to explain to Clarissa that it was a question of proximity. Gentle Doe was going with me when I called on the Sioux and the other tribes of Dakota, and we were in each other's company twenty-four hours a day. I didn't have the slightest intention of being unfaithful to Clarissa, but I couldn't help responding to Gentle Doe's advances. That's the way I'm built. The affair was a separate, meaningless incident in my life, and it had nothing to do with my relations with Clarissa. I have tried to explain to her that at no time have I stopped loving my wife and that I want no other woman on earth."

"As I told your mother," Lee said, "I can understand your position and sympathize with it. It's much harder for any woman to sympathize with you, but it seems to me that Clarissa owes you the chance to make amends to her."

"To be blunt about it," Toby said, "she's giving me no chance to show her my real feelings. I told her that I may be offered a position of some kind in Idaho, and I asked her if she and Tim would come with me, but she sidestepped the question and wouldn't give me a straight answer. And to be candid about it, she avoided me in bed last night."

"That's unfortunate," Eulalia said. "I believed— and I still believe—that your wife loves you, Toby. If she hasn't come around and forgiven you yet, you've got to be patient and give her more time. I'm surprised, because I thought she was too sensible to carry a grudge or feel resentment, but in time I'm sure she'll soften toward you."

"What more can I do to change her and persuade her to forgive me?" Toby asked, a slight note of bitterness creeping into his voice. "I've apologized, and I've explained as best as I can. I can't do much more than that. I'm not capable of crawling to her on my hands and knees."

"I'm sure she doesn't expect such treatment, Toby. Be patient. It's always possible that something else is responsible for Clarissa's attitude," Eulalia said, "but I don't want to complicate your own thinking by even discussing the possibility. Hang on, Toby, and I'm sure everything will work out for the best."

Slightly heartened by his mother's encouragement, Toby remained at Fort Vancouver until Cindy came home from a picnic she was attending with some other young women and soldiers at the fort. Cindy was the most popular girl at Fort Vancouver, though she remained totally faithful to Hank.

It was late afternoon when Toby, having had a chance to exchange warm greetings with his younger sister, took the ferry across the Columbia River to the Oregon shore. Dusk was beginning to gather as he made his way toward the Holt ranch, taking his time and giving his stallion its head.

Suddenly, as Toby was approaching his property, a rifle shot sounded from the depths of the forest to his right. A bullet whistled passed him, missing him by mere inches.

Reacting instinctively, Toby crouched low in his saddle and started in the direction from which the shot had come. Rapidly retreating hoofbeats told him that his would-be killer was trying to escape.

Gripping his own rifle grimly, Toby followed him. One fact above all others impressed itself on Toby's mind: He had been the subject of a deliberate attack. He now knew that this was the second time that he had been assaulted, the first time being in Utah when Beth Martin had been the unwitting victim.

He had no idea who was trying to kill him or what motive the murderer might have, but the only thing that mattered at the moment was that he succeed in catching the villain.

Toby quickly learned that the fleeing culprit was an excellent horseman. The large, broad-shouldered stallion Toby rode found it difficult to push through the dense forest, and the fleeing man managed to keep a safe distance from his pursuer. The hoofbeats continued to drum steadily, and to Toby's dismay they grew somewhat fainter.

He was determined not to lose the killer, however, because he had no clue as to the man's identity or the reasons that the man sought to kill him. Pushing on doggedly, Toby at last came into a clearing, and in the dying light of day, he saw the other rider far ahead of him.

The foothills of the mountains that lay to the east were relatively bare, and Toby could see the man racing toward the heights. He increased his own pace to a rapid gallop and, crouching low in the saddle, urged his stallion to achieve greater and yet greater speed.

Toby held one advantage in the grim race: He had grown up in these mountains; his father had taught him tracking and hunting, and they had played games of hide-and-seek in these heights. He knew every turn, every peculiarity, every dangerous ridge, and every shortcut in these mountains. Consequently, he more than held his own, and for a while he seemed to be closing the gap between himself and the would-be assassin.

As the chase went on, dusk gave way to night. Intermittent clouds covered the stars and the half-moon more often than not, occasionally parting to allow some light to fall on the craggy ground below for a few moments before more clouds appeared.

Toby was forced now to depend on his hearing alone to determine the location of his quarry. He strained his ears and could make out the sound of the other's horse as the animal, dodging and twisting, made its way toward much higher ground. The danger of losing the man completely was very great, but by demonstrating great agility and taking advantage of several shortcuts that he knew, Toby managed to keep pace with the man. Then, when another heavy layer of clouds blotted out the moon and stars, the sound of hoofbeats ahead halted abruptly.

Toby was not surprised when he saw the other man's tired gelding standing quietly, its reins looped over a stunted pine tree. But then Toby realized that he was faced with a new and even more dangerous situation.

Actually, he thought, the move had been exceptionally clever. From here upward, the climb was erratic, and there were no real trails, which meant that someone trying to shake off a pursuer would stand a far better chance on foot than mounted on horseback.

With great reluctance, Toby dismounted, looped his stallion's reins around another stunted pine, and headed toward the heights up a narrow, twisting path.

The advantage that had been his had suddenly shifted, and the odds now favored his foe. By taking advantage of the uneven terrain, the fugitive could dash in and out of half-hidden places, could conceal himself behind boulders and small evergreens. Unless the night sky became clearer, Toby would lose the other person.

Not only was his pursuit more difficult now, Toby realized, but his role of pursuer and that of the fugitive could be reversed suddenly and unexpectedly. The hunter could become the hunted again, and he could expect another shot to be fired at him at almost anytime.

Knowing that the rocky slope he had just come to rose for about one thousand feet, Toby began to climb steadily, hugging the ground in order to diminish his visibility as a target. Fortunately, he was wearing dark trousers and a dark shirt, making him even harder to see, as well as his old, battered ten-gallon hat, which had become dark gray with use.

Eventually he reached a small plateau that overlooked a ravine, and there he halted and listened carefully. He could hear nothing. Putting one ear to the ground, he listened again, but there was no sound other than that of the wind whistling mournfully through the mountains.

At that moment the clouds once again dissipated briefly, and Toby caught a clear, quick glimpse of his quarry. The man was on higher ground, perhaps twenty feet above the spot where Toby himself was crouched, and was standing erect as he looked down, searching the mountainside for some sign of his pursuer. Then the cloud cover returned, and the figure of the man was blotted out by the darkness.

Toby knew he should refrain from shooting until he at least had a very good chance of striking his pursuer. But his seething anger made him impatient, and he broke one of the inviolable rules his father had taught him. Raising his rifle to his shoulder, he squeezed the trigger, firing at the spot where the man had been standing.

The roar of his rifle echoed across the mountains.

Toby heard the scraping of leather against stone too late, and he realized then that he had missed his shot and the man was again escaping from him, making his way to still higher ground. Hitching up his trousers, Toby followed, determined to finish the feud. He knew that this chase would end only when one of them died.

Whip Holt had been noted for his remarkable ability to make no sound while climbing mountains, and he had taught the art to his son. Now Toby snaked upward silently, staying close to rocks, taking refuge whenever possible behind boulders, and peering through the gloom for some sign of motion that would tell him his enemy was near.

Never had there been a stranger chase, one more handicapped by obstacles. Then, all at once, the breeze freshened, and the clouds that obscured the sky were blown away and did not reappear. It became clear enough for Toby to make better time, for he could see ahead sufficiently well to be somewhat less concerned about his safety. Nevertheless, he continued to observe the rules of the hunt, never exposing himself to potential enemy fire for more than a moment or two at a time.

His caution served him well. Just as he slid behind a boulder, a shot sounded from somewhere directly ahead of him on about the same level, and a piece of rock at the edge of the boulder was chipped away. The spot was only inches away from his face.

Toby felt a vast sense of relief from the tension that had gripped him since the beginning of the hunt. At last his foe had declared himself and, by firing again at him, had indicated his own whereabouts. Now Toby knew what to do.

On the ledge ahead, a long string of boulders stretched out at the edge of a steep precipice. Between the boulders and the rock wall of the mountain itself was a space of twelve to eighteen inches. Toby instantly decided to adopt daring tactics and squeezed into the opening and inched his way forward. It was impossible for him to move rapidly because he lacked the space. Occasionally the opening was so narrow that he had to turn his head sideways as he inched through,

scraping his shirt and trousers either on the boulders
or on the more solid wall of the mountainside. He
took care to go forward as silently as possible and
was reasonably satisfied with the progress that he was
making. It was unlikely that his quarry would look
for him in this narrow space. This was just as well,
because he had no room here to raise his rifle, much
less to aim and fire it.

Relief flooded him when he saw the opening
widen some feet ahead. As nearly as he could judge,
his gamble had paid off, and he had gained an advantage over his quarry.

He inched toward the wider opening, eager to
get out of the confining space. But suddenly his blood
froze: Directly ahead of the opening, the man was
looming up on level stone ground. Toby was seen at
the same moment, and the man raised his rifle to his
shoulder. Toby stood defenseless, unable to crouch
lower or raise his own weapon to protect himself because of inadequate space.

Again the sound of gunfire echoed through the
mountains.

Toby blinked when he found himself still alive.
His attacker had missed.

While the man frantically started to reload his
rifle, Toby moved sideways little by little, step by
step, toward the wider space. Never had he known
such an agony of suspense. Never had he been so
helpless while facing certain death. At last, finding his
way into the open before the man finished his reload-
ing, Toby raised his own rifle to his shoulder and
squeezed the trigger.

To his disgust nothing happened. Apparently
while squeezing through the narrow space, he had
somehow dislodged dirt, which had fallen into the firing pin of his weapon and had jammed it.

He lost no time bemoaning his situation, however. Grasping the weapon by the barrel and wield-

ing it like a club, he stepped forward and swung it, intending to strike his foe.

The man managed to duck, and in so doing lost his grip on his own rifle, which clattered down the steep precipice behind him, echoing as it tumbled to the waters of a mountain stream that flowed far below.

This was the opportunity that Toby had awaited. Dropping his own useless rifle to the ground, he stepped forward, flexing his hands.

The man was desperate and braced himself for a final, climactic struggle.

In the moonlight, Toby examined the man more closely and was somewhat puzzled. He was burly, heavyset, and looked strangely familiar. Toby knew their paths had crossed somewhere at some time, but he couldn't place the incident, and this was not the time to think of such things. He had the fight of his life awaiting him.

The arena for the struggle was the worst of all possible places. The ground was hard stone, with patches of rubble here and there. There were no trees, no cover of any kind. Behind the stranger was a precipice that dropped at least a thousand feet to a narrow gorge below, and anyone who fell or was pushed down it was almost certain to be killed. The stranger made his own plans clear when he reached out and tried to grab Toby hard by the arm. Had he succeeded, Toby well might have been pulled forward and then yanked over the precipice.

Instead, however, the other's move was too obvious to be effective, and Toby braced himself, ducked, and then drove his fist into the man's face. Bone met bone, and he felt rather than heard the crunching sensation that meant he had broken some bone in the man's face.

The man shook off his injury, though, and lunged forward, groping for his opponent, who was tall and solid but not as heavily built. He caught hold of Toby and, employing his greater weight to good advantage, the man bore him to the ground. They rolled over and over, each of them pummeling ferociously and trying to drive a knee into the other's groin.

Toby had an infinite capacity for absorbing and enduring punishment, but so did his foe, and both were merciless as they smashed at each other's faces, shoulders, and torsos. But Toby was far more disciplined a fighter than his opponent, and eventually that discipline turned the tide somewhat in his favor. He began to gain the upper hand, and the other man's blows became feebler.

"Why have you—tried to—kill me?" Toby demanded.

There was no reply; the man passively stared back at Toby.

Suddenly Toby froze. He found himself looking down past his opponent's shoulder, and he saw himself staring into the abyss that loomed far below.

All at once he understood his quarry's passivity. At an appropriate moment the man would try to heave him over the edge.

Quickly Toby inched his way back to safety and then climbed to his feet.

The man also rose, slowly, painfully, and wavered back and forth unsteadily. Then he unwittingly took two backward steps in order to get away from the grimly determined Toby Holt, tripped on a stone, and losing his balance, went plunging off the precipice.

Toby could hear stones rolling and the cracking and breaking of tree branches jutting from the side of the abyss as the man plummeted toward the mountain stream at the base of the ravine.

The end of the fight had come so suddenly that Toby was unprepared for it. Standing still while he regained his strength, he realized the fight was over. His foe was dead.

Toby was ready to start down the mountain when he noticed a strange, bulky object on the ground near his feet. Stooping and picking it up, he found it was a wallet that his opponent had been carrying and that obviously had fallen out of a pocket during the fight. It was too dark to read now, and so Toby dropped the wallet securely into his own pocket as he began his descent from the mountain.

Gripping his rifle again, he told himself that he would most likely find in the wallet some clue regarding the man's identity, perhaps some indication of his reason for attacking him.

Taking his time because he was too weary to hurry, Toby labored his way carefully down the rocky slope and came at last to his stallion and, not far away, the other man's gelding. Mounting his own horse, he began his homeward ride, leading the other horse behind him. After he had ridden a short distance, he came to a running stream where he stopped, dismounted, and while the horses watered, bathed his head, face, and hands in the cold water. Feeling considerably refreshed, he started out for the Holt ranch, again leading the gelding. The night seemed to grow brighter as he approached level ground, and overcome by curiosity, he opened the wallet. In the moonlight, he could see it was filled with newspaper clippings.

Toby drew out a stack of the clippings, and as he leafed through them, his blood ran cold. Each of them was a news item about Clarissa. The man appeared to have followed her entire life in the West through the newspapers. There was the notice of her marriage to Toby and another of the birth of their son. There was an interview she had given a national news service about the significance of marrying into the Holt family and how it felt to be related to a liv-

ing legend. In fact, every item that had ever appeared
in print about Clarissa Holt seemed to be in the wallet.

Toby looked no further. Anger grew within him,
threatening to explode, and stuffing the newspaper
clippings back into the worn leather container, he returned it to his pocket. Clarissa, who had made such
a strong fuss about his relations with Gentle Doe, had
a great deal to explain herself.

Was it possible that this man was an admirer of
Clarissa's and that he had tried to do away with her
husband in order to set her free to marry him? There
was no way of telling from the objects in the wallet,
but Toby had a real clue now and intended to get to
the truth as soon as he arrived home.

The journey to the ranch seemed endless, and his
anger grew with each step that his horse took. His
raging temper caused him to forget the exhaustion
from which he had been suffering, and his mood
turned very bitter as he approached the ranch.

He rode to the corral adjacent to the stables,
which was located near the kitchen, and threw the
reins of both horses to a waiting ranch hand. "You
might check the sheriff's office tomorrow and see if
anybody in the area is missing a gelding that meets
this horse's description. If not, we've added a lively
gelding to our stock." He did not wait for an answer
and instead turned and walked to the house.

A deeply worried Clarissa awaited him in the
kitchen. "Where have you been?" she asked. "I expected you to return from Fort Vancouver in time for
supper, and I've been so afraid—" She broke off
abruptly and gasped when she saw the cut under his
eye and his swollen lip. "What happened to you?"

"Never mind all that now," Toby replied
abruptly and pointed to a kitchen chair. "Sit down."

She was struck by the harshness in his voice, but
she asked no questions and obediently went to a

chair. Nevertheless, her concern persisted. "Can I get you a drink and something to eat?" she asked. "At the very least, let me fix a poultice for your cut and another for your lip—"

"I want you to explain something to me first," Toby said, opening the bulging wallet. He spread the clippings in front of her. To his disappointment the wallet contained no other documents, no money, and no indication of its owner.

Toby seated himself opposite Clarissa and began to speak in a staccato tone. He told her again about the accidental death of Beth Martin and of his own certainty that he had been the intended victim. Then he related how a shot had been fired at him this very evening as he returned home, how he had followed the would-be assassin into the mountains, and finally how his pursuit had culminated in their climactic fight there.

Clarissa grew pale as she listened, and Toby noticed that her hand trembled as she raised it occasionally to her mouth. Suddenly she covered her face with both hands, burst into tears, and sobbed uncontrollably.

Toby watched her silently. He felt sorry for her in her obvious distress, but he knew he had been right. She did have some connection with the would-be killer. He could not allow himself to forget that there had been two serious attempts made on his own life and that Beth probably had been killed by this very man.

He continued to say nothing, however. It was best that Clarissa reveal whatever she had to say in her own good time.

Gradually her sobs subsided, and at last she rasied her head and looked at Toby, her expression miserable, her eyes red. "I see it all now," she said. "If it was the same man, then I'm responsible for the death of Beth Martin. It was my fault." She began to weep again.

"I don't see how that's at all possible," Toby said. "Suppose you tell me about it from the beginning."

Eventually she regained sufficient poise to tell her story, beginning with the dramatic reappearance of Otto Sinclair from the dead. Holding back nothing now, she told Toby about her first husband's threats and demands for money.

"I realized," she said, "that he was blackmailing me, but there was nothing I could do about it. Legally, I'm a bigamist, and that makes Tim illegitimate."

"I think not," Toby said calmly, "but go on."

She went on to tell him about her last visit from Sinclair and about his intention to return for more money. It was after that visit that Clarissa had decided the only thing she could do was leave Toby and the baby and go back East. But in the meantime, Sinclair had not reappeared. Obviously it was at that point that he decided to pursue Toby Holt himself. Clearly, if Toby died, Clarissa would inherit not only the Holt ranch but also the half-interest in the Montana gold mine and the property in Washington. Once these assets were safely in her hands, Sinclair would show up, claim her as his wife, and take possession of all that had been Toby's.

Now Toby remembered where he had seen Otto Sinclair before: It was in the saloon outside Ogden!

He let out a great sigh. "Then your coolness to me had nothing to do with my affair with Gentle Doe?" he demanded.

"Not directly," Clarissa replied. "I forgave that indiscretion long ago and tried to put it out of my mind. But when Otto reappeared, I was afraid that you'd take advantage of my bigamy to leave me and dissolve our marriage. I . . . I suspected that, because of your affair, you didn't really want to be with me anymore. Then I began to think that the only course of action open to me was to leave you and Tim and to go back East."

Toby raised an eyebrow. "That isn't what you wanted?"

"It was the last thing on earth that I wanted!" she replied. "I was afraid Otto would follow me, and the very idea of that terrified me. I hated every moment of our marriage. As I told you when we first met, I felt no grief, no sense of loss when the War Department reported him killed in action—I felt only a sense of great relief that I had been delivered from him. That he was still alive has been the worst nightmare I've ever been forced to endure."

"I believe I can set your mind at rest," Toby told her. "When you thought yourself a widow, you acted in good faith on the basis of official information given you by the U.S. government. Sinclair succeeded in fooling the War Department, and I see no reason why you should be penalized for it. We'll go to see Judge Ernie von Thalman together tomorrow morning, and we'll find out precisely where you stand and how you can protect yourself. In the meantime, you have nothing to fear. When Sinclair went tumbling down the precipice, his schemes died with him."

A flicker of hope crossed Clarissa's tortured face. Circuit Judge Ernst von Thalman certainly was familiar with the law. Perhaps, indeed, he knew a way to overcome the problem.

"Sinclair will never cause worry to anyone on earth ever again," Toby said.

It dawned on her slowly that Otto Sinclair had met his just deserts and that the threat hanging over her head had been removed. "Do you think that we had better go into town and talk to Judge von Thalman tonight?"

Toby shook his head. He rose from his seat and came round the table to his wife. "The information will keep until morning," he said, lifting her from her chair. "I have better ways of occupying myself this evening." He brought her to him, holding her tightly as he kissed her on the mouth. At first she was too numb to respond, but then feeling him against her, feeling his ardor, she knew all was right with their world once again. She put her arms around his neck and returned his kiss with equal hunger, equal passion. At last they separated, both breathless.

"I've been waiting a long time—a very long time—to sleep with my wife," he said, grinning.

All at once a beatific smile wreathed Clarissa's face. "That can be arranged," she said, her voice husky. "Definitely! But first I'm going to bathe your face and see to those injuries. From now on, I'm going to take care of you as I never have before. I love you, Toby, and I'm never going to let anything hurt you again!"

Judge von Thalman received the young couple in his book-lined chambers in the federal courthouse in Portland. He listened intently to Clarissa's hesitantly told story, to which Toby added an occasional comment. When she was finished, he stared out the window for some time.

"Sinclair," he said, "has met his just reward. I don't think you have any cause for concern, thanks to Toby's prowess as a fighter. You really are a chip off the old block, Toby."

Toby accepted the compliment gracefully but nevertheless was somewhat disturbed. "What worries us," he said, "is the question of our son's legitimacy. If Sinclair was still alive at the time we were married, that invalidates our marriage and means that Tim was born a bastard, even though we believed we were married at the time."

"I see your point," Judge von Thalman said, "and I can sympathize with your concern. But I believe we can get around that problem very easily. If you'll be good enough to dictate the story you've told me to one of my secretaries, we'll have her transcribe the document, and then we'll go on from there."

The reunited Toby and Clarissa went off into another chamber, where they dictated to a legal secretary the whole story of Clarissa's nightmarish experience. By noon the document had been neatly transcribed, and both Toby and Clarissa signed it.

Judge von Thalman immediately went into action. He issued a court order stating unequivocally that Otto Sinclair was legally dead and that his reappearance, as per the story that Clarissa had outlined on paper, in no way changed that fact. Therefore, he decreed, the marriage of Clarissa and Toby had been valid from the start, and the birth of their son was totally legitimate. He signed the document with a flourish.

"That," he told them, "should dispose of your problems."

The relieved couple profusely expressed their thanks, but the judge waved aside their expressions of gratitude. "I was glad to do it," he said. "You two have suffered enough needlessly, and poor Beth Martin was most likely killed by the same man who caused your troubles, an unscrupulous man who met justice at the end of his life. Now go home and put the whole incident out of your minds!"

The message delivered by the courier from Fort Vancouver was specific. It was imperative, General Blake wrote, that Toby Holt come to the fort for dinner that same day. Not wanting to be separated again from the wife with whom he had just been so happily reunited, Toby wrote back that he would come, accompanied by Clarissa and little Tim.

They crossed the Columbia River and arrived at the house of the commanding general in midafternoon.

Eulalia took one look at her beaming son and equally happy daughter-in-law and was elated. She had no idea how a rapport had been achieved, but it was obvious that Toby and Clarissa had put their difficulties behind them. She insisted that they accept glasses of sherry before dinner, and while she played with her grandson, General Blake returned from his office. He kissed Clarissa, then shook hands vigorously with Toby. "I'm glad you've come," he said, "and I won't mince any words. I just received a telegram signed by President Grant." He reached into an inner pocket of his tunic and produced a folded slip of paper, which Toby read.

REQUEST THAT TOBY HOLT COME TO WASHINGTON EARLIEST CHANCE AT GOVERNMENT EXPENSE. EAGER TO SEE HIM AND TO DISCUSS IDAHO SITUA-TION. SIGNED, GRANT

Toby handed the slip of paper to Clarissa, then both of them looked to General Blake for a further explanation.

"We've all been expecting something of the sort," the general said, "ever since you met that government agent before you left Utah. I don't presume to know exactly what the President has in mind, but I assume that he does indeed want to send you to Idaho to make the territory safe for settlers, for the railroad, and for those prospectors of precious metals, who are there in fairly large numbers."

Toby's stepfather smiled grimly. "Unforunately," he went on, "the government of Idaho has been a joke for the past decade. A new governor has been appointed every year, and most of them have either resigned while in office or have literally vanished from the face of the earth. I suspect, although I don't know, that those who've disappeared have given in to the natural cravings of men for riches and have joined in the hunt for gold, silver, copper, and other metals. Theoretically, Andy Brentwood's regiment is responsible for maintaining order there, but Andy is stretched too thin as it is and has no troops to spare for duty in Idaho. I've got to find some other competent cavalry and infantry units that I can assign to permanent duty in the territory and have them assist the governor in maintaining peace. The Nez Percé and the Shoshoni are both kicking up their heels. The territory has attracted more than its share of criminals, ranging from murderers to petty thieves. All in all, it's a very rough land."

Toby smiled reassuringly at Clarissa, then he sobered as he turned back to General Blake. "As I think you know, sir," he said, "I've never hesitated to do my duty when my country has called me before now. I've always responded to the call and have been glad of the opportunity. But Clarissa and I have been through some very difficult times, and we're looking forward to spending time together and mending our relationship. I'll go as the President asks, and I'll pay a visit to him in Washington in the immediate future. I'll not only go by train, but I intend to take my wife and my son with me. But I must tell you flatly that if the President wants me to proceed alone to Idaho and states that in his opinion conditions there are too unsettled for me to be accompanied by my family, I shall be obliged to refuse his request. My first duty now is to my family. I'm sorry, but that's the way it is, and if you care to notify the President by telegram accordingly, he may want to cancel my visit."

"Thanks for being so forthright, Toby," General Blake said. "I'll pass your message along to President Grant, and we'll see what he has to say."

Lee Blake wired the President, and the following morning received a succinct reply:

Toby promptly engaged space on the next day's
steamer to San Francisco. From there he would engage sleeping quarters for himself and his family on a
train traveling across the continent to the nation's
capital. He was somewhat mystified by the insistence
of President Grant in seeing him and reasoned that,
having made his position clear, he could not refuse
the President's urgently expressed desire for a meeting.

In San Francisco the Holts made a stopover of
twenty-four hours so that they could enjoy a reunion
with Rob Martin, who was completely installed in his
fine new house on Nob Hill.

They went to dinner with Rob and Kale Salton at
a hotel. At first Kale did not want to go, saying her
place was at home with little Cathy. In truth, she felt
like an intruder at the gathering of old friends.

But Rob insisted she come with them. "You're as
much my friend as Toby and Clarissa," he told her as
she sat on the edge of the bed in her room, looking
miserable. "You're a part of the group, and there's no
reason to cloister yourself in the house. Irma can look
after the baby. She's already looking after the Holts'
son."

Clarissa, who had regained all her former self-
confidence and forthrightness, had never met Kale
but took an instant liking to her. Perhaps she didn't
recognize the depth of Kale's feelings for Rob, but
she did know that the other woman occupied a
special place in Rob's life, and she therefore added
her own voice in encouraging Kale to come out with
them. For this, Kale was grateful, and she was glad,
too, to note that Toby and Clarissa appeared very
much in love, even after their long separation.

The evening at the Palace Hotel passed pleasantly, and Rob told Toby how fortunate they were. "According to Chet Harris, the gold in our mine shows no sign of giving out. It promises us a substantial income for many years to come."

"That's wonderful," Toby replied.

Toby had already explained that he had just been called to Washington to see President Grant on a matter concerning the Idaho Territory. "The question now is what you're planning to do with your future, Rob. Your finances are assured, and between the gold mine and our lumbering property, you're in a good position."

"A *very* good position," Rob said, smiling, "but I don't expect to sit idle. I bought the house in San Francisco for a good reason. I intend to go to work in Chet Harris's firm. In fact, I have an appointment with him tomorrow."

"That's just great," Toby said, and proposed a toast with their glasses of wine. "Here's to us," he said. "To a bright future for each and everyone of us!"

Early the next morning the Holts were on their way to the train station, and Rob went to his appointment with Chet Harris. The wealthy businessman was delighted to see his young friend and listened with great interest as Rob proposed he go to work for the firm.

"I'd be happy to have you work for me, Rob," Chet boomed. "There's a real future in this company for you."

"That's wonderful, Chet," Rob replied. "Kale will be just delighted."

Chet raised an eyebrow. "Kale Salton?"

Rob knew what he was thinking and replied defiantly, "Yes. She's taking care of my infant daughter."

Chet instantly backtracked, looking regretful. "Oh, yes, Miss Salton," he said. He fingered the gold watch

fob that dangled from his waistcoat pocket, then said,
"Rob, perhaps it's best if you look for a position with
another firm. Of course I'll continue to look after your
interests in the gold mine and your investments in the
Northern Pacific, but it wouldn't do to have whispers
about a junior partner coming up regarding this firm.
We're a bit old-fashioned."

Rob knew he was thinking of the scandalous reputation that Kale had acquired in San Francisco. He
could no more expect Chet Harris to believe that his
relationship with Kale was innocent than he could expect anyone else to accept such a view. Well, so be it.
It looked as if his decision to stay in San Francisco
might not have been a wise one.

Washington City had grown so much in the past
decade that it was virtually unrecognizable. The War
and Navy departments had burst their bounds in the
years of the Civil War and now occupied whole rows
of temporary buildings. The Treasury Department,
increasingly powerful, was about to move to a new
building, as was the State Department, which had
achieved considerable prominence two years earlier
when Secretary of State William H. Seward had arranged for the purchase of Alaska.

There were so many bureaucrats employed by
the government that housing was now at a premium.
Restaurants, taverns, and hotels were crowded at all
times of the year. Even now when Congress was not
in session and its members had gone to their homes,
the city bustled as it never had before.

Toby and Clarissa Holt encountered no difficulty
in acquiring appropriate accommodations, however. A
reservation had been made for them in a first-class
hostelry, and there were flowers in their sitting room
bearing a card from President and Mrs. Grant, together with an invitation to supper that same evening
at the White House. The hotel was pleased to provide

a competent and responsible middle-aged woman to look after Tim.

The lavish hotel suite, the flowers, the invitation to supper all thrilled Clarissa, who was making her first visit East since her marriage to Toby Holt. Life's pleasures now seemed boundless after all that they had suffered, both separately and together, and Clarissa was determined to keep things wonderful always.

In the meantime, a note from a presidential secretary awaited Toby, requesting him to appear for a meeting with the President at his earliest convenience. Toby wasted no time, and leaving the unpacking to Clarissa, he hurried to the White House, where armed sentries stood guard as they had since the era of President Lincoln. He presented his credentials; his name was found on the accredited list, and a secretary appeared from the White House and led him across the lawn to the building.

The President was meeting with several members of his cabinet, Toby was told, so he was made comfortable in the office of the secretary, who brought him a cup of coffee and was most solicitous of his welfare. He realized he was being given the treatment accorded important visitors, and his curiosity regarding his reason for being summoned there increased still more.

After a brief wait, he was admitted to the President's inner office, and Ulysses Simpson Grant rose from an oversized, cluttered desk to shake hands with him. Toby had last seen Grant in 1866. At that time Grant had been a general and Toby had been assigned to work in Dakota to make peace with the Indians.

The burdens of the last few years were telling on Grant. His dark hair and full beard were generously flecked with gray, and there were circles of fatigue beneath his penetrating eyes. It seemed odd to Toby,

who had last seen Grant in uniform, to find him
dressed in civilian clothes.

"Welcome, Toby. Good to see you again!" he said
in a loud voice in which his midwestern accent was
clear. He waved Toby to a visitor's chair opposite his
desk. "Damned if you don't look more like your father
every time I see you!"

"That's a compliment, sir," Toby answered
proudly. "Thank you."

"I'm convinced there is a great deal to be said for
heredity," Grant said. "I admired Whip Holt enormously, and I thought there was no one like him in
all the world. But it appears that his son is following
in his footsteps."

Toby flushed and shook his head. "You're very
kind, Mr. President," he said, "but I'm still nowhere
near the man my father was. If I can grow into his
footsteps by the time my career is finished, I'll be well
satisfied."

Grant lighted the stub of a foul-smelling cigar
and blew a cloud of blue-gray smoke across his office.
"You have an opportunity in the immediate future,
Toby, to add to your reputation and to your accomplishments. I'm speaking of Idaho. What do you know
about things there?"

"Well," Toby said, "the mountains are higher,
and the valleys are greener and richer than they are
in most mountain territories. The rivers flow more
swiftly, and the changes in climate are more violent.
In fact, in spite of the scenery, which is second to
none anywhere in the United States, the territory is a
land of violence. According to General Blake, two Indian nations, the Nez Percé and the Shoshoni, are
kicking up their heels and defying the U.S. government, although I'm none too sure of their reasons, and
I don't know if they've been approached to make
peace. I understand that the riffraff that's been drawn
to the West has all concentrated in Idaho now, that

there are more criminals, major and minor, per square foot than there are anywhere else and the decent citizens are having hell's own time, if you'll pardon the expression, sir. In other words, Idaho is a mighty mess."

"Your information is correct," the President told him, "although I can add some rather grisly details to it. Do I understand correctly that in spite of the upset conditions there, you'd be willing to go there to try to establish peace and the authority of the U.S. government provided you could take your wife and your baby son with you?"

"When I went to Dakota, Mr. President," Toby replied slowly, "I operated virtually on my own. Not until the end of my stay did Andy Brentwood finally come along with his regiment and help me to establish law and order at the point of a bayonet. I'm sorry, Mr. President, but I can't just automatically accept an appointment to serve the government in Idaho unless I have some factors very clearly understood in advance."

Ulysses Grant pulled a sheet of foolscap toward him and picked up a pen. "What are they?" he demanded politely. "Just what are your conditions?"

"First of all," Toby replied, "I'd need the full-time assistance of at least two battalions of troops, one of cavalry and one of infantry. I'd want seasoned veterans, not recruits, and men on whom I know I could rely."

To Toby's astonishment President Grant was taking down every word that he said.

"Don't get me wrong," Toby said earnestly, "but I wouldn't be satisfied with Andy Brentwood's regiment on a part-time basis. Those troops are already promised to too many other places in the West, and they're drawn so thin that you can't depend on them when you need them. I'd want the two battalions assigned to permanent duty in Idaho, and if I had my way, I'd like to have them under my direct command. That's not easy, I know, because I left the army with the rank of captain, and both of the battalion commanders would outrank me."

The President smiled but made no reply.

"I'm not being fresh, sir," Toby went on, "but I resent being placed under the ultimate authority of a territorial governor, some politician from the East, who has no real understanding of the facts of the mountain territories and who makes impossible demands. Life there is tough enough without complicating it with the dos and don'ts of a political superior."

Grant was reminded of his own reaction when President Lincoln had appointed him to the overall command of the entire Union Army during the war, and he chuckled reminiscently.

"I'd also like some sort of guarantee of adequate quarters for my wife and child, and although this may be asking for too much, I'd like them provided with some sort of around-the-clock security." He paused for breath.

"Do you have any other requirements?" Grant asked mildly.

Toby was somewhat surprised by his own temerity. He was giving a list of requirements to none other than Ulysses S. Grant, the man who knew his own mind, never hesitated to express it, and who gave orders, not received them. "At the moment, Mr. President," he said boldly, "I can think of only one addition to the list. It would be very helpful if you were to sign an executive order authorizing the execution of those who—in my opinion—break the law. I'd be very careful in using that power, but I'd like to have it, if you know what I mean. Hang a couple of rogues, and it has a very strong effect on every other rogue within shooting distance."

"You have some novel ideas, Mr. Holt, ideas that should be very effective," the President told him. "I imagine that I'll have no trouble in accommodating you."

Toby became hesitant. "A great deal will depend, sir, on the identity of the territorial governor. If he's a broad-enough minded man that he's willing to share a measure of responsibility with me, there should be no problem. But if he wants to gather the reins of authority firmly in his own hands, then I'll be hog-tied from the outset, and I'd rather bow out now than create an impossible mess later on."

"I envision no troubles for you on that score, Mr. Holt," the President said quietly. "You see, the truth of the matter is that there is no governor at the moment, and if you're willing, I intend to appoint you as military governor of the Idaho Territory."

Toby stared at him in openmouthed astonishment.

"Obviously," the President told him, "I anticipate some problems from various senators from the northeastern states who have their own candidates for the territorial governorship. They're sure to try to block your appointment. Fortunately, however, the farther west one travels, the more weight the name of Holt carries, and I've been assured by the majority leader in the Senate that no matter how violent the fight, your confirmation will be assured. Before you accept, however, let me issue a warning to you. The position of military governor is no sinecure. If you're the least bit aware of the history of the position, then you know that Idaho has had a new governor as frequently as once in every year. Several have resigned in utter disgust. Others have disappeared and have gone off to the mountains to make their fortunes. For all we know, they've found gold or silver or whatever it is they were looking for, and they've become very wealthy and are living very happily ever after. I have no idea. It's also possible that they have lost their lives violently. I wouldn't be the least bit surprised about that. If you can keep the job for more than a year, you'll be doing exceptionally well, and that's all I can ask of you."

"If you meet my needs, Mr. President," Toby said firmly, "I'm sure I'll be able to last a good deal longer than one year on the job. Before I accept, however, I'd like the opportunity to discuss this with my wife."

"By all means," Grant said, and then added, "You can let me know your decision when you and Mrs. Holt come back here this evening for dinner. I'll eagerly await your decision."

Toby's head was spinning as he returned to the hotel suite he was sharing with Clarissa and their son. His wife took one look at his troubled face and immediately became concerned.

"What's wrong?" she demanded.

"Nothing—and everything. It depends on one's point of view. I've had a very remarkable offer from the President. I've been offered the position of military governor of Idaho, and I'd have to serve for at least a year on the job."

"I—I'm overwhelmed," Clarissa said, and Toby couldn't tell whether she was laughing or crying.

"I'm more than slightly stunned myself," Toby admitted, "but the post is no great plum. Ten men have been governor there in the last ten years, and they've either thrown up their hands in disgust and walked out, or they've given in to various pressures and have walked out on the job and have vanished without a trace. It'll be hard work at best, and the rewards will be very few."

Clarissa looked up at him. "All I want to know is if Tim and I will be able to go to Idaho with you and to live there with you."

"I have the President's unequivocal assurance on that point," Toby told her. "I don't know where we'll live, but I gather there's a suitable residence for the governor."

"You agreed to take the position, no doubt," she said.

He shook his head. "Actually, I've given him no answer. I wanted to explain the whole thing to you and let you make the final decision."

"But that's unfair," Clarissa protested. "Your career is at stake, and you're the one who'll have all the hard work to do if you accept. You'll have to make your own choice."

Her husband grinned at her. "No, ma'am," he said. "You'll make it, and I'll abide by it."

"In that case," she said slowly, "I see no real choice. Of course you'll accept. It's not only flattering to think that your country thinks enough of you that you're considered to be one man capable of doing the work of military governor, but you know and I know that that estimate of you is correct. When we go to the White House tonight, give the President your answer. Tell him we're pleased to be going to Idaho."

The fortunes of Ulysses S. Grant had changed violently from year to year since the early 1850s. A career military officer, he had retired from the army in 1854, rather than face court-martial charges for drunkenness. After failing in several attempts at business, he had accepted a post in his father's leather store in Galena, Illinois, for a salary of eighteen hundred dollars a year. Recalled to active duty by President Lincoln, he had become one of the great field commanders in the history of the U.S. Army. He had defeated his one-time colleague, Robert E. Lee, and had won the war. Serving under President Andrew Johnson as secretary of war, he had responded to popular demand and had been elected to the presidency by an overwhelming vote.

Mrs. Grant had accepted adversity and success with equal, unflappable equanimity. No one had heard her complain in failure, and no one had known her to put on airs in success.

Now, as the nation's first lady, she stood on the portico on this warm summer evening and greeted her guests with dignity, poise, and charm. She seemed especially happy to greet Clarissa and Toby Holt, who were different from the politicians who made up the better part of the guest list.

Clarissa fell completely under Mrs. Grant's spell and soon was feeling at home. She looked without awe at several senators and two cabinet ministers who were among the guests, and she was not in the least uncomfortable in the company of anyone present. Her husband, she decided, was the equal of any man at the gathering.

Before the group proceeded into the dining room, Clarissa saw the President draw her husband aside and listen intently as Toby spoke to him earnestly for a moment or two. President Grant smiled, clapped him on the shoulder, and then drifted away. There was no further private talk between them.

When the group adjourned to the dinner table, a butler refilled the glasses of the gentlemen with whiskey as was President Grant's custom, and the ladies were served small glasses of a light, sweet sherry. To the surprise of the company and without forewarning Toby, Grant rose to his feet. "Ladies and gentlemen," he said, "I want to offer a toast to a new official of the government, a man who has just joined us in one of the most demanding posts in this administration. I give you the new military governor of the Idaho Territory."

Everyone drank to Toby's success, and Clarissa, sitting on the President's right, looked down the table proudly at her husband. Not only were their personal troubles behind them, but Toby was about to start a new career of great promise.

The headlines in the Portland newspapers were triumphant:

PRESIDENT NAMES TOBY HOLT
MILITARY GOVERNOR OF IDAHO

The patient in room 17 of the Portland hospital looked at the newspaper avidly, holding it in bandaged hands, and his eyes burned. Mr. Thomas, as he was known to the doctors and nurses of the staff, was something of an enigma. He had been discovered in a hotel room in the city, barely able to walk, so dazed and battered that it was almost a miracle that he was able to stand on his own two feet.

Somehow he had managed to survive and to reach his hotel, where he was living under his assumed name, after suffering a severe fall from his horse, or so he told members of the staff. In truth, he had fallen from a mountain, but his fall had been miraculously broken by trees along the side of the cliff.

He had ample funds to pay for his hospital care. For days he had been under the care of the staff of the hospital and had been treated with great concern until gradually he had recovered his health. And as Otto Sinclair's bruised and battered body healed, his mind grew sharper. Now it was filled with all of his old zeal, which was compounded by a fresh hatred.

Toby Holt had left him for dead in the mountains, and Sinclair was determined, if he did nothing else on the face of the earth, to do away with the man he considered responsible for all of his suffering.

So Holt—and Clarissa—were being sent to Idaho as military governor and first lady of the territory. The news seemed almost too good to be true. Holt would be in one place and should be an easy enough target, as he would be making innumerable public appearances.

But Otto Sinclair was in no hurry to leave the hospital. He was safe there and each day grew stronger. So he was content to wait until he was in top health again. Only then would he take his leave, go north to Idaho, and do away with Toby Holt. Obviously by now Clarissa had told her second husband about Otto and his threats, but it was also equally obvious that the Holts believed him dead after the fall in the mountains and they would not expect him to show up again.

That was where they were wrong. This was to be a fight to the end, and Otto Sinclair, who had already proved himself a survivor, was determined to survive once again.

Kale Salton felt strangely uncomfortable, very much out of place in the house on Nob Hill in San Francisco. She fervently wished that she and Rob had left this town, but it was too late for that now, and she guessed she had to make the best of it.

Taking care of little Cathy occupied only a portion of her time, and she was glad that the baby kept her as busy as she did. At least Kale was safe in the house for those hours.

The rest of the day she was at loose ends. Rob, who had been boycotted by most major firms in the city because of his controversial living arrangement with a former courtesan, continued to look for a position that would challenge and occupy him, but he met with no success. He was listless and unhappy, and it pained Kale to see him this way, all the more so because she believed it was her fault.

Kale suffered equally whenever she left the house to go shopping or do errands. No matter how circumspectly she dressed, no matter how properly she behaved, she was recognized as Kale Salton, the prostitute. Men stared at her and sometimes even followed her into stores, attempting to pick her up.

Worse than the men, however, were the ladies of standing in the town, who treated her like a leper. They moved to one side when she passed them and stared and talked in hushed tones. Even shopgirls began to recognize her and treat her with disdain.

Whether these women imagined that she and Rob were actually married or not she did not know, and it did not much matter. It was enough that they avoided her and gossiped about her, and she knew that sooner or later there was certain to be an explosion. Perhaps people would fabricate an incident; perhaps they would try to drive her from the town. Whatever the case, that explosion would mark the end of her relationship with Rob.

Now, feeling relieved because no grave incidents had marred her trip into the city, she returned meekly to the house. For the moment she could breathe somewhat more easily. She instructed the driver to take the horse and carriage to the stable at the rear of the house and then bring her packages into the kitchen.

To her astonishment Rob had returned early from making his rounds of the large San Francisco firms and was sitting at the kitchen table, a broad smile on his face. Kale looked at him curiously. "You bear a strong resemblance," she said, "to the cat that ate the canary."

"That's the way I feel," he replied. "I know you haven't been any too happy here, and I've certainly been at loose ends. But now we're being given an opportunity to start all over again in fresh surroundings."

"What do you mean?" she asked.

He took a letter from his inside coat pocket. "This just came for me today, arriving by special rail messenger. It's from Toby, and he wrote it from

Washington City. President Grant has appointed him as military governor of Idaho, and he wants us to join him there. He says he needs me as his deputy."

A sense of infinite relief flooded Kale. "You'll go?" she asked eagerly.

"Sure," he said. "It's a great challenge, and I hate to turn that down. We can always return to San Francisco when it's time for Cathy to attend school, but in the meantime, it's a golden opportunity. Besides, I know it's what you want."

She had difficulty in refraining from throwing her arms around his neck and kissing him. She was indeed being given the opportunity to start once again, in a raw frontier community, with the slate wiped clean. Maybe in Idaho she could at last make something of herself—and maybe, just maybe, she would win Rob, too.

The hatchet man, Wang, had spent a profitable but easy morning and was well satisfied with his efforts. Having learned from his superiors that the members of a recently formed rival tong were about to challenge the authority of the group he represented, he had paid a "business call" to them, and it had done much to reestablish his standing.

Even though he had been discredited when he returned to San Francisco from Utah, his mere appearance at their headquarters had filled them with terror. Four or five of them had fled when they saw his enormous bulk and his grim expression; they did not wait to find out what he might have to say or what he proposed to do. That reaction had restored much of the pride he had lost when Toby Holt had compelled him to lose face.

The remaining members of the rival tong's security-guard division had watched him in wide-eyed silence as he raised his hatchet above his head and brought it down sharply, splitting an oak desk in half with a single blow. After that exhibition, it had been necessary for him to say only a word or two.

As his own superiors had directed, he ordered the new tong to disband at once or to suffer the consequences. Then, removing his hatchet from the shattered desk, he strolled out to the street, certain that his single-handed efforts had been enough and that the new tong would be no more by the end of the day.

Wang was in a cheerful mood as he returned to the headquarters of his own tong. Dutifully, proudly reporting to the elders of his tong on his morning's activities, he walked into the kitchen of the San Francisco Chinatown restaurant that they owned. The chief cook gave him an enormous meal that befitted his great bulk, and he ate it with gusto.

Finishing his meal, he wandered into the office and, with nothing else to do, picked up an English-language San Francisco newspaper. He glanced idly at the front page.

All at once the photograph of the man he hated more than anyone else in all the world seemed to rise up from the page. He found himself staring at a picture of Toby Holt, and his eyes narrowed.

Slowly, laboriously, the hatchet man read the accompanying article and managed to glean from it that Holt had been appointed as military governor of the Idaho Territory, which was described in the article as "the most lawless area in all of the United States."

Leaning his enormous bulk back in his chair, Wang exhaled slowly through gritted teeth. An opportunity better than any he had imagined previously was opening to him.

He would not have to go to Portland after all to do away with Toby Holt. He would wait until he read that Holt had actually arrived in Idaho, and then he would obtain a leave of absence from his position and would take his hatchet on a very personal mission. Idaho, unlike Portland, was wild, uncrowded, and uncivilized, and his mission would be incredibly easy. Toby Holt's days were numbered.